Available
from Mills

SNOWED IN WITH THE BOSS

from Mills & Boon® Intrigue

He'd very nearly given in to temptation and kissed Sophie.

What was more, she would've welcomed his kiss; he'd seen it in her eyes, felt it in the tension-laden air. Griffin prided himself on his discipline and self-control. So what had happened in that moment with Sophie?

The attraction was there, had been there from the first moment she'd walked into his office. He'd managed to tamp it down to an awareness and she'd hidden the fact as well. Most of the time, anyway. But that moment in front of the fireplace had shattered their pretence of disinterest.

This was going to complicate things. Big-time. And not just over the next couple of days while they were trapped inside, but over the long term, too.

Now, as Griffin worked his way out to the place where the bridge had collapsed and nearly killed them, he realised he was probably out of luck retrieving their suitcases.

For the duration of the storm, it looked as though he and Sophie were going to be down to borrowed clothes and doused PDAs.

And each other.

CRIMINALLY HANDSOME

The only way for Miguel to guarantee she'd be safe would be to stay here himself.

Suddenly she turned to look at him and beamed an unexpected smile in his direction. The worry in her face disappeared. Her blue eyes shimmered like sunlight on a mountain lake.

The analytical side of his brain shut down. As he stared at her, he forgot the potential danger that had brought him here.

For just a minute, he almost felt like they were on a date.

"Thank you for coming over here so quickly tonight."

"My pleasure." Earlier he'd been thinking he should stay at her house as a bodyguard. Now he had another reason altogether. He *wanted* to be here, *wanted* to be with her.

"I should get going to the café, pick up that order."

Shyly, she bit her lower lip, then said, "Hurry back."

And those words gave him every reason to want to.

All the characters in this book have no existence outside the imagination of the author, and have no relation whatsoever to anyone bearing the same name or names. They are not even distantly inspired by any individual known or unknown to the author, and all the incidents are pure invention.

First published in Great Britain 2010
Harlequin Mills & Boon Limited,
Eton House, 18-24 Paradise Road, Richmond, Surrey TW9 1SR

Snowed in with the Boss © Harlequin Books S.A. 2009
Criminally Handsome © Harlequin Books S.A. 2009

Special thanks and acknowledgement are given to Jessica Andersen and Cassie Miles for their contributions to the Kenner County Crime Unit mini-series.

ISBN: 978 0 263 88254 4

46-0910

Harlequin Mills & Boon policy is to use papers that are natural, renewable and recyclable products and made from wood grown in sustainable forests. The logging and manufacturing processes conform to the legal environmental regulations of the country of origin.

Printed and bound in Spain
by Litografia Rosés S.A., Barcelona

SNOWED IN
WITH THE BOSS
BY
JESSICA ANDERSEN

CRIMINALLY
HANDSOME
BY
CASSIE MILES

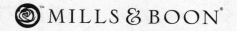

SNOWED IN
WITH THE BOSS
by
JESSICA ANDERSEN

CRIMINALLY
HANDSOME
by
CASSIE MILES

MILLS & BOON

SNOWED IN WITH THE BOSS

BY
JESSICA ANDERSEN

Chapter One

"We'll reach the estate soon," Griffin Vaughn said to his executive assistant, Sophie LaRue, as their rented SUV thundered down the Colorado highway, headed into the mountains.

He was driving; he preferred to drive himself rather than hire limos because he disliked putting his safety in someone else's hands, professional or not. Sophie sat in the passenger seat, her entire attention focused on the breathtaking Colorado scenery. The sweeping vista was shadowed by the distant Rocky Mountains, and the entire scene was overhung by an ominous gray winter sky.

At Griffin's words, she glanced over at him. "I hope so. We need to be done at Lonesome Lake and back down off the mountain before the weather hits."

In her mid-twenties, with wavy, dark blond hair and light brown eyes almost the same color, Sophie was a knockout, hands down. The cinnamon-colored sweater she wore beneath a stylish wool coat accented her undeniable curves, and her neatly tailored pants managed to be simultaneously professional and sexy. Even a cynical, "been there, done that, got the scars to prove it" businessman like Griffin could appreciate the aesthetics. However, that didn't change the fact that she was a dozen years younger than his thirty-nine, and she was his employee, both of which meant she was way off-limits, even if he was looking. Which he wasn't.

Yet he kept feeling the need to fill the silence that stretched between them as the highway unwound beneath the rental's wheels. The fact that he bothered trying to make small talk, which he wouldn't have done with Sophie's middle-aged, über-experienced predecessor, Kathleen, just went to prove what Griffin already knew: he was badly off his game.

He was tired, hungry and irritable. His meeting in New York City had started off bad and had gotten worse the longer he and Sophie stayed, forcing him to pull the plug after only two days of negotiations. He'd decided to return home to San Francisco and see if things went better long-distance, only to have his private jet delayed several hours on the tarmac while air traffic control tried to reroute them around a series of major snowstorms that were blanketing the Midwest.

The frustrations and delays had all added up to Griffin being in an admittedly foul mood by the time they'd finally taken off. That was why, when he'd gotten the voice-mail message that renovations to his Rocky Mountain retreat in the Four Corners region of Colorado had been delayed yet again by another "accident," he'd ordered his private plane to set down near Kenner County. Griffin had suspected for some time that his contractor, Perry Long, was taking him for a ride, and it was past time to deal with it.

The pilot, Hal Jessup, had warned him that there was some serious weather on the way, but Griffin had been adamant. He might not have sewn up VaughnTec's acquisition of the HiTek memory module he was jonesing to get his hands on, but he was going to get *something* done on this trip, damn it. He was going to deal with Perry Long, once and for all. The swindling contractor wasn't going to know what hit him.

Besides, according to the weather forecast, they had a few more hours before the blizzard hit. That should be plenty of time for him and Sophie to drive out to the estate, get a look at the renovations, and then drive back down into Kenner City, where Sophie had already booked them into a decent B and B. She had also arranged for them to meet with Perry the following day, weather permitting. And it damn well better permit as far as Griffin was concerned. He was done with the contractor and his excuses.

"Looks like someone's getting a jump on being stranded in the snow," Sophie said as they rounded a corner and an accident came into view up ahead. Behind a row of cherry-red flares, a battered pickup truck was stuck partway in a ditch off to the side of the road. A police cruiser and tow truck were on-scene, their lights flashing brightly in the gloom. Several men were huddled around the rear of the entrapped vehicle, working on securing a winch to the rear axle.

"Don't let the weathermen talk you into blizzard-

induced hysteria," Griffin said. "They're in cahoots
with the grocery stores, trying to sell out all the bread,
eggs and milk."

She grinned a little and lifted a shoulder. "I'm a California girl. I've never been in a snowstorm before. Until
three days ago, I'd never even been on a plane."

Griffin stifled a wince at the reminder of just how
green his new executive assistant was. He'd told the
retiring Kathleen to find her own replacement—someone
efficient with no social life to speak of, who wouldn't
mind working the crazy-long hours required by his
position as head of VaughnTec. He hadn't bothered reminding Kathleen that his new assistant should be
middle-aged and highly experienced, because he'd
figured that would've been a given.

Yet Kathleen had hired green, gorgeous Sophie LaRue
and disappeared on her retirement cruise. Worse, she
had either left her cell phone behind, or she was ignoring
his calls, in a blatant signal of "Don't call me, I'll call
you." Griffin should know; he was a master with that line.
But he'd given up after a while anyway, because what
good would it do him now to bark at Kathleen? She'd
retired. What happened next was up to him.

He'd been tempted to un-hire Sophie the moment
she'd walked through his office door, introduced herself,
knocked him for a loop with an instant blast of sexual
chemistry, and five minutes later spilled most of a pot
of coffee on a stack of important papers. But Kathleen
had already shown the new executive assistant the basics
of the job, and Griffin was in the middle of delicate ne-

gotiations to acquire a memory module that was vital to his newest handheld computer PDA. All of which meant he didn't have the time to interview or train another assistant. Besides, he trusted Kathleen, and figured she must've seen something in Sophie, some reason she thought the two of them would click. Kathleen had always had a knack for reading people, and predicting which employees would work well together. Trusting that even if he didn't see it right off the bat, he'd let his new assistant stay on the job, and they'd both done their best to make it work.

He'd overlooked her occasional bouts of inexperience and nerves, and the clumsiness those nerves seemed to bring out. For her part, she'd worked the long hours without protest, and often took paperwork home with her when she left for the night. And if he'd caught a hint or two that Sophie reciprocated the raw physical attraction he felt for her, they were both doing a fine job of gritting their teeth and ignoring it. They'd been working together nearly a month now, and they'd achieved a functional, if tenuous, boss-and-assistant relationship.

"The cop's waving for us to pull over," she said now as they rolled up to the accident. "I hope your license is good."

"If it's not, I'm blaming it on you," Griffin said, only halfway joking as he stopped the rental and lowered the window.

"Afternoon, folks," the cop said, taking a not-very-casual look from Griffin to Sophie and back. "If you're planning on spending the night in the hotel, you missed the turn by about a mile. Nothing much up this way except pines, rocks and ice." The officer looked to be in his late thirties. He was tall and dark-haired, with vivid blue eyes that were cool and assessing, and didn't look like they missed much.

Griffin saw the edge of a pointed star on the cop's uniform shirt beneath his heavy parka, and made the connection. "Sheriff Martinez?"

The cop's eyes narrowed. "Do I know you?"

"We spoke on the phone when your people needed access to my estate. I'm Griffin Vaughan." Griffin nodded in Sophie's direction. "My assistant, Sophie LaRue." When there was no immediate response from the sheriff of Kenner County, a flutter of long-unused instinct stirred the fine hairs at Griffin's nape. "Do you want to see our IDs?"

Martinez shook his head, and finally relaxed a degree. "No. It's fine. Sorry. Things have been…complicated around here lately. We're giving everyone a second and third look." The sheriff paused. "Are you two headed up to Lonesome Lake?"

Griffin's new estate had been named for the large, spring-fed lake on the property, one of only a few open bodies of water in the immediate area. The lake was located near the main entrance to the sprawling grounds; the driveway cut straight across the middle, running over a sturdy cement-pylon bridge. The promise of summer-time fishing, along with a hell of a mountain view, had sold Griffin on the place. The lowball price hadn't hurt, either, though in retrospect it should've been a red flag. Since he'd taken possession of Lonesome Lake, the property had been one long-distance headache after another.

Griffin nodded in answer to the sheriff's question. "Just a quick in-and-out. I gave the live-in couple the month off because of the reno, and the construction crew has undoubtedly gone home to wait out the weather, but I wanted to get a look at the place before we sit down for a meeting with Perry tomorrow."

"You picked a hell of a time to visit." Martinez glanced at the sky. "They're saying this storm could take a couple of days to blow through, maybe more."

"We'll be back down in the city before it starts," Griffin said. "I don't have any desire to be snowed in up there until after the reno is complete." And certainly not with his executive secretary. Lonesome Lake was intended for family, not business.

Griffin had bought the estate to be a getaway for him and his three-year-old son, Luke, and Luke's male nanny, Darryn, both of whom were waiting for him back in San Francisco. The estate was intended to be a luxurious "just the guys" cabin, a place that would let him retreat from the hoopla that came with being a multimillionaire under the age of forty who made regular appearances on the Steele Most Wealthy list and almost all of San Fran's "Most Eligible Bachelor" roundups.

Those lists invariably included personal tidbits such as his divorce from songwriter Monique Claire, his single father status, and the fact that he'd been a decorated marine technical specialist before taking over struggling VaughnTec and making it into a megacorporation.

Back when Griffin had been in the military, he'd built weapons and tracking tools out of whatever he'd been able to scrounge from the field. As a civilian, he focused more on handheld computers, but the gadget-building theory was the same, and the self-discipline and ruthless logic he'd learned in the battle zones had served him well in the business world.

Unfortunately, his military service only added to his dossier as far as the San Fran socialites were concerned. That, combined with his net worth and dark good looks, had made him the target of too many gold diggers to count. In fact, he'd stopped counting the wannabe Mrs. Vaughns around a year ago, right around the time he'd stopped dating. His lack of interest had only increased the pressure from the gold diggers, which was why he'd bought Lonesome Lake. He needed to get the hell away from his work and the city he'd grown up in, and he wanted someplace comfortable to do it.

Which was great in theory, but so far had been seriously lacking in practice, due to the construction glitches.

Griffin had hired Perry as his general contractor based on the Realtor's recommendation and a handful of local references, and had signed off on a basic updating of the forty year-old structure. At first, the contractor's reports of things needing immediate repair or replacement had seemed reasonable enough. As the months had dragged on, though, and the schedule had doubled, and then tripled, Griffin's patience had decreased in direct proportion to the budget's increase. Now he just wanted to put an end to whatever the hell was going on up at the estate, regardless of whether that meant a sit-down with Perry…or lining up a new contractor.

"We should get moving if we're going to beat the storm," he said pointedly to the sheriff.

Martinez glanced up the road, though Lonesome Lake was a good ten miles further along the two-lane track leading into the foothills. "Do me a favor and call me when you get back to Kenner City, so I know you made it down off the mountain safely, okay?" The sheriff rattled off a number. "Got that?"

Sophie nodded and entered the number in her sleek, sophisticated PDA, which was one of VaughnTec's newer designs. "Got it." Once she had the number keyed in, she tucked the handheld into the pocket of her stylish wool coat, keeping it close at hand.

Still, Martinez didn't look satisfied.

Getting the distinct impression that the sheriff wasn't at all happy with their plan, Griffin lowered his voice and said, "What aren't you telling us?"

Martinez grimaced, and for a moment, Griffin didn't think he was going to answer. But then the sheriff said, "Look, there have been some…incidents in this area lately. First, there was that body that turned up, the dead FBI agent?" At Griffin's nod of remembrance, he continued, "Well, after that, we found an abandoned car with a baby in it. A *baby,* for God's sake. And then one of our crime scene analysts was attacked the other day not far from here, further on toward Lonesome Lake. The weather's been playing hell with our ability to process the scenes, which is logjamming the investigations…and to top it all off, the Feds think there's a chance that Vincent Del Gardo might still be in the area." The sheriff shook his head. "Logically, those incidents probably aren't all connected, but… Just be careful up there, okay?"

Griffin muttered a curse under his breath, but nodded. "Will do."

"Call me if you need anything." The sheriff stepped back and waved them on their way, but his eyes remained dark as he watched them pass.

His figure had barely begun to recede in the distance before Sophie said, "Who is Vincent Del Gardo?"

Griffin knew he probably should have told her about the recent problems near Lonesome Lake, but to be honest, he'd all but forgotten about them. Between the HiTek negotiations, Kathleen's retirement and various other business matters he'd been juggling against his responsibility as Luke's father and his desire to be involved in as many pieces of his son's life as he possibly could be, he simply hadn't given much thought to the issues in Kenner County. He'd assumed the matter would be settled by the time the estate was completely renovated and he brought Luke and Darryn out for a visit. So he hadn't bothered updating Sophie on the situation.

Besides, it wasn't like he'd planned to bring her out to Lonesome Lake. Between the stalled negotiations, the air traffic delays and the continued problems up at the estate, it'd just been the most practical solution under the circumstances.

More or less, he thought, glancing at the ominous sky

overhead and considering just how much of his decision to drive out had been motivated by practicality, and how much had been the bloody-minded stubbornness Kathleen had accused him of more than once. He could feel the storm gathering, and a piece of him wondered if they might not be better off turning around and heading back down to the city without doing a walk-through of the lake house. But he was bound and determined to get *something* done today, and besides, the best Doppler money could buy said they had a few hours' leeway.

So instead of calling it off, he answered her question, saying, "Vincent Del Gardo is—or *was*—head of the Del Gardo crime family in Las Vegas." Griffin recalled what Martinez had told him a few weeks earlier, when the sheriff had called to ask for permission for the county's newly assembled crime scene unit, the Kenner County CSU, to search the estate and surrounding property. "About three years ago, Del Gardo was put on trial for ordering a hit on Nicky Wayne, head of the rival Wayne crime family. Del Gardo was convicted, but he escaped from the courthouse jail and disappeared. A few months ago, the body of Special Agent Julie Grainger, who'd been working the Del Gardo case, was found on a Ute reservation near here. Since then, Sheriff Martinez's people, the KCCU, the Feds and the reservation police have been investigating the murder. About a month ago, they figured out that Del Gardo used to own Lonesome Lake, and came to suspect that he might've been hiding out in the area."

"You bought your getaway from the Mob?" Sophie

asked. She had a faint wrinkle between her eyebrows, which he'd learned signaled that she'd just made a mistake, or thought he had. He'd actually learned to pay attention to the tiny frown, because when she wasn't dumping coffee on him, she had pretty good instincts.

"No way." He shook his head in adamant denial. "Del Gardo owned the property through a shell company. It was well-hidden, and not something that even the best due diligence would've turned up. The Del Gardo family went into a financial skid after Vincent disappeared, so they liquidated a bunch of assets, including Lonesome Lake. My purchasing the place was totally on the up-and-up. Once the Feds figured out the connection between Del Gardo and Lonesome Lake, though, and given that Agent Grainger's body was found in Kenner County, they wanted the KCCU to go through the house, just to be sure Del Gardo wasn't hiding there. They searched the mansion backward and forward and didn't find anything. I think they even did a few flyovers of the mountainside, looking for infrared signatures and such. Nothing. Del Gardo is long gone."

Sophie pursed her lips. "Sheriff Martinez seems to think otherwise."

Griffin glanced over at her, but beyond her faint frown, he couldn't read her mood from her face. He'd noticed before that for a young woman who by her own admission hadn't seen much of the world, she had an unusual ability to hide her feelings.

"The place is clean, but if you're worried about Del Gardo, you can stay in the car while I look around," he offered. "I just want to see what's finished and what's not, and check whether the problems that Perry has been reporting are actually as bad as he says, or if there's something else going on up at the estate. It shouldn't take more than an hour, and then we'll head back into Kenner City."

But she shook her head. "You wanted me to come along to take notes and pictures, and that's what I'm going to do. It's my job." She said the last with a hint of defiance.

Griffin nodded and slowed as the road curved and a set of pillars came into view, flanking a crushed stone driveway. "Here we are." He turned the SUV between the pillars and followed the gravel drive, which quickly gave way to the lake-spanning bridge. He eased up on the gas and let the rental roll to a stop at the edge of the bridge. "Welcome to Lonesome Lake."

Even in the gray light of the approaching storm, it was just as gorgeous as he remembered from the one time he'd visited prior to buying the property. On that day, several months earlier, the lake had been clear and blue beneath a perfect sky. Now, it was a flat expanse of white, wearing a dusting of snow over the frozen surface. The bridge, which arrowed straight across a narrow point of the lake, was a wide expanse of brick-inset concrete, with knee-high brushed-steel railings on either side to prevent cars from swerving into the water. On the far shore of the lake, the driveway went back to crushed stone and continued up through the tree line, where the lowlands merged with the foothills of the Rocky Mountains.

Partway up, rising above the level of the trees surrounding it, the large estate house looked as though it was built into the side of the mountain itself. The structure, which followed the angle of the earth beneath it, was a blend of rustic logs and modern glass. It ascended the mountain, level by level, and was topped with a partially finished solar-paneled roof. When the roof was completed, the solar panels would catch the sun and help power the massive home. For now, the estate relied on two huge diesel generators, which ran everything except the propane stoves and the well water and filtration system, which used battery-powered pumps. Off to the left of the main house, the roofs of the detached guesthouse and large barn were just visible, as well. Several smaller structure, including the lean-to that housed the generators, as well as a woodshed where the firewood was kept, were below the level of the trees, hidden among the pines.

Griffin was proud that he was able to offer his son such a cool getaway, and a place where they could be just a family, away from the pressures and posturing of San Fran society. He glanced at Sophie. "What do you think?"

"It's lovely," she breathed.

"Yeah," he agreed, the view reminding him why he'd bought Lonesome Lake rather than one of the other half dozen places he'd considered. He'd liked the isolation, yes, and he'd been able to picture himself fishing in the lake with Luke, year after year. But he'd also been drawn to the wildness of the location, the grandeur of the views and the sheer presence of the architecture.

It was a hell of a place, that was for sure.

Suddenly anxious to get inside the buildings and take a look around at what had—or hadn't—been done, he hit the gas and sent the SUV thundering across the bridge.

They were halfway across when he heard a banging noise, as though the SUV had backfired.

Moments later, the concrete surface ahead of them cracked, then sagged. Adrenaline jolted through Griffin as the SUV dropped a few inches, tilting. The damned bridge was giving way!

"Hang on!" he shouted as he hit the gas hard, flooring it. The SUV's tires screeched and the vehicle lunged forward, but it was too late. They were already sinking. Falling.

Sophie screamed as the steel railing gave way with a screech and groan. The nose of the SUV yawed downward. Griffin locked up the brakes, but that didn't help. Nothing did.

The vehicle slid ten or fifteen feet, then dropped straight down and smashed into the frozen surface of Lonesome Lake.

The crash noise roared inside the vehicle, counterpointed by Sophie's choked-off scream. Ice chunks flew up on either side of them and the airbags detonated with a *whumpf,* cushioning the force of the impact, but also pinning Griffin back against the driver's seat as the SUV nosed beneath the lake surface. Cursing, he fought the springy airbag, fought his seat belt, trying to get free.

The spiderwebbed windshield crumbled inward under the water pressure and frigid water poured in over the dashboard, dousing him. Freezing him. A clock started up in his head, timing how long they'd been in the water, and how long they could stay there, which wasn't long at all.

The SUV paused for a moment, hung up on a chunk of pylon, then slewed to the side and started to sink once again.

Griffin didn't know how deep the lake was at that location, didn't want to wait around and find out. They had to get out of the vehicle, had to reach the mansion and get themselves dried off and warm, or else hypothermia would set in quickly. He didn't know why or how the bridge had given way just as they were crossing it—maybe the passage of the construction trucks had weakened it, or the last freeze-thaw cycle had done irreparable damage. But that didn't matter just then. What mattered was getting him and Sophie to safety.

Knowing they'd gone from a business drive to a life-or-death situation in an instant, Griffin shoved his business persona aside and drew on the man he'd once been, the soldier who'd saved lives, and taken them. Fighting past the airbag, he kicked the windshield all the way out, letting in a new gush of water but clearing the way for escape. "Come on," he said. "We can—" He broke off, cursing bitterly as he got a good look at Sophie.

She was out cold. And the water was rising fast.

ON THE OTHER SIDE of the lake, the bald man leaned up against a tree and watched the SUV sink into the frozen lake.

He would've liked a cigarette to congratulate himself for a job well done, but his wife had nagged him to quit a few years back. So instead, he stood there and watched as the ice-laden water rose up around the heavily tinted rear windows of the four-by-four.

He couldn't see in through the tint, but there was no sign of the vehicle's occupants trying to escape. If Vaughn and his secretary were in a position to get out, there would've been doors flying open, and occupants scrambling out to safety. Which meant they were already dead, or close enough to it that the distinction was academic.

It was for the best, really, he thought, feeling no grief or guilt for the dead, but rather the sense of another box checked off on his to-do list. He didn't have anything against Vaughn and the woman. They had simply been in the way of more important things.

Satisfied, the man pantomimed flicking an imaginary cigarette butt to the ground and pretended to grind it into the frozen soil. Then he settled his loaded knapsack more comfortably on his back and turned away, headed back uphill toward the barn at the rear of the house.

He had a job to do. It was as simple as that. And anyone who got in his way was going to become a statistic, real quick.

Chapter Two

Sophie awoke to panic and pain. The panic was locked in her chest, squeezing her lungs and keeping the screams inside. The pain was in her head, making her dizzy and weak. And she was freezing—not just a little "time to go put on a sweater" chill—but a deep, bone-hurting cold that surrounded her, consumed her.

She struggled against the sensations, trying and failing to push away from whatever terrible nightmare gripped her. Then the world shifted, reeling around her. Light intruded, forcing her to squint against the stabbing glare.

"That's it, Sophie. In and out," a deep, masculine voice said from very close by. "You can do it. Breathe in and out."

The pressure on her lungs let up, and some of the pain cleared. The world stopped spinning and she could move again. Moments later she could see again, though seeing didn't do much to clear her confusion, because she found herself lying on her back, with her handsome boss, Griffin Vaughn, leaning over her.

In his late thirties, with short dark hair that was frosted

with silver at the temples, Griffin was a hard, no-nonsense businessman with chiseled features and elegantly arched brows. He was clipped and to the point, and rarely let his face show the slightest hint of emotion. Which was why it was shocking to see worry in his dark green eyes, and hear it in his voice when he said, "Hey. Welcome back to the land of the living. You scared the heck out of me."

"Sorry," she said inanely, too aware that his face was close enough that if she reached up just a little, they'd be kissing. Which was the sort of thought she usually relegated to the "don't go there" section of her brain, along with thoughts of her mother's illness and her own crippling debt load.

She stared up at him, blinking, trying to figure out what had happened. As she did so, she realized she wasn't really even that cold anymore, just numb, almost going to warm now, kindling to heat. She smiled, dazed. Griffin didn't smile back, though. Instead, he touched her cheek, though she barely felt it. "You're freezing."

"Not really. I'm actually sort of warm." Her voice sounded strange, a deep rasp she wasn't used to, and her throat hurt with the effort.

His expression went hard. "That's even worse, because it means you're going into hypothermia. We've got to get moving. Come on. Your arms and legs are working fine—nothing's broken. I could carry you, but I think it'd be better if you walked and got your blood moving." He eased away from her and stood, then reached down to pull her up. The world tilted beneath her feet and she sagged against him, feeling his hard, masculine muscles beneath his sopping-wet button-down shirt.

Wait a minute. Why was he wet?

Her fuzzy brain finally sharpened and she became suddenly cognizant of the fact that he wasn't the only one who was wet to the skin. Her own clothes were glued to her body, cold and soaking. And it was freezing out; a sharp wind cut through the pitiful protection of her wet clothing, and as she watched, a few fat flakes of snow drifted down from the leaden sky above. *The blizzard*, she thought, heart kicking with belated panic. *The bridge!*

She gasped as she remembered the accident, the pop of the airbags, and then—

What then?

Heart hammering, she pulled away from her boss and looked at the lake. The bridge was a wreck, with a big section missing from the middle and chunks of cement hanging from mangled steel reinforcements. There was no sign of the SUV.

"Wha-t-t-t…" The last word turned into a stutter when huge shivers started racking her. With the exertion of standing and beginning to move around, the numbness she'd been feeling had changed to a huge, awful coldness. Wrapping her arms around her body as her muscles locked on the chills, she turned to Griffin. "You pulled me out-t-t?"

"Come on." He slid an arm around her and urged her uphill. "We've got to get up to the house."

He was shivering, too, she realized. She could feel the tremors racking his large, masculine frame, could hear them in his voice, warning her that the two of them were far from out of danger. They could very well freeze before they reached safety.

As if called by the thought, a storm gust whistled across the lake and slammed into them, nearly driving them to the ground. Wind-driven snow peppered them, the icy pellets stinging Sophie's hands and face. The pain was a sharp heat against the background of bone-aching cold.

"It's not supposed to s-start snowing until l-later," she stuttered, not even able to feel her lips moving.

He didn't answer, just started walking, keeping a strong grip on her waist and urging her onward. Knowing he was right, they had to get moving, she put one foot in front of the other, forcing herself to keep up with his long-legged strides.

From the feel of gravel beneath her low-heeled boots—which were *not* designed for snow trekking—she figured they were following the driveway. She couldn't see it, though; it was covered with a layer of white. Snow had already blanketed the ground and frosted the trees, and more of the cold, wet stuff was plummeting down from the sky every second. Sometimes it drifted along, white and fluffy, looking almost pretty. For the most part, though, it blew sideways with stinging impact, eventually forcing her to slit her eyes against the storm. She put her head down and tried to shut out the cold and the snow, tried not to focus on anything but trudging along.

You're still on probation for this job, whether he's admitting it or not, she told herself. *Now is not the time to wimp out*.

Granted, she could argue some seriously extenuating circumstances, and even a terrifyingly in-control man such as Griffin would have to give her a pass on losing it just now. But thinking about it that way, like it was a test she needed to pass, gave her the strength to keep pushing forward.

She needed this job more than he had any reason to understand. She knew he thought she was too young and inexperienced to fill Kathleen's size-ten shoes, but she was bound and determined to do just that, because if she lost this job…

No, she wouldn't think about that, either. She'd just keep walking, keep proving herself.

They struggled against the wind, headed toward the mountainside house, which had seemed very close when they'd been driving over the bridge, but now felt very far away. Eventually they passed into the tree line and the wind abated slightly, but the steady incline of the driveway sapped Sophie's strength, and the temperature was dropping with the incoming storm. She'd all but stopped shivering, which she knew was a bad sign, and a glance at Griffin showed that his face reflected the gray of the sky, and his lips were tinged with blue.

They didn't have much time left.

He caught her look, met her eyes, and in his expression she saw only determination, and a flat-out refusal to admit defeat. Sounding far more like a drill sergeant than the efficient businessman she'd come to know over the past month, he growled, "Move your ass. That's an order."

If he'd coddled, she might have given in. Instead, the grating rasp of his voice had her stiffening her spine, gritting her teeth and forging onward as the snowfall thickened, going from stinging ice to fat flakes that whipped around them, swirling and turning the world to white. They were no longer a mismatched pair of boss and assistant—they were just two very cold human beings struggling to reach the basics: shelter and warmth. Safety.

Sophie's breath burned in her lungs, and her muscles felt dead and leaden. She stumbled and caught herself, stumbled again and would've fallen if it hadn't been for Griffin looping a strong arm around her waist. His silent strength urged her to keep going, not to give up.

Then, miraculously, the snow-covered surface beneath their feet changed, going from gravel to rough-edged cement bricks. Sophie jerked her head up and peered through her ice-encrusted lashes, and gave a cry of joy when she saw that they'd reached a parking area that encircled a central planting bed. Beyond that was the modern, pillar-fronted house.

"Come on, we're almost there!" Griffin said, shouting encouragement over the howling wind.

Through the whipping ice pellets, she could see the details that distance had obscured: the touches of stained glass on either side of the carved main doorway, and the intricate stonework and terraced landscaping leading up the walk. There were no lights, no sign of habitation, but that didn't matter. What mattered was the promise of getting out of the wind and—please, God—getting warm and dry.

The possibility spurred her on, and she felt a renewed burst of energy from Griffin, too. Together, they hurried up the wide stone steps leading to the front door. She grabbed the knob and twisted, her fingers slipping in the icy wetness. Her breath hissed between her teeth. "It's locked. D-do you have a key?"

"It's in the lake with the rest of our stuff." He cast around, kicking at several half-buried rocks that were frozen into the planting beds on either side of the entryway. When one came loose, he grabbed it, returned to where Sophie was waiting and used the rock to smash one of the narrow stained glass panels. The glass held against the first two blows, then gave way on the third, shattering inward in an act of destruction that would've bothered Sophie under any other circumstance, but in this case seemed very much like Griffin himself—direct and to the point.

He took a moment to clear the sharpest shards away from the edges, then stuck his arm through, and felt around.

"No alarms?" Sophie asked.

"Not yet," he replied, face set in concentration. "Too many workmen to bother. Besides, the cops are, what? Half an hour away? Forty minutes? Not worth it."

The reminder of how isolated they were, even more so with the incoming storm, brought a renewed chill chasing through Sophie. If Griffin hadn't gotten them safely out of the SUV, it might've been days, maybe longer before rescue personnel arrived. By then it would've been far too late.

Then again, if they didn't get warm soon, the same logic could very well apply.

The click of a deadbolt followed by the snick of a door lock came through the panel. Sophie twisted the knob, and nearly fell through when the door swung open beneath her weight. Griffin grabbed her and they piled through the door together. He kicked the panel shut at their backs, closing out most of the storm. The air went still, save for the draft that whistled through the broken window.

But it wasn't the sudden quiet that had Griffin cursing under his breath. It was the sight that confronted them, laying waste to any hope of an easy fix to their predicament.

"Oh," Sophie breathed, because there didn't seem to be much else to say.

The place was a wreck.

They were standing in a grand entryway—or what might've been a grand entryway in a previous life. Just then, though, it was bare studs and two-by-four construction, with electrical wiring spewed haphazardly around and the flooring pulled back to the plywood subfloor. The skeleton of a stairwell rose up to the right, leading to a second floor that wasn't much more than framework, and Sophie could see straight through to the back of the house, where nailed-down tarps seemed to be substituting for the back wall.

Worse, it wasn't much warmer inside than out, and she didn't hold much hope for a working heat source if the rest of the place looked as rough as the entryway. No doubt the hot water heater was off-line. Probably the electricity, too.

"Son of a bitch." Griffin took two steps away from her and stood vibrating with fury, his hands balled into fists. "That thieving bastard. Look what he's done to this place. That no-good, lying—" He snapped his teeth shut on the building tirade, and shook his head. "Never mind. I'll kill him later."

Sophie was startled by the threat, and by how natural it sounded, as though her slick businessman boss might actually be capable of hurting his contractor. Then again, she realized, looking at him now, this wasn't the Griffin Vaughn she'd grown more or less used to over the past month. He was wet, cold and angry, and should've looked like an absolute mess in wringing wet business clothes furred with globs of melting snow. But he didn't. He looked capable and masculine, and somehow larger than before.

He glanced over at her, his eyes dark, but softening a hint when he looked at her. "Let's get moving. There's got to be at least one room that still has walls and a working fireplace. That may be the best we can hope for."

Sophie nodded shakily. Trying to force her rapidly fuzzing brain to work, she said, "The housekeeper and her husband live here, right?"

He snapped his fingers. "Good call. Gemma and Erik are gone, but they've been doing the repairs to their quarters personally. Erik didn't want anyone else messing with his space. Which means there's a good chance that their apartment is in better shape than this disaster area. It's probably even still got electricity." He gestured off to the left, where drywall had been hung in a few places, though not taped or mudded. "Their quarters are in the back corner."

She expected him to head off and leave her to follow, reverting to business as usual now that they were, at the very least, out of the whipping wind. Instead, he took her arm, which probably meant she looked as bad as she felt. Telling herself she could be tough and self-reliant once they found someplace to hunker down and get warm, Sophie leaned into him as they walked down a short hallway, skirting drop cloths and torn-up sections of flooring.

"Obviously the generator's not running, but it's a standard model. I should be able to get it going again," Griffin said, sounding as though he was thinking aloud. "If not, hopefully Gemma and Erik's fireplace will be usable. I'd say we should try the guesthouse if we don't have any luck here, but Perry stripped it last month after the pipes froze and burst, and the barn and woodshed have zero in the way of amenities." He shot her a wry look. "If worse comes to worst, we can lay out some kitchen tile and build a campfire on it. There's plenty of scrap wood."

"True enough," Sophie murmured.

Moments later, they reached a closed door. Griffin tried the knob. "Locked." He glanced at her. "In this case, expediency trumps privacy."

Putting his shoulder to the door, he braced against it, half turned the knob and then gave a sort of combined jerk-kick that looked as if he'd practiced it to perfection. The door popped open, swinging inward to reveal a simply furnished sitting room.

"Thank God," Sophie breathed. Telling herself not to wonder where he'd learned how to pop a door off its lock without breaking any of the surrounding wood, she stumbled through the door.

Gemma and Erik's apartment proved to be a small, simply furnished suite done mostly in neutral beiges and browns, with accents of rust and navy. There was a kitchen and bathroom off to one side of the sitting room, and two doors leading from the other side. Sophie made a beeline for the doors. One opened into a small office filled with landscaping books and magazines. The other yielded pay dirt, not in the neat queen-size bed and southwestern-print curtains, but in the dresser and his-and-hers closets, which were full of clothes.

Wonderful, warm, dry clothes.

There were also photographs everywhere, scattered around the room in a variety of wood and metal frames. Even though she was freezing, Sophie couldn't help pausing for a quick scan of the pictures. She'd always been fascinated by families, and that was clearly what these photographs chronicled: a man and woman's lifetime together.

The earliest of the pictures showed the couple mugging for the camera from atop a pair of bored-looking horses in Western tack, against a backdrop of purplish mountains and a wide-open sky. The woman looked to be in her early twenties, dark-haired and pretty, with regular features and an open, engaging smile. Her eyes twinkled with mischief. The man was maybe a few years older, blond and fair-skinned, with the beginnings of a sunburn. He was looking at her with an expression of complete and utter adoration.

The other photos showed the couple at different points in their lives together—their wedding; a baby, then two; family candids as the children grew. The man's hair went from blond to white, while the woman's stayed relentlessly—and perhaps unnaturally—dark brown, but her face softened with age, and living. There were other weddings, other vacations, until the last photo, which sat on the beside table and showed just the man and the woman, in their late fifties, maybe early sixties, wrapped around each other at the edge of Lonesome Lake, with the now-demolished bridge in the background.

The woman's expression still twinkled with mischief. The man still had eyes only for her. That love, and the sense of family unity that practically jumped out of the photos, put an uncomfortable kink in Sophie's windpipe, right in the region of her heart.

"Here." Griffin appeared in the doorway behind her and tossed an armload of terrycloth towels on the bed, having apparently raided the bathroom. He moved past her and rooted through the dresser and closet, coming up with jeans, a shirt and thick sweater, along with two pairs of wool socks and a worn men's belt. Then he headed back out, saying over his shoulder, "You take this room, I'll change in the office." Then he paused in the doorway. "What's wrong?"

"Nothing." She made herself move away from the bedside photo and start picking through the dresser. "I'm guessing we're out of luck in the shower department?"

"Sorry. The pump is battery-powered, so we've got running water, but it's going to be cold. I'll have to get the generator going for hot water. First, though, I want to get us dry and see about starting a fire."

Sophie nodded. "Of course." As he left the room, she pawed through the dresser, telling herself not to waste time feeling squeamish about going through a stranger's things. The worst of the bone-numbing cold had eased now that they were out of the storm, but getting dry and warm was still a major priority.

"I'll reimburse them for the clothes," Griffin said unexpectedly from the other room. "So stop stalling. If I don't hear you getting naked in the count of ten, I'm coming in and doing it for you."

From another man the words might've been a tease, or a threat. Coming from laconic Griffin Vaughn, who didn't seem to suffer from the same zing of chemistry Sophie felt every time she was within five feet of him, they were simply a fact. As far as she could tell, he hadn't even noticed she was female—theirs was purely a business relationship. Or rather, the possibility of one, if she worked very hard and managed not to dump any more coffee on him.

Unfortunately, she got clumsy when she was nervous, and something about the way he looked in the throes of negotiation—all stern-faced and dark-eyed, with a flash of excitement when he moved in for the coup de grâce—well, that made her all too aware that he was male. Which made her nervous, and therefore clumsy.

"Sophie?" Griffin called, and his low-voiced inquiry buzzed along her nerve endings like liquid fire, the heat brought by the thought of him undressing her, and focusing all that dark-eyed intensity on her.

But the threat got her moving, and she started stripping out of her wet, clinging clothes. "You don't have to come in," she called after a moment. "I'm naked." She blushed at the echo of her own words, bringing stinging warmth to her cheeks. "Never mind. Forget I said that, okay?"

She grabbed the towels he'd left for her and scrubbed them over her skin, warming some life back into her chilled flesh, which seemed strange and disconnected, as though it didn't belong to her anymore. Soon, though, life began to return—pins and needles at first, then stinging pain. Skin that had been fish-belly-white moments earlier flared to angry red, and she hissed with the return of feeling as she drew on a pair of borrowed jeans and a turtleneck, socks and thick sweater.

She soon realized that she and Gemma were built very differently: the other woman was taller and significantly narrower in the hips and bust. Doing the best with what she had, Sophie rolled up the cuffs to deal with the too-long jeans, and hoped the sweater was loose enough to disguise how tightly the clothes fit across her chest

and rear. Like Griffin, she skipped borrowing under-
wear, instead going commando beneath her clothing.

Logic said that shouldn't have felt daring under the
circumstances, but she was acutely aware of the chafe
of material against her unprotected skin as she left the
bedroom. Not that he would notice, because he was all
about business. Which was a relief, despite the fact that
she'd developed a mild crush on him. Indeed, she only
allowed herself the crush *because* he wasn't interested.
After what had happened at her last job, where she'd
been romanced and played by a jerk of the first degree,
and said jerk had set out to destroy her career options,
the last thing Sophie was looking to do was get roman-
tically involved with her boss. No thanks, not going
there again.

Heading out of the bedroom into the main sitting
area, Sophie found Griffin crouched by the fireplace.
Kindling and mid-sized logs were neatly organized in
a burnished copper tub to one side of the hearth, and a
small drift of ashes and charred wood inside the fireplace suggested it was fully functional, which was very
good news indeed.

Griffin had used some of the kindling to build a neat
teepee, with crumpled paper in the center, and a trio of
larger logs crossed in a tripod arching over the kindling.
The setup, like the hip-check he'd used to open the door,
looked practiced and professional, which didn't fit with
the image of the polished businessman she'd spent the
past month assisting.

The Griffin Vaughn she worked for wore custom

suits and monogrammed shirts, yet cared little for fashion. His entire focus was centered on VaughnTec. He was seeking to grow the company by shrinking their products even further while increasing the functionality of each unit. VaughnTec, which was part R & D, part mass market, combined cameras, computers, phones, music, video games and a host of other functionalities into small handheld units so simple that even the technologically challenged could figure them out within a few minutes. It was Griffin who'd moved the company in that direction when he'd taken it over from his uncle, Griffin who'd made it into the powerhouse it was today. He was ruthless without being cruel, cold without being unfriendly. But even when he was being his most cordial, she'd noticed, he maintained a thick barrier between him and the world, a reserve that she'd only seen soften when he was talking to his young son, Luke, on the phone.

Despite the pressures of Sophie's job situation—i.e. that losing it was a real threat yet absolutely not an option—she had grown, if not comfortable with Griffin's business persona, at least confident that she knew where she stood with him. He was polite but not terribly friendly, and had made it obvious that he considered her too young and green for the position. But at the same time, he'd been clear about his needs and wishes, and had given her ample room to perform the tasks Kathleen had laid out for her, which had mostly consisted of scheduling his travel and juggling calls, retrieving information and hunting up the occasional meal. All of those things were well within the skills she'd learned in the courses she'd taken for certification, and if she'd fumbled a few times when nerves had overcome training, he'd seemed to let those instances go. All in all, she'd found him a tough but fair employer. Yes, he was far too attractive for her peace of mind, but she thought she understood the Griffin Vaughn she'd been working for.

However, she didn't know the Griffin Vaughn who was crouched down in front of the fireplace wearing a fisherman's sweater and faded jeans, blowing a small ember into a flame, then feeding it strips of kindling until the fire flared up and lit the teepee he'd built so carefully. Logic and what she knew about her boss suggested that he should've looked like a man completely out of his natural element. Instead, he wore the borrowed clothes like they were old familiar friends, and he moved with neat economy as he built the fire up, coaxing it to accept the first of the logs. His towel-dried hair was engagingly rumpled, making him seem younger, though his face still gave away little of the man within.

Illumination from the flames danced across his forbidding features. The warm light was a welcome contrast to the dimness outside, where the world had gone to grayish-white and the day was fading hours earlier than it should have.

The fire drew Sophie forward, even as nerves warned her not to get too close to this new version of Griffin Vaughn. She stood beside him and stretched her hands out toward the fire, but felt little relief from the cold.

"It'll need to warm the brickwork before much heat starts bouncing out into the room," Griffin said.

"Were you an Eagle Scout or something?" she asked, unable to help herself, because too many things weren't quite lining up between this Griffin and the one she thought she knew.

"Or something." He rose, dusting the ash from his hands, and wound up standing very near her. Too near.

She could see the hints of hazel in his green eyes, saw them darken when tension snapped into the air between them. She was suddenly very aware of his height and strength, and the way the smell of wood smoke fit with the sight of him in jeans and a sweater—raw, masculine and elemental. And in that instant, she realized she'd been wrong about at least one thing: Griffin most definitely knew she was a woman. The knowledge was in his eyes, which were more alive than she'd ever seen them.

Heat flared suddenly, not from the fireplace, but within her. The warmth spread from her core to her extremities, which still tingled with the aftereffects of the freezing conditions, and the danger they'd survived together.

Maybe it was that danger that had her leaning into him, maybe it was the attraction she'd told herself to ignore all these weeks. Either way, she was suddenly very close to him, and he to her, their lips a breath apart.

A log shifted in the fireplace, sending sparks. The noise startled her, breaking through the sensual fog and slapping her with a shout from her subconscious. *Danger!*

Grabbing hold of herself, she took a big step back, away from the fireplace. Away from the man. As she did so, she was aware that he did the exact same thing, levering himself away. In that moment, she saw the shields drop back down over his expression, distancing him more surely than the floor space now separating them. Suddenly, he was no longer a regular guy starting a fire in the fireplace; he was a millionaire businessman who ate small companies for breakfast, and just happened to be wearing a sweater and jeans.

More important, he was her boss.

Heat rushed to Sophie's cheeks and she berated herself for being stupid, for getting too close to the line with the man who had far too much control over her future, more than he even realized. "I'm sorry," she whispered. "I shouldn't have—"

"I'm going out," he interrupted, heading for the door, where he grabbed a pair of tired-looking boots and a heavy, bright-red waterproof parka, borrowing more of Erik's clothing. "I want to look around a little and get the generators going. There are a bunch of outbuildings—barns, a guesthouse, that sort of thing. I want to make sure they're as secure as they're going to get before the main force of the storm hits. I'd appreciate it if you'd check the kitchen and see about some food. Do you still have your PDA in your coat?"

A unit of his own design, the PDAs combined a phone, computer and GPS functionalities into a single small unit.

Sophie nodded. "Yes, I do. But won't it have shorted out?" They were seriously useful little machines, but still, they were machines.

"Sometimes the little buggers come back to life after they've gotten wet. Say, for instance, after a toddler tries to flush one of them." His expression softened a hair at the tangential mention of his son, but his eyes stayed cool on hers, as though he was waiting to see what she would do next, how she would handle herself in the aftermath of the sensually charged moment they'd just shared.

She was going to ignore it, that was what she was going to do, Sophie decided on the spot. Just as he'd done.

Plastering a neutral expression on her face, she tried to drop herself back into the executive assistant's role, even though it didn't seem to fit quite right under the circumstances. She nodded. "Food and PDA. Got it. If I get the phone up and running, do you want me to call Sheriff Martinez and let him know what happened?"

Griffin glanced through a window, at the whiteout conditions outside. "Definitely. See if he can get someone out here to pick us up." He lifted a shoulder. "It's a long shot, but you never know. Maybe this is just a squall before the blizzard."

A howl of wind hit the side of the mansion and rattled the windows in their frames, seeming to mock the idea. Somewhere else in the house there was a crashing noise, suggesting that Perry and his work crew hadn't secured the construction zone sufficiently against the force of the incoming blizzard.

Griffin winced, but didn't say anything, just jerked on the borrowed boots, shrugged into the coat and headed for the door.

He paused at the threshold and looked back at her. "I want you to lock the deadbolt after me, and keep it locked."

He was gone before she could ask why that would be necessary, given that they were alone in the mansion. She flipped the bolt as ordered, but couldn't help wondering who he was trying to guard her from. Himself? That didn't make any sense.

She heard his footsteps recede, heard a distant door slam. Moments later, she caught a flash of his red parka as he headed, not around the generator shed, but rather straight across the parking circle and down the driveway.

He was going to look at the crash site, she realized, and the realization brought a shiver of fear as she clicked onto the one question she hadn't yet asked herself about the situation—not how they were going to manage to wait out the storm, or what would happen if she and Griffin ended up face-to-face again and they weren't smart enough to step away, but rather the all-important question they hadn't had the time to ask before. Why had the bridge given out beneath them? Was it just bad luck?

Or had it been something more sinister?

Chapter Three

The wind was sharp as hell and Griffin's core temp wasn't all the way back to normal, but he kept moving down the driveway, his booted feet sliding in the rapidly deepening snow. The visibility wasn't great, but he was certain he could make it down to the crash site and back up to the mansion before the conditions became impossible. Besides, the longer he waited, the less likely he was to find anything useful.

If, of course, there was anything to find.

Maybe it was just a flat-out coincidence that he and Sophie had been in the SUV that broke the camel's back, so to speak. Maybe it was simply that their vehicle had finally overloaded the time-stressed cement bridge and brought it crashing down.

Thing was, he wasn't a big believer in coincidence. That lesson had been hard learned in the service, and his years in the business world had only reinforced his conviction that everything happened for a reason, and that anything could be prevented from happening twice if he was smart enough, disciplined enough. Controlled enough.

At the thought of control, he flashed back to what had just happened in front of the fireplace, when he'd almost lost the self-discipline he prided himself on. He'd very nearly given in to temptation and kissed Sophie. What was more, she would've welcomed his kiss; he'd seen it in her eyes, felt it in the tension-laden air.

The attraction was there, had been there from the first moment she'd walked into his office. He'd managed to tamp it down to an awareness, and she'd hidden the fact, as well. Most of the time, anyway. But that moment in front of the fireplace had shattered their pretense of disinterest. And damned if that wasn't going to complicate things, big time, not just over the next couple of days if they wound up snowed in together, but over the longer term, as well. He couldn't afford to get tangled up with another woman who wanted to trade affection for a step up in life.

It wasn't that he thought Sophie was playing him, either. His instincts said she was exactly what she seemed: a young, relatively inexperienced woman who was getting a late start in the workforce for whatever reason, and was earnest in her efforts to do a good job. But that didn't mean she wouldn't set her sights higher if he gave her reason to think it was a possibility.

That wasn't ego talking, either. It was just the way he'd learned the world worked. And if that felt faintly disloyal to the memory of his own childhood, it couldn't be helped. His parents had met and fallen in love in a very different time, and they'd been lucky to find a perfect match in each other. He'd tried to find the same sort of match and failed. Worse, the last failure had hurt his son, as well. There was no way he was putting Luke—or himself—through another such ordeal.

They were fine on their own. There was nothing wrong with it being just the guys. In fact, the only thing wrong with the arrangement was the extensive traveling Griffin had to do for work, while Luke stayed behind in San Fran with Darryn. Then again, it was a huge relief knowing Luke was safe at home, especially given that Griffin didn't yet know exactly what sort of a situation he was dealing with.

His musings had occupied him on the half-mile trek down to the bridge. Now, as he got within sight of the wrecked span, he once again replayed those last few moments before it had given way. He remembered a banging noise, like a backfire. Or maybe an explosion. But seriously, what were the chances someone had rigged the bridge? And why?

Unfortunately, he could make an all too plausible case for the "why." When Sophie called to set up the meeting with Perry, she'd mentioned that she and Griffin were planning to tour the estate that afternoon, before the storm hit. What if the contractor was more than just shoddy or a little crooked? What if the delays were only the surface of the problem, and Perry was actually up to something even more devious, something that he couldn't afford to let an outsider see? The theory might seem pretty farfetched, but the contractor had given Griffin some seriously negative vibes the last few times they'd spoken. At the time, Griffin had assumed

Perry was spooked by his run of bad luck on the project, and rightfully fearing for his job.

Now, as Griffin worked his way out to the place where the bridge had collapsed, testing each step as he went, he wondered whether Perry had perhaps been afraid of something else entirely, like his employer finding out about dire doings up at Lonesome Lake. And if so, whether the contractor had decided to slow him down, or worse.

When Griffin reached the edge and looked down, he cursed, giving up any hope he might've had of recovering his and Sophie's suitcases or computer bags. There was no sign of the SUV, save for a rough patch where it had broken through the ice, and even that was rapidly smoothing over to snowy sameness.

"Son of a bitch," he grated, liking the situation even less than he had before. For the duration of the storm, it looked like he and Sophie were going to be down to borrowed clothes and a doused PDA.

And each other.

As TIME PASSED and Griffin still didn't return, Sophie kept herself moving because she figured it was better than working herself into a state of panic.

Deciding she'd give her boss another half hour before she went out looking for him, she turned to the tasks he'd given her: pulling together some food and rebooting her PDA. She started by making a survey of the supplies in Gemma's pantry, and quickly realized they were in pretty good shape in the nonperishable food department. The shelves were crammed with canned goods, along with glass jars of pasta sauce and home-made preserves. There was plenty of dried pasta, along with pancake mix and coffee, and even powdered eggs and milk.

"Looks like you're prepared to be snowed in for the entire winter," Sophie said to the absent housekeeper. The thought wasn't particularly cheering.

Deciding to keep it simple, in case the meal had to wait while she went out looking for Griffin, Sophie added tap water to a can of condensed tomato soup, and broke out a box of mac and cheese, knowing firsthand that it tasted fine made with powdered milk and no butter. Once she had the pasta cooking, she headed out into the main room, where a welcome sight greeted her, namely the telltale wink of an LED light from her PDA.

"Aha. A sign of life." Relieved by the thought that they might not be completely cut off from the outside world, she crossed to the unit and pressed a few buttons, shutting down the handheld computer and then power-ing it back up to see if it would come fully online.

When it did, it showed her a half charge on the battery and a weak but tenable network signal. Crossing her fingers that the call would go through, she phoned Sheriff Martinez.

He answered on the second ring. "Ms. LaRue? Are you back in the city? That was quick."

"Hi, Sheriff. And no, we're not even close to being down off the mountain." Sophie sketched out the situa-tion, trying to give the facts as calmly as she could, even though it wasn't easy to keep a tremor out of her voice as she described their plunge into Lonesome Lake and the harrowing trek up to the house.

There was a long pause after she finished, and then Martinez said, "Okay, here's the problem we're going to be facing. That snow out there? It's the real deal. The blizzard got here faster than predicted and is likely to be here for a good long time. Two days, maybe three. More importantly, the road up to Lonesome Lake goes through a pass that's impossible to keep clear during a storm. Which means you're going to be stuck there until the blizzard blows itself out."

She heard something else in his voice, and asked the same question Griffin had earlier. "What aren't you telling me?"

There was another, longer pause. "Maybe Vaughn should call me when he gets back in."

"We'll have to conserve the battery on this phone," she said, too aware that unless Griffin managed to rescue their chargers from the SUV, they were going to have to make her half-charged battery last. "So why don't you just tell me whatever it is that you'd rather tell him?" Nerves had her edging toward irritation more quickly than she would have otherwise. "I *am* a fully functional grown-up, you know."

"Yes, ma'am," the sheriff said politely, "but you're not a highly decorated marine TecSpec with some serious combat experience."

Her breath whistled between her teeth at that. "Are you saying that Griffin is?"

"Yes, ma'am. It popped up on the background check we ran as part of the Del Gardo investigation. So the way I'm figuring it, if you had to be stranded up at Lonesome Lake for a few days, you picked a pretty useful guy to be stuck with."

"I didn't pick him," she murmured automatically, but her brain was spinning.

Eagle Scout, indeed. He'd been a marine, had he? Well, that probably explained the skills he possessed that were decidedly non-MBA-approved, and the quiet reserve that sometimes seemed as much about survival as it did business. And yeah, under their current circumstances it helped her to know that he could deal with dangerous situations better than the average tycoon— if there was such a thing. But at the same time, the revelation put a serious shiver down the back of her neck.

She hadn't known about his military service. What else didn't she know about him?

A tap at the door to the apartment had her spinning with a gasp. She relaxed only slightly when Griffin's voice said, "It's me."

"What's wrong?" the sheriff asked quickly, still on the phone.

"Griffin's back." She unbolted the door and let him through, then held out the phone. "The sheriff wants to talk to you."

He nodded and shucked out of his gloves and parka, and hung them near the door, where a mat was set out to catch the wet. When he reached for the phone, his fingers brushed against Sophie's. Warmth kicked at the contact, but she forced herself not to jerk away, forced herself to act as though she hadn't felt a thing.

From the way his green eyes darkened, though, he knew. And he'd felt it, too.

So much for there being a safe distance between them. She had a feeling the next few days were going to be very dangerous to her equilibrium. But she needed this job. She needed to be able to stay in San Fran near the facility where her mother was being treated now, and she needed to make a good enough salary to cover more than the bare minimum payments on her various loans. Which meant she couldn't risk making the same mistake she'd made at her last job. What was more, she couldn't risk Griffin knowing about that mistake. Kathleen had overlooked the rumors and hired Sophie anyway, but Sophie had a feeling Griffin wouldn't be nearly so sanguine about it. The members of upper crust San Fran society tended to stick together.

After a moment, Griffin nodded, though neither of them had said anything. Then he took the phone, headed into the office and shut the door behind him.

Sophie stood for a moment, staring after him. Irritation rose. Granted, he was the boss, and he certainly had the right to take private calls in private. Hell, he'd have that right even if their roles were reversed. But what could possibly be private about a conversation with Sheriff Martinez? Whatever the sheriff was telling Griffin, it had to be related to the situation out at Lonesome Lake…and that most definitely involved her.

Setting her teeth, she marched toward the office. She

wasn't sure what she was going to do when she got there, but that didn't matter because the door opened before she reached it, and Griffin stood there, filling the doorway with his face set in harsh, unyielding lines.

She halted an arm's length away, tension coiling in her stomach. "What's wrong?"

"Perry's wife hasn't spoken to him since right after you called to tell him we were coming to meet with him." He paused, and held up his hand to show her a slender wire attached to a round, circular metal scrap, which he held pinched between his thumb and forefinger. "And I found this down by the bridge."

She stared. "What is it?" she asked, even though on some level she already knew.

"A piece from a radio-controlled detonator. The bridge didn't just give way. Somebody blew the damn thing out from underneath us."

GRIFFIN WATCHED Sophie's color drain and hoped she didn't pass out on him. If she did, though, he'd deal with it, just as he was doing his best to deal with the situation that was developing around them.

After finding the detonator scraps and evidence of a blast pattern, he'd raced back to the mansion, hoping to hell he'd find Sophie intact, that the bomber hadn't been waiting for them to split up before he made his move. But there was no sign of the bomber, no evidence of another move.

So what now? He didn't know.

His first instinct had been to not tell her about the

bomb, which was why he'd talked to the sheriff in private. That wasn't because he was trying to keep her from worrying, either. It was more that he was used to keeping the most important pieces of information to himself. Whether in battle or in business, information was power. Besides, he was used to being alone, dealing with things alone, and didn't see any need to share.

After talking to the sheriff, though, the business side of him had overtaken the soldier, and he'd reconsidered. Logic said that Sophie needed to know about the potential danger. What if the bomber was still somewhere on the estate? Given how quickly the storm had come up, that seemed like a distinct possibility. If he—and Griffin was assuming it was a he, based on general chauvinism and his gut-level belief that his contractor was the culprit—had stashed a truck on one of the rear access roads that wound through the forest surrounding the estate, he might've gotten away before the blizzard hit. But if not, there was a good chance that he'd gotten caught in the storm just as Griffin and Sophie had been…and in the same location.

So Griffin told Sophie about the bomb, showed her the detonator cap, and described the crash scene and what he'd noticed of the blast pattern, even though a piece of him wanted to shield her from the ugly truth.

As he spoke, a range of emotions crossed her face, shock and understanding, followed by a flash of anger and then outright fear.

"Somebody tried to kill us," she said softly.

"Yeah." He didn't try to sugarcoat. "Looks like it."

She was badly shaken; her light brown eyes were wide in her pale face, and she leaned a shoulder against the door frame as though that was the only thing holding her up. The chivalry his mother had worked to instill in him said that he should go to her, comfort her. Instead, he stayed put. He didn't trust the protective feelings that had kicked in the moment he realized she might be in danger, didn't like how they had threatened to overwhelm the logic that said he and Sophie were far better off keeping a professional distance.

After a moment, the shock started to fade and he could see Sophie begin to think it through. Her faint frown crinkled the skin between her eyebrows, and she said, "Did the sheriff have any idea who might've set the explosives?"

"He's reserving judgment." Actually, Martinez had cursed his head off, cursed the storm, and then cursed Griffin for being a pigheaded idiot who'd insisted on driving into the teeth of an oncoming blizzard.

Griffin couldn't argue with any of his points, either. However, what was done was done, and they could only go forward from there. Which meant figuring out who had tried to kill them, and whether he was still on the property. Either way, they needed to fortify the apartment, get it as safe as they possibly could, and then hunker down to wait out the storm.

Martinez seemed to think that the sophisticated detonator suggested the work of a professional, but Griffin disagreed. Just about anyone with a military background and a passing familiarity with explosives could've

bought and used the device. That was one of the down-
sides of the Internet. And surprise, surprise, when
Griffin had pressed, Martinez had admitted that Perry
was ex-army. The sheriff's reluctance had also warned
Griffin of something else, namely that Martinez and the
contractor were friendly.

Which, in his experience with smaller jurisdictions,
meant that the sheriff might be less than forthcoming
with important information. Indeed, the sheriff hadn't
wanted to tell Sophie about the contractor's apparent
disappearance, he'd waited to tell Griffin, then let him
decide whether to share the info. That was probably
less about Martinez being a small-town cop and more
about him not wanting to frighten Sophie more than
necessary, Griffin figured. He'd told her, though. She
needed to know what they were up against.

Sophie's eyes narrowed as she looked at him, guessing something from his expression. "You think you
know who it was, don't you?" She straightened away
from the door frame. "Is someone after you? Is this
about the HiTek acquisition?" But she shook her head,
answering her own question. "No, that doesn't make
sense. They're out in New York, and they wouldn't have
known we were coming here. Which means it's someone here, either someone who wants to hurt one of us—
presumably you, because I'm not the sort of person
who'd pop up on anyone's radar screen—or someone
trying to keep people away from Lonesome Lake." Her
eyes snapped to his. "Vincent Del Gardo."

Frankly, Griffin found it unnerving that her thought

process had taken her there so quickly. He'd known she was intelligent—there was no way she could've picked up the vagaries of his work and the business research he'd been asking her to do without being smart. But he never would've expected her mind to work that way. "Let's not jump to conclusions, especially when even Martinez admitted there's no evidence that Del Gardo has been anywhere in the vicinity for several months. Besides, there's another alternative. Perry Long."

The wrinkle between her eyebrows deepened. "You think your contractor tried to kill us? Why, so you wouldn't figure out that he's been billing you for repairs while gutting the house and selling off the material? Because that's sure what it looks like he's been doing."

"He'd think of the bomb as a way for him to protect himself," Griffin countered. "Especially if there's more to it than just the renovations. What if he's got something going on up here that he doesn't want anyone to know about? Something he thought he could be done with by the time I wanted to come out and see the place?"

"Such as?"

"I don't know," he admitted. "But I intend to find out. Martinez said he'd have two of his people, a Callie MacBride of the KCCU and forensic investigator Ava Wright, go back over the evidence they collected when they searched the estate, and see if they can come up with any ideas. In the meantime, we need to dig in and get ourselves prepared to wait out the storm."

Sophie nodded, pale but resolute. "Tell me what to do and I'll do it. We're in this together."

He glanced around the room. The soldier in him liked the ground-floor location, which gave them escape options. But he didn't like the idea of someone outside being able to see in, without being seen in the swirling snow. "I want you to pull all the shades and keep the lights to a minimum when it gets dark. I saw some kerosene lanterns in the office, and some candles in the bedroom."

"I found a couple of flashlights in the kitchen," Sophie volunteered.

"Good, I'll take one, you keep one. Conserve the batteries, though. We won't know about electricity until I check out the generator and the electrical panel."

"You didn't do that while you were out there?" she asked, sending him a sidelong look.

"I wanted to get back here and see about the PDA. Figured Martinez needed to know about the bridge ASAP." Griffin left out the part where he'd nearly panicked, thinking he'd left her alone in the house, wide open to attack.

He'd only responded that way because she was his responsibility. Logically, she wouldn't be in this situation if he'd listened to her and put off the trip to Lonesome Lake. Instead he'd dragged her straight into danger, albeit unwittingly. But unwitting or not, the danger was a fact, and it was up to him to make sure she didn't suffer because of his miscalculation.

"The signal's weak and I've got maybe half a charge on the battery," she said about the PDA.

"Leave it out so I can call home a little later, okay?"

"Will do. You want me to hold the food until you've restarted the generator?"

"Please. And there's another thing." Griffin headed for the bedroom and pulled out one of the drawers on Erik's side of the dresser. Just as Martinez had said it would be, there was a .45 nestled in the back, beside a box of ammo. Returning to the main room, Griffin loaded the weapon while Sophie's eyes got big. He held it out, butt first. "I want you to keep this with you while I'm gone. Just in case."

She held up her hands in a "no thanks" gesture. "You take it. I wouldn't know what to do with it."

"It's easy. This is the safety, this is the trigger." He pointed them out, then pantomimed the actions as he said, "Safety off, point the gun, pull the trigger. Boom, done."

She stared at him, expression clouding. "You think he's still up here, don't you?"

"It's a possibility," he hedged. In reality, his soldier's instincts, which he found were coming back online quickly even though he'd been a civilian for nearly seven years now, had started chiming a warning on his hike down the mountain. Finding the detonator had only confirmed what his instincts were saying: he and Sophie weren't alone.

"Then I should come with you. I can stand lookout while you work on the generator."

"You'll distract me," he said bluntly. "Cover the windows, stay near the center of the space and keep the gun with you. I'll be quick, I swear, and when I get back we'll rig a trip wire around the perimeter, so we'll have some warning if anyone tries to get at us."

It took a long moment, but finally she swallowed hard, nodded, and took the .45 from him. "Okay. Make it quick."

"I will." He suited up again in Erik's boots and parka, thinking for a moment of the man who usually wore the clothes, and how he might feel under the circumstances, having to leave behind the woman he'd been married to for nearly three decades. "Lock up behind me," Griffin said, his voice rasping on the words.

"Of course." Sophie crossed the distance between them, and though he knew she only intended to throw the deadbolt once he was gone, he had a fleeting thought that she was going to kiss him goodbye, or good luck.

That would be what a man like Erik could expect, the sort of man who had the love of a good woman, one who would kiss him goodbye and welcome him back again when he returned. And for a crazy moment, Griffin wanted to be that man. He wanted to kiss Sophie, wanted to know she'd be waiting for him, and that they'd have the long winter's night ahead of them, together in the fire-lit darkness, with the storm doing nothing more dangerous than insulating them from the outside world for a few days.

And, Griffin thought, he'd clearly hit his head when the SUV fell through the bridge. He didn't remember doing so, and didn't have a bump on his scalp, but that was the only rational explanation for the completely irrational urge.

There was no arguing that Sophie was a lovely woman. More than that, she was vivid and alive, and proving to be so much more than he'd thought upon first meeting her. She was clever and interactive, and a stronger business asset than he'd expected. And yes, she was gorgeous and single, and he was a red-blooded human male, and just about any guy would have a few "let's get closer" thoughts under the circumstances. But that was just it, he wasn't just any guy, and he had more than just his own needs to think about.

"Lock up," he repeated, pushed through the door and slammed it at his back. Though his survival instincts were shrilling for him to get out of there and do it fast, he stopped and waited, needing to hear the deadbolt click safely into place before he left.

But it didn't click. Instead, the door opened and Sophie stepped through, wearing Gemma's boots and parka, and carrying the .45.

"What in the hell do you think you're doing?" he demanded, glaring at her.

She lifted her chin and glared right back. "I'm watching your back, that's what I'm doing. You can accept it and we can move on, or I can pretend to listen when you order me back inside, and then I'll follow you from a distance. Your choice. Either way, I'm coming with you. It's stupid for me to stay behind when I could be helping."

He glared a moment longer, but saw that her mind was made up. And truthfully, she had a point. Yes, he'd be distracted if she was there, but he'd be worried about her regardless. And a lookout was never a bad thing.

"Fine." He snapped off a nod. "Don't slow me down. And for crap's sake, don't point the gun at me."

Flicking on his flashlight and keeping the beam low, he started moving down the hallway, headed for the corner of the building closest to the generator shed. He heard her footsteps and the rustle of clothing right behind him as she fell into step, bringing up the rear of their two-person army.

And damned if he didn't feel a little better, after all.

THE MOMENT THE BALD MAN slid open the door to the barn, where he'd been hiding out in a corner of the loft, he knew he'd miscalculated. Not because the snow was still whipping down from a gray-cast sky, though that would certainly slow him down, but because he smelled wood smoke.

Someone had lit a fire nearby, most likely at the main mansion, which was the only structure even halfway to livable, and at that, only in the servant's quarters. Since the staff was long gone, that could only mean one thing: he'd left the scene of the crash too quickly. Griffin Vaughn and his secretary must've somehow gotten to safety, after all. Lucky them.

Too bad for them, their luck had just run out.

Chapter Four

Sophie couldn't decide if she was proud of herself for taking a stand, or appalled at the stand she'd chosen to take. Granted, if the bomber was still in the area there was no guarantee that the apartment was any safer than elsewhere…but the walls and locked door had certainly provided the illusion of safety, if nothing else.

Instead, she was out in the main house, following practically in Griffin's footprints as he searched the mansion from bottom to top and down again, making sure they were alone in the huge, gutted structure. As they searched, he was also gathering construction detritus that he deemed useful—mostly scrap metal and rope—and piling it near the apartment for use in setting a perimeter defense, or at least an early warning system. They didn't find any evidence of there being anybody else in the house, though there was a broken upstairs window that hadn't been tarped over, making Griffin wonder aloud if it had been smashed after the workmen left the site.

Sophie tried to make as little noise as possible as she

followed him from room to room, but where he seemed
to move soundlessly, gliding across the plywood subfloor and among the scattered drop cloths, she felt like
she was making a major racket, clumping along in
Gemma's too-large boots. Griffin didn't shush her,
though. He didn't say or do anything to acknowledge
her presence, hadn't done so since they'd left the apartment. She wondered if he'd tuned her out completely,
focusing on the search. If so, she envied him the ability.

She would've liked to shut her brain down, forcing
it to focus on the task at hand—watching the doorways
as they passed, staying alert for any sign of malevolent
company. Instead, she felt as though she was fighting
to corral her thoughts when they wanted to scatter in a
dozen different directions.

Her blood hummed from her standoff with Griffin,
and with fear of the man who might be stalking them,
the man who had already tried to kill them once. She
was aware of the solid, intimidating weight of the gun
she carried with her. And she was acutely conscious of
Griffin walking an arm's length ahead of her. His long-
legged strides carried him effortlessly along, and his
shoulders were straight and square beneath the
borrowed parka, making him seem larger even than
before, as though he'd grown with the need to recall his
days as a soldier.

In some ways it made her feel better, knowing that he'd
been a marine. But at the same time it left her unsettled.
The one picture she had of her father was one of him in
uniform, square-shouldered, square-jawed and capable-

looking. Like Griffin. Over the years, she'd come to associate that picture with the family she'd wished she had, the one her mother had been unable to provide.

Focus, she told herself, and shifted her grip on the .45 as they came to a renovated exterior door that still had strips of protective adhesive on the brass hardware. Griffin glanced at her. "The generator shed is on the left. Cover me from the doorway. If anything happens…" He trailed off. "Well, just try not to shoot me, okay?"

He waited for her nod before he turned the deadbolt, put his shoulder to the door, and shoved it open.

A gust of wind nearly tore the doorknob from his grasp. The gale whipped through the opening, bringing a slash of stinging ice pellets and a deep, biting cold Sophie hadn't been prepared for. She'd thought the unheated house was frigid, but that dry cool was nothing like what she stepped into as she followed Griffin through the door and out into the storm.

The whole world was white and cold and angry, the noise and power of the storm frightening. There was snow everywhere, drifting against the side of the house and over lumps and bumps of landscaping rendered unidentifiable by a thick layer of white.

The wind slammed into Sophie, sending her reeling, but her feet stayed stuck in the shin-high snow. She nearly overbalanced, would have if Griffin hadn't grabbed her free arm, stopping her mid-fall. He leaned in, so his face was close to hers, and shouted, "Forget about staying back. The storm's stronger than I thought it would be. We'll stick together."

She nodded rather than trying to out-shout the storm. Hanging on to each other for balance, and so they wouldn't lose each other in the limited visibility, they headed for the generator shed. Each step was a huge effort, each yard gained toward their destination a small victory.

Sophie's heart was pounding and the frigid air was burning in her lungs by the time they reached the narrow exterior room that housed the generators. It was an elaborate lean-to built off the main structure, with metal sheeting she assumed was a firebreak separating it from the rest of the mansion. There were large vents at either end, no doubt intended to keep the generator fumes from building up.

Those vents also let in the cold and the blowing snow, she realized as soon as Griffin had cleared the double doors and opened the slider enough for the two of them to squeeze through. The interior was sheltered against the wind but the inside air wasn't much warmer than outside, and small drifts of white powder had collected beneath the vents.

"Not very weatherproof in here," she noted, taking a look around the narrow room, which housed two big machines, along with assorted wiring and heavy dials.

"We won't stay long," Griffin said. "Just keep watching."

"Watching what? You can't see three feet in front of yourself out there." But she took position by the open door, squinting into the too-white world of the storm.

Griffin took a circuit around the room, checking another set of doors at the far end of the lean-to, and paying close attention to one set of dials. Seeming satisfied, he turned to the nearer of the two big machines and started fiddling with the control panel. Catching Sophie's glance in his direction, he called, "There's no sign that it's been tampered with, and no sign of charges or a timer having been set. I think we're okay to start it up."

Since she hadn't been worried about the possibility of the big generators being sabotaged until just that second, she could only nod, and then close her eyes when he hit the button to start the generator.

The machine purred to life, and she let out a relieved breath. "Next time you think there's a chance something might blow up on us, warn me, okay?"

He raised an eyebrow. "Would it have helped you to know ahead of time?"

Probably not, she admitted inwardly. Aloud, she said, "Did you do this sort of thing a lot when you were in the marines?"

"Who told you about that?"

"The sheriff, on the phone." She let her earlier question hang. It was prying to ask about his time in the marines, she knew. But she wanted to hear him say that what they were going through was no big deal, that he'd survived worse. She didn't even think she would care if it was a lie, as long as she could pretend everything was going to be okay.

Seeming to understand, Griffin crossed to the doorway and stopped very near her, close enough that she could see the beginnings of a beard shadowing his jawline, and the uncompromising glint in his dark green eyes. "I was a TecSpec, which means I was the gadget guy, the one who could get anything running, rig a security system out of spare parts, make a working firearm out of three broken rifles, and get us home despite a busted GPS unit. I was the guy who fixed things and helped get my team home safe and sound, mission accomplished."

Sophie found it difficult to think of him as part of a team when he so adamantly held himself apart from everyone except his son. But that didn't really matter under the circumstances, did it?

"Can you fix this?" she asked, meaning the situation, and the threat that might or might not hang over them, depending on whether the bomber was still at Lonesome Lake.

It was a long moment before he said, "I can't promise you that nothing bad is going to happen to us, Sophie. But I can and will promise to do everything I can to get us both out of here in one piece."

It wasn't a simple, easy answer, but she wouldn't have believed him if he'd gone with simple or easy. Because he'd gone with honesty instead, she took a deep breath to settle the nervous quiver in her stomach, and told herself that would have to be good enough. She nodded. "Okay. What's next?" She shot a look at the generator, which had settled into a good working rhythm of engine noise. "Do we need to find fuel?"

"The generators draw from a pair of underground tanks, and the building inspector said they checked out fine. I had them topped up before construction started, so we should be all set in that department." He didn't say "unless someone has tampered with them," but she knew they were both thinking it. He continued, "Now that the generator is running, let's go back inside and test the lights. If the power is still off, we'll head for the basement and check the electrical panel."

She offered the .45. "Take this. You know what to do with it. I don't."

He took the weapon without comment, tucking it beneath the parka, at the small of his back. The small action bore the ease of familiarity, which she found both reassuring and unsettling. It was reassuring in that it made her feel that much safer, knowing he was armed. Yet it was unsettling in that it kindled a core of warmth in the pit of her stomach. Apparently, she was turned on by a guy with a gun. Who knew?

Then again, odds were it wasn't the gun. It was Griffin. Had been from the first moment they'd met.

He glanced at her and lifted an eyebrow. "Ready to brave the elements?"

Ignoring the dangerous warmth of an attraction she had no business feeling, even though they were in a situation and place far out of their normal reality, she pulled her parka more securely around her body, and nodded. "Ready as I'll ever be."

The storm slapped at them the moment he slid open the door of the generator shed, but she was more or less braced for the blizzard's fury this time. Hanging on to each other, they slogged across the short distance to the mansion entrance without incident.

Once they were back inside, though, their luck ran out.

When Griffin tested the power, nothing happened.

"Damn it." He jiggled the switch, checked that the overhead chandelier had bulbs, then tried another nearby. Still nothing. "The wiring in here looks complete. Let's hope we just need to flip some circuit breakers."

"Basement it is, then," Sophie said, though the idea dragged at her.

She was running out of steam fast; they'd skipped out on the food she'd prepared, and she tended to weaken quickly when her blood sugar got low. Add to that the bumps and bruises from the accident on the bridge, and the overall drain of the stress and the cold, and she was just about done in. Not that she was going to admit any such thing to Griffin. *Probation*, she reminded herself. *You need this job*.

Oddly, the mantra didn't work nearly as well as it had earlier in the day. Maybe it was because she was tired, maybe because of the threat of danger, but she found herself needing an added incentive to keep going. *Don't give up*, she told herself. *Don't let Griffin down*.

And yeah, she knew it was skirting close to the edge of stupidity, venturing too near that closed-off part of her brain where she put impossible things, but she'd had a hard day. She'd give herself a pass this time.

They headed back across the huge house, stopping at a solid-paneled door. Griffin swung it open to reveal a stairwell that led down into darkness. The blackness and the faintly stale smell coming from the basement raised the fine hairs on the back of Sophie's neck, but when Griffin glanced at her as if asking whether she was all set, she nodded. It was just a basement, after all.

Still, she was comforted to see him draw the .45 and hold it cross-handed with the flashlight as he played the light over what they could see of the basement from the top of the stairs. The steps ended in a smooth cement floor, where, inexplicably, someone had placed a woven mat that had the word *Welcome* imprinted on it. The rest of the space immediately surrounding the stairwell was clear, looking almost swept clean.

"Seems harmless enough," Griffin muttered, more to himself than to her.

Sophie followed him down the stairs, trying not to crowd too close. Although the area immediately surrounding the stairs was clear, the basement itself proved to be a labyrinthine maze of pylons and load-bearing cement-block walls designed to support the massive weight of the mansion. The supports divided the space into a series of interconnecting rooms that proved to be empty and echoing, and nearly identical to one another. Within minutes, Sophie questioned whether she would be able to find her way out again. Faint light came from narrow windows set near the ceiling, the snow-filtered illumination casting the scene with a strange blue glow.

"What is this place?" she whispered.

Griffin lifted a shoulder. "The Realtor said the previous owner used it for storage. Given who that owner turned out to be, I'm not taking any bets."

She suppressed a shiver. "How do you know we're going the right way?"

"The panel's in the northwest corner of the building, which is the side sunk into the mountain," he answered, as though that should explain everything. Which it might have, if Sophie had ever needed to think of things in terms of north and west. As it was, she'd lived pretty much her entire life within a hundred-mile radius of San Fran, and knew how to get where she was going without a compass.

Gritting her teeth, knowing that was no excuse, she started counting doorways and turns, and scuffing her feet in the thin layer of dust that had accumulated in some of the doorway corners, marking the way they'd come in. Not because she thought Griffin was likely to abandon her, but because it was something active she could do, and made her feel as though she was taking an iota of control.

Eventually, they came through a doorway and found themselves in a larger space, where two outer structural walls joined in a right-angle corner. Two other doorways led off along the main walls, leading to darkness beyond. Griffin flashed his light on a large gray box that was bolted onto the wall and had a profusion of wires and conduits running into and out of it. The door of the electrical panel hung open, revealing rows of circuit breakers, all of them in the off position.

"Now there's some good news," Griffin said, heading for the panel. "If we just flip the breakers, we should have lights and—"

A blur erupted from the darkened doorway to their left. Sophie turned, gasping at the sight of a man in jeans and a heavy parka. He wore a knit cap pulled down low over his brow and a muffler up over his chin, so only his cold blue eyes were visible, and then only for the split second it took her to focus on the heavy crowbar he held in leather-gloved hands.

"Griffin!" she screamed as the man raised the crowbar and swung it straight at her head.

Chapter Five

Griffin lunged for Sophie's attacker, not stopping to think or plan, his only goal to get the bastard away from her. He deflected the crowbar with his forearm, ignored the searing pain of impact, and drove his shoulder into the other man's chest.

The tackle sent the men sprawling through the nearest doorway into darkness. Griffin had lost his flashlight, but belatedly realized he'd kept hold of the .45. He brought it to bear just as the other man jabbed at him with the crowbar, digging the tip in to his ribs.

Griffin's breath whooshed out. He grabbed the end of the crowbar with his free hand, preventing a follow-through blow, but didn't dare start shooting. Not with the two of them sandwiched together on a cement surface, and ricochet an all-too-real possibility.

"Take this," he called to Sophie, and sent the weapon skidding in her direction. He didn't hear an answer, which wasn't a good sign. Had the bastard gotten her with the crowbar?

Rage spiked alongside the fighting adrenaline that

had Griffin's blood hammering in his veins. He might not be that young, brash marine who'd taken out the enemy on his CO's orders anymore, but he wasn't the staid businessman, either. He was both of those men, and something in between—someone smarter and more controlled, yet willing to kill in order to protect.

Roaring a curse, he twisted out from underneath his heavily muscled attacker and fought to rip the crowbar from the other man's hands. The men wrestled, grunting curses, landing elbows and knees as they struggled in the darkness. Searing pain exploded in Griffin's upper arm, but he didn't let go. He dragged himself to his feet, fighting for leverage.

Suddenly, his opponent released the crowbar and jumped back. Overbalancing, Griffin crashed to the side with a yell. He blinked against the pain, and too late, saw a bare fist coming his way. He tried to duck the punch, caught the blow on his temple, and sagged, dazed.

"Get away from him!" Sophie shouted. She aimed the .45 and pulled the trigger. The gun roared, and the other man cried out in pain, grabbing at his right side.

Griffin lunged and snagged the other man's coat, grunting as the pain in his arm slashed to agony. His adversary yanked away and bolted, getting through the far doorway a split second before Sophie's next shot slammed into the wall nearby and pinged with a dangerous ricochet.

"Cease fire!" Griffin shouted, ducking.

When the gunshot echo faded, he could hear the sound of running footsteps, followed by a grating noise.

Then there was nothing but the sound of rapid, rasping breaths. Griffin's own. Sophie's.

"Are you okay?" he asked, fighting to marshal his breathing and not let on that his right arm was rapidly going numb. The bastard hadn't had a knife, so Griffin had to assume he'd been nailed with the crowbar and hadn't noticed immediately in the heat of battle. It happened that way sometimes.

"I think…" Her quivering voice trailed off, and he heard her take a deep breath. When she spoke again, her tone was steady, if weak. "I think I shot him."

"I think so, too."

Something in his voice must've tipped her off, because she turned, clicked on her flashlight and shone it on him. "You're hurt." Dull horror filled her tone. "I didn't shoot you, too, did I?"

"No. Guy nailed me in the shoulder with the crowbar. I don't think anything's broken." The last was a lie meant to reassure them both, because even if it was broken, there wasn't much they could do about it. And he was right-handed. If he lost full use of that arm, it would seriously limit their defensive options, which were going to become crucial now that they knew for sure they weren't alone in the mansion.

Sophie's voice carried a fine tremor of nerves—or maybe incipient hysteria—when she said, "We should get you back to the apartment and take a look at it."

"You're okay?" he asked again, needing to be sure. "He didn't get you with the crowbar? I thought he might've hit you in that first rush."

"No." She shook her head. "But after he missed me, he took a swing at the fuse box before you got to him."

Griffin took one look at the electrical panel, and cursed bitterly. The thing was a write-off. No fuses meant no power to the apartment, and no juice he could use to rig pieces of the old security system into something that would protect them from their attacker.

A warning bell sounded at the back of Griffin's brain, because taking out the bridge and the electricals smacked of military strategy. Or the work of a professional.

"Come on. Let's see if we can follow the bastard." Griffin retrieved his flashlight from where it had fallen during the fight, clicked it on, and sent the beam skimming down the dim corridor where their attacker had disappeared.

"Did you recognize him?" Sophie asked, joining him as he moved along the corridor. "Was it Perry?"

"Not sure. Could've been." The man's face had been obscured. His height had been about right, but that didn't mean much.

The hallway floor was clean—maybe too clean?—providing little in the way of evidence. Griffin found a couple of drops of blood, but absolutely no sign of where their attacker had gone, how he'd disappeared. It was a mystery.

Nodding to the weapon Sophie held at the ready, Griffin said, "At least we've still got the gun. I'd guess we're one-up on him in that department given that he used a damned crowbar as a—" He broke off as he realized something.

"What is it?" Sophie said quickly. "What's wrong?"

It wasn't what was wrong, he knew. It was that something had finally gone their way. Maybe. "We need to bring the crowbar back with us, but wrap it in something before you touch it."

"Why not?"

A grim smile touched his face as he remembered the sight of an incoming fist. A *bare* fist. "The bastard lost one of his gloves during the fight. He must've grabbed it when he left, but I had the crowbar, so he couldn't take that. If he left a usable fingerprint, and we can find some way to get an image of it over to the CSU, Martinez's people should be able to tell us who we're dealing with."

"That's assuming the prints are on file."

"Perry was in the army. He'll be in the armed forces database." And Vince Del Gardo would be in AFIS, Griffin knew, but he didn't want to voice that alternative if he could help it.

The idea of being stalked by a contractor in self-defense mode was bad enough. He didn't want to think how much worse things could get if it turned out that their enemy was a cold-blooded fugitive.

WHEN THEY GOT BACK to the apartment, Griffin checked inside and out for signs that their attacker had been there. When he found no signs of tampering, he hid the crowbar—which might or might not hold valuable evidence—and went back outside the apartment to string the rope and scrap metal at strategic points in the hallway. Once he was done with that, he braved the storm to do the same outside the windows.

All the while, Sophie followed him with the .45, watching his back. She hated the weight of the weapon, and the faint smell that clung to it, and to her. Intellectually, she knew she'd done the right thing, that she hadn't had an option other than shooting the man. But that didn't stop her from replaying the moment over and over again in her head, feeling the kick of recoil and hearing his cry of pain. She couldn't stop seeing the blood trail in her mind's eye, and knowing she'd been the one to cause it.

That knowledge dragged her down, and had her close to tears by the time Griffin finally finished, and declared the apartment safe. They both knew he meant, "as safe as I can get it under the circumstances."

Mindful of his injured arm, which he favored when he thought she wasn't looking, she packed several large snowballs and piled them just outside the apartment door, figuring the main house was close enough to freezing that they'd stay frozen. They wouldn't last as long as an icepack, but they'd be better than nothing.

Back inside the apartment, they went around to each of the rooms to draw all the curtains and pull the shades, closing out the world. The four-room space was warm from the fire, and orange and yellow light played from the mismatched candles and the kerosene lanterns as the early storm dusk turned to full dark.

Under other circumstances, Sophie knew, it might've been a scene set for romance. Under the present circumstances, she felt vulnerable and exposed. Their enemy had used explosives once before, what was to say he wouldn't do the same again?

As if she'd said the words aloud, Griffin crossed to her, gripped her shoulder and squeezed it in a gesture of support. "If he had the means to attack us in here, he would've done it already. Besides, he's wounded. He'll need tonight at least to deal with the injury."

Because that thought was both reassuring and disquieting, she changed the subject. "How's your arm?"

He rotated it, then grimaced. "It's pretty sore," he admitted. "And my fingers are tingling."

She pointed to the bathroom. "In there, shirt off. Let's see what we're dealing with."

That gave him pause. "You've got medical training?"

"I can hold my own in the first-aid department," she said evasively, having no wish to discuss the decade-plus she'd spent becoming an expert in home health care, when her mother's medical problems had rendered her practically bedridden, yet the doctors they'd been able to afford weren't able—and frankly didn't care enough—to provide a solid diagnosis or useful treatment suggestions.

Griffin held her gaze for a long moment, as though asking if she was sure this was a good idea.

She raised an eyebrow. "Shy?"

He snorted. "Not hardly."

"Then get in the bathroom and strip, boss." She said it that way in an effort to be funny, and also to remind herself of their respective roles.

Still, there was a hum of warmth in her core and an unfamiliar beat in her blood as she followed him into the apartment's single bathroom, which was done in the same neutrals in the main room, with splashes of color in the southwestern-themed towels and a touch of femininity in a soapstone bowl of potpourri beside the sink.

Sophie turned her back on Griffin and busied herself looking in the medicine cabinet for painkillers at the very least. All the while, she was acutely aware of Griffin's presence filling the small room, and the rustle of movement and hiss of pain as he pulled off his borrowed shirt and sweater.

The medicine cabinet yielded ibuprofen, as well as an arnica cream that would help take the sting out of any bruising, and help speed the healing process. That was assuming it was a bruise. If he'd broken or cracked the bone, there was little she could do beyond stabilizing the spot and telling him to use it as little as possible, which wasn't really feasible given their situation.

And she was stalling, she knew.

Taking a deep breath, she swung shut the mirrored door of the medicine cabinet, which then gave her a clear view of her own flushed face, and the half-naked man standing behind her.

If she'd ever consciously wondered whether the delicious golden undertones of his skin were from the sun, her question was answered now in glorious expanse of gold-burnished skin that stretched across his powerful chest. Since she knew he wasn't one to lie out and work on a meticulous tan, she could only

assume he looked like that all over his body. Which
was a thought she absolutely, positively shouldn't
have, and one that stuck in her mind and echoed in
the heat that chased through her veins, even as she
noticed the angry red spot on his upper arm. The bur-
geoning mark was already turning purplish-black,
suggesting that it was a deep bruise, maybe something
worse.

His eyes met hers in the mirror. "You sure this is a
good idea?"

It was as close as either of them had come to admitting that there was a bite of chemistry between them. Or
rather, that there was a great big ravening gulp of chemistry, at least on her part.

But she nodded. "I don't like the looks of that bruise.
No offense, but I'll feel far better if you have full use of
both arms."

"And you can help with that?"

"I'll do my best." She turned around finally, so they
were face-to-face, and she forced herself to drop into the
caretaker's role that was all too familiar. She directed
him to sit on the closed toilet lid, and moved in to
inspect the damage the crowbar had done to the flesh
and muscle of his upper arm.

She didn't stare at his broad chest, or let her eyes
follow the faint trail of masculine hair that dusted across
his pecs and led downward, disappearing into the waist-
band of his borrowed jeans. Instead, she kept herself
busy and businesslike, testing his grip and range of
motion, and probing at the edges of the bruise, then

using the snowballs from out in the hallway to ice the injury and bring the swelling down as far as she could.

All the while, she was acutely aware of the warmth of his skin, and the heat that seemed to be pouring off his body and curling inside hers.

Griffin stared straight ahead, his jaw locked.

"I'm pretty sure it's just a bruise," she said finally, "though the word 'just' probably feels relative from where you're sitting. I bet it hurts like hell."

"It doesn't tickle," he said, and flicked a glance at her. She saw reflected heat in his eyes, and felt an answering flare within her. But his voice was cool and casual when he said, "Where'd you pick up the medical stuff?"

"I spent some time looking after a family member," she answered vaguely. She handed him the ibuprofen. "Take these—no more than four to start with, then two every couple of hours. It should keep the pain down to a dull roar." She reached for the arnica cream and squeezed some into her palm. "This'll help, too."

"What is it?"

"Arnica. It takes out the sting and helps speed healing." Seeing that he didn't look convinced, she said, "It works. Trust me."

"I do trust you," he said, and then looked surprised to have said it. Trying to cover whatever slip he'd just made, he kicked up the corner of his mouth and said, "You haven't dumped any scalding liquids on me in a while, after all."

He had a point, she realized. Whatever she was feeling right then, it wasn't nerves. At least not the kind that

made her clumsy. More like the kind that brought a
flush to her skin and a spin to her head, and made her
want to step toward him rather than away. She was too
close to him already, standing behind him and to the
side, where she had easy access to his injured arm, and
entirely too good a view of his broad, muscular back.
She couldn't make herself move away, though, held
transfixed by the intimacy that had grown between them
over the course of the day, whether either of them
wanted to acknowledge it.

He'd saved her life down by the bridge, and fought
to protect her just now in the basement. She'd guarded
his back and helped him when his reserves finally gave
out. They weren't the same people they'd been that
morning when they'd gotten on the plane, planning on
spending the night at their respective homes in San Fran.

Instead they'd be spending the night at Lonesome
Lake, together by candlelight.

"Go ahead," he said, turning slightly away from her
so she could apply the cream. "You're the doctor."

She complied wordlessly, unable to come up with
anything witty, or even mildly intelligent, to say. First,
she smeared the arnica gel along his heavy shoulder
muscle, then worked it down to where his bicep joined.
There, in the natural indentation that was so much more
defined than she would've imagined in a man she
thought of as having a desk job, was where the worst of
the bruising had bloomed.

"This is probably going to hurt," she warned.

He said nothing, simply waited. Knowing there was no

use putting it off, she started working the gel in to his skin, turning the application into a light massage that would break up some of the bruising as it formed, and help the medication get to the damaged tissues more easily. As she did so, she told herself this was no different from easing the aches and pains that had plagued her mother's joints for so long. Only it was very, very different.

She loved the feel of his skin beneath her fingertips, and the warmth of his body up close. She reveled in the leashed strength of his muscles, and fought not to inhale his spicy, male scent.

And, she realized, she needed to stop it, right now.

Griffin wasn't hers, wouldn't ever be hers, and to think otherwise was just foolishness. They were in an artificially intimate situation. It wouldn't do her any good to create unrealistic fantasies out of it.

Dropping her hands, she took a big step back, away from him. "And, um, that's pretty much it. Keep up with the ibuprofen, and you should feel a big improvement by morning."

He didn't meet her eyes, just kept staring straight ahead. "Thanks. I owe you one."

"I'll, um, go reheat our lunch," she said. "Which I guess is dinner now." But she didn't move.

"Okay." He didn't move, either. At least she didn't think he did. But if that was the case, how come it seemed that they were closer to each other than they'd been before?

Then, abruptly, he stood and moved past her, stalking out of the bathroom into the main room of the apartment. She didn't follow, didn't think her legs would support her just then if she'd tried. In fact, she stayed in the bathroom until she heard him opening dresser drawers, looking for another shirt in the bedroom.

Relieved to avoid facing him just then, she escaped to the kitchen, and went through the motions of reheating the food from earlier, clicking on the propane stove, and stirring in some condensed milk when the macaroni and cheese looked less than appetizing the second time around.

"We could toss it and make something else," Griffin suggested from very close behind her.

Sophie jolted. She hadn't realized he'd come into the kitchen, hadn't realized he was so near, practically looking over her shoulder.

Steeling herself to ignore the warmth that kindled in her blood at his proximity, she shot him a look. "Spoken like a man who's never had to make a box of Kraft stretch a couple of days."

"Try one who can't remember the last time he ate anything that came solely from a box and a couple of cans, finished off with a side of tap water."

"Right." She nodded and concentrated on stirring the noodles so they wouldn't stick. "You probably grew up in a place like this is going to be once the renovations are finished. A mansion with three pools, a cook and a live-in nanny." As soon as the words came out, she regretted them. It'd sounded more like an accusation than an observation, and it was seriously none of her business either way. "Sorry," she said, a beat too late. "If it's all the same to you, I'd appreciate it if you'd pretend I didn't just say that."

He didn't respond for a moment, just stood there too close to her. She didn't dare turn, didn't dare look at him. She wasn't even entirely sure what she was afraid of seeing in his eyes, whether it was his potential for anger that had her nerves humming...or something else entirely.

After a pause that seemed like it went on forever, he moved away from her and sat at the small table on the other side of the eat-in kitchen. For a few seconds she was relieved, thinking he'd taken her at her word and was pretending she hadn't just sniped at him for being born into a wealthy family, when she'd grown up in anything but.

Then he said, "No nannies or cooks, actually. My dad and my Uncle Will started VaughnTec when I was ten, maybe eleven, trying to get in on the early wave of VCR technology. They went with the beta format, which never caught on, and it was pretty much like that for them all along. They had the right ideas, but they were always a little too late, or sank their money down the wrong R & D path."

Don't pry, Sophie told herself firmly as she dished up for both of them. "Yet no dinners out of boxes."

"My mom cooked," he said simply. "She cooked, she gardened, she wrote poetry...and she made life fun. She was younger than my dad, and very different in temperament, but somehow they were the perfect match." He paused, and though she hadn't asked, said, "She and my dad died six years ago in a car accident. It was one of those things—a big rig blew a tire and swerved...and that was it."

Sophie hesitated in the midst of setting their soup bowls out on the table, then forced herself to keep moving. She set out the last of the food, then sat opposite him and picked up her spoon before she said, "I'm sorry."

Because really, what else was there to say? She didn't know him well enough to suggest he should be grateful for having had a steady nuclear family for so long, didn't have the right to lay that on him just because a streak of nasty jealousy had reared up at the thought of a mother who cooked, gardened and wrote poetry, never mind the thought of childhood being fun.

Those were her problems, not his.

He nodded. "Thanks." He dug into his soup, then gestured with his spoon. "What, no quid pro quo? Not going to tell me why you're an expert at minimizing bruises and resuscitating macaroni and cheese? Nice job on both of those things, by the way."

"Thanks. And no, I think I'll skip the life-story portion of today's entertainment."

That had him putting down his spoon and giving her his full attention, which was exactly what she'd been hoping to avoid. "And she continues to surprise me," he said as though in an aside to himself. To her, he said, "Most of the women I've had occasion to share a meal with would've jumped at the chance to tell me all about their lives."

"Then I guess I'm not like those women."

"No," he said, drawing out the word reflectively. "No, you're not."

He picked up his spoon again and kept eating, and for a few minutes they sat in companionable silence. Just when Sophie was starting to relax, though, he said, "So tell me something else about yourself. What do you really want to do with your life?" He held up a hand to forestall her immediate defensive response. "Let me rephrase, because obviously the PC answer is 'be your executive assistant for ever and ever, Griffin.' If you could do anything at all, if money were no object and you had all the time in the world, what would you do?"

"I'd become a lawyer," she said, the words popping out before she was aware that she'd decided to share that unrealistic dream. "Then, since you said money was no object, I'd become an advocate. I'd help low-income single parents and marginal families fight for proper medical coverage, and—" She broke off, knowing she'd already revealed too much on the "story of my life" front. She lifted a shoulder. "And that's it. If I won the lottery or whatever."

Needing badly to move, she popped up from her chair and started clearing the table.

Griffin rose when she did, and reached for her plate. "You cooked. I should clean up."

"You realize there's no hot water, right? No electricity, no dishwasher."

"I'll manage."

She was tempted, but in the end waved him off. "You go on. Call your son and then rest your arm. Something tells me that tomorrow could be a very long day." She paused, suddenly gripped by the knowledge that they couldn't really think about tomorrow until they'd made it through the night, and there were no guarantees on that front. "What are we going to do?" she finally asked, unable to keep her voice from going thin.

"The best we can," he said, which wasn't really an answer, but was somehow calming nonetheless. After a moment, he continued, "I truly do believe he'll lay low tonight, though I'll walk the perimeter every hour or so, and I sleep very lightly, so if anything hits the trip wires, I'll know it. As for tomorrow..." He trailed off. Shrugged. "Let's get some sleep and see what the day brings, okay?"

She nodded. "You're the boss."

He left the kitchen, taking one of the kerosene lanterns with him, and she puttered in the kitchen far longer than she needed to, stalling. By the time she finally made it out into the main room, he was off the phone and sprawled out on the sofa cushions, which he'd laid out end-to-end near the fireplace, where it was warmest. He was fully clothed, and his boots were close at hand.

What was more, he'd carried the mattress out of the bedroom, into the living room, and set it up on the other side of the fireplace.

Sophie stopped dead, staring at it.

"Don't freak," he said without moving or opening his eyes. "It's not an indecent proposal. If we have to move fast for whatever reason, I don't want to lose time going into the bedroom after you."

She stared at the mattress a moment longer, then nodded. "Of course. No problem." But as she got ready for bed, copying him by staying clothed and keeping her boots within reach, she wondered what he would do if she gave him another piece of her life story, namely that this would be the first time she'd ever slept with a man. Literally or figuratively.

She lay down and stared into the fire, expecting that her racing brain would keep her wide awake. Instead, soothed by the regular sound of his breathing, the crackle of the fire, and even the howl of the storm winds outside, she drifted off.

A HALF A MILE AWAY, deep in the hidden tunnel system that bracketed the mansion and a large portion of the estate, the bald man leaned against the rocky tunnel wall and shone a flashlight on the hole the bitch had blown in his side.

It was deep and ugly, flushed red at the margins, and it hurt like the devil. His head was spinning from the loss of blood, and he was too disoriented to make another try for his targets tonight. He needed rest and fluids. Then, when he was feeling steadier, he'd be back on the hunt.

Griffin Vaughn and his secretary might've gotten lucky a second time, but their luck would run out soon enough. And then they'd be dead.

Chapter Six

Sophie slept deeply, not even surfacing all the way when, every few hours, Griffin rose, pulled on his boots, and checked the perimeter he'd set up around the apartment.

Each time when he returned, he reassured her in a low voice, telling her there was no sign of anyone out there. Then he tossed another log or two on the fire, keeping the room toasty warm. By the time he'd returned to his pallet, she'd dropped back to sleep.

When she finally came all the way awake, it was tough to tell at first whether it was morning or not, because the room was still dark, so she climbed up off the mattress and crossed to the window. Pushing the drape aside a bit, she peered out into a leaden gray world of whipping ice and wind.

It was morning, and the storm definitely hadn't broken.

"Sorry," Griffin said from his side of the room, his voice thick with sleep. "I don't think we're getting out of here today."

No matter how many times she'd told herself that the sheriff was probably right, that the blizzard would last another day at least, a knot of disappointment tightened in her gut, wrapping itself around the ball of fear that said the next time they went up against their enemy, they might not be as lucky as they'd been so far.

Worrying about it, though, wasn't going to help. She needed to do something more productive, more active.

"Go back to sleep," she told Griffin, knowing he hadn't gotten much actual rest during the night. "I'll wake you if I hear anything."

He muttered something that she thought was assent, and settled back into his makeshift bed. Forcing herself not to watch him sleep, or think the things she shouldn't be thinking in the light of day, she headed for the kitchen and started coffee. While it brewed, she powered up her PDA and placed a call to Sheriff Martinez.

"Martinez here," the sheriff answered.

"Sheriff, it's Sophie. We've had some developments up here." She briefly outlined what had happened the night before, ending with: "So that confirms it. Whoever is up here with us wants us out of the way."

There was a long pause as the sheriff digested the new information. After a moment, he said, "Can you give me a description?"

"Sorry, not really. Average height and weight, jeans and a parka, and he was wearing a hat and had a scarf wrapped around his face, so I couldn't see anything. The light wasn't good, either." She paused, holding onto their one thin hope. "Here's the thing. He was wearing gloves when he first attacked us, but he lost one of them during the fight."

"You've got the glove?"

"No. But we've got the crowbar, and Griffin is pretty sure the guy grabbed on to it with his bare hand. He thinks it's worth checking out, anyway."

"I would agree wholeheartedly if it weren't for this damned storm," Martinez said irritably. "It's got us completely shut down here. The Del Gardo investigation is at a standstill, and with every inch of snow that falls, we're losing crucial evidence at our various crime scenes. It's a bloody mess down here. Which, I know, doesn't help you and Griffin one bit. But that's where I'm at."

Thinking of what Griffin had said, Sophie asked, "Is there, I don't know, some way we could process the prints ourselves and e-mail you some pictures?"

Martinez muttered a curse, then said, "Sorry, that was aimed at me, not you. I got so caught up in thinking about the storm and being frustrated that I can't get anyone up there to help you, that I wasn't thinking outside the box. Let me transfer you to the KCCU. You're going to be talking to one of the best we've got, investigator Callie MacBride. Okay?"

"Yes. Thanks so much."

"Keep in touch. And be careful."

On one hand Sophie was pleased the sheriff had stopped doing the "don't scare the pretty, very young-looking lady" routine. On the other, she suspected it was because he was out of options. Which wasn't a very encouraging thought.

Sophie heard a couple of clicks on the line, and then a soft beep and the phone on the other end started to ring. Moments later, the line went live and a crisp, businesslike female voice said, "Crime scene unit. This is Callie MacBride."

Sophie introduced herself and explained the situation, trying to keep it to just the facts—partly because she instinctively sensed that the investigator was both busy and to-the-point, and also because she was a little afraid that if she let the emotions seep in, she'd lose her cool completely. She finished by repeating the request she'd made of Sheriff Martinez, for help lifting the fingerprints and seeing if they could ID their attacker long-distance.

When she was done, there was a long, drawn-out silence on the other end of the phone. Then Callie's voice came back, much softer than it'd been before. "You poor thing. I can see why Patrick—that's Sheriff Martinez—is about killing himself trying to figure out a way to get you and Vaughn down off the mountain."

Sophie's voice shook a little when she said, "Can you help with the fingerprints? I think...I think it'd be better if we knew who we're up against."

"Yes, I think we can do something. What I'm actually going to do is have you call Ava Wright. She's a forensic specialist who's also working on the Del Gardo case. Her knowledge base is a little more esoteric than mine, so I think she'll have a better idea of what household powders might work to provide the detail we're going to need." Callie recited the other woman's number.

"Got it. Thanks."

"Good luck, Sophie."

Ava Wright picked up on the first ring, and Sophie

described the situation. Ava proved to be a warmer, bubblier version of Callie, and made Sophie feel as though she and Ava had been friends for some time. Ava talked her through the fingerprinting procedure and suggested some kitchen and bathroom items that might serve as fingerprinting powders.

After they were done discussing the actual lifting protocol and what Sophie should use to provide sufficient contrast for the photographs she planned to take using her PDA, Ava sighed and said, "For your sake I really hope it's not Del Gardo. I know Patrick is dead set against it being Perry, since they know each other some, but at the same time, I'd say your hunky exmarine is probably a better match for an ex-army contractor than a mob boss."

"My hunky ex-marine," Sophie repeated, suddenly thinking of all that golden skin, and the feel of warm man and muscle beneath her fingertips.

"I researched him on the Internet, found some society-type pictures. Nice. Might not be much of a hardship being snowed in with a guy like him." Ava paused, as if inviting gossip. When Sophie didn't say anything, she continued, "Then again, he's your boss, right? You probably don't want to go there, huh?"

"I…I don't know what to say," Sophie confessed. "Do you need to know this for the case?"

"Nope, just being nosy. Pregnant woman's prerogative." Ava paused and her voice went soft. "And you sound like you could use someone to talk to."

Sophie choked up and nodded, which was silly

because Ava couldn't see a nod through the phone. So she managed to say, "Thanks. I...thanks."

"You go ahead and try those prints now, okay? Call me if you need help. Or even if you just need to talk. And remember, you and the hunka-hunka might be on your own up there at the mansion, but there are a whole bunch of us down here worried about you, and pulling for you, and trying to figure out some way to get to you. You're not alone in this. Okay?"

"Okay," Sophie whispered into the phone, as a fat tear trickled down her cheek. "Thank you."

Once she'd hung up and powered down the PDA, she just sat there at the kitchen table for a long moment, soaking in the feeling of community, which was something she'd never really experienced in San Fran, though she'd lived there her entire life. Maybe it was because she'd spent so much of her time dealing with her mother's illness, or maybe she herself had never made enough of an effort, but even in the neighborhood where she'd grown up, she'd always felt like an outsider looking in. Yet in the space of a single day, the cops of Kenner County had accepted her more warmly, and were worried about her more deeply than anyone back home ever had.

It's because of Griffin, a small inner voice said sourly. *You've got to be rich in order to get attention in this world.* And maybe that was true, but for the moment she was simply grateful that Patrick Martinez, Callie MacBride and Ava Wright were on her side.

"Okay." She drew a deep breath and scrubbed both hands across her face. "Time to get to work."

Energized by the thought of doing something useful, she searched the kitchen and bathroom, and assembled a likely-looking collection of spices, makeup and talcum powder, along with clear packing tape and paper in several different dark colors, in addition to plain white. She completed her kit with a worn-looking blusher brush that was the closest she could come to the fine, natural-bristled paintbrush Ava had recommended.

Throughout it all, Griffin slept deeply, apparently trusting her to rouse him if there was any sign of trouble.

Figuring she should practice first, she pulled down a pair of juice glasses, gripping them tightly with her fingertips to make prints. Then she got to work, starting with cinnamon and working from there.

Ten minutes later she had a halfway decent lift of one of her own fingerprints, in blusher on black paper. Holding her breath, she powered up the PDA and used it to photograph the print. It worked.

Her heart was tapping at her ribs as she retrieved the parka-wrapped crowbar. Holding her breath, hoping against hope that this would give them some answers, she bent over the crowbar and started dusting. An hour later, she had twenty lifted prints. She could see that some were the same, some were different. The best part was that she thought she had three thumbs. Even if two were Griffin's, the other one should—maybe?—belong to their assailant.

Blood humming with excitement, she photographed the prints, then scrolled down the list of recently connected numbers to call Ava back. It wasn't until the second ring that she looked at the display and checked the number.

It wasn't Ava's local number. She'd missed and hit the wrong redial.

Sophie groaned when she recognized Griffin's home number in San Francisco. She'd scrolled down too far, darn it! And the call put her in an awkward situation, because Griffin had made it very clear that his home and family were off-limits to her under any but the most extreme circumstances. And while the current situation was certainly dire, it had nothing to do with Darryn and Luke.

By then, though, it was too late to disconnect, because someone was already picking up.

"That you, Griffin?" a pleasant, male voice said.

"Sorry, no. It's Sophie. Is this Darryn?"

"That'd be me," the male nanny agreed cheerfully, but then his tone changed to one of concern. "Everything okay out there?"

She paused, because she didn't have a clue how to answer. She'd only met Darryn once, when Griffin had asked her to stop by his house and pick up an important document. On first impression, Darryn was a warm, fun-loving guy who'd taken a break from college to, as he called it, "get my beer goggles off and figure out what I want to be when I grow up." In the space of maybe two minutes, she'd also learned that he was a cousin of Griffin's, removed a time or two, and had gladly taken on the offered role of childcare to Luke, because, as Darryn had said, the job gave him breathing room, and both Griffin and Luke were "cool dudes."

The meeting had been brief, but Sophie had come away liking Griffin's cousin very much. She'd also gotten a glimpse of three-year-old Luke, who had popped his head around the corner just as she was leaving. The boy's short, blond hair and shy smile had tugged at her, as had his wide-eyed stare. But when Griffin had sent her over to the house, he'd made it clear—not in so many words, of course, but clear nonetheless—that she was part of his business life, not his home life, and should get herself in and out with a minimum of chitchat. He'd softened the order by admitting that Luke missed Kathleen, and he didn't want the child to get too attached to her replacement. Sophie suspected there was more to it than that, but hadn't pressed, because really, Griffin's home life was none of her business.

Mindful of that, she didn't answer Darryn's question directly, instead saying, "I'm sorry, but this is actually a wrong number. I scrolled down too far and pulled up this number from when Griffin called you guys last night."

"He wanted us to know you two would be stuck for a few days. Said for me to have the helicopter at the closest flyable airport, ready to buzz in and pick you guys up the moment the storm breaks, because otherwise it'll be a few days more before the roads are clear."

"That's about the sum of it," Sophie said, lying through her teeth, because Griffin obviously hadn't wanted his cousin or son to worry about the full extent of the problems up at Lonesome Lake. "Sorry to bother you with the misdial."

"No prob. You going to call your family now?" Darryn asked, apparently in no rush to get off the phone.

What family? she thought, feeling the lack with a sharper pang than usual. "Nope, it's all business. I need to follow up on something we've got going on down here."

Darryn groaned theatrically. "Dude, I know how that is. Or rather, I know how Griffin is. The man's a total workaholic. Do me a favor and talk him into making a snowman or going sledding or something. The guy could use a snow day."

"I'll do that," Sophie said, which was a total lie. Even if they'd simply been stuck together in a snowstorm, she couldn't picture herself talking Griffin into anything, much less something as frivolous as a toboggan run or a snow angel. Pushing aside a quick, wistful image of doing just that, she said, "I'm sure he'll call you himself later. Bye."

She was about to scroll back to Ava's number and make her call when something drew her attention to the doorway—a noise, maybe, or the sort of sixth sense she seemed to be developing when it came to her boss, a preternatural awareness of where he was, and what sort of mood he was in.

Nerves shimmered to life, running in fine currents just beneath her skin. Sure enough, when she looked over, she found Griffin standing in the doorway, staring at her, his expression unreadable.

His hair was wet, his skin pale, suggesting that he'd taken a cold shower. Where the beginnings of beard stubble had humanized him the day before, now his strong jawline was clean-shaven, making him look more like the businessman she'd been working for than the rougher, more down-to-earth soldier she'd started getting to know the day before. The change created a distance, putting them back to boss and assistant rather than two people working together in an effort to survive.

He looked pointedly at the phone. "Talking to Darryn?"

"Sorry. I scrolled down too far and hit your number rather than the KCCU's. Then I didn't want to worry Darryn by hanging up."

Griffin's eyes didn't warm. If anything, they chilled further. "Long conversation for a wrong number."

Irritation prickled. "I thought you'd want him to think everything was okay here. So, yes, I chatted for a minute rather than telling him I had to hang up right away and call the Kenner County CSU because I wanted to send them some fingerprints that might belong to the guy who's been trying to kill us."

He glanced at the kitchen table, which was littered with the leftovers from her fingerprinting project, along with the sheets of black construction paper on which she'd affixed the lifted prints. He nodded shortly. "Good work. Get those to the CSU pronto."

"Hello? That was what I was trying to do." Her nerves were jangling now, mixed with annoyance, because she hadn't done anything to deserve his attitude. "And for the record, I know you require a strict boundary between VaughnTec and your son, and I'm not looking to change that. I don't appreciate you implying otherwise."

"It's your job to follow orders, not dictate their tone.

We might be stuck here together, but that doesn't make us friends."

Sophie drew back, stung. She bit her tongue on the first handful of responses that came to mind, though, because he was partially right. His delivery stank, but she had started to relax her guard around him, and lose sight of the boundaries. It was probably a good thing that he'd reminded her to keep her distance. They were neither friends nor—in the VaughnTec power structure, anyway—equals.

What was more, she absolutely couldn't risk losing this job. For whatever reason Kathleen either hadn't known or had chosen to ignore the rumors that Sophie had been blackballed by one of San Fran's most elite families. Sophie doubted she'd get lucky a second time if she got herself fired from VaughnTec.

So she swallowed the burn of anger, shoved the irrational hurt deep down inside, and nodded. "Fine. We're not friends, and I'm to stay away from Darryn and Luke. Got it. If there's nothing else, I'll go into the other room and send Ava the prints." She could've done it from the kitchen, but she didn't really want to be around him just then.

He nodded, unspeaking, his face a blank mask as she turned, grabbed the fingerprint-covered pages off the table and ran. She didn't care if it looked like retreat or escape, she just wanted to be away from him before she did something stupid. Like cry. Or grab on to him and shake him until the businessman went away and the soldier came back.

GRIFFIN FUMED his way through his first cup of coffee. By the time he started his second cup, he'd leveled off; caffeine had that effect on him, whether he liked to admit it or not. By his third cup, he wanted to kick himself.

Instead, he went in search of Sophie.

She wasn't in the bedroom or sitting room, and the bathroom was empty. He had to assume that even if she was furious with him—which she had every right to be—she wouldn't have left the apartment and gone off on her own. So, hoping to hell she wasn't crying, he knocked on the office door, and then, without waiting for an answer, pushed through.

She was sitting at Erik's desk, staring out the window into the driving snow. She'd pulled the curtains back, but the visibility was so poor it seemed as though there must be another layer of curtains on the other side of the glass, creating a flat white exterior marked with occasional billowing ripples of wind and grayness.

At Griffin's entrance, she turned and looked at him. Her eyes were dry, and filled with a mix of wariness, hurt and anger.

"I'm sorry," he said simply. "I was out of line."

She looked startled for a moment, then her eyes narrowed. "Yes, you were, but I didn't expect you to admit it. Why the change of heart?"

"You want the explanation or the excuse?" Though in reality he wasn't proud of either.

"I want the truth."

"It's a little bit of both. The excuse is that I'm flat-out

inhuman before my first cup of coffee. Ask Darryn. He'll back me up on that."

"I'm not supposed to talk to Darryn," she said sweetly, but with an edge to the words. "So I guess I'll have to take your word on it."

"Which brings me to the explanation." Since she was firmly entrenched behind the big, masculine desk, he moved a pile of landscaping magazines off a nearby chair and sat down. "At the risk of dragging out my apology, I'd like to tell you about Luke's mother."

Sophie shifted, crossing her arms protectively over her chest. "You don't need to. As you correctly pointed out, we're not friends. I'm your executive assistant, nothing more, nothing less."

"I was being an ass. We both know there's more be-tween us than a business relationship, and has been since day one. We've ignored it as best we can, but that doesn't mean it's not there."

She said nothing, simply stared at him with an ex-pression of shock that almost bordered on horror, as though by alluding to their mutual attraction he'd yanked open a big old can of worms. And maybe he had, but after the two sensually charged moments they'd shared the day before, and the fact that it looked like they'd be stranded together another day at a minimum, he had a feeling this was the way to go. Maybe if they talked it out, the tension would disappear. If not, at least the elephant would leave the room.

That was the theory, anyway.

"Be that as it may," Sophie said carefully, avoiding

his eyes as color rode high on her elegant cheekbones. "I thought we agreed not to trade life stories."

"I'd still like you to understand why I'm so protective of my home life." When she didn't say anything, he took it as tacit agreement and continued, "I told you my parents died in a car accident six years ago. I was just back from the marines, had just started getting my feet underneath me at VaughnTec, and then, *wham*. It was just me and Uncle Will left, and, well, suffice it to say neither of us was in a very good place for a long time after it happened." He paused, remembering both the good and the bad. "Ironically, the first couple of buy-ins I made after they died paid off for the company in a big way. Where VaughnTec had barely been making payroll before, suddenly the money started rolling in. Since Will and I were too miserable to do anything but keep working, we plowed every penny back into the company, and it exploded. We were suddenly both very wealthy men."

He broke off, wondering how it could be that such a crazy, awful, wonderful, terrible time in his life could boil down to just a few simple sentences.

"I take it that in this case, wealthy didn't equal happy?"

"Yes and no. Eventually, the shock of it all started wearing off. Will woke up one day, realized he wasn't getting any younger, married the woman he'd been dating on and off for a few years, and asked me to buy him out of the company. I did, of course, but once he was gone, I was damned lonely." He twisted his lips into a completely humorless smile. "I tried to fill the gap with flings and parties, but that wasn't doing it. Then I met Monique." She'd been young, vivacious and pretty. And the way she'd made him feel had reminded him of the way his father had looked at his mother. It'd taken him too long to realize he'd married that memory instead of Monique, who was someone else entirely. "Long story short, we got married too fast, before I figured out that we'd been looking for very different things. I wanted a family like the one I grew up in. She wanted a rich husband."

"The two are not necessarily mutually exclusive," Sophie pointed out.

"They were in this case, except that I didn't have a clue what she was really like, what she was really up to, until I happened to intercept a message from an upscale women's clinic, confirming her appointment for a D & C." He paused, still in disbelief at how close a thing it had been. "I confronted her, and she didn't deny it. Hell, maybe she wanted me to find out, maybe that was how she'd decided to get out of the marriage with a decent enough payoff. Uncle Will had insisted I use a good prenup, so she either had to stay married to me, or she had to come up with some leverage."

"Luke."

"Luke," Griffin confirmed. "I quite literally bought him. In exchange for a hefty payoff, Monique carried the baby to term. She had a C-section as soon as the doctors would let her, had the best plastic surgeon my money could buy give her a nip and a tuck while they had her on the table, and whisked herself away to an exclusive spa to recover from her 'ordeal.'" He paused, and his voice went ragged. "She never even looked at him."

Sophie let the silence linger for a second, broken only by the background howl of the storm winds. Then she said, "No offense, and I don't mean to cross the line—wherever the hell it's been redrawn—but did you ever stop to think that she did you both a favor by being completely out of your lives? Some women shouldn't be mothers, period."

A thread of steel in her expression warned him not to push. Since he was the one who owed the apology, he didn't press, instead saying, "I'm not willing to go so far as to call it a favor, but yeah. I've accepted that Luke and I are significantly better off on our own."

"That wasn't exactly what I said."

"But it's the point I'm trying to make." Griffin leaned forward in his chair, propping his elbows on his knees. "After the initial drama from Monique died down, I started dating again, and I was honest about what I was looking for, someone old-fashioned, who wanted to be a wife to me and a mother to my son. I thought I'd found the right woman about a year ago. Cara was great with Luke, and she said and did all the right things. But when she found out I wanted a prenup, she bailed. She'd been in it for a lucrative lifestyle with the promise of an equally lucrative divorce. She didn't even bother to try pretending otherwise."

"So you've, what? Sworn off dating?" Sophie asked, and he couldn't gauge her thoughts from her voice or expression.

"I've sworn off all of it until Luke's older. When Cara left, he was heartbroken. For a while, any woman he saw, he called her mama, with this hopeful look on his face like he was trying to figure out where she'd gone, or what he'd done wrong. The same thing happened with Kathleen. He's been moping ever since she retired, even though he only saw her now and then. Which is why I don't want you around him. No offense, but we both know that this job is only a waystop for you. You'll be moving on when you're done dealing with whatever you're dealing with. It might be a year from now, it might be three. Who knows? All I know is that I'm not making my son say good-bye again. Not until he understands how life works."

"Or your version of it, anyway," she murmured, and there was a glint in her eyes that he thought might be irritation.

"Look." He spread his hands. "I'm doing the best I know how to do. Luke's doing great with Darryn and me. He doesn't need anyone else. As for me…" He shrugged. "Running VaughnTec and raising my son are my only two priorities right now. I don't have the time or energy for anything or anyone else. Which is why this…this thing between us, this chemistry, or attraction, or whatever, isn't going to go anywhere. But even knowing that, I'm still attracted, which frustrates the hell out of me. And it's largely because I'm frustrated that I snapped at you earlier. I want you, but I don't want to want you, if that makes any sense."

The frustration kicked even higher once he'd said the

words, as though some part of him was hoping she'd throw up her hands, relieved that he'd finally admitted that he wanted her, and jump him.

Instead, she nodded calmly. "Believe it or not, that's exactly how I feel about you. Only I apparently deal with frustration far more politely that you do."

He waited for her to continue. She didn't. "More secrets, Sophie?" he asked quietly when it was clear she didn't intend to elaborate.

She tipped her head. "Not secrets. Privacy."

He wanted to ask more, but knew damn well he didn't have the right. "Fine, then. Privacy." He blew out a breath, discomfited to realize that the tension hadn't faded. If anything, it'd gotten worse.

The need for her churned in his belly, attuning him to her every move, her every breath. The previous night had been torture, with her touching his shoulder, soothing his injuries. He'd been rock-hard, and it'd been all he could manage not to reach for her. And now, it was all he could do not to ask her for a repeat performance, even though his arm felt fine.

"So. What next?" she asked, regarding him steadily, as if in challenge.

We get naked, he wanted to say, but that wouldn't do. So instead, he said, "I'm willing to keep trying the working together thing if you are."

And he was a little surprised to realize it was true. He was honest enough with himself to admit that at least part of his on-again, off-again thoughts of firing Sophie had come from a desire to avoid dealing with his inconvenient attraction to his too-young executive assistant. Having gotten it out in the open might not have mitigated the attraction, but it forced him to acknowledge that it was totally unfair to fire her for being young and pretty, and because he couldn't keep his thoughts where they belonged when it came to her.

That was his problem, not hers.

"I was assuming that much, since you just gave me enough ammunition to make a pretty good case for sexual harassment," she said dryly. "I was actually asking 'what next' in the context of keeping us alive long enough to get back to civilization and a more or less normal working routine."

"Again, that is so not what the women I'm used to dealing with would say under the circumstances," he murmured, continuing to be both baffled and charmed by her, and to a degree that was beginning to worry him.

"And again I'll reply that I'm not those women," she said. "So. What's the plan?"

He wanted to call her on the change of subject, wanted to know what she thought about the two of them, how she was managing to tamp down the attraction. He knew she felt it, too. That wasn't ego talking, it was a fact, gleaned from her nerves and clumsiness, from the faint catch of her breath when they inadvertently touched, and from the almost palpable tension that had hummed in that tiny bathroom, where he'd imagined taking her in his arms and kissing her, putting her up on the edge of the vanity and sliding home.

But he couldn't call her on the subject change any

more than he could follow up on the fantasy. So he answered her question with a question: "What did Ava say about the prints?"

She frowned and shook her head. "I couldn't get through. The signal is seriously weak. Maybe the battery's getting low?"

"Doubtful. If it's powering up, it's got enough juice to send and receive. More likely the storm is messing with the reception."

"Either way, I dropped the files to Martinez's e-mail, which I pulled off the sheriff's department Web site. That way I could turn off the PDA and the pictures should still be in queue."

"Good thinking." Griffin nodded, trying, and mostly succeeding, to make himself focus on their immediate issues rather than the larger complications. She was right, priority number one had to be getting through the rest of the storm, and getting home. Then they would see what might happen between them. Or not. "I think the next step is hitting the woodshed and restocking. I tossed the last log on the fire when I got up, and it's too damn cold to go without."

She nodded and stood. "Then the woodshed it is."

He paused. "Maybe you should stay here. I'm going to go back down into the basement and see if I can find the hidden door. There's got to be one—that's the only explanation for how that lead-fisted bastard got away last night."

"Are you sure I'll be safe here?"

Of course not, and she knew it. He was being selfish,

looking to get some time away from her, to clear his head. But she was right. They were safer together than apart. Period.

He nodded shortly. "Fine. Let's go."

They suited up in silence, but once they were ready to go, he paused by the doorway. "The woodshed isn't far, but it's on a bit of an incline, and I'm betting the drifts are going to be bad. Choose your footing carefully, and if it comes down to a choice, drop the wood rather than hurting yourself, okay?"

She nodded, skin pale in the storm light. "Will do. And Griffin?"

"Yeah."

"Thank you. For telling me about Monique and Luke. I didn't think it would, but it helps to know why you want me to keep my distance from your family."

Too late, Griffin realized he'd let himself get close to her again. They were standing near the door, inside each other's personal space, her face upturned to his in earnest conversation, and all he could think about was how easy it would be to lean down and touch his lips to hers. His blood fired at the thought, his skin tightened and his flesh hardened, making him all too aware that his head might be trying to make the right choice, but his body had other ideas.

Very deliberately, he stepped away from her. He inhaled, trying to settle himself, but that only made it worse because the air carried her soft, feminine scent and the spark of the tension that had existed between them from the first moment, when she'd walked into his office, wide-eyed and nervous, and trying so hard to control her nerves, which had only served to make it worse. His brain had told him to transfer her to another department, but his body must've overruled the logic, because he'd made excuses instead of making the transfer. And now, here they were, closer to each other than his brain liked, not nearly close enough as far as his body was concerned.

Knowing they'd better get moving before he did something to tip the fragile balance, he unbolted the apartment door and yanked it open. "Come on."

At the moment, a short hike through the blizzard was sounding like a very good idea, threat or no threat.

THE STORM WINDS seemed slightly less ferocious to Sophie than they had the day before. Either the blizzard had eased a fraction, or her California-girl self was getting used to bundling up in multiple layers just to venture outside, and spending the rest of the time huddled next to a fireplace.

Or else, she admitted inwardly as she followed the path Griffin was breaking through waist-deep snow, it was easier to think about the weather than it was to think about what had happened back in the apartment. She wasn't sure which information was more staggering in the grand scheme—that he'd bought his son from his gold digging ex-wife and had pretty much sworn off women until Luke was older…or that that she and Griffin had admitted to their mutual attraction.

She probably ought to have felt uncomfortable about

that, but she didn't. She felt empowered. Feminine. And more than a little daring.

Griffin had admitted that he wanted her sexually. He didn't want to want her, granted, but the attraction was there. After what she'd been through with her recently ex-sneak-around-almost-lover, Tony Spellman, and his evil fiancée, Destiny, it was nice to know that a powerful, virile man like Griffin could desire her and be honest about it, without all the subterfuge she'd experienced in that other non-relationship.

Smiling secretly to herself from deep inside the hood of her parka, behind a woolen muffler, she labored through the snow as Griffin reached the woodshed and started kicking snow away from the door, shoving it off to one side. Just as she reached him, he jerked back with a curse.

"Don't look!" He turned and grabbed her and tried to drag her away, but she stayed rooted in place, her eyes locked on to the grisly sight he'd uncovered.

There, leaning up against the woodshed, was a man's body, cold and blue and frozen. He was wearing dark clothes and one glove, with a woolen cap pulled down over his forehead, and a muffler dangling below his chin. His eyes were open and staring, sightless and frozen. Even worse, at least as far as Sophie was concerned, was the patch of red-stained snow near his side, where he'd been gut-shot.

"It's Perry," Griffin said, his voice rough, and sounding too loud in a momentary lull of the storm winds.

"I killed him." At first Sophie didn't know if she'd

said the words or merely thought them, but when she felt Griffin curl his arm around her shoulders despite their earlier conversation about keeping things all business between them, she knew she'd said them aloud. And he wasn't arguing. Worse, he was holding her.

Which meant it was real.

She had killed a man.

Shock rattled through her, freezing her in place. Self-protection or not, the contractor was dead because of her. He had a wife and kids waiting at home for him. Somehow that knowledge made her actions all that much more awful.

"I should have—" She broke off, because what could she say, really? If she hadn't acted, he might have killed her and Griffin. Yet...

"You saved our lives," Griffin said softly, from very close by. Which made her realize that she'd turned toward him, that she was clinging to him, her fingers digging into his parka, her heart drumming in time with the pulse at his throat. In her shock she had reached for him, and he'd let her. More, his arms had come around her and locked on, offering support when she so badly needed it.

Always before, she'd been her own anchor, the one who'd been in charge of things, even when she'd been little more than a child herself.

Now, for just a second, she gave herself permission to cling. She turned her face into Griffin's neck. And wept.

Chapter Seven

Griffin held Sophie, wrapping his arms around her, wishing he could take away what she'd just seen, and the knowledge of what she'd done.

Worse, he wished he didn't notice how right she felt against him. This wasn't the time or place. But he was painfully aware that she was soft and warm and curvy, and fit against him just right, with her head tucked beneath his jaw, her hair brushing against his face and throat. He'd opened his parka so her arms were looped around him beneath the coat, and he'd automatically wrapped the edges of the parka around her, bringing her into his body heat.

He would've liked to get her away from the scene, get her back inside the house, but the trail through the deep snow was too narrow for them to walk together, and he didn't want to let go of her yet.

They stood there, locked together, for a long moment that seemed far simpler than it actually was. The storm lull made for an eerie sort of quiet, an expectant hush.

After a few minutes her sobs passed, and she loosened

her grip on him and pushed away from him. Avoiding his eyes, she said, "I'm sorry." Her voice was low and husky, with a faint tremor of emotion. "That was—"

"Completely understandable," he said, cutting her off. "Come on. Let's get you back to the apartment. I'll take care of the wood."

Inhaling deeply, she scrubbed both hands across her face, leaving her skin rosy pink and her eyelashes heavy with the memory of tears. In that moment, she looked very young and very lost. But then her expression firmed and she shook her head. "No. We're in this together. Tell me what to do."

In reality, the best thing would be for her to go inside and let him have room to do what needed to be done. But the jittering energy that was suddenly pouring off her suggested that she needed to do something active, something more than stand at the window and watch him examine the man she had quite likely killed. So he said, "You're on wood detail. Haul as many loads as you can and stack them just inside the hallway. I'll carry it from there. When you run out of steam on that, maybe you could pull some food together? I don't mean to put you on kitchen detail, but—"

"I don't mind," she said quickly. "Wood. Food. Got it." She moved to pass him, but he caught her arm. Through the layers of clothing and parka, he could feel her trembling.

"Sophie, look at me," he said, and waited until her eyes connected with his. Tension vibrated through her body, and her eyes were dull with shock, yet bright with frenetic energy. He understood both, though wished like hell he could've spared her from it all.

When he didn't say anything right away, she said, "The wind's picking up again. I should get going."

He tightened his grip. "I need you to know that this isn't your fault. You didn't do anything wrong, you hear me? You. Did. Nothing. Wrong."

The tears that had been brimming in her light brown eyes welled up and a single droplet spilled over, tracking down her cheek, which was already wet from the snow and her earlier crying jag. "Please," she whispered. "Just let me go."

Something deep within him said, *I don't want to*. It was that small, seditious voice that had him dropping her arm and taking a big step back, away from her. But he said softly, "We'll talk later."

She nodded, unspeaking, and headed for the wood-shed door, deliberately averting her eyes when she passed Perry's corpse.

Griffin watched, wishing to hell he'd left her down in Kenner City the day before. He wasn't sorry he was there—Lonesome Lake was his property, his responsibility. If there was something shady going on there, it was his duty to fix it, especially before he brought Luke out for a visit. But he regretted having involved Sophie, regretted the things she'd been through over the past forty-eight hours, regretted the things she'd been forced to see and do.

"This damn well better be over now that you're dead," he said as he knelt down beside Perry's body.

Problem was, he needed to be sure. Occam's razor suggested that there had been just the single threat, that Perry had gotten into something he hadn't wanted Griffin to know about. But experience, both on the battlefield and in the boardroom, had taught Griffin that human nature didn't necessarily conform to the simplest explanation. Humans were complicated creatures, and because of that, made dangerous enemies. What if Perry wasn't alone?

That was why Griffin decided that his and Sophie's immediate situation trumped police procedure, even though he suspected Martinez and the CSIs would disagree. Still, he was there and they weren't, and he needed to be sure Perry was the man who'd attacked him the day before.

Hunkering down in the stomped-down snow, Griffin examined the body, looking for any evidence that could explain what the contractor had been up to, and whether he'd been working alone or not. A search of Perry's pockets turned up a billfold and some loose change, along with a small, dog-eared spiral-bound notebook containing punch lists, measurements and terse notes about molding and electrical wiring. Which was about what he would've expected from a contractor, and didn't tell him a damn thing about what was going on at Lonesome Lake.

As Griffin searched, he was aware of Sophie passing to and fro, lugging armloads of wood. On her next pass, he called, "That's probably good for now. I'll meet you inside."

She turned back to look at him, her eyes dry, but hollow with shock and grief. "What don't you want me to see?"

"Just go on. Trust me."

She stared at him a moment longer, then nodded. "Okay. But are you certain the apartment is safe?"

They both knew he'd be lying if he said yes. But his gut instinct said they were alone in the mansion now, so he nodded. "You'll be fine. I won't be more than a few minutes behind you."

She nodded and left, though reluctantly.

When she was gone, Griffin focused on the body. The contractor's face was covered with snow and gray with death, but Griffin thought he saw red marks and the beginnings of a bruise along the side of Perry's face, which was consistent with Griffin's adrenaline-jacked memory of struggling with his attacker the day before. Griffin didn't see or feel any evidence of head trauma, and the only blood appeared to have come from the region of the contractor's waist.

Grimacing, Griffin stripped aside Perry's jacket and clothing so he could get a look at the injury. It was a bullet wound, all right, a through-and-through shot at the level of the contractor's right kidney, with the exit wound in the front. It would've been a fatal wound, Griffin knew, as the bullet had most likely taken out the renal artery. There wasn't as much blood as he would've expected, but he had to assume that was a function of the snow having washed it away. Martinez had been lamenting how the blizzard was destroying evidence. Now Griffin could relate.

It had been many years since the last time Griffin had been this up close and personal with death, and never before with the added element of the cold. In a way, the freezing temperatures made it easier, robbing the body of the rubbery, not-quite-warm-enough feeling of the freshly dead. But at the same time the weather complicated things, obscuring any footprints or other evidence, and confusing the blood pattern. He couldn't get past thinking there should've been more blood, but maybe not. It wasn't like he was an expert. The CSIs would be able to get a better idea of what had happened, once the storm broke and they were able to get in and recover the body for processing.

For now, all he could say for certain was that the bullet wound and bruises seemed consistent with what had happened down in the basement the day before.

As he'd been examining Perry, the wind had grown worse and the sky was darkening once again, warning that the lull had only been temporary, and there was more blizzard yet to come. Figuring he'd learned all he was likely to from the body under the circumstances, and also figuring he'd already done enough damage to the scene, he decided he wouldn't compound that by moving the body inside. Instead, he climbed to his feet and slogged back to the house, squinting against a sudden, stinging spray of ice pellets.

Once he was back inside the mansion, he grabbed a huge armload of the wood Sophie had left just inside the door. As he did so, the fine hairs on the back of his neck stayed quiet, and there was an easing of the heavy weight that had been pressing on his lungs ever since he'd realized the bridge collapse had been no accident.

His gut instincts seemed to think Perry had been the sum total of the danger. And he'd never had reason to question his instincts before—at least not on the topic of personal safety. When it came to women, that was an entirely different story. But it was exactly that subject at the forefront of his mind as he headed back to the apartment: women. Or rather, one particular woman.

Sophie had impressed the hell out of him over the past two days. She was gentle, kind and loyal, yet with an unexpectedly fierce fighting spirit, and enough backbone to stand up to him when she deemed it necessary. Yes, she was relatively inexperienced in the business milieu, and far from worldly, but she balanced him in ways he hadn't realized he needed. What was more, there was an aspect of her inexperience that he hadn't even consciously let himself think about before. But now that they had acknowledged the chemistry between them, a small voice deep inside him dared to whisper the words, *Vaughn virgin.*

There was a story on his father's side of the family, a myth, really, passed down from father to son. It said that the Vaughn marriages that worked, the love matches that truly lasted, were to virgin brides.

When Griffin's father had first told him the story, he'd been thirteen and the idea of marrying anyone, virgin or otherwise, had seemed ridiculous. A few years—and a few girlfriends later—he'd all but plugged his ears when his dad brought it up again, because the conversation had involved his mother, and he so hadn't wanted to go there.

The last time they'd talked about it had been a few weeks before the accident. Griffin had been in his early thirties, fresh out of the marines, and ready to take his place within VaughnTec. The idea of settling down and starting a family had been crossing his mind more and more often, at least in an abstract "some day" sort of way, so he'd asked his dad about the legend, and what it meant in real terms.

"I'll keep it general, so I don't skeeve you out again by talking about your mom and me," his old man had said, for which Griffin had been profoundly grateful. "The way I see it," his father had continued, "you'll have to modernize the legend however you see fit. It's not a rule, or even something you should be using as a criterion. But the fact remains that the happiest Vaughn marriages have involved a relatively inexperienced bride. Which isn't to say," his dad had said with a sly grin, "that they don't catch up extremely quickly when they do start gaining some experience."

Which had ended that conversation with Griffin making outraged gagging noises and his father busting a gut. In the aftermath of the accident that'd shifted his world on its axis, Griffin had pretty much walked away from the idea of finding his own Vaughn virgin. Monique hadn't even been close to virginal, but she'd played the role of domesticity so well that he hadn't caught the disconnect until it was too late for their relationship, and almost too late for Luke. Similarly, Cara had proven to him that there was a big difference between ingénue and innocence.

I'm not like those women, Sophie had told him, twice now when he'd compared her responses to those of the other women he'd known. And maybe that was the point.

Which wasn't to say that this the time or place to explore the possibility, Griffin acknowledged inwardly as he thumped a toe against the closed apartment door and called, "Sophie? It's me. Can you get the door?"

But although the circumstances were far from perfect, Griffin thought there was something approaching perfect about the way his heart kicked a little at the sight of her when she opened the door and waved him in, and the way the smell of wood smoke and soup combined to make him feel settled and grounded. Like it or not, he was a traditional man raised by parents who'd held very traditional family roles. Was it any wonder he found himself gravitating toward the same thing in his own life, despite all his intentions to remain apart and alone?

"Thanks." He stacked the wood and fed a couple of logs into the fireplace.

The wind howled outside, and ice pellets dashed themselves against the windowpanes, but for the first time since their arrival, the noise made the apartment seem cozy rather than vulnerable.

"There's soup and baked beans ready to go in the kitchen," Sophie said. "I didn't dish up, because I wasn't sure how long you'd be."

"I'll eat after I've brought in the rest of the wood."

Griffin looked over at her, and saw the remnants of tears on her face, the dull horror still in her eyes. She was being as brave as she knew how, but Perry's death was digging at her. He wished he could tell her she would forget about it in time, that it would matter less because it'd been self-defense, but he couldn't honestly say that. Seven years out of uniform, and he still sometimes saw the faces of the men he'd killed. So instead he said, "Do you want to talk about it?"

She shook her head. "Not really. In fact, I'd really like to turn it all off for a while and take a nap."

He noticed that she'd dragged the mattress back into the bedroom, and returned the sofa cushions to where they belonged. It made sense, given that it appeared as though they had no need to stay away from the windows anymore, and the fire kept all four rooms warm enough. Still, Griffin felt a faint pang, not of disquiet, but of disappointment at the distance it put between them. The message was clear: they would each sleep alone that night.

Which was fine. It was what he wanted, right? It was sure as hell what he'd told her that morning, laying out the bare facts of why there was no future for them, trying his best to convince her when he'd really been trying to convince himself.

She had no way of knowing he'd started to second-guess himself, started to think maybe she was what he'd been looking for—or at least what he should've been looking for—all along. And she didn't need to know it now, either. She was exhausted, physically and emotionally drained. The last thing she needed right now was for him to start changing the rules.

So he waved her to the bedroom. "Go, please. Rest. Recharge. It's been a hell of a couple of days."

She went, but hesitated in the bedroom doorway. "Promise me you won't go out and investigate on your own?"

He wasn't sure if she was afraid of being left alone, afraid he'd get in trouble without her to watch his back, or afraid she'd miss out on part of the impromptu investigation they'd fallen into. Her success at Mickey-Mousing the fingerprints that morning suggested he wasn't the only one who enjoyed the occasional episode of *CSI*. Figuring it covered all three options, he nodded and said, "I'll stay in here until you come back out. I promise."

The rest of the wood could wait, and the thought of the fingerprints had reminded him that he needed to check the PDA and see if he could get through to the sheriff. The sooner he reported Perry's death, the sooner he could see which way Martinez intended to play it, and whether one of the VaughnTec lawyers would need to get involved in order to make sure Sophie didn't suffer any repercussions when the shooting had been pure self-defense.

Sophie nodded, stepped into the bedroom and closed the door softly at her back. But even though she was gone, the cheerful crackle of the fire remained, as did the smell of a hot lunch and the sense that he wasn't alone. Which was something he thought he could get used to. And if a piece of him wondered whether he was getting ahead of himself, creating things that weren't real simply because the two of them were in such an unreal situation, he ignored it as he headed for the kitchen, grabbed a bite to eat, and sat down with Sophie's PDA.

The good news was that the signal strength was decent. The bad news was that the battery side of the equation was less robust, which meant they should start thinking about conserving, in case they were there another day or two.

He found Martinez's number in the PDA's memory, and made the call. The sheriff answered on the third ring, sounding harried. "Martinez here."

"Sheriff, it's Vaughn. How's the weather looking?"

"Another twenty-four hours of heavy snow, minimum. Damn storm system's stalled right on top of us." Martinez paused. "How's it going up there?"

Griffin sketched out the discovery of Perry's body.

When he was done with his report, there was a long silence on the other end of the phone line. Then Martinez sighed. "I'll be honest with you. Part of me hoped it'd go the other way. Not that I'd wish it on anybody to be stranded up there with Vince Del Gardo, but because Perry's one of us. He's a local. And this is going to about kill his wife."

Griffin refrained from pointing out that Perry had very nearly killed both him and Sophie. Instead, he said, "What are the chances he was working with someone up here? Not just on the renovations, but on something he wouldn't want an outsider to see?"

After a moment, the sheriff said, "It's possible, I suppose."

"But you don't think it's likely," Griffin guessed from his tone.

"Honestly? It doesn't play for me. I know you've had troubles with Perry, but before all this happened I would've sworn to you that he's a good man and a good worker. He was the type who hates getting behind schedule, hates not finishing a job to his absolute satisfaction. I would've said that if he told you he was having problems with the reno, then he was having problems, hands down."

Which was consistent with Griffin's initial impression of the man, and why he'd hired him in the first place. But it wasn't consistent with the evidence. "Be that as it may, the bruises and the gunshot wound prove he was the one I fought with down in the basement. And the fact that he attacked us down there seems to make a good argument for him being the one who blew the bridge, too. He didn't want us up here, whatever the reason."

"Goddamned storm," Martinez muttered. "If it weren't for the snow, I'd have the CSU out there. They'd get straight to the bottom of what's going on."

"Did you get Sophie's e-mail?"

"E-mail hasn't exactly been our first priority around here."

"Sophie sent scans of some fingerprints she lifted off the crowbar. Most of 'em are probably mine, but there's at least one thumbprint that isn't. Can you have Ava check them out? She can e-mail Sophie if there's anything else you'd want us to do."

"I think I hear a 'but' in your voice," Martinez said.

"That'd be the part where I'm thinking it's not a priority for her to cross-check the prints. My gut says we're in the clear now that Perry's gone."

"What's your gut's general accuracy rating?"

"Pretty good, except where it comes to women."

"I hear that. Or at least I did until I met my Bree." Martinez paused, and Griffin heard the squawk of a radio in the background. When the sheriff spoke again, he sounded rushed. "Look, I've got to take this. I'll tell Ava to e-mail when she gets the results or if she has any questions. Other than that, you two sit tight for another day or so, okay? We'll get the roads cleared as soon as we can."

The sheriff hung up without waiting for a response, but that was fine with Griffin. He'd done what he'd needed to do, and put the necessary wheels in motion. And, having gotten the sense that Perry was well-liked in the community, and his death would be a shock, Griffin extrapolated that it'd be a good idea to bring in the lawyers sooner than later.

Hitting the batteries for one more quick call, he phoned home and let Darryn know that when the helicopter made it through to pick them up, it should come equipped with a VaughnTec lawyer. After that, Griffin had a quick, garbled conversation with Luke that made him long to be back home with his son. Then, having done what he could do long-distance, Griffin powered down the unit to conserve what was left of the batteries.

He cleaned up his lunch dishes, grabbed a paperback at random from Erik's bookcase, and settled down on the sofa with his feet to the fire. Although part of him was jonesing to get back into the basement and find the hidden passageway that logic said had to be there, he was mindful of his promise to Sophie. She'd needed to know that he was going to be there when she woke up, so that was exactly what he intended to do.

And, thinking that, he dozed off with the book on his chest, alert to sounds or alarms, but otherwise letting himself drift, and think of what might be. Those thoughts kept circling back to Sophie. And instead of pushing them away, as he would've done before, he went with the flow, into a world of warmth, soft sighs, and innocence.

He awakened some time later, jolted back to full consciousness by a hint of sound, a furtive movement. The light was dimming toward the quick winter dusk, darkening the already low illumination afforded by the storm skies. But the cool blue light was sufficient to show him Sophie, standing in the bedroom doorway. She was wearing a too-large T-shirt that covered her nearly to her knees, with jeans below, as though she'd slept in the T-shirt and pulled on the jeans before coming out of the bedroom. Her hair was loose, tumbling to her shoulders and her expression was wary.

Griffin was on his feet and across the room before he was aware of moving. He stopped near her and looked past her into the bedroom, but saw nothing amiss. "What's wrong?"

"I've been thinking."

He winced. "About Perry. Look, I know it'll probably

be a while before you're ready to believe it, but you didn't have a choice. It was him or us. I see it that way, and the law's going to see it that way." If not, the VaughnTec lawyer would make sure of it.

Her eyes went hollow at the mention, but she shook her head. "I wasn't thinking about what happened to Perry. Or at least not directly. I was thinking about everything you said this morning, about how we should just keep working together and ignore the attraction."

"About that," he began. "I've been thinking—"

She lifted her hand and touched her fingertips to his lips, silencing him. "Don't. Please. Not until I've finished saying what I want to say to you. It took me nearly an hour to gather the courage to come out here. If I derail now, we might not get another chance at this."

Griffin's blood thrummed in his veins as he got an inkling of where her thoughts had taken her. And although he liked to think he wouldn't have even considered it, would've stopped her there, if he hadn't been doing some major rethinking of his own, the reality was that he couldn't be sure. He wanted her that much. But because he *had* been rethinking things, when she took her hand away from his mouth, he nodded encouragement. "Go on. I won't interrupt."

The hollow look drained from her eyes, to be replaced with a spark, one he suspected was a reflection of the heat that had roared to sudden life inside him. Her lips curved as she said, "Something tells me you're catching up."

"The sheriff says it'll be at least another twenty-four hours before the storm lets up."

"Then that's twenty-four hours that we can both agree will cease to exist once the storm breaks and we get back to reality." She paused, then said softly, "I can't help thinking that it could've so easily been you or me, or both of us, out there leaning up against the woodshed, dead and gone. And I decided that life's too short, and I've spent too much of it already doing the things I ought to do, or that I have to do. I want to take something for myself. I want to take *this* for myself, even if it's nothing but a memory by the time the storm breaks."

Griffin knew he should say something, to tell her that he'd been an idiot that morning, and that he hoped whatever they were about to start could last beyond their time together at Lonesome Lake. But his voice had stopped working, and his brain could form only one coherent thought as he stood there, looking down at her and seeing the faint hint of wariness along with a spark of challenge in her light brown eyes.

That thought was: *I want.* There was no other rationality than that. Nothing mattered beyond it.

And because he had no voice, and no thoughts other than of her, and because he, at least, knew there might be more than a single night for them, he did what he'd wanted to do from the very beginning.

He leaned in. And touched his lips to hers.

The first moment of the kiss was a shimmer of warmth, the second a bite of electricity, just as Sophie herself was soft innocence covering an edge of excitement. She parted her lips on an exhalation of surprise and pleasure, or maybe the surprise and pleasure were his, he didn't know anymore where his desire left off and hers began.

He crowded closer and deepened the kiss, slanting his mouth across hers and delving with his lips and tongue, suctioning gently, asking for access.

If he'd expected to have to cajole a response, he was way off base. She met him head-on, headlong, opening to him on a murmur of pleasure and leaning into the kiss. She slid her tongue along his, shaping his lips with hers and bringing a sharp wash of sensation he hadn't expected, wasn't prepared for.

They touched at only two points—where she held his hand against her cheek and where their lips met in ever-increasing fervency—but raw need roared through him as though they were twined together, horizontal, tearing at each other's clothes.

Heat flared and his blood pounded in his veins, tensing him, hardening him, bringing him close to the point of madness. He wanted her naked, wanted her pressed against him, underneath him, above him, hell, pinned against the wall; he'd take her any way he could get her, any way that was humanly possible.

The compulsion hammered through him, driven higher when she curled her fingers around his hand, anchoring them together. He lifted his free hand, needing to touch her, to undress her.

That was when she stepped back and smiled at him. And led him into the bedroom.

Chapter Eight

When Sophie's mother had spoken to her about sex, she'd talked about power and the things a woman could make a man do for her in exchange. Sophie's high-school girlfriends used sex to be popular, or rebellious, or whatever. And when she'd finally gotten out from underneath the burden of being her mother's primary caregiver and the sole supporter of their two-person family unit, she'd focused on her studies, then her new job. Tony had been an aberration, and though he'd seemed sincere, she learned soon enough that to him, sex was a game. Never once, really, had she understood sex as it was touted in the media, as a transcendental experience. Nor had she had sex with Tony, or anyone before him, simply because it hadn't felt right.

Until now.

She led Griffin into the bedroom, which was dark with the dusk and the storm, illuminated only by the single candle she'd lit when she'd awoken from her nap with two thoughts pounding in her head, in her veins: Griffin wanted her, and she wanted him.

She'd thought it through, and had tried to argue herself out of the decision, only to come back to the basic reality that there wouldn't be another night like this, a night out of their normal realm. Danger had brought them together, and violence had made her step back and look at what might've happened, what experiences she might've died without.

It was time. It was right. With him.

When they reached the side of the bed, she slid open the bedside table to reveal the box of condoms she'd found there. They were obviously a joke gift to Erik; each packet had some version of a saying about the wearer being over the hill. If she'd believed in karma she might've taken the presence of condoms in a retired couple's bedside table as a cosmic sign that she was making the right decision. As it was, she'd simply been grateful for the find.

Griffin's lips twitched, and his dark green eyes sparked with self-deprecating humor. "I'll do my best to prove that the sayings don't apply."

"They haven't hit their expiration date," she said, speaking of the condoms, because their ability to do their job was really all she cared about. Not only because the last thing she needed was another complication in her life, but also because of what Griffin had told her about his past experiences, and the women who had tried to manipulate him. The last thing she wanted would be for him to ever put her in that category.

He grinned. "Hopefully, I haven't hit my expiration date, either."

That had her tipping her head to one side. "The age gap bothers you?"

His grin faded as he shook his head. "No. Trust me, it doesn't. I'll tell you why later. Right now I have other things on my mind."

Then, though she'd been the one to offer the invitation and lead him into the bedroom, he took charge. Not by making a forceful move, or by dominating her physically, but by simply being there. With her. Because she'd asked.

"Sophie," he said, just her name, and leaned in and touched his lips to hers.

The heat came instantly, springing from the well of desire she'd kept tucked away where she'd thought he couldn't see it, and gaining an edge of desperation from their recent brush with death.

He changed the angle of the kiss, slanting his mouth across hers and requesting access, demanding it. She softened on a sigh of rightness, a click of connection, and his tongue swept inside to touch hers. In that moment, rationality disappeared, and reality ceased to exist.

Her blood roared in her veins, skimming through her body and tingling at the points where he touched her, lifting his hands to skim up her arms, brush along her temple and jaw, and then finally settle around her, encompassing her and urging her into the warmth and strength of his big body.

She stepped into him, fitted herself against him, and nearly reeled at the added sensations: her breasts pressing up against the wall of his chest; the hard ridge of his erection settling against her; and the continued magic of his hands playing over her, shaping her, caressing her through the thin nightshirt, then beneath it to her skin.

"Touch me," he groaned, his tone caught somewhere between a plea and a demand, and she complied gladly, sliding her arms around his waist, then beneath his shirt where it had come free as he'd slept.

Running her hands up the strong columns of muscle on either side of his spine, she pressed into him as she'd imagined doing the day before, when he'd been bare to the waist and she'd wanted to put her hands on him, her lips.

As though he'd read her mind, he pulled away and yanked his shirt and sweater off over his head with a powerful, impatient move. That impatience was echoed in his intense, focused expression as he reached for her once again, kissed her once again, and his intensity brought an echoing spear of desire stabbing within her.

"Come here," he said softly, and drew her down to the unmade bed, where she'd woken an hour ago, thinking of him. Wishing they could be together despite their differences.

Now, as she followed him down and lay beside him, touching him, kissing him, there was no gap between them in age or station—she was woman to his man, softness to his strength. There was a definite gap in experience, but he seemed to instinctively understand that, though maybe not the degree. Regardless, when she paused or fumbled, unsure of where her hands belonged, or whether she was doing things right, he smoothed over the moments by guiding her, or simply by holding still and letting her find her way.

She touched his chest, following the hard ridges of muscle and delighting in the contrast of smooth, warm skin and wiry, masculine hair. He lay back, fisting his hands in the bedclothes as she moved to trace the same paths with her lips, learning the taste of him, the feel of him.

His harsh breathing quickened. She could feel the tension vibrating through his big frame, and knew he was giving her this time, giving her himself, because he knew she needed it. And with each touch and kiss her nerves smoothed and the heat coiled higher within her. She grew brazen, brave, and when lips and hands weren't enough anymore, she sat up away from him and drew her shirt off over her head.

He just lay back, anchored by the grip of his hands in the sheets. And looked at her in the candlelight.

She saw the approval in his eyes and reveled in it. Chills chased across her bare skin and tightened her nipples when he whispered, "You're beautiful, Sophie."

Other men had complimented her looks before. But he was the first to really know her before he complimented her, to really see *her* as he was saying the words. So instead of blushing or covering up, as she might have done otherwise, she stayed there, rocked back on her heels on the mattress above him, and let him look his fill. And when he released his anchoring hold and reached up to trace a fingertip along the edge of one of her breasts, she shivered against the heat and sensation brought by the caress, but didn't move. She stayed still, letting him learn her body as she had begun to learn his.

He drew her down and touched his lips to her mouth, her cheeks, and the sides of her throat. And all the while, he caressed her, skimming his hands along her ribs and waist, across the sensitized skin of her stomach and up to cup her breasts and then away again, each time making her hotter, bringing her higher.

Desire raged in her, and impatience took root. Soft, gentle kisses and touches ceased to be enough. She wanted more.

Emboldened now, no longer fumbling or frantic, she guided his hands to the button of her borrowed jeans, and helped him strip the last of her clothing away. He unhooked his belt and skimmed out of his jeans, as well, then lay back down beside her, so they were just barely touching. She reveled in the heat pouring off his slick skin, the quick tap of the pulse at his throat, and the absolute focus in his eyes, which let her know he was entirely in the moment, there with her.

Crowding closer to him, so they touched and twined together from nose to toes, she pressed her lips to his, opened her mouth beneath his, and poured herself into the kiss. Another time, if there was another time for them, she would touch and taste him again, learning the lower half of his body as she had learned his upper half. But now, this time, she was ready for more. Beyond ready. She was burning, pulsing with desire and caught in a building wave of intensity that fired her heart to a frenzied cadence.

Make love with me, she wanted to say, but didn't because she knew what they were doing wasn't love, not really, and didn't want to dress it up as such. Yet she couldn't bring herself to offer a coarser version of the invitation, either, because she had to believe this was more than the sex her mother had used as power, the "getting it on" the girls had giggled over in high school, or the mean, hurtful thing Tony had twisted it into.

So in the end she said nothing. Or rather, she let her body speak for her. *I want this,* her lips said to him, *I want you*.

He shifted against her, sliding his hand down to grip her hip, her upper thigh, and then her knee. He guided her leg up and over him, so her calf was hooked around him and she was open to his soft, whispering caresses.

She arched against him, opened to him and let herself ride the rising tide of sensation. He kissed her, whispered hot promises, praise and the things he wanted to do with her. Restless now, she reached for him, taking hold of his erection and reveling in the feel of soft, velvety skin over hot, hard flesh.

A groan ripped through him and his body tensed to rigor for a second, then eased, letting her know just how hard he was fighting to go slowly, to make it last. To make it matter.

Warmth rolled through her, sweeter than the heat, though no less powerful. She opened her eyes—when had they drifted closed?—and found his face very near hers, his expression intent. When their gazes met she felt a new flare of heat, an added click of connection that let her know that this was good and right for her, that it was what she wanted and needed.

"Are you sure?" he asked in a whisper, offering her a last out.

But there was no turning back for her, hadn't been since the moment she'd finally risen from the bed and gone out into the main room to take what she wanted. He was what she wanted, in that moment, all other considerations aside.

She let him see the heat in her eyes, the need and the confidence he'd given her, and that she'd taken for herself. "I'm very sure."

He smiled, and it seemed to her that the warmth in his eyes was more than desire when he said, "I'm glad."

He reached past her, covering her with his body for a moment as he retrieved one of the condoms. He ripped through the silly slogan, pulled out the latex sheath and covered himself in a practiced move that was somehow more elegant than she had imagined it being. Then he was rising over her again, settling himself between her legs and pausing, as if to give her a chance to get used to his weight. But she was done with pausing, done with taking it slow. She reached up and kissed him, openmouthed and inciting, a wordless demand for completion.

Take me, the kiss said. And he did.

He surged against her, into her, breaching the slight resistance of her virginity in a pinch of pain that was quickly lost to the strangeness of having a piece of him inside her, filling and stretching her.

"You okay?" he asked, his voice rough with tension, and maybe something else.

She looked into his eyes, looking for surprise or accusation and finding something much more complicated, more compelling. In answer, she kissed him and hooked a leg around his, urging him to move.

And, on a long, shuddering exhale, he did. She could almost see the restraint fall away from him, could feel it in the surge of his body as he withdrew from her and thrust home, and in the fervor of his kiss.

The sensation of his penetration went from strangeness to pleasure, then kindled to a flame. She moved against him, matching his thrusts and then demanding more as the tempo increased and the power of the act coiled tightly inside her. She grabbed on to him, dug into him, and in answer he hooked an arm at her knee and raised one of her legs, spreading her, baring her to the slide of his body against hers.

She cried out at the sensations that brought, and again when her body somehow clamped onto him, tightening around the point of their joining. He spoke to her, urging her on, telling her to trust him, to trust them. She heard his voice but didn't process the words; her entire being was focused on the pleasurable tightness inside, and the sense that there was something bearing down on her, something huge and important.

They surged together and apart, together and apart, and she clung to him, giving herself over to the feelings they made together, until finally she reached that huge place inside her, or it reached her, she wasn't sure which, or even where she was, or who. Pleasure coalesced into a hard knot at the point where she and Griffin connected, growing tighter with each thrust until the balance tipped and the hard knot went nova, bursting into a brilliance of heat and sensation that had her bowing back on the bed, her mouth open in a silent scream.

Griffin moved urgently against her, drawing out the moment. Then, just as she was coming down from the peak, he picked up the tempo once again, thrusting surely and rhythmically, his hot cheek pressed against hers. A hollow groan built in his chest and became her name, and then he was shaking and driving into her, shouting as he found his own release. His excitement put her over again and she came a second time, shuddering in his arms and holding on to him, using his solid strength as her anchor.

The pleasure drained then, going from urgency to a background hum of completion. They were both breathing hard, and Sophie was aware of fine tremors running through her body, little post-coital bursts of satisfaction.

Griffin whispered something—praise, perhaps, or maybe simply her name—and rolled off her to one side. He gathered her against him, fitting her close as her breathing slowed and her skin cooled.

"Cold?" he murmured, and drew a blanket up over them before she could answer, once again seeming to know what she needed before she did.

Sophie had never felt so in tune with another human being. Or, for that matter, with herself. She knew reality would intrude soon enough. The storm winds were still blowing outside, lashing icy snow against the window-panes in a dusk that had gone to night. But the weather would break eventually, and they would have to deal with Perry's death, and saying good-bye to what they'd found together at Lonesome Lake, both the good and the bad. For now, though, she was determined to stay in the moment, with the man she'd claimed for herself, if only for a short time.

Cuddling into him, she threaded her fingers with his, turned her face into his throat, and let herself drift. She should probably say something, she knew. And she'd get around to it, in a moment. For right now, all she wanted to do was lie there with him, feeling deliciously and thoroughly taken, and pretend for a few seconds that the rightness she was feeling could last forever.

GRIFFIN LAY AWAKE a long time after Sophie drifted off to sleep. He listened to the storm winds and the beat of his own heart, and waited for guilt to descend, along with its close cousins, regret and panic.

Except they didn't come.

The lessons hard learned in his past suggested that it would be a mistake for him to get involved with a woman, any woman, even one as genuine as Sophie. But at the same time, he couldn't ignore the inner resistance of her maidenhood, sure evidence that she'd come to him a virgin.

The responsibility of that, expressed or implied, should've had him up and out of the bed, and halfway down the mountain, blizzard or not. Instead, he stayed cuddled up against her, idly wondering which he should do first, scrounge for food or wake her up and see if he could ease her into round two.

As he did so, two words worked their way inside his skull, in a voice that sounded like his father's. *Vaughn virgin*. And again, something that probably should have freaked him out, failed to do so.

She was what he'd been looking for, he realized on a burst of wonder, along with something that might quickly become love. He'd wanted his match, his Vaughn virgin, and hadn't even known it.

Satisfaction expanded within him, stretching his chest and putting a wide smile on his face. Feeling primed and ready for more, yet conscious that she might not be, he eased away from her and crawled from the bed. He cleaned up and disposed of the condom, thinking with an inner smirk, *So much for those over-the-hill slogans*.

Pulling on his jeans and taking the candle for light, he headed to the kitchen and did what he could to assemble a snack from the canned provisions in Gemma's pantry. When he returned, Sophie stirred and woke, blinking in the candlelight.

He stopped in the doorway, feeling his heart give an uncharacteristic thump in his chest as he searched her face for evidence of regret. "Hey."

She smiled, her expression one of hesitant pride. "Hey, yourself."

And somehow, that was all that needed to be said. He crossed the room and set the snacks within reach, though he suspected it would be some time before they got around to eating. Then he slid back beneath the covers. And into her arms.

They ate eventually, slept little and talked even less. The entire night was given over to their bodies, and the pleasure they found together, which filled a hollow inside him that he hadn't even acknowledged before.

When dawn broke and still the storm raged on, he found a piece of himself wishing it would never end. But at the same time, he wanted to get back to civilization, and deal with the inevitable fallout from what had happened to him and Sophie at Lonesome Lake. They would need to do that before moving forward.

For a while the day before, he'd been thinking he would resell the estate, that he'd never want to return, and certainly not with Luke. Now, though, he was starting to reconsider. Something terrible had happened to him there, it was true. But something wonderful had happened, too.

Touching his lips to Sophie's temple, he eased from the warm bed into the chilly winter air of the apartment. *The fire must've died*, he thought. And no wonder, because he'd had things on his mind other than keeping the fireplace going.

Whistling softly so as not to wake Sophie, who was deeply asleep, he got dressed and tiptoed out to the main room to resuscitate the fire. As it slowly came back to life, he headed to the kitchen for his first cup of coffee, figuring he'd save Sophie from his early morning ogre routine, though he was feeling damned civilized, considering the lack of caffeine.

Maybe that was what love did to a guy, he thought.

Then he stopped dead, and waited again for the panic, and the knee-jerk "no way in hell, not me" reaction. Only it didn't come.

And okay, maybe two days stranded together in a blizzard, and one night spent together, was too short a time to fall in love, but what about the month prior to that, when they'd been circling around the attraction, and learning each other's rhythms and quirks? Maybe, for him and Sophie, at least, that had been a sort of courtship.

Trying on the idea of love and a future, and finding that it fit far better than he would've expected, he snagged her PDA off the counter and powered it up. He wanted to check in with Martinez and see how much longer they'd be stranded up at the estate, and whether the lawyers needed to be doing anything in the interim.

The coffeemaker started bubbling as the PDA came online, showing that there was no current phone or Internet signal, but there were two e-mails in Sophie's inbox.

Figuring they were from Ava Wright, confirming that the fingerprints Sophie had lifted from the crowbar came from Perry Long—or at least didn't match Vince Del Gardo—he clicked over to the e-mail and opened the first message.

He skimmed a few lines, and froze.

Dear Sophie, However did you manage to hook yourself up with Griffin Vaughn? Does he know what kind of a schemer you are, how you tried to black-mail your last boss and nearly got away with it? Does he know that you're maxed out on three different credit cards, in default on your student loans and looking for an easy way out? I suspect not. Quit now, leave town, and he'll never have to find out. If you stay, I'll make sure he knows everything. I won't let you do to him what you tried to do to me.

The message was unsigned, the address a generic jumble of initials and numbers, hosted by one of San Fran's major providers.

Griffin just stood there, stunned, coffee forgotten as the morning's foolish joy curdled to anger.

Sophie might've been a different sort of woman from the others, but she'd played the same game. And he'd damn well nearly fallen for it again.

SOPHIE AWOKE sore and satisfied, without a hint of regret or remorse. There were some nerves, though, mainly at the thought that she and Griffin could very well make it down off the mountain by nightfall, and she'd have to deal with what came next.

Though a foolish part of her wanted to believe that Griffin's tenderness the night before had been affection, that his whispered promises of a future had been real, she knew those wishes belonged locked up with her dreams of a law degree and a chance to fight for the rights she and her mother had been denied. Her wistful fantasies of a future with Griffin were just as lovely, and just as unlikely. She had to at least try to be realistic.

Still, she couldn't help feeling a bubble of optimism

as she raided Gemma's closet and dresser for another shirt and a clean pair of jeans. She felt different. Hell, she *was* different.

Granted, there was a darkness in her heart that came from having found Perry's body the day before. She was grateful that she and Griffin were safe, but wished that could've come at a price other than a man's life, even a man who had attacked them, and probably would have killed them if she hadn't pulled the trigger. Self-defense or not, she knew she would carry the weight of his death for a long time to come. But somehow that didn't over-shadow the specialness of what she and Griffin had found together. The two very different emotions existed side-by-side. Or maybe the joy she'd found in her own body was helping her deal with the guilt and sorrow. She didn't know.

What she did know, however, was that she was starv-ing. She could smell coffee, and even that was enough to get her stomach rumbling. Grinning at the thought of what she'd done to work up that appetite, she headed for the kitchen, trying not to feel strange about seeing Griffin in the light of day, after the things they had done to each other in the darkness.

The snappy greeting she worked up died the moment she stepped into the kitchen and got a look at his dark, brooding countenance.

She crossed the room, reaching for him, but some-thing in his eyes had her stopping a few feet away, her hands dropping to her sides as her stomach did barrel rolls and hunger turned to nerves. "What's wrong?"

He didn't answer right away, just sat there at the kitchen table, staring at her. Her PDA lay on the table beside his hand, next to an empty coffee cup. The presence of the handheld computer suggested that he'd gotten terrible news. But what was it? Possibilities cascaded through her mind, all having to do with the estate and the police, and the body that sat where it had fallen, out in the snow. Her heart shuddered in her chest. "Is Martinez going to press charges?"

The sheriff had to follow protocol, she supposed, and in a fair world she wouldn't have anything to worry about. Unfortunately, her own experiences had taught her that life was far from fair. Worse, a few minutes earlier, she would've said that Griffin would be on her side if it came to a court battle. But now, looking into his eyes and seeing nothing of the man who'd made love to her the night before, she wasn't so sure.

Her voice dropped to a whisper as she forced the words through a suddenly closed throat. "Griffin, say something. You're scaring me."

"When were you going to tell me about your debts?" His voice was flat and rough. Accusatory.

The question was so far from anything she might've expected him to say, that it took her brain a moment to catch up and process the words. And even then, all she could do was stare at him in shock. "Excuse me?"

He spun the PDA to face her. It was down to its last bar of battery power, but that wasn't what caught her attention. No, it was the e-mail address that had her heart clogging her throat and a kick of desperate tears filming her eyes.

The address belonged to Destiny Marlowe. Or rather, she supposed the name was Destiny Spellman now, because she and Tony had married recently, hadn't they?

It had been Destiny who'd tracked Sophie down based on an errant phone message, Destiny who'd revealed that Sophie and Tony's almost-affair had been nothing more than his pre-wedding jitters, a last fling that the powerful up-and-coming lawyer had turned into a game. It had been Destiny who hadn't been satisfied with Sophie breaking off the relationship, Destiny who had been determined to drive her out of San Francisco altogether, not understanding that it wasn't an option for Sophie to leave town, not with her mother finally installed in a state-subsidized longterm care facility.

Sophie had hoped Tony's vengeful bride would be satisfied at having used her high-placed family's considerable connections to have Sophie blackballed, not only at the employment office of the business school where she'd graduated at the top of her class, but also at just about every major company in the metro region except for VaughnTec.

And now she'd ruined even that. Sophie could see it in Griffin's eyes.

She scanned the message, though she could've guessed what it contained—the same blend of half-truths and evidence Destiny had used elsewhere. The words almost didn't matter. What mattered was that Griffin had undoubtedly checked and learned that yes, indeed, Sophie was way over her head in debt, with little hope of digging her way out on her present salary.

And because of what Monique and Cara had done to him before, and the way his mind worked, he'd convicted her without the benefit of a trial, or even an opportunity to speak on her own behalf.

Anger and disappointment rolled through her, along with the crushing weight of grief. "So this is how it's going to be?" she asked softly, hoping against hope that he'd soften, even slightly, and ask for her side of the story.

"No," he countered, "I'm about to tell you how it's going to be. When we get out of here, I'm terminating your employment at VaughnTec. My lawyers will help you deal with any fallout from Perry's death, because the fact remains that you saved our lives by shooting him. But that's where my responsibility ends, understand? I'm not paying you a damned dollar beyond your salary, and I had better not hear the first hint of any sort of sexual harassment talk. You try that garbage on me and you'll be seriously sorry."

Sophie wanted to crumble beneath his words as he piled rage atop anger atop accusations she could only defend if he chose to believe in her.

Tears filled her eyes and spilled over, tracking down her cheeks, born from both sorrow and anger. A few months earlier, in the aftermath of what had happened with Tony, she'd thought she'd hit the lowest point in her life. Clearly she'd been wrong, because the pain that echoed in her chest now was ten times worse than what she'd felt when Destiny had shown up at her workplace, told her about Tony's perfidy and gotten her fired, all within the space of twenty minutes.

The emotions she'd felt back then had been a mix of hurt and shame. The grief that slammed into her now, threatening to drive her to her knees, was made of both those things, along with a keening sense of loss and betrayal.

Struggling not to sag beneath that burden, she lifted her chin and used her sleeve to wipe the streaming tears away. "Please give me a chance to explain."

"Explain what? I checked the facts. Evidence doesn't lie."

She sniffed back a fresh bout of tears, seeing from the cold rage in his eyes and the uncompromising set to his jaw that there would be no use talking to him now. His mind was made up, not just by the anonymous e-mail he'd happened to stumble across—which must have recalled how he'd learned of Monique's planned abortion—but also because he'd confirmed the so-called evidence.

She could've told him that he was no CSI, that even hard evidence could be interpreted in different ways, but what would be the use? He'd gotten where he was in life by being stubborn and hard-nosed, and wasn't likely to change.

Bowing her head in a vain attempt to keep him from seeing how upset she was, she whispered, "Fine. No harassment charges." She never would've gone after him for harassment, especially given that she'd arguably been the aggressor the night before. Heck, she'd never seriously considered going after Tony for harassment. Not that Griffin would believe her if she told him that, though. He'd made up his mind.

Suddenly unable to stay in the apartment a moment longer, she spun and fled the kitchen. She didn't stop to think or plan; she just stuffed her feet in the boots she'd been using, and grabbed Gemma's parka off the rack.

She had her hand on the apartment door when Griffin said from behind her, "Where do you think you're going?"

"Out." She unlocked the deadbolt and yanked the door open.

"That might not be such a good idea."

"Oh?" She spun on him, letting loose some of the fury she was trying to keep inside, knowing that if she set the anger free, the rest of the emotions she was fighting so hard to keep in check would soon follow. Advancing on him, hands fisted at her sides, she grated, "And what would you prefer I do? Stay in here with you?" When she saw the answer in his eyes, she shook her head. "I didn't think so."

"Don't leave the mansion," he said. "I don't want you freezing to death on my watch."

With the implication that she was welcome to do exactly that once they were away from Lonesome Lake.

"I can take care of myself." God knew she'd been doing it since she was thirteen.

Knowing if she stayed a moment longer she would lose it completely, she turned her back on him and stepped out into the hallway. It was empty, of course, but it didn't feel lonely until she heard the apartment door close, and heard the deadbolt click into place.

For the first time since their arrival, she was alone outside the relative safety of the apartment perimeter.

But Perry was dead. And, as she'd said to Griffin, she could take care of herself. Realistically, all she had to do was find someplace to wait out the last bit of the storm. Once she'd picked a likely spot to hunker down, she'd return to the apartment for some supplies—food, some pillows, maybe a chair and one of Erik's books. A lantern. The basics.

Feeling a little more settled having a plan of sorts, she headed down the hallway and across the mansion, toward the far wing, where she remembered seeing some rooms with actual walls and flooring, and one even with sunny yellow paint on the walls.

She figured she could use a little sunshine right about then.

When she came to the door leading to the basement, she couldn't help looking at it, shuddering and hurrying past. She was halfway down the corridor leading to the yellow room when she heard a board creak behind her.

She spun with a gasp, but it was already too late.

Something slammed into the side of her head, and darkness rose up to claim her.

Chapter Nine

Griffin knew he'd done the right thing. He'd called to check out the e-mailer's story before confronting Sophie, hoping against hope that it'd turn out to be baloney, or something that could be easily explained, but had gotten blown out of proportion in the anonymous e-mailer's mind.

But he'd had no such luck. He'd burned through almost all of the PDA's remaining battery power making the calls, only to learn that Sophie owed nearly fifty thousand dollars split among three credit cards, on which she'd been paying no more than the minimum. She'd taken out student loans for her business courses— not just for tuition, but for living expenses, as well. Those loans were several months in arrears, and headed for collections.

Despite her apparent lack of financial smarts, however, she'd aced her classes, graduated and had taken a job at the prestigious law firm of Wade & Kane, where she must've met—and apparently come close to seducing—her boss. Not that Griffin had been able to get that information prior to business hours, but given that the other facts matched with the e-mail, he'd been forced to assume that one did, too.

Besides, she hadn't denied it.

"Goddamn it." Griffin scrubbed a hand across his chest, which hurt with a steady, insistent ache he wanted to say was a pulled muscle, but suspected was his heart.

He was on his third cup of coffee, but neither the anger nor the hurt had faded with the influx of caffeine. If anything, the ache had gotten worse.

Scowling, he punched in a familiar number, figuring he could bark at Kathleen's voice-mail, if nothing else.

To his surprise, she answered on the second ring. "Hello? Sophie?"

Something dark and nasty twisted in his gut. "It's Griffin."

There was dead silence, then a quiet, "Oh. Hell."

Since he didn't remember ever hearing his former assistant curse, that was another surprise, but the effect was lost to a roaring sense of betrayal. He'd thought Kathleen's lack of response to his occasional voice-mails meant she'd left her PDA behind as part of retiring, or maybe that she never checked her messages. Not that she'd been screening.

Of all the women in his life, she'd been the one he'd trusted. And even she, it seemed, had a hidden agenda. Anger spiking hot and ugly, he growled, "So you're taking her calls and not mine, is that it? Any particular reason for that?"

"Actually, Sophie's never called me, though I encouraged her to do so if she had any trouble with you," Kathleen said in the level, faintly chiding voice she'd perfected over her nearly six years of working for him. "So I figured if she was calling me now, it was important."

"And my calls weren't important?"

"You needed a clean break so you'd give her a chance." Kathleen paused. "Since you're calling from a work number that's popping up her name on the caller ID, can I assume that you at least haven't fired her yet?"

That hit close to home, roughening Griffin's voice when he said, "Please tell me you didn't know about what happened at her last job."

"Tony Spellman? I knew about him."

Disbelief heightened his outrage. "And her debts?"

"I figured between the blackballing and the money she owes, she'd be likely to stick with you long after most of my other choices would've quit. It's not like you're an easy guy to work for, you know."

She'd told him that time and again over the years, with varying degrees of amusement. But there was zero humor in it for him. Not now. "Why her, Kath? There had to be a dozen older, better qualified applicants for the position. I may be a pain in the ass, but I pay well."

There was such a long pause he thought she wasn't going to answer. Then she sighed and said, "There's something about her, isn't there, Griffin? She has this quality that makes you feel as though she's completely in the moment, experiencing life as though everything is fresh and new. I wanted that for you, Griffin. I wanted it for you and Luke."

Suddenly the storm wasn't raging outside anymore. It was inside him, tearing at his chest. "You were *matchmaking*?"

"Don't sound so horrified. It wasn't like you were going to meet the woman of your dreams at one of those chi-chi charity balls. You tried that. It didn't work. So I found you a good girl. If you didn't notice her, so be it." Her voice went sly. "I'm guessing you noticed her."

"Actually, my complete lack of response is over you calling her a 'good girl.' For crap's sake, she's up to her neck in debt, and she seduced her last boss!" Or had tried to, anyway. He knew firsthand that it hadn't gone all the way. Which was something he was trying very hard not to think about just then.

"The seduction was the other way around, despite rumors to the contrary," Kathleen corrected. "Which, by the way, were started by his ticked-off bride-to-be. As for the debts, the vast majority of them are from her mother's medical issues, which Sophie has been dealing with since she was thirteen." A pause. "Is it worth me pointing out that you should've asked her this yourself rather than calling me?"

"I—" Griffin began, and then broke off, partly because he had absolutely no defense, and partly because the PDA had started emitting the rhythmical beeping noise that indicated he had three minutes left on his battery. "Long story. Look, I'm losing my battery, and I have one more call to make."

He was about to hang up when Kathleen said, "Griffin, wait. I want you to do me a favor."

"What?"

"Give her a chance. Whatever is or isn't happening between you two, give it a chance, okay? That sweet boy of yours needs a woman's touch, and so do you."

He hung up without answering, because what could he say? He couldn't believe that Kathleen had picked Sophie, not as his executive assistant per se, but as someone he might fall for. And yeah, he'd noticed her, all right. He just wasn't sure yet whether that was a good or bad thing, because even though Kathleen seemed to think Sophie's debts and past behavior were no big deal, he was far from sure about that.

In his experience, women who needed funds—or, really, anyone who needed funds—looked to get them the easiest way possible. Which in this case meant through him.

The PDA beeped again, derailing his already chaotic thought process. He was down to two minutes.

Cursing, he dialed Martinez's number.

The sheriff picked up immediately. "Sophie?"

"No. It's Vaughn. I wanted—"

"What the hell took you so long to call?" the sheriff snapped, interrupting. "Where's Sophie? Is she okay?"

A massive chill crawled down Griffin's spine. "Why? What happened?"

"Didn't you get Ava's e-mail?"

Griffin cursed under his breath, remembering that the nasty-gram about Sophie's past had been the first of two in her inbox. "No. What have you got?"

"The prints weren't Perry's and they weren't Vince Del Gardo's. But they were in the system."

Griffin's gut tightened. "One of the construction crew?"

"No. A professional killer by the name of Boyd Perkins."

"A hitman?" Griffin snapped, disbelief racheting his volume up. "What the hell does a hitman have against me?"

"Not you. Del Gardo. Boyd Perkins often works for Nicky Wayne, head of the Wayne crime family in Las Vegas. They're the Del Gardo family's biggest competitors, and Nicky Wayne has hated Vince Del Gardo's guts ever since the botched contract kill that got Del Gardo convicted—Wayne was the target. If Perkins is up there, he's gunning after Del Gardo on behalf of Nicky Wayne."

"But why here?" Griffin demanded. But then, realizing that "why" wasn't the most important question, he said, "Never mind. Do you think Perry Long was working for this hitman?"

"Maybe. Or maybe he just got in the way and made a convenient body."

Griffin understood exactly where the sheriff was going with that, and his blood iced in his veins. They'd been fooled by a damned decoy, and Sophie was somewhere out in the mansion. Alone. Unprotected. He shot to his feet and hurried across the apartment. As he yanked on his borrowed boots, he snapped into the phone, "How long before you can get people up here?"

"It'll be at least three more hours before the skies clear."

Griffin cursed. "Get here as fast as you can. And bring dogs if you've got them. I think there are secret passages or something in this house, maybe in the mountain itself. If Del Gardo and Perkins are up here, playing cat-and-mouse, that's where they're hiding."

"Where's Sophie?"

The call was cut off before Griffin could respond to the sheriff's question, but he answered anyway, growling the words into the empty apartment. "I don't know, damn it. But I'm going to find her."

BOYD DUMPED the unconscious woman in the unfinished tunnel he'd chosen to serve as her and Vaughn's grave, then bent over her motionless form, cursing and pressing a hand to the wound in his side as he breathed through the pain.

He was a mess. His face hurt from the bruises Vaughn had pummeled into him the day before, and damned if he wasn't bleeding again. But at least his plan was working. It had needed a few necessary adjustments, granted, but it was working.

He'd arrived a week ago, and had arranged to bump into Perry Long at a bar down in Kenner City. A few beers and some negotiations, and Boyd had secured an invite up to Lonesome Lake, ostensibly as a newly hired worker, though Long believed he was a journalist trying to dig up dirt on the estate's prior owner, Vince Del Gardo.

Boyd had paid the contractor well for information about the estate, and had smirked when Perry had complained about the rash of accidents and setbacks the project had endured. That sort of thing was trademark Vince Del Gardo, and had only served to reinforce Boyd's conviction that his mark was hiding somewhere on the estate. The question was, where?

It hadn't been until just the day before the storm that the contractor had said something about the rumors that the estate was haunted. The workers had been going on about footsteps and missing tools and lunches, he'd said, inviting Boyd to laugh along with the joke. Only Boyd hadn't been laughing at all, because it made perfect sense. Del Gardo was a gutless rat. It figured he'd be hiding in the walls like a rodent. Once he knew what he was looking for, it hadn't taken much for him to find a way into one of the hidden passageways. After that, he'd just needed some uninterrupted time for searching. The blizzard had been convenient, offering him a few days when there would be no workers around, giving him ample opportunity to get in there, find Del Gardo, force him to divulge where he'd stashed the fifty million dollars he'd hidden from the government, and then kill him.

When the crew had cleared out of the mansion, Boyd had doubled back with his gear. He'd set up his camp in a high, shadowed nook of the barn and had been headed into the mansion for a first look-see when Perry's car had come screaming back up the driveway. Perry had been surprised to see him, but Boyd had made up some excuse about forgetting his notebook and Perry had been too preoccupied to care. He'd been in a dither because Griffin Vaughn, the rich-boy homeowner, was on his way up to see the project, and it was a mess.

Once Boyd had ascertained that there was no way Perry could talk Griffin Vaughn out of the visit, he'd walked him around the side of the building and tried to convince him to return to wait out the storm. Which would've worked fine, except that Del Gardo, apparently thinking the place would be deserted for the duration of the blizzard, had chosen that moment to walk by an upstairs window.

Perry had freaked, thinking the ghost was for real. Boyd had pulled his piece and shot out the window, aiming to wound so he could question Del Gardo about the missing fifty mil. He'd missed the bastard, cursed, and grabbed Perry before he could flee. Knowing he couldn't trust the contractor to keep his mouth shut, Boyd had broken Perry's neck and stashed him just inside the tunnel entrance he'd found in an outbuilding behind the main house. At the time he hadn't realized the body would prove useful; he'd just been looking for someplace inconspicuous to hide the corpse while he wired the bridge, figuring he could take out the richy-rich homeowner and Del Gardo's main escape route simultaneously.

But even the slickest plans sometimes had their kinks. Boyd hadn't realized until too late that Vaughn and his secretary had survived the explosion, and by the time he'd figured that out, the two had been firmly entrenched in the housekeepers' apartment. Since Boyd hadn't planned on tunnels or rock work, he'd only brought a limited amount of C4, which meant he couldn't simply blow the apartment. And once the blizzard hit, it had put a serious damper on any hope of sniping them through the windows. Besides, the guy, Vaughn, had skills. He'd covered the windows and set a perimeter, which had meant Boyd couldn't get to them easily. He'd had to wait for them to come to him.

Unfortunately, he hadn't expected to surprise them in the basement. It had been a miscalculation on his part to attack with nothing but a crowbar, but he hadn't realized the woman was armed. Worse, his 9 mm had jammed when he'd tried to fire, which meant his best recourse had been retreat.

The bitch had shot him in the back.

Scowling now, he nudged her motionless form with his toe. Not that he could blame her for the shot—he'd have done the same. And really, whichever way he looked at it, it was all business. It was his business to kill them, find Del Gardo and make his retrieval and his hit. And it was her business to try to stay alive, even if that meant shooting a man in the back.

Not that she knew she'd shot him. She thought she'd shot Perry, thanks to a little scene-setting and the extra bullet hole Boyd had put in the corpse and painted with his own blood. He'd thought it rather clever. And sure enough, Vaughn had dropped his guard, and he and the woman had split up. It would've been easier if Boyd could've captured Vaughn first and then gone after the secretary at his leisure, but things hadn't worked out that way, so he'd just have to improvise.

Humming softly, Boyd turned away from the woman and headed back for the surface. He had some more scene-setting to do.

SOPHIE WOKE SLOWLY, and for a long moment had no idea where she was or what had happened. All she knew was that it was very dark, she was very cold and she was lying on something hard, with her arms and legs twisted awkwardly behind her. She rolled and stretched, trying to work out the kinks, but her limbs didn't unkink. They were bound behind her.

Memory returned on a flash of pain and a scream that she choked off at the back of her throat. She remembered fighting with Griffin, and the memory brought a fresh wash of tears and pain. Worse, though, was the realization that she was in the exact situation they had tried so hard to avoid: in the power of the man who'd tried to kill them. But who could that be? Perry was dead. Maybe he hadn't been working alone; maybe the contractor had been nothing more than a decoy, she didn't know.

All she knew was that she was scared and alone, and she wanted Griffin. She didn't care if she got the soldier who'd protected her, the man who had loved her through the night, or the cynical businessman who had hurt her so deeply by not giving her a chance to defend herself against his accusations. He was a piece of all of those men—or more accurately, they were each a facet of his personality, all summing to the man who she trusted to get her out of danger, though she'd learned the hard way that she couldn't trust him with her heart.

"Damn it, Griffin," she muttered. "Where are you?" Surely he'd noticed by now that she wasn't in the mansion?

Not necessarily, a sly, hurtful voice whispered from

within her. And it was right, she realized. He'd been so furious with what he'd seen as her betrayal, that it was quite possible he wouldn't go after her until it was time to leave.

The thought that he might not even be looking for her was almost more than she could bear. Ever since they'd arrived at Lonesome Lake they'd been a team, coordinating their efforts and working together as best they could, despite—or maybe because of—the circumstances. And now all that was gone, taken from her by a nasty, rich woman who wanted to punish her for Tony's lies, and by the fact that Griffin couldn't find it in himself to trust her, or even listen to her side of the story.

Tears welled up and spilled over, tracking down Sophie's cheeks and cooling rapidly in the chill air. She couldn't see anything in the darkness, couldn't move, couldn't do anything, really.

Or could she? Her attacker hadn't gagged her, which suggested that he didn't think there was much of a chance that anyone would hear her if she screamed. But what if he was wrong?

Refusing to give up without a fight, she filled her lungs and cried out. She'd intended it to be a long, drawn-out scream, but what emerged instead was a single word. A name. "*Griffin!*"

CURSING STEADILY, fighting to keep from attacking the wall with his bare hands because he knew that wouldn't do a damn bit of good, Griffin worked his way around the basement, scanning each section of cement for evidence of a hidden doorway. He didn't see a damn thing, but there had to be a door, didn't there? Perkins had been in the basement one moment, gone then next. He'd vanished into thin air. But how the hell had he managed it?

Griffin pointed his flashlight down at the floor, looking for a trapdoor, a set of footprints—something, anything that would give him a clue. But the floor appeared to have been swept recently. That made sense if Perkins—or Del Gardo, for that matter—had been trying to hide evidence of foot traffic.

Which left Griffin exactly nowhere. It was nearly 1:00 p.m. and he hadn't seen Sophie since ten that morning. He knew where she'd been; he'd found scuff marks on the plywood subflooring, suggesting that there had been a struggle. The sight had hurt, deep inside him. The marks had been in the hallway just past the basement door, which had been unlocked when he was sure he'd locked it the day before. Which meant—

"Wait a minute." Griffin stopped dead as the pieces failed to line up. He knew he had secured the basement door, which only locked from the hallway side, not the side facing the stairs leading down. Which meant it'd been unlocked from inside the mansion. And that meant Perkins was using more than just the hidden entrance in the basement. He had to have some other way of getting into the mansion, at least one other access point. But where else had they seen evidence that they weren't alone?

Griffin racked his brain, thinking it through first as a

soldier, looking at it strategically. When that didn't get him anywhere, he tried to think it through analytically, as though it was a business deal. But that didn't work either.

"Damn it." He sank to his knees, kneeling on the cold, hard cement flooring of a basement that refused to give up its secrets. "Please. Where is she?" He didn't know who he was talking to, whether he was invoking some nebulous higher power, or trying to wrestle the information out of his own subconscious. "Where is Sophie?"

He thought of her as she'd been that morning, sleeping deeply amidst the rumpled covers. Her lips had been swollen from his kisses, her eyelids shadowed a delicate purple from lack of sleep, though she'd slept deeply once they'd finished with each other, replete and exhausted.

He'd wanted to go to her then; he'd wanted to touch her, to wake her, and tell her about his parents and the legend of the Vaughn virgin. He'd wanted to tell her all about Luke, about how he loved Spider-Man and video games, and called nearly every woman he met mama because he so wanted one of his own.

Instead, he'd decided to let her sleep. He'd gone into the kitchen and powered up the damn PDA, and everything had gone to hell. He still didn't know what to think about Sophie's debt or what had happened in her last job. But it didn't seem nearly so cut-and-dried as it had earlier that morning, when he'd decided to cut his losses, defend her against whatever came of Perry's death, and—

And that was it, he realized. Not Perry's death, but Perry himself. That was what his subconscious had been trying to tell him. His gut told him that Perkins had probably been the one to kill the contractor, and he'd set him near the woodshed as a decoy. Which meant Perkins himself had been somewhere near the woodshed.

Maybe even *in* the woodshed.

It was thin, Griffin knew, but he'd searched the basement thoroughly, to no avail. Rising to his feet, he sent a quick plea skyward, this time unashamedly aimed at the higher power he'd spent very little of his lifetime considering. "Please let her be okay. Please don't let me be too late."

With that, he took off for the woodshed at a dead run, charging up the basement stairs two at a time, and bursting out into the hallway. He slammed through the exterior door, and was instantly driven back against the wall of the mansion, lashed by storm winds that seemed, if anything, to have gotten worse than they'd been before.

Hoping to hell this was the blizzard's last dying gasp, Griffin fought the force of the driving snow, slogging one step at a time along the faint depression that showed where he and Sophie had walked the day before. Or maybe the track had been beaten down more recently— he couldn't tell. The windblown snow erased the evidence immediately, even wiping out his footprints almost as soon as he made them. He couldn't see Perry's body anymore; it had become the base for an enormous snow drift that covered almost one whole side of the shed.

When he reached the door leading to the shed, he thought a single word. *Please.* That was all. Just "please." Holding that prayer in his heart, he opened the woodshed door, braced for an attack and hoping he wouldn't see something far worse, like Sophie leaned up against the wall, frozen and still.

He got neither. The woodshed was just a woodshed— a ten-by-ten expanse with huge piles of split wood stacked in precise rows, with no deviation in the pattern. Except one.

Griffin's eyes were immediately drawn to a section in the corner, where the stacking seemed more hapha- zard than elsewhere, as though it'd been restacked far less precisely than elsewhere. Barely daring to hope, or to breathe, Griffin approached the section and shined his light all around the area.

The thin flashlight beam picked out a seam in the floor, a spot where the boards joined just slightly askew, forming a rectangular shape on the floor. A trapdoor.

Griffin's heart pounded in his chest, sending adrena- line through his system. He felt like the soldier now, and the man. He wanted to find Sophie, unharmed and alive. And he wanted to kill Perkins for daring to touch her.

Pulling the .45, which he'd tucked at the small of his back, he slipped the safety. Then, following a set of scuff marks in the sawdust, he pressed on a small, ir- regular section of flooring off to one side of the trapdoor.

The panel popped up soundlessly, working on a well- oiled mechanism.

Moving as quietly as he knew how, Griffin eased up the trapdoor. He shielded the light at first, listening intently in case Perkins was waiting for him down below. At first he heard nothing.

Then he heard a single word. His name, called softly in Sophie's voice.

He practically lunged through the trapdoor, but held himself in check and went step by step, testing the short ladder and the narrow passageway below, alert for traps. But all he found was a tunnel cut into the side of the mountain itself, running maybe fifty feet underground from the shed before it hit a T-intersection. One side dead-ended almost immediately. The other continued on beyond the reach of his flashlight beam, but he thought he saw movement just at the edge of the darkness.

Risking it because he couldn't stand it any longer, he whispered, "Sophie?"

"Griffin!"

He lunged toward her, weapon at the ready, but there was nobody to fight. She lay on the ground with her hands and feet bound behind her. Her face was pale, her lips bordering on blue. But her eyes were alight and alive, and filled with joy at the sight of him.

Relief hammered through him. What had happened between them earlier didn't matter right now. All that mattered was that she was okay, that he'd found her. They'd deal with the rest of it later.

"Sophie." He dropped to his knees beside her and yanked at the ropes, unknotting them quickly and freeing her. Then he dragged her up and into his arms, and hung on tightly as she sagged against him. "I was afraid I wouldn't get to you in time."

"So was I." Her voice trembled; her whole body trembled. "I wanted to have a chance to explain—"

"Me, too," he said, cutting her off. "Later, though. Let's get the hell out of here. The storm's almost over. The chopper should be cleared for takeoff in another hour or so."

She nodded against his throat. Keeping hold of her, he climbed to his feet and helped her up, and together they stagger-stepped along the tunnel toward the glow up ahead, where light filtered down through the opening.

They were maybe ten feet away when the trapdoor slammed shut.

"No!" Griffin shouted. He shoved the flashlight and .45 at Sophie, raced up the short ladder and slammed his shoulder into the panel, but to no avail. "Let us out!"

"Sorry, Vaughn," a man's voice said from up above. "I'd intended to finish you two off nice and neat right now, but I've just seen a rat pop his head out of a hidey hole. He's priority numero uno, so you'll have to wait."

There was a clattering roar as the hitman toppled one of the stacks of wood onto the trapdoor, weighing it down. Griffin roared a curse and shoved at the hatch, but it didn't budge upwards. If anything, it sagged down, bowing as the weight of the wood stressed the hinges and latch. There was no way Griffin could lift it from below.

Which meant they were caught in the tunnel, with no way out. Stuck there, waiting for the killer to return.

Chapter Ten

Sophie watched numbly as Griffin slammed his body up into the trapdoor twice more, following his progress by the thin flashlight beam.

She'd slipped the safety on the .45 and stuck the gun in her pocket, and held the light in both hands, clutching at the source of illumination. Even as dull shock reverberated through her at the realization that rescue had so quickly turned to renewed danger, she was pitifully grateful for light. She'd never thought of herself as afraid of the dark before, but she'd also never been tied up in a narrow dirt-and-stone tunnel before, either, left alone in the pitch darkness for hours in the freezing cold.

When Griffin sagged away from the trapdoor, breathing hard, she said softly, "You came looking for me. I wasn't sure you would."

"I don't blame you for wondering." He lifted his eyes to hers, and in the wan yellow light, she saw rage and regret, and a complicated mix of emotions she couldn't begin to identify. His jaw was darkly stubbled with the beginnings of a beard, and the tension coming off him in waves belonged entirely to the soldier. Yet there was an unusual gentleness about him as well, and she got the sense that although he was furious that he'd let their enemy get the drop on him, he was also aware of her, and worried for her. Worried about her.

In that moment he was both the soldier and the man who'd made love to her, and maybe even a little bit of the businessman who had judged her and found her lacking. He was all those things and more, the sum of the pieces becoming a larger whole.

She was unable to look away from his eyes, from the intensity of them and his searching gaze, which seemed to be simultaneously asking and telling her something, though she wasn't sure of either the question or information. She wanted to believe he'd come for her because he'd been worried, not because he'd felt it was his responsibility. But in the end, did it really matter? He'd come for her. That was the most important thing.

"Do you think there's another way out?" she asked softly.

"Perkins doesn't seem to think so."

"Who is Perkins?"

A humorless smile touched the corners of Griffin's mouth. "A hitman most likely on the trail of Vince Del Gardo, who, it appears, is still in the neighborhood after all. Perkins left the fingerprints you lifted off the crowbar. Which I would've known if I'd read both of the e-mails in your inbox, because Ava sent the info last night." He paused. "For what it's worth, I'm sorry."

For which part? she wanted to say, but couldn't

because there was too much information coming at her too quickly, and she didn't know what to focus on first.

Wobbling on legs made unsteady by the cold and lack of blood flow, along with shock, she let herself sag down to the tunnel floor, so she was leaning back against the rough rock surface of the tunnel wall. Griffin followed her down and sat cross-legged opposite her, facing her full-on. That was good because she could see his expression, but also bad, because she found she couldn't look away when he leaned in and touched a finger beneath her chin, tipping her eyes up to his.

"I'm sorry for missing the e-mail from Ava. If I'd gotten it, we would've known it wasn't safe for us to split up yet."

"But if Perkins left the fingerprints," she said, trying to work it through, "that means he was the man in the basement, right?"

"Right. The relative lack of blood on Perry's body bothered me at the time, but I didn't know enough to say for sure. With this added evidence, I think it's reasonable to figure that Perry was already dead, and Perkins shot him to mimic his own wound and get us to let our guard down."

If yesterday she'd had an inkling that she might be exonerated so thoroughly for Perry's death, she would've been relieved to the point of tears. Now, though, she felt only numbness. "And that was Perkins up there?"

Griffin nodded. "He mentioned a rat popping its head out. I'm guessing he saw Del Gardo and decided to go after him rather than finishing us off."

Sophie shivered at the thought. "So what do we do

now?" She pulled out the .45 and looked at it. "Wait until he comes back for us and try to kill him before he kills us?"

Three days earlier, it would've been unbelievable to think that she could say such a thing and mean it. But over the course of those three days, many things had changed.

"If necessary. I'd prefer to look for another way out, first. It doesn't make much sense to have a tunnel that doesn't lead anywhere."

"Unless it's more of a storage spot than a passageway," she pointed out.

"Let's take a look and see."

Relieved to have even that small of a plan, Sophie stood when he did, handed over the .45, and moved to join him as he started testing the walls of the tunnel, sweeping his hands over the rough rock surface and pressing on any likely-looking bulges. She took the other side of the tunnel, and they worked their way from the ladder to where the tunnel branched to the left and right, but came up empty.

Griffin cursed and banged on the wall. "I bet this was supposed to go to the basement and join up with another hidden door."

"Another? You found the one he used the other day?"

"No, but I know it's there. I'm betting Del Gardo had them built. They could be anywhere, lead anywhere. Except for this one, which doesn't lead to a damn thing." His expression was hollow. Haunted.

Sophie wanted to touch him, to fold herself into his arms, but didn't know if she dared. Too much had been said between them, and even more had been left yet unsaid.

So instead of being weak when she so badly wanted

to be, she forced herself to think. The tunnel walls and ceiling were made of a mix of rock and soil. She asked, "Do you think we could dig our way out?"

Griffin thought about it for a long moment before shaking his head. "I don't think we dare. Even if we managed to punch through the permafrost—and that's a huge 'if'—we have no way of ensuring that we come out underneath a spot where the snow has blown thin. The last thing we need is for six feet of the stuff to come down on top of us and smother us to death. I'd rather take my chances fighting Perkins when he comes back, thank you."

"If he shot Perry to fake the wound, that means he's got a gun," she pointed out.

"So do I." But they both knew Perkins had the advantage. He could open up the trapdoor and fire down on them from above.

"Well, that's something, anyway." Sophie paused, taking stock and getting a glimmer of an idea. "So…you're the gadget guy, right? What do you think you could make out of the ropes I was tied with, plus the stuff we're wearing?" She was thinking along the lines of a pulley system or something, though wasn't clear on how that would help when what they really needed to do was push up on the trapdoor hard enough to break the door latch and shift the woodpile.

But a gleam kindled in Griffin's eyes. "I don't think I can do anything with the ropes or our clothes. The gun might be another story, though. The weight of the logs has already stressed the door…" He led the way back to the trapdoor, which had clearly buckled beneath the force pressing down on it from above. "If we can weaken the hinges or the latch enough, the wood might punch right through."

The awful pressure on Sophie's chest lightened a little. "You're going to shoot the door?"

He shook his head. "My aim would have to be dead-on, and the shot might still ricochet. I think it's too risky to use up the bullets that way."

"Then what?"

He pulled the .45, flipped open the cartridge and dumped the bullets into his palm. "Erik is a real do-it-yourselfer. He packs his own bullets, which probably means he adds a few extra grains of powder for more kick. It's what guys do. If I pull the grains out of the bullets, use the hammer and the caps to rig a detonator, I might be able to make some noise."

"You want to use the gun to build a mini-bomb and blow the trapdoor hinges?" Sophie asked, incredulous because it actually made sense. She stared at the metal cylinders resting in his palm. "Will six bullets be enough?"

"I've got another six in my pocket." Which wasn't really an answer.

"Can you hold a couple aside in case it doesn't work, and we need the gun for when Perkins comes back?"

"We could, but I'll need to disassemble the firing mechanism, too." His eyes were steady on hers. Soldier's eyes. "What do you think?"

He wouldn't do it if she objected, she knew. Fairness dictated that they both agree to effectively sabotaging their one means of defense, in the hopes of getting the heck out of there. So it was up to her.

She nodded slowly. "Let's do it."

He held her eyes for a long moment, as if assessing whether she really understood what she was agreeing to, and then tipped his head in acknowledgement. "I'll need you to hold the flashlight."

He dropped to sit cross-legged, pulled off his belt,and started using the tongue as a makeshift screwdriver to disassemble the .45. Sophie sat opposite him. She tried to follow his actions with the light, but found it difficult to minimize the shadows.

Worse, she had a feeling the batteries were on their way out. The cone of light, which had been yellow-white the day before, was headed more toward amber now. She could only hope they'd have enough light for Griffin to complete his work and get them out of there. God willing.

"Talk to me," he said absently. "Tell me a story."

"Any sort of story in particular?"

"How about the story of why you're nearly a hundred thou in debt and made yourself a powerful enemy."

She tensed. "Why now?"

"Kathleen. She told me that I should give you a chance to explain." He paused. "I was headed in that direction even before I talked to her, though. Things happened between us so quickly last night, and the situation in general has been so out of the norm, that there wasn't really time for you to tell me about it, was there?"

"It wasn't the first thing on my mind under the circumstances," she agreed, but something inside her was saying, *I wouldn't have told you regardless. It's my business, and I only asked you for one night.* Still, he was offering her an opportunity to explain Destiny's e-mail. It was what she'd wanted, what she'd begged him for earlier. And it was clear that he'd been hurt by finding out the way he had. He had lashed out, but there had been pain beneath the anger.

Deciding she owed it to herself, at least, to give him her side, she said, "My father died when I was very young, a month before he and my mother were supposed to get married. He'd been in the army, and died during a training exercise, but since they weren't married…" She lifted a shoulder. "No widows' benefits, no medical coverage."

Griffin frowned and glanced at her. "There are mechanisms in place to cover situations like that."

"Technically, yes. In reality, the people my mother contacted were very discouraging, telling her all the things she couldn't do rather than what she could. And her health was shaky even back then. The doctors gave it all sorts of names over the years, but none of them really stuck, and none of the treatments they tried worked for very long. She'd lost touch with her family—their fault, hers, I've never been sure, haven't been able to find them with the limited resources I've had access to." She lifted a shoulder. "When I was thirteen, it got to the point where she couldn't even get out of bed. Practically overnight, I went from being a normal kid to being a nurse."

"You could've gotten help," Griffin said bluntly. "You should've talked to a teacher, called DSS, something."

"I wasn't dropping the dime on my own mother. There were foster families in the apartments on either side of ours. Trust me, I was better off where I was." In the wan yellow light, she saw the dull horror on his face, and found herself resenting it. "Not such a pretty story, is it? So forgive me if I don't go around telling it to everyone I meet." She caught herself before she let rip with the deep resentment she carried toward people who worked within the system rather than trying to fix it. "Anyway, I learned the system as best I could, got her to as many doctors as I could, but none of it helped. My grades dropped, I missed lots of classes and eventually dropped out." Those years existed largely as a blur of days, chores, and crushing emotions. "I split my time between working crappy jobs that didn't cover all our expenses, keeping Mom comfortable, and going to the library, where I studied up on how to get the system to sit up and listen to me. Fast forward to eighteen months ago, when I finally, *finally* got her into a state-supplemented long-term care facility."

"Good for you." Griffin nodded that he understood, but how could he? He'd lost his parents, yes, but he'd had a long, happy childhood, and an uncle to lean on. She'd been completely on her own.

"Once she was being taken care of, I knew I had to find a job that would pay off our debts and cover my part of her care. But I'd been working mostly minimum-wage jobs, and never lasted more than a few months because I missed days dealing with her issues. How was I supposed to make headway on that sort of salary?

So I took a chance, took out some loans, and did a nine-month certificate in executive support."

"And went to work for Wade and Kane," Griffin said neutrally.

"That's not what you want to know about, though is it? You want to know about Tony. Fine. I worked with him, dated him, and would've slept with him first instead of you, if his fiancée hadn't shown up at the office, screaming bloody murder about the wedding and her daddy's money. It didn't matter to Destiny that I didn't know he was engaged, didn't matter that Tony had played her as much as he'd played me. She wanted me out of town before the wedding. Failing that, she wants me gone before the next election, when good old Tony plans to start his political career. I think Destiny lives in fear that one or more of his indiscretions is going to show up at an inconvenient time."

"With good reason, apparently." Griffin's tone and expression were unreadable. "She wrote the e-mail?"

"Yep. And leaned on her father's contacts to black-ball me pretty much citywide."

"Sounds like a charmer."

Sophie allowed herself a small smile. "Let's just say she and Tony deserve each other. And no, I won't be voting for him." It did feel a little better to have told Griffin the bare bones of the situation, she realized. And in telling it, she'd been reminded of the wide gap that existed between her and Griffin, not just in age and experience, but in their priorities. He'd done his service to his country. She was just gearing up to start. "And that, dear boss, is the long and short of it. I've got debts, yes, but they're my debts, and I'm not looking for someone to pay them off for me. Though I wouldn't say no to winning the lottery. And Tony…well, he was a mistake."

"Are we?" Griffin asked, focusing intently on the pile of parts he'd created from the disassembled .45.

"Are we what, a mistake?" She pinched the bridge of her nose, where a heck of a headache was forming. "Does it matter? It was just one night. Once we're out of here, it'll go back to business as usual. And if we don't make it out…well, it was just one night either way."

"What if I want it to be more?"

Something kicked in the region of her heart. "You swore off relationships, remember?"

"I've been reconsidering." His attention stayed on the creation that was taking shape beneath his quick, clever fingers, but she suspected his focus was as much an evasion as necessity. He continued, "There's a legend in my family. A correlation. Whatever you want to call it. Anyway, down through the generations, Vaughn men have had two types of marriages—absolute bliss or total disaster. The happy marriages, like my parents' and the one my Uncle Will is in now, have always involved a certain gap in age and experience, and have fallen along very traditional lines." He lifted one shoulder in a half shrug. "So I'll have to admit that the more we got to know each other over the past few days, the more I started to wonder if I'd been dating the wrong kind of woman. Or rather, if I'd been killing time, waiting for someone like you."

She stared at him, dumbfounded. "Is it my imagination, or did we just go from talking about a one-night stand to talking about marriage?"

"Obviously we'd have to spend more time together once we're out of here," he said, making it sound like a foregone conclusion, which she appreciated, even if the topic of conversation was making her twitchy and upset. "But yeah, I am. Which was one of the reasons I overreacted when I found out about your debt load and prior relationship. Except that wasn't fair, because I hadn't clued you into what I was thinking. I just figured, given the chemistry and the way we've been getting along, that you'd be interested in something longer term."

And she would've been, except that she wasn't entirely sure he wanted her. It seemed like he wanted an ideal, someone with her relative lack of experience in the bedroom, but with a similar lack of experience in other facets of life. Not to mention what he'd told her about his first marriage, and how he'd been looking for someone to keep his home and raise his son. Which wasn't wrong, necessarily. But she wasn't sure it was her.

He glanced over at her, expression wary. "Nothing to say?"

"I think…" She trailed off, trying to line it up in her head, struggling to figure out where the boundary between dreams and reality fell. "I think that if I believed you wanted a true partner, I'd be interested. But you said it yourself—you want a wife who will make you a home and help you raise Luke."

His hands stilled in the process of reassembling the

gun parts into something else entirely. He looked at her, eyes hooded. "What's wrong with that?"

"I have goals of my own, Griffin. Once I've paid off my debts and gotten ahead some, I'm serious about going to college, and from there to law school. I want to help people like my mother and me get the help they need."

He scowled and returned his attention to his project. "You don't need a law degree to advocate. Not if you've got VaughnTec money behind you."

Now it was her turn to go very, very still. After a moment, she said softly, "Yet you blame the other women for only wanting your money."

"Monique sold me her son," he bit off.

"But what about the others, Cara and the ones you've dated since? Did you ever stop to think that it wasn't so much them wanting the money, as much as it was the one thing you thought you could offer?"

It started coming clearer to her now. Clear and very sad. So much for her occasional thoughts that money could solve everything. Apparently, it just created a different set of problems.

"You made the company a success," she said softly, "but it didn't bring your parents back or save your marriage. You've bought this place, but it won't change the fact that Luke is growing up without a mother." She paused, aware that she'd not just stepped over the line, she'd shot and buried it. Since it was too late to retreat, and because she thought it needed to be said, she continued, "You don't want me, Griffin. You want some idealized version of what your parents had. I don't want that, not at this point in my life. I'm sorry."

Though she knew she was being as honest as she could, something tore in her chest at the words. She'd never known security, and had only really had a skewed version of love. Though Griffin hadn't said the word, she knew he'd primed himself for the emotion by slotting her into the family pattern. Would it really be so bad to live the life he could offer, and be loved by a man like him?

She didn't have an easy answer for that. All she knew was that she hadn't yet had a chance to live. Griffin was looking to make his world smaller at a time when hers had just begun to open up. One of these days she was going to get those debts paid off, and then, look out, world! She had a mark to make.

It was odd to realize that exhilaration could exist alongside heartache, but apparently it could. "I'm sorry," she whispered again, hating the pain she could see beneath his stern facade.

"Well. I guess that clears up a few things, doesn't it? My mistake."

"No," she said quickly. "No. It was…" But then she trailed off, because really, what could she say?

"It's okay. Really." He looked at her, and she saw from his eyes that he was trying to make it be okay. "I know I should be saying that I'd support whatever you want to do, that we can make it work. But I'm not sure that's in me. I want the Vaughn dream, Sophie. I want the wife and kids, the home cooking and the flowers on the table when I get home. And yeah, I know I can hire someone for most of that, but I don't want to. I want a woman who loves me so much that she just does stuff like that because she knows it'll make me happy, just like I'd do anything in my power to make her happy."

Except accepting that she wants to have a life of her own, Sophie thought. She didn't say it, though, because what would be the point? Instead, she said, "How's that contraption coming? We should probably get out of here."

He sent her a long look through shuttered eyes, then nodded. "Yeah," he said softly. "We probably should."

He stood, taking his makeshift mini-bomb with him, saying over his shoulder, "Come on. I'll need the light for this."

Trying to think of nothing but their escape plan, nothing but the moment at hand, Sophie held the dimming flashlight at a helpful angle as he affixed his device to the trapdoor. She didn't know what he'd done or how the thing was meant to work, but she didn't figure she needed to. What mattered was that he thought it was worth a shot.

She might not trust him to let her live her life, but she trusted him to save it, or die trying.

When he was done, he took her arm and urged her away. "We'd better get in the cross tunnel. I don't think the blast will reach that far, but better safe than sorry."

As they retreated from the immediate area of the trapdoor, he played out the rope she'd been bound with. One end of it was connected to the device, the other was looped around his wrist.

When they reached the T-intersection, he pushed her behind him and backed in, so she was shielded behind his big body.

Heart clutching a little at that quiet protection, she touched his arm and said softly, "I'm sorry. I wish things were different."

He held himself still for a long moment, before he exhaled a long breath and turned to face her. "Yeah. Me, too." He leaned down and touched his lips to hers in the briefest hint of a kiss. When he straightened away, he had a sad smile on his face. "For luck."

"For luck," she repeated, knowing that one way or the other, it would be their last kiss.

"Plug your ears," he said in warning. Moments later, he jerked on the rope.

There was a split-second pause, just long enough for her to fear that his device had failed. Then there was a sharp bang of detonation, followed by a huge crash.

"I think it worked!" He grabbed her and they hurried to the other end of the tunnel.

The air was thick with dust and a sharp, burning smell, but even as far back as the corner, they could see daylight up ahead. His plan had worked exactly as they had hoped; the trapdoor had given way and the logs had fallen through. He shoved the piled timber out of the way, then grabbed one stick and held it as a makeshift club as he scrambled partway up, stuck his head through the opening, and took a cautious look around. Moments later, he ducked back down and waved to her. "It looks okay. Come on."

She grabbed on to his outstretched hand. He helped her scramble up the teetering pile of logs, and kept hold of her hand as they headed across the woodshed. Sophie didn't mind the grip, though, because it anchored her in a world that suddenly seemed far too bright.

She blinked, figuring it was because of the difference between the dark tunnel and the gray light of day. But when her vision cleared, she didn't see grayness at all. Through the open door of the woodshed, she saw a patch of dazzling white snow, a drift-shrouded corner of the mansion…and blue sky.

The blizzard had passed.

Griffin turned to her, expression guarded. "Two sets of tracks lead into the mansion, one from this building, one from around the side. I don't think we dare try heading for the house or we'll risk getting caught in the crossfire. But that might play in our favor, too, because if Perkins is preoccupied with tracking his mark and figures we're pinned down in the tunnel, he might not be keeping an eye on the driveway. What do you say we make a run for it, heading downhill, and meet the chopper on its way up from the city?"

Sophie sucked in a breath past the huge lump her heart had made in her throat. Some part of her must have thought that once they made it out of the tunnel, and once the storm passed, they'd be home free. But they weren't. He was right. They couldn't go back to the mansion, couldn't stay where they were. But there was a very real flaw in his plan. "What if the helicopter gets delayed, or another snow squall blows up?" They would be stuck out in the open, with no supplies or protection.

Griffin held her eyes with his. "I promise I'll do whatever I can to keep you safe."

He'd made the same promise to her before, as they had struggled up the driveway, wet and cold and shivering, not realizing that their problems were just beginning. She had believed him then, and she believed him even more deeply now. Griffin was a good man, a man of his word, and she trusted him implicitly.

The realization gave her pause, because if that were the case, then why had she so thoroughly rejected the thought of a future with him? He was a proud and stubborn man, yes, but he was also rational. A businessman as well as a warrior. If he came to love her, and they decided to make a life together, it would be a negotiation, not a dictatorship. Maybe, just maybe, in this case she was the one who had knee-jerked a response based on her own past. What if, in an effort to protect her own freedom, she was in danger of throwing away something that would make that freedom so much better?

"Griffin…" she began, but then trailed off, because now was neither the time nor the place. "Never mind." She squeezed her fingers on his. "I trust you. Down the hill we go."

He looked at her intently as though he, too, wanted to say something more. But in the end, he simply nodded and said, "Stay close."

They came out the door hand-in-hand and hit the ground running. The snow had blown mostly clear to one side of the shed and they headed that way, moving fast and aiming downhill. As they cleared the woodshed, Sophie caught a blur of motion out of the corner of her eye, but it was already too late.

A rough hand grabbed her and yanked her back, tearing her hand from Griffin's. A strong forearm clamped across her throat and cool metal touched her temple. A gun.

"Griffin!" she screamed, fearing that this time not even he would be able to save her.

Chapter Eleven

Griffin spun and nearly launched himself at the man who held Sophie, but froze the instant he saw the gun. Very slowly he dropped the firewood club and raised both hands, palms out, showing that he was unarmed.

The man who held Sophie was in his early forties, bareheaded and bald, with strong features and the cold blue eyes of a killer. He was wearing a winter camouflage snowsuit and held a 9mm to Sophie's temple with the ease of familiarity. His age matched that of hired killer Boyd Perkins, not fugitive mobster Vince Del Gardo. Which meant that maybe, just maybe, the hitman could be bought with a better offer.

"Think it through," Griffin said calmly. "I've got money, and the only thing I want to do is get the hell out of here, and take my assistant with me." He deliberately downgraded Sophie to her professional role, lest Perkins use their relationship as added leverage.

Because they *did* have a relationship, damn it, and he was going to do whatever it took to make sure that relationship had a chance of moving forward. Fairness forced him to admit—inwardly, at least—that she was right about some things. Maybe he had been trying to fit the women in his life into the mold of the Vaughn virgin and his parents' marriage. But if he could admit it then he could work to change it, if that was what it took to keep Sophie in his life.

Perkins smirked faintly at the offer of a bigger buyout. "Sorry, Mr. Vaughn. I stay bought, and I can't afford witnesses."

His finger tightened infinitesimally on the trigger in prelude to the killing shot. Griffin lunged forward, his heart stopping dead in his chest, shouting, "No!"

Perkins shifted to avoid the charge. As he did so, Sophie drove her elbow into his right side, just above his hip.

The hitman shouted in pain and staggered back. Griffin grabbed Sophie and ripped her away from the other man a split second before the gun roared. The bullet sang harmlessly into the trees as Griffin fell on Perkins, shouting.

Rage suffused Griffin, along with a territorial possessiveness he'd never experienced before. He pummeled the bastard, hammering him with his fists for scaring Sophie, for threatening her. For nearly killing her. The hitman fought back, but he was favoring his injured side. Griffin took ruthless advantage of the fact, digging his knee into the spot and landing a roundhouse punch when Perkins screamed in pain.

Griffin yanked the 9 mm from the hitman's lax fingers, and tossed the gun in Sophie's direction. "Take this." He didn't want Perkins getting it back and didn't want to hold it himself because it'd be a serious temptation to use it on the bastard.

Then he dragged Perkins to his feet and got in the dazed, semiconscious man's face. "Let's see how you like being tied up and stuck in a hole for a few hours while we wait for the sheriff!"

He was dragging Perkins toward the woodshed when he heard Sophie scream, "Griffin, look out!"

She started racing toward him, struggling through the snow, her attention fixed on an upper floor of the mansion.

Griffin jerked his head up just in time to see a glint of metal and motion from the broken second-story window. Screaming his name, Sophie threw herself at him just as the crack of a high-powered rifle echoed in the crisp winter air.

She slumped and crashed into him as deadweight, driving him to his knees. He lost his grip on Perkins, who ripped away from him and fled. Two more rifle shots sounded in quick succession, both missing Perkins, who disappeared into the tree line behind the woodshed.

Then, as Griffin had known he would, the man in the second-story window trained his rifle on him and Sophie. *No witnesses*, Perkins had said, and the same held true for the second man. Griffin couldn't see his features, but had to assume it was Del Gardo.

Griffin ducked and braced himself, trying to cover as much of Sophie's still form as he could with his own body.

"Go!" he thought he heard her say.

"I'm not leaving you," he growled. "Not ever." He closed his eyes and waited for the sound of a gunshot.

Instead he heard the rhythmical thump of a helicopter's rotors. Moments later, a small, light chopper came over the tree line, proudly bearing the VaughnTec logo on its doors. Help had arrived!

There was a swirl of motion as Del Gardo shouldered the rifle and disappeared from the window.

Griffin barely noticed, though. His entire focus was locked on the woman in his arms.

Sophie's exertion-flushed face was rapidly draining to waxen with pain and shock. He held her close, and didn't have to look to know that the warm wetness on his hands was her blood. She'd been shot pushing him out of the line of fire. She had, quite literally, taken a bullet for him.

"Hang on," he said urgently. "The cavalry's here. We'll get you back to Kenner City pronto and get you patched up. Just think, fresh food and hot water. Come on, stay with me. You don't want to miss out on a burger and a shower, do you?"

In response to his nonsense, her eyelids fluttered and then lifted, and her light brown eyes focused on him. The corners of her lips trembled. "You're okay."

That brought it all crashing down around him. A moan of pain ripped from his throat, and came out sounding like a sob. "I shouldn't be. You never should've gotten in the way. I'm the one who's supposed to protect you."

She started to say something, but broke off when her breath rattled in her lungs. She coughed slightly, bringing a wince of pain and spots of blood to her lips. The sight just about broke his heart, and when she tried to talk again, he shushed her with a kiss. "Hush. We can talk later."

She shook her head. "What if there isn't a later?" Her words were stronger now, as though she'd found another reserve, or was reaching the end of it. "If I've learned anything over the last few days, it's that we shouldn't assume there's going to be a tomorrow."

"But I want there to be," Griffin said, feeling it all start to slip away from him. As close to panicking as he'd ever been before in his life, he said, "I'll do anything, give anything to make sure there's a future for us."

"I believe you," she said, and his heart shuddered in his chest when he saw the sheen of love and acceptance in her eyes. "I was wrong before."

"No, I was."

"Fine, we both were. The thing is, I do want a future with you. I don't know how we'll make it work, but I want to try."

"It's a deal," Griffin whispered as her eyelids fluttered shut once again. He kissed her cheeks, then her lips, not a soldier or a tycoon now, but simply a man who held his woman in his arms and prayed that that he hadn't found her only to lose her that same day. Pressing close to her, he whispered, "Why did you take that bullet?"

He didn't expect an answer, but he got one, a thready whisper of, "Because this isn't about you protecting me. It's about us being a team."

That was the last thing she said.

The helicopter landed nearby and Sheriff Martinez

leaped out, followed by a half dozen others, which was more than the small chopper was rated for.

Griffin gathered Sophie in his arms and lifted her, trying not to see how much blood had spread in the snow beneath them. As he carried her limp form to the waiting helicopter, he called to the sheriff, "You'll see Perkins's trail leading off behind the woodshed, and Del Gardo was in the upstairs bedroom with the broken window no more than three minutes ago. Do whatever you need to do with my property, I don't care. Just find the bastards."

Then he climbed into the chopper with Sophie, barking for the copilot to get the first aid kit, pronto. The pilot had them in the air in no time flat, radioing ahead to find the nearest hospital helipad and warn the emergency doctors of an incoming gunshot victim. Griffin leaned over Sophie, talking to her, trying to stop the copious blood flow that was coming from a bullet wound in her upper chest.

He was wholly focused on the woman who in a few short days had become, in his heart at least, part of his family. He glanced back once as the helicopter flew away from Lonesome Lake, and saw the investigators fanning out in search of Boyd Perkins. A part of him wished he'd killed the bastard himself, but another, more civilized part of him was content to leave it to Martinez and his people. It was time to begin a new chapter in his life. Starting now.

Leaning down, he brushed a tendril of dark blond hair from Sophie's brow, and whispered, "Hang in there, beautiful. You can do it. You can do anything you want."

SOPHIE FLICKERED in and out of consciousness for what seemed like a long time, though her sense of time felt seriously out of whack, as did the rest of her body. She was light-headed and giddy half the time, crushed with pain the other half. She barely knew her own name, never mind where she was, or why. The only thing she did know for sure, the only constant she came to rely on, was the presence of the big, solid man at her bedside, his silver-shot hair standing up in finger-rumpled spikes, and his eyes tired and full of worry.

Griffin was there constantly, day and night. When she opened her eyes, he whispered words of praise and love, or updated her on what was happening in the outside world, though she didn't retain any of it when she slipped back under again.

Then, finally, she woke all the way and felt clear-headed, though weak and sore. It was daylight, though she couldn't have said what day, and Griffin was there, moving into her line of sight immediately, his mesmerizing green eyes full of hope. "Hey. How are you feeling?"

"Capable of speech, which is an improvement," her words came out barely above a whisper, and the effort sent a twinge of pain through her chest, but all of that was still better than it had been.

As her eyes adjusted, she became aware that they weren't alone. Sheriff Martinez stood at the end of the bed, next to a wiry, light-complexioned stranger with black hair, piercing blue eyes and a scar on his chin.

"Hey, Sheriff," she said, her voice sounding a little stronger this time. "Did you get Perkins?"

She saw the answer in Martinez's frustrated expression, but it was the other man who spoke, saying, "Ms. LaRue, my name is Dylan Acevedo. I'm with the FBI. We were just starting to discuss our findings with Mr. Vaughn here. Is it okay if we continue? Then, if you're up to it, maybe you could answer a couple of questions?"

Griffin shook his head and moved toward the men. "I don't think—"

"Wait." She caught Griffin's hand. "I'd like to hear what they have to say."

He stopped, but shot her a dark, disgruntled look. "You had a bullet taken out of your right lung. You think you could maybe take it easy for a day or two?"

Though her heart stuttered a little at the confirmation that she'd been seriously injured, though she'd already guessed it from the number of monitors and the length of time she'd been incoherent, she squeezed his fingers. "I promise that if it's too much, I'll either kick them out or fall asleep on you guys mid-sentence."

She was pretty sure she'd done the latter a couple of times in recent days. The corners of his mouth twitched, confirming it. "Okay. You win." His eyes warmed a notch. "Guess I'd better get used to that, huh?"

Her pulse kicked at the reminder of the things they'd said to each other up at Lonesome Lake, but she figured that was a conversation better held in private, so she looked back to Sheriff Martinez and Agent Acevedo. "Go on. I think you've got at least five minutes before I conk out again."

The agent inclined his head. "Then to keep it short, Mr. Vaughn here has already confirmed from a photo lineup that Boyd Perkins was the man who attacked and imprisoned the two of you. All of the evidence collected from the estate, by myself as well as Callie and Ava, indicates the presence of two men—Perkins, and another man whose height and weight are roughly consistent with that of Vince Del Gardo. Unfortunately, both of the men remain at large, and the second storm meant we weren't able to bring up the equipment needed to find any other access tunnels."

Sophie made a face and glanced at Griffin. "Another storm?"

He nodded. "At least this time we're in Kenner City where we belong."

"Actually, I'm pretty sure we belong in San Francisco."

He lifted a shoulder. "I had Hal take the jet and pick up Darryn and Luke. They're here now, which makes it feel a lot more like home."

Sophie searched his eyes, trying to interpret the undercurrents in that statement, and failing.

"What we were hoping to get from you," Martinez said, redirecting her attention, "is a description of Del Gardo."

She frowned. "You don't know what he looks like?"

"There's some speculation that he may have changed his appearance through plastic surgery. We were thinking you might be able to give us something more to go on."

"Sorry." She shook her head, though it was starting to throb as she hit the end of her small reserve of strength. "I just saw movement, and the rifle. A man's figure in the broken window. Nothing else."

"That's all I saw, too," Griffin said, gripping her hand in support. He looked over at the sheriff and FBI agent. "I think that's enough for her for now."

Sophie didn't protest, because she was already sliding toward sleep.

When she awoke next, she looked automatically to the chair beside her bed. For the first time since she'd woken up in the hospital, Griffin wasn't there. In his habitual place sat a slick, cool-looking blond woman in her mid-thirties. Beside her, in a second visitor's chair, sat a petite redhead with porcelain skin and vivid blue eyes. Both of them were wearing street clothes, but the blonde had a badge hung around her neck, identifying her as a member of the KCCU.

At first, Sophie assumed they were there to ask her more questions. But the air between the two women crackled with excitement, and their eyes shone, making Sophie think that something other than business had woken her. "What's up?" she asked, figuring that was more polite than leading with, *Who the heck are you?* For all she knew, she'd met the women earlier during her recovery and had blanked on it.

"Welcome back to the land of the living," the blonde said. "I'm Callie and this is Ava. You talked to us on the phone from Lonesome Lake? We wanted to meet you in person after all that long-distance stuff. And we wanted to let you know that if you're ever looking for a job, you might think of crime scene analysis. That was a hell of a set of fingerprints for using pancake makeup and packing tape!"

Sophie laughed, feeling the same instant connection to the two women that she'd felt during their phone conversations. "I'm happy to put faces to the voices! Now, tell me what I just missed. I'm guessing it was something big."

Ava's eyes sparkled. "I was just telling Callie that Ben—that'd be FBI agent Ben Parrish—just proposed, and we're going to tie the knot this weekend!"

"Wow," Sophie said. "Congratulations!"

Ava patted her stomach, drawing Sophie's attention to the gentle swell of a baby bump. "I know it's pretty hurry-up on the wedding end of things, but we're sort of doing this out of order."

Sophie smiled shyly, feeling more than a little out of her element as she realized that, just as she'd gone a long time without a man in her life, it'd been years since she'd had any real female friends to speak of. "Congratulations. Really." She glanced at Callie, who seemed to be the more reserved of the two. "Is there any news on the investigation?" Sophie faltered. "I mean, that you can tell me about? If you can't it's no big deal. It's just—" She broke off and blew out a frustrated breath. "Never mind. It's just that you guys made me feel like one of the team when we were on the phone together. I have to remember it's back-to-reality time."

Callie grinned. "You'll find we're a fairly relaxed group. Within reason, of course. So I'll tell you that we've got a ton of questions and no real answers right now. Given the amount of snow the second storm dumped on the mountains, there's not much we can do up at

Lonesome Lake at the moment. And yeah, we liked talking with you, too. That's part of why we're here. We wanted to put in a vote that you and your hunky millionaire boyfriend, and his super adorable kid, should stick around. Maybe not up at Lonesome Lake, at least not until we've fully cleared it. But maybe in Kenner City."

Sophie felt the prickly heat of a blush cover her cheeks. "My boyfriend, huh? Seems like a strange term for a guy who's…well, not a boy."

That got some eyebrow wiggles from her new friends, but any further conversation was interrupted by the sound of male voices in the hallway, followed by the door swinging open. Griffin stood in the doorway, with Luke at his side. Luke was gripping a file folder with careful concentration.

"I think that's our cue." Callie rose, pausing to jot something on the bedside pad. "That's my number. If you're going to be in town for a while, give me a call and we can get together some time."

The women filed out, greeting Griffin and tousling Luke's hair on the way by. When the door swung shut at their backs, Sophie used the remote control to raise the head of her bed, allowing her to sit partway up.

A quiver took root in the pit of her stomach, warning her that this could be a major moment in progress. The thing was, she didn't know which way it was going to go. She and Griffin had connected up at Lonesome Lake, but how much of what they'd said to each other had stuck once his helicopter had dropped him back in reality?

Sure, he'd stayed by her side, and yes, he'd hinted at there being a future for them, even in front of the sheriff and Agent Acevedo. But what shape would that future take? Would Griffin try to ease her into the role of his fantasy wife, or would he be open to negotiating?

Unable to guess any of the answers from his expression, she said, "Hey, guys." Then, focusing on the child at Griffin's side, she said, "Hi, Luke. I'm…" She faltered, knowing that one of Griffin's biggest hang-ups was his son getting too attached too quickly. "I'm Sophie."

Luke, who even with short blond hair and brown eyes somehow managed to look like a miniature version of Griffin, looked up at his father. "Now, Dad?"

"Yeah," Griffin said, his voice soft and a little rough. "Now would be good." He kept his eyes fastened on her as Luke crossed the room, stopped near Sophie's beside and held out the file folder. "These are for you."

"Thank you." She took the file, though she hadn't a clue what it contained. His job completed, Luke scampered back to his father's side.

Griffin, however, crossed the room and took his usual seat, then hoisted his son up onto his lap. Griffin was wearing jeans and a cable-knit sweater the same color as his eyes, and he seemed far more relaxed than she'd ever seen him before. He wasn't the soldier, the tycoon or the lover now. He was the father. The family man.

And somehow she instinctively knew this was the man she'd been trying to find inside him all along. The man who was brought to the fore by his son. But it wasn't his son he was looking at right now with all the love in the world plain for her to see in his eyes.

No, he was looking at her.

"Open it," he said. "And please do me a favor and hear me out before you get mad."

"Oh, well. With a lead-in like that…" Faint butterflies churned in her stomach as she flipped open the file.

The first page was a terse e-mail sent from Tony's account at Wade & Kane. All it said was, "Done."

She glanced at Griffin. "What's done?"

His eyes hardened to those of the soldier. "I told both he and his wife that they would sorely regret it if they ever contacted, spoke or even thought about you ever again." He paused. "And if you want to accuse me of throwing my weight around, then yes, that's exactly what I did. But she started it."

"Yes, she certainly did." Sophie tried not to feel a slice of satisfaction that he'd dealt with Destiny in such a way. She failed, because it *was* satisfying. "Sometimes it just takes the right weapon to do the job." She smiled at him, sharing her approval with Luke. "Thank you both."

"Keep going," Griffin said. "Or better yet, let me explain first."

"Okay, now I'm nervous."

"Trust me, not nearly as nervous as I am." And for the first time since she'd known Griffin, he looked less than a hundred percent confident.

"You're not going to drop coffee on me, are you?"

"I'll try not to." He blew out a breath. "Here goes. I've cleared your debts. All of them." He held up a hand to keep her from interrupting, not seeming to understand that all the breath had just left her lungs. "I know you didn't want me to, and you're probably thinking I did it to control you, or make you feel like you owe me, or something like that. And I could see how it might look that way. But I'd really rather you consider it hazardous duty pay for me dragging you up to Lonesome Lake. Anything but an effort to make our relationship into something other than a fifty-fifty partnership."

It wasn't until the last sentence that the pressure in her chest eased. Those, it seemed, were the magic words. "Fifty-fifty, eh?" She arched an eyebrow. "And what, exactly, am I going to be doing with my fifty percent of this relationship?"

"Whatever you want," he said with quiet simplicity. "If you want to go to law school, I'll pack your lunch. So to speak, anyway. What you saw up at the mansion was about the sum total of my cooking skills. On the other hand, if you want to use our money to springboard yourself straight to advocacy, or open an office that employs a half dozen lawyers dedicated to your cause, then that's what we'll do. Hell, I don't care if you want to knit doilies or run for President. I'll support you no matter what."

All of a sudden, it sounded too big, too huge for someone like her. "I don't know if I can do all that."

"Then we'll do it together," he said. "All I'm asking is that you stick around and get to know Luke and me as a family, and Darryn, because he's family, too. And that while you're doing that, you consider marrying us."

Her throat closed and her eyes filled with tears. "I will."

He went very still. "You will what? Stick around, or marry us?"

"Both," she said, and there wasn't a single qualm in her heart. "I love you."

His features eased, as though he'd been braced for something else. As though he'd feared that even after all they'd been through together, the family of his dreams would stay beyond his reach. Exhaling on a gusty sigh, he said, "And I love you."

Bringing Luke with him, he leaned over the bed and kissed her, very gently, still mindful of her injuries.

Sophie wept a little and clung, and couldn't help thinking that not in a million years would she have predicted this based on her first day of work, when he'd scowled at her and she'd dumped a pot of coffee in his lap. But it turned out that Kathleen had been right, even though neither of them had known the retiree had been matchmaking. It might have taken them a three-day blizzard and harrowing danger to figure it out, but in the end, the reality was inescapable.

They were a perfect fit.

* * * * *

CRIMINALLY HANDSOME

BY
CASSIE MILES

Though born in Chicago and raised in LA, **Cassie Miles** has lived in Colorado long enough to be considered a semi-native. The first home she owned was a log cabin in the mountains overlooking Elk Creek with a thirty-mile commute to her work at the *Denver Post*.

After raising two daughters and cooking tons of macaroni and cheese for her family, Cassie is trying to be more adventurous in her culinary efforts. Ceviche, anyone? She's discovered that almost anything tastes better with wine. A lot of wine. When she's not plotting Intrigue books, Cassie likes to hang out at the Denver Botanical Gardens near her high-rise home.

Chapter One

Emma Richardson folded her arms on the desktop in her home office and laid down her head. At nine o'clock in the morning, it was too early for a nap. But she was tired, so very tired.

I'll only rest my eyes. Only for a moment. While the house is quiet....

Reality faded as a psychic vision seeped into her mind. Daylight shimmered and vanished, transformed into night.

She was in a forest.

A cold wind rattled through bare branches, and the shadows shifted beneath her feet. Beside her, to the east, the dark waters of a wide, wild river crashed against rocks and boulders, spewing a deadly froth.

A tall woman appeared. She wore an FBI jacket. Her eyes were hollow. Her lips were white and dead. She spoke only one word. "Run."

Emma didn't ask why. She knew. He was coming closer. The danger was coming closer.

She scrambled over the rocks at the river's edge. This was no good; she needed to seek open ground. Turning to the west, she fought her way through thicket, pine and cottonwood. The trees dissuaded her. West was the wrong direction. On the medicine wheel, west meant death.

She slipped, caught hold of the slender white trunk of an aspen. The bark felt warm, full of life. The branches were green with leaves. This tree had saved her balance, kept her from falling.

With a final effort, she crawled into the open. As she ran, her sneakers dug into the moist earth, still saturated from the recent blizzard. She vaulted over low shrubs and patches of snow, running hard, running for her life.

The muscles in her thighs throbbed. Her blood pumped so fiercely through her veins that her ears were ringing. But she had to keep going. If she stopped, he'd catch her.

Straight ahead, she saw a car, and she heard the cries of an infant. She had to protect him. She veered toward the south—the direction of safety—leading her pursuer away from the precious child.

He was gaining. So close that she felt his hot, fetid breath on the back of her neck. His hands grabbed her jacket. There was no escape. He had her. She fell.

He was on top of her. Shadows hid his face but she saw his necklace. A leather medallion with a black bear claw design. He held a knife. Moonlight gleamed on the silver blade.

Through the ringing in her ears, she heard him say, "Aspen got away. But you will die."

As the blade descended toward her throat, her eyelids closed....

She woke with a start, jolted back in the swivel chair. April sunlight poured through the window. The screen saver on her computer showed a random lightning bolt pattern. Though Emma knew she was safe at home, the aura of danger lingered. Her heart raced as if she had actually been running.

Finally, she'd had a vision. Finally, her gift as a medium might help her find her cousin.

Before the images faded in her memory, she grabbed a piece of paper and wrote down all that she could remember. Her pen flew across the page, making sketchy notes: Woman in FBI jacket. The river to the east. The green aspen leaves. Running to the west. The car with the baby. Turn to the south. His knife. His leather necklace. She drew the bear claw design.

Lifting her pen, she looked down at the paper and saw that she'd unintentionally drawn a second design. Leafy with vines, it looked like a logo. Three letters twined together. VDG.

Where did that come from? And what did VDG stand for? Very Damn Good? Vines Do Grow? Or the *V* could stand for Virgin. She winced. *Don't go there.* This vision wasn't about her personal life. These images pertained to the disappearance of her cousin, Aspen Meadows.

Aspen. She circled the word. The aspen tree in her vision was leafy and warm, still flowing with sap. And the pursuer said that Aspen got away. Emma wanted to believe those words, wanted to believe that her cousin had survived the attack. But where was she?

Five weeks ago, just before a spring blizzard blanketed the southeast corner of Colorado with several feet of snow, Aspen's car had been found in a ditch just outside Kenner City. Her six-week-old son, Jack, was safe in his car seat, but Sheriff Patrick Martinez suspected foul play. When he placed Jack in Emma's care, he had warned her to be prepared for the worst.

But that couldn't be. Aspen wasn't dead. Whenever someone close to Emma passed on, she knew. The dead came to her from the other side, spoke to her, showed her visions or symbols. Ever since she was ten years old and her deceased grandmother warned her about the fire, she'd been a medium—able to communicate with the dead. At age thirty, she trusted her spirit visions almost more than reality.

For five long weeks, she'd been hoping that her psychic senses would give her a clue to Aspen's whereabouts, but nothing had come into her mind. Until now. The spirit who showed her this vision had to be the tall FBI woman—a dead woman. Who was she? How was she connected to Aspen's disappearance?

Emma closed her eyes and concentrated. *Who are you?*

Nothing came. Not a sound. Not a symbol.

Please tell me. Who are you?

Still nothing.

Are your initials VDG?

She heard a faint echo. *Julie.* Then silence again.

"Okay," Emma said as she opened her eyes. "Your name is Julie."

It was a start. Sometimes, Emma was able to reach out to these spirits, and they'd respond. She communicated often with her grandma Quinn and her aunt Rose, both of whom had been popping in to offer advice on how to care for Aspen's infant son. They observed and commented and nagged about how Emma was doing everything all wrong. If the spirits of Grandma and Aunt Rose had been able to change diapers, life would be so much easier. But no. Emma was the sole caregiver. Definitely not a job she'd signed up for.

She figured that the main reason she hadn't had a vision about Aspen's disappearance was severe sleep deprivation from baby Jack's every-few-hours feeding schedule. He was a cuddly little bundle of stringent demands: Feed me. Change me. Carry me. Rock me. Dealing with an infant was far more time-intensive than she'd ever imagined. Also, she had to admit, more rewarding.

Though she learned—from the dozens of baby care

books she'd purchased online—that Jack's change of facial expression could be nothing more than a reflex or a muscle twitch, his smile was amazing. And the random sounds he made—other than the full-throated crying—tickled her. In his wide-open eyes, she saw the wisdom of the ages. She had to find Aspen, to reunite her with this little miracle named Jack.

Finally, she had a vision to work with. Emma grabbed the phone on the desk and punched in the number for Sheriff Martinez. He owed her for a couple of cases where she'd used her skill as a medium to help him find missing persons. Now, it was his turn to help her.

MIGUEL ACEVEDO, a forensic investigator for the Kenner County Crime Lab, rode in the passenger seat beside Sheriff Patrick Martinez. Miguel hated that his analysis of a crime scene was being called into question. By a psychic? "This is a waste of time, my friend."

"Don't be so sure," Patrick said. "Over the years, Emma has helped with missing person cases. She's saved lives. Everybody around here trusts her and knows she's not a fraud."

"Why haven't I heard of her?"

"You don't know much about Kenner City. Your crime lab has only been here for a year."

Though the Four Corners area covered a huge territory in four different states, the small-town populations were insular. The people in Kenner City were slow to accept change, even slower to warm up to strangers. Miguel hardly knew anyone outside law enforcement. "Tell me about one of her cases."

"Remember last fall when that boy disappeared from his mother's house? Emma told me where to look."

"The boy was with his father." And it didn't take a visionary to figure out that the estranged dad snatched his own son. "Wasn't he your first suspect?"

"You bet, but Emma said they were in Durango. In a room with a wagon wheel in front. And she saw the number seven."

"Was she right?"

"Close enough. The name of the motel was the Covered Wagon. And it was room seventeen." Patrick reached up to adjust the brim of his Stetson. "Trust me. She's the real deal."

"A real psychic. Those two words are opposites. If something is real—as in reality—how can it be psychic?"

"You're a real pain in the ass, Miguel."

"It's my *primo* talent."

"And she's not really a psychic. She's a medium."

"What's the difference?"

"She talks to dead people."

"Muy loco." He lowered the window and pushed his open palm against the wind. A fresh coolness rushed inside the cuff of his denim jacket and plaid cotton shirt. A few weeks after the blizzard, there were still patches of snow on the shady side of the street and at the curbs where the snow plows had piled up little mountains. Today's temperature was already in the fifties. By noon, it would be sixty. The weather felt like spring. His favorite season. He felt like a kid instead of a thirty-three-year-old man, felt like he should stick his head out the window like a collie and let the wind blow through his hair.

He ran his fingers through that thick, black hair which was seriously in need of a trim, then turned toward Patrick. "Tell me, my friend. Did Emma the fortune teller predict that you'd fall in love with Bree Hunter?"

At the mention of his fiancée's name, the big tough sheriff melted like chocolate in *mole*. "Emma isn't that kind of psychic. She doesn't read a crystal ball."

"Exactly what kind of *bruja* is she?"

"She's not a witch," Patrick said. "There are scientific theories about paranormal abilities and mediums. Why are you so threatened?"

"She's no threat. Just a waste of my time."

He'd already done a thorough analysis of the vehicle abandoned by Aspen Meadows. From the skid marks left by tires and a high-impact dent on the rear bumper, he determined that Aspen's car was forced off the road into a shallow ditch. He'd found no fingerprints or other trace evidence in the car, other than those of Aspen and a few close friends, which led him to believe that she'd climbed out from behind the steering wheel and took off running—probably searching for help or trying to divert her pursuer from harming her baby.

Then Aspen disappeared. She was either purposely in hiding or dead. No matter what Emma Richardson said.

Patrick cleared his throat. "Do me a favor. Don't tease Emma."

"Why not? The *bruja* is sensitive?"

"Aspen is her cousin. They're close. They grew up together on the rez."

The nearby Ute Mountain Ute reservation took up thousands of acres on these high plains. Patrick's fiancée, Bree, was a detective on the tribal police force. "I didn't know Emma was Ute."

"Partly. She doesn't look it. Her hair is brown, not black. Her eyes are blue."

It must have been tough to live on the rez and not look like everybody else. Miguel would have felt a twinge of sympathy if he hadn't thought this whole psychic thing was crazy. "I won't give her a hard time, unless she asks for it."

"She's a good woman. When I told her about Aspen's disappearance, Emma stepped up and took responsibility. She's the temporary guardian for Aspen's baby."

"What about the father?"

"Aspen never said who he was."

"We could run the baby's DNA," Miguel said. "The father might be in the database."

"The guy obviously doesn't care. Baby Jack is better off with Emma."

The sheriff pulled into the driveway of a pretty little ranch-style house, white with black trim and a shake roof. The lot was huge and well-landscaped with indigenous pines and spruce. Empty flower boxes at the windows waited for their spring planting.

"Nice place." The cleanliness and normality surprised him. He'd halfway expected a haunted house with cobwebs draped across the windows and a graveyard in the back. "What does this medium do to earn her living?"

"Some kind of consulting or editing. She works at home on her computer." Patrick issued one last warning. "Be nice."

"I'll be on my best behavior, and that's saying a lot. I used to be an altar boy."

Like that churchgoing boy from so many years ago, he trudged along the sidewalk, dragging his feet. He'd rather be somewhere else. Back at the lab, he had work piling up and a new piece of audio analysis equipment he wanted to play with. He waited on the front stoop while Patrick rang the bell. From inside, he could hear a baby crying, which didn't exactly reassure him about Emma being a good mother substitute.

The door swung open. Miguel found himself staring into the huge blue eyes of a slender woman with straight, silky brown hair that fell across her forehead and was cut in a straight line at her sharp, little chin. He saw hints of her Ute heritage in her dusky complexion and high cheekbones. Her lips pulled into a wide, open smile as she greeted Patrick. Though she balanced the fussing baby in her arms, she managed to shake his hand when the sheriff introduced them.

"Pleased to meet you, Miguel."

"Same here."

His first impression was all good, *muy bueno*. As he entered her house, he studied her more closely. As a CSI, he was trained to notice details. Her silver earrings and the necklace around her long, slender neck had a distinctive Ute design. Her beige turtleneck, almost the same color as her skin, and her jeans resembled the typical outfit worn by most people in the area at this time of year. But the fabric of her turtleneck was silk. He didn't know much about women's clothing, but he suspected that she shopped in classy boutiques.

In her sunlit kitchen, she offered them coffee.

With a glance at Miguel, Patrick said, "We probably shouldn't waste any time."

"No rush," Miguel said.

"Oh, good," Emma said as she bounced up and down with the whimpering baby, gently stroking the fine hair on top of his head. "Because it's time for Jack's feeding. I just finished heating the formula."

"I'll take the baby."

Miguel held out his arms. Back home, he had a growing herd of nieces and nephews. Though his family lived only a few hours' drive away from Kenner City, his schedule didn't leave much time for visits, and he missed them.

When she handed over the baby, dressed in footed pajamas, he wrapped the blanket snugly around the infant's tiny legs and cradled him in the crook of his arm. "Hush, *mijo*."

The baby looked toward him. As soon as Miguel took a seat at the kitchen table, the fussing stopped. "How old is he? About three months?"

"Eleven weeks." Her jaw literally dropped. "How did you get him to settle down?"

"He's curious. Is that right, *mijo?* You're figuring out who I am before you start making noise and complaining."

"Let's get him fed before that happens."

She maneuvered in her kitchen with a graceful economy of motion. Her age, he guessed, was probably about thirty—the prime of womanhood, old enough to be done with girlish giggles and young enough to be open to new experience. The more he saw of Emma Richardson, the more he liked her.

After she handed him a bottle full of formula and placed two coffee mugs on the kitchen table, she said, "I made notes of what I remembered about my vision. I'll go get them."

As soon as she left the room, Patrick said, "No rush? I thought you were in a big hurry."

He smiled down at the baby, who smacked his little lips as he sucked down formula. "You didn't tell me she was pretty. How does a woman like that get to be in her late twenties and still unmarried?"

The sheriff sipped his coffee. Wryly, he said, "Maybe because she's a witch, and she turns her lovers into toads."

That was a chance Miguel might be willing to take if it meant spending more time with Emma. He settled Jack into a baby seat on the tabletop and kept the nipple plugged into his mouth. With the other hand, he lifted his coffee mug. The brew was lightly flavored with cinnamon, just the way he liked it.

Emma returned with a sheet of paper, which she placed on the table in front of her. "I'm not quite sure how to interpret everything I saw, but I believe Aspen is alive."

Miguel's infatuation slipped a few notches. Crazy wasn't appealing. "Why?"

"Two reasons. I saw an aspen tree with green leaves.

And the man who was chasing me in the vision said so. He said, 'Aspen got away.' I assume that means he failed to kill my cousin."

"What else?" Patrick asked.

"I was next to a river. For me, water is a symbol of life. The river was to my right, to the east." She frowned at her notes. "Directions seemed to be important, but I'm not sure why. It might have something to do with the medicine wheel."

"The medicine wheel?"

"I'm part Ute. I was raised by my aunt Rose on the rez, and the medicine wheel is part of my culture. The east where the sun rises is associated with good things, new life. I always orient my desk toward the east so my work will go easier. West is the opposite. North is negative. South is positive."

"This vision of yours," Miguel said, trying hard not to be sarcastic. "Was it a road map to find your cousin?"

"I'm not sure what the directions mean. I'm hoping that if I take a look at Aspen's car, I might get a clearer picture of where she is."

"Like a psychic GPS system?"

Anger flashed in her blue eyes. Though Patrick had told him to be nice, Miguel couldn't help teasing. Not when she left herself wide-open with such an irrational theory.

Her tone was curt. "You're a forensic investigator, right?"

"Correct."

"Here's something specific for you to work with." She pushed the paper toward him. "The man who was chasing me wore a leather necklace with a bear claw design. This is what it looked like."

"A grizzly paw." His gaze slid down the page and saw the words in quotation marks: *Aspen got away. But you will die.* Emma hadn't mentioned that second part. Was that the way visions worked? Pick one thing and ignore another?

He also saw another scribbled design using the initials

VDG. That was a symbol he recognized; it was important to another investigation. "What's this?"

"I didn't see it in my vision. When I started making notes, I just drew it."

He adjusted Jack's bottle. "You don't know where it came from? You've never seen it before?"

"Not that I recall."

Her smile was a treasure. So beautiful, *muy bonita*. And so crazy, *muy loca*.

He needed to inform the FBI about the VDG symbol.

Chapter Two

On their way to the impound lot where Aspen's car was being held, Emma rode with Miguel in her little gas-saving hybrid so they wouldn't have to switch the baby seat in and out of the sheriff's cruiser. Though they were in her car, she let Miguel drive so as not to further affront his authority. His sarcasm clearly told her that he didn't much care for mediums, psychics or spirit visions. The only thing that sparked his interest was that VDG scribble.

She stole a glance at this dark, lean man with the shaggy black hair and dark green eyes—the color of a cool, deep forest. When he wasn't making smart-alecky comments, he was attractive. And she wasn't the only one who thought so. Baby Jack adored him; they'd bonded in seconds. After finishing his bottle, Jack wiggled cheerfully in Miguel's arms and made gurgle noises that sounded like an alien language. Riding in the backseat, Jack still hadn't stopped burbling. His was the only conversation in the car.

Emma couldn't think of a word to say. Though she'd always been terminally shy, this long silence was ridiculous. She cleared her throat. "The snow is melting fast."

"Yeah, it's about time it started feeling like spring," he said.

More silence.

"So, Miguel, are you new to Kenner City?"

"I've been here about a year. I was one of the first employees at the new crime lab."

"Where are you from?"

"You tell me." He shot her a wry glance. "You're the psychic. You're supposed to know these things."

Usually, she paid no attention to those who doubted her visions or—even worse—those who treated her with great deference as if she were the Oracle of Delphi. But she wanted Miguel to accept her. Maybe because he was good with the baby. Maybe because he could help her find Aspen. And maybe…just because. "Are you challenging me?"

"Go ahead. Astound me."

"Fine." She studied him for a moment. His identity shouldn't be so hard to figure out.

The sheriff had mentioned that most of the employees at the lab were from Colorado. She assumed that Miguel wasn't newly transplanted from a big city like Denver; his cowboy boots were well-worn and looked like his habitual footwear. He didn't have the roughened hands of a cowboy or a farmer from the San Luis Valley, but she noticed calluses on his fingertips, typical of a guitar player.

She figured that he'd gone to college to study forensics. But where? Which school? She remembered that when he looked at the design on her pursuer's necklace, he identified the marking as a grizzly claw. Not a bear, but a grizzly. And the grizzly was the school mascot for Adams State College in Alamosa.

"I'm not sure if you were born there," she said, "but you lived in Alamosa."

"Correct." He arched an eyebrow. "The sheriff told you, right? Everybody thinks Patrick Martinez is the strong, silent type, but he can't keep his mouth shut."

"I never heard your name until I met you this morning."

He pulled up at a stop sign, pushed his sunglasses up

on his forehead and stared at her with an intensity that she found both intimidating and sexy. As his gaze scanned her face, searching for a hint that she was lying, she faced him without flinching.

He asked, "What else can you tell me?"

"You play guitar."

He held out his right hand. "You saw the calluses."

"You've got a fresh grease stain on your jeans. Maybe you ride a motorcycle."

"A Harley," he confirmed. "You're using logic. Not psychic intuition."

"Does it matter if I find the answers with logic or by a vision?" she asked earnestly. "Both are methods of observation. Different paths that lead to the same truth. You'd understand if you could be inside my head, walk a mile in my shoes."

He glanced at her feet. "Purple sneakers with white stars? I don't think so."

"They match my jacket." She ran her fingers down the zipper of the purple leather jacket she'd bought on her last trip to New York. The style was so *not* from the Southwest, but she loved it.

As her tone lightened to match his teasing, she realized that she was enjoying this conversation. Moments ago, she'd been tongue-tied. Now her wits were fully engaged. How lovely to talk to an adult who wasn't a nagging ghost. "We have more in common than you think, Miguel. We're both investigators."

"But you see things that aren't visible to the naked eye."

"So do you. Every time you look into a microscope."

"You make a good point." His brow furrowed. "So much of forensics, like DNA testing and trace evidence analysis, isn't readily visible."

"Paranormal phenomenon is the same thing. It exists,

but nobody has invented the tools to accurately reveal these signs and symbols."

Until someone created a reading device, it was up to people like her—psychics and mediums—to interpret.

They parked outside the ten-foot-tall chain-link fence surrounding the police impound lot. The person in charge wasn't a police officer in uniform, but a crusty gray-haired man who looked like he knew his way around a junkyard. As soon as Miguel showed his badge, the old man unlocked the gate and slid it aside.

After a brief discussion, Miguel agreed to hold the baby so she could concentrate, but he refused to wear the color-fully patterned designer baby sling she'd ordered online. Instead, he tucked the baby in the crook of his arm as he answered his cell phone.

Emma picked her way across the gravel lot where most of the snow had melted. Some of these tightly parked cars and trucks looked like they'd been here for years with their tires gone flat and the paint jobs dulled by constant exposure to the elements. Aspen's beat-up sedan seemed new in comparison.

The last time Emma saw this vehicle, shortly after her cousin disappeared, she'd felt confusion and fear as she imagined the desperation Aspen must have experienced as she fled. Similar emotions roiled inside her, but this fear came from her own terrible foreboding that her cousin was never coming back. *Please, Aspen, you have to be alive.* She had so much to live for. Her son. Her new job as a teacher on the rez. After years of struggling and working lousy jobs at the Ute casino and in Las Vegas, Aspen had finally finished college at the University of Nevada. She'd been so close to reaching her dreams.

Miguel strolled up beside her. His calm, no-nonsense attitude reassured her. "That was Patrick on the phone. He has other police business and won't be joining us. When we're done here, can you give me a ride back to the lab?"

"Sure." She circled the hood of the car, hoping to get a clue that would lead to her cousin.

"What are you doing?" he asked.

"Sometimes, when I touch things, I can tap into a spirit energy. In my vision, I saw the car. It must be important."

"If your cousin isn't dead…" He shook his head. "I can't believe I'm saying this."

"Keep going," she encouraged. "A mile in my shoes."

"If your cousin isn't dead, what spirit are you hoping to contact?"

"I saw a woman wearing an FBI jacket. I'm not sure, but I think her name is Julie."

He reacted with a start. "And she's dead?"

"Yes."

His jaw tensed. "Don't play games with me, Emma. You heard something about the FBI investigation. Correct?"

"I haven't heard anything. Why would I?"

"The sheriff mentioned it. Or you heard local gossip."

His accusations irritated her. "I've barely been out of my house for five weeks, ever since Jack came to live with me."

"What about before that?"

"I live alone, and I work at home. When I get together with friends, we don't discuss FBI investigations." She confronted him directly. "Who is Julie?"

"Agent Julie Grainger. She was murdered in January."

She heard the cry of a bird and whirled around. Crows symbolized death for her. When her aunt Rose passed away, a flock of the big black birds had blanketed her yard. Their cries had been deafening.

She looked up, searched the blue skies and saw nothing. No birds at all. But she'd heard something.

There was another chirp, and she realized the sound

came from Jack. Miguel stroked the baby's head. "It's okay, *mijo*. You're a good boy."

"Did you know Julie?"

"A little." His jaw unclenched. "Are you okay, Emma? You look pale."

"As if I've seen a ghost?"

When he smiled, his demeanor changed from hostile to gentle. "I guess that happens a lot to you."

"Too much." She glanced at Jack when he made another chirp. "Maybe you should take the baby back to my car. I don't want to frighten him."

"Are you going to do something scary? Roll around on the ground? Squawk like a chicken? Do a voodoo dance?"

When she glared at him, he grinned.

"You like to tease," she said.

"Life is too sad not to laugh. I mean no disrespect." He rested his hand on her shoulder. His touch was steady and strong as an anchor in a storm. "Do whatever you need to do. I'm here for you. Nothing bad is going to happen."

A dark mist rolled in at the edge of her vision. She'd just told him to go away, but now she wanted him to stay close, wanted to maintain physical contact. "Don't go anywhere."

"You got it."

She laid her palm on the hood of the car. Her sight narrowed. Though still aware of the cars and snow in the impound lot, she seemed to be peering down a tunnel. At the end, she saw the tall woman in an FBI jacket. Julie Grainger. Beside her was a teenage girl in a lovely white gown. Words and images raced through Emma's mind. Rapid-fire. Like film on fast-forward.

Then the vision was gone.

"What is it?" Miguel asked.

Her brain sorted the jumbled impressions. The aspen had been leafy and green. *Her cousin was still alive.* Julie told her Aspen had escaped. Then she'd made a weaving motion with her hand. A river? A snake? "A trail," Emma said. "I should start at the beginning and follow the trail."

"From the crime scene."

"Yes. We should start there." Emma had also seen the VDG symbol again. "VDG is important."

Again, Miguel's interest picked up. "Is VDG connected to your cousin's disappearance?"

"It could be."

She remembered the girl in the white dress. Her presence had nothing to do with Aspen. *She was Miguel's sister. Teresa.* She had died young, less than a year after her *quinceanera,* the ceremony and party that celebrated the fifteenth birthday of a young woman. Teresa wanted her brother to know that she was all right, that she'd found the light and gone to the other side. Teresa believed that Miguel would understand.

But Emma wasn't sure. Though Miguel seemed more open to her ability as a medium, he might not be ready for contact with his tragically dead sister, and she didn't want to alienate him. She needed Miguel to help her find Aspen.

Looking into his eyes, she measured her words, trying to find a balance between proving to him that she wasn't a phony and not freaking him out. Teresa had shown her a family photo with Miguel standing beside his brother, who appeared to be the same age. She said, "You're a twin."

He nodded slowly.

"Fraternal, not identical. Alike, but different."

The silver medal he wore around his neck on a chain glittered in the sunlight. Though she couldn't make out the design, it didn't appear to be a saint. Instinctively, she reached toward it. When her fingers touched the surface, her hand glowed. She identified the image on the front: El Santuario de Chimayo, near Taos in New Mexico.

"Chimayo," she said. A legendary healing place like Lourdes. The words etched on the back of his medal were *Protect and Heal*. Teresa wanted her to know that Miguel had been near death, close enough to see the light.

His near-death experience was why her ability to communicate with dead people threatened him. He knew she was telling the truth, knew there was something beyond this world. He'd been there.

IN THE BACK OF HER CAR, the baby had begun to fuss, and Miguel knew their time for further investigating was limited. He didn't want to believe that Emma's pronouncements were anything more than random guesses, but he couldn't ignore her accuracy. How the hell did she know he was a twin? How had she described his relationship with his brother, Dylan, so accurately? Alike but different. That pretty much summed it up. They were both in law enforcement, but Miguel relied on forensic science while Dylan was a supermacho FBI agent.

Emma reached toward the backseat, hoping to calm Jack. "I should get him back home."

"Mijo," Miguel said. "Give us a break. You'll be okay."

Immediately, Jack's cries modified to quiet little sniffles. He was a good baby, a good boy.

"Amazing," Emma said. "I can't believe the way he responds to your voice. It's almost like you're his father."

"His father is a pig. If *mijo* was my baby boy, I would never abandon him. Family is everything."

"But you're not married."

"Don't remind me." Though he and his brother were thirty-three, neither of the Acevedo twins had found a wife and settled down. "I get enough nagging from my mama."

The leftover snow had melted enough that he could pull onto the shoulder at the edge of the road. This area—where

Aspen's vehicle had been found—was outside Kenner City, but there were houses within sight. There had been no witnesses, no one who stepped forward and said they heard her scream.

"This is it," Emma said. "The start of the trail."

"We won't find anything here. I did the crime scene analysis. There's nothing more to be learned."

Not unless she did that weird vision thing. When she'd touched the car in the impound lot, he'd felt the tension in her body. She seemed to catch her breath. Her blue eyes went blank as a corpse. *Muy loca,* like a trance. But it had lasted less than a minute. If he hadn't been standing beside her with his hand on her shoulder, he wouldn't have noticed.

She shoved her car door open. "I want to take a look around. Jack seems okay. We can leave him in his car seat."

Reluctantly, he joined her. If she managed to somehow turn up evidence that had been overlooked, he needed to be with her to verify and to maintain proper procedure.

Her gaze scanned from left to right and back again. What could she possibly hope to find? The blizzard had erased any footprints. He and the other crime scene investigators had already measured and photographed the skid marks on the pavement.

She lifted her chin and gave a sniff.

"Now what?" he asked. "Are you channeling a bloodhound to scent the trail?"

Instead of bristling, she chuckled. "Might be handy to have a ghost dog. I wouldn't have to pick up the poop."

"You made a joke, Emma."

"But you didn't laugh."

"On the inside, I'm in stitches."

"Seriously," she said, "were search dogs involved?"

"There wasn't time before the blizzard hit." And he regretted that they hadn't been able to call on that resource to locate her cousin. "We only had a few hours to process the scene, and the sheriff's first concern was taking care of Jack."

"I know. As soon as he checked the car's registration, he came to me with the baby." Guilt furrowed her brow. "I should have been here, should have gone out into the snow to look for my cousin. But I was overwhelmed. I wasn't prepared to care for an infant."

"You managed."

"Only because I could order all the baby equipment online. I hired someone to come in four hours a day so I can get my work done, but I'm still sleep-deprived. Sometimes I'm so exhausted that I think I'm losing my mind."

"Losing your mind?" He couldn't resist teasing. "How can you tell?"

"Very funny," she said. "Laughing on the inside."

She walked to the intersection, turned and walked back toward him. Her purple sneakers dug into the snow and mud. Then she went in the opposite direction.

Noises from the baby seat in the back of her SUV reminded him that they didn't have much time. "We can come back here later."

She hunkered down beside a pile of dirty snow. "Over here."

He joined her. The dark leather of the medallion stood out against the snow. The black design, etched into the leather, was a grizzly paw print.

Chapter Three

The coffee at the Morning Ray Café on the main street of Kenner City wasn't as good as the cinnamon-flavored brew at Emma's house, but Miguel signaled the waitress for a refill as he checked his wristwatch. Dylan was more than fifteen minutes late.

It wasn't like his by-the-book, precise twin to be off schedule by more than a couple of seconds. Ever since Dylan had arrived in Kenner City, he'd been preoccupied; the inside of his head was crammed full with old guilt and new grief. *Numero uno* was the recent murder of Dylan's friend and colleague, Agent Julie Grainger. He and three other FBI agents were working overtime on their investigation of Vincent Del Gardo, the former Las Vegas crime boss suspected of Agent Grainger's murder.

Miguel gave a nod to the cute, red-haired waitress who filled his coffee mug. When she grinned and crinkled her nose, her freckles danced. "How are things at the lab? Solve any big crimes lately?"

"Have you committed any?"

"Not today." She took her order pad from her apron pocket. "What else can I get you?"

"Nothing now, Annie."

She was one of the few people in town he knew by name.

He ate a lot of his meals at this cozy little diner where the burritos were good, and the posole was *primo*. The head cook and owner was Nora Martinez, the sheriff's mother.

Because it was after three o'clock with the lunch rush over and only four other people in the place, Annie lingered at his booth. "Waiting for somebody?"

"My brother."

"The FBI agent." Her smile grew ten times brighter. "He's really cute."

Women had always responded to Dylan as if he were a rock star, which never made sense. They weren't identical twins but resembled each other a lot, and the *chicas* never threw themselves at Miguel. "Better not let Dylan hear you call him cute. That's a word for baby ducks and puppies."

Annie laughed. "Handsome is a much better word."

If anyone had heard about the FBI investigation, it would be Annie or the people in the café, which was frequented by many of the local law enforcement people. "How much do you know about Dylan's investigation?"

"An agent got murdered. A woman agent. One of the other FBI guys was showing her picture around, asking if we'd seen her or noticed her talking to anyone."

"Thanks, Annie."

Miguel thought Emma might have picked up Agent Julie Grainger's name from talking to someone at the café or someone else who had seen the photograph. That'd be a logical explanation for how she came up with Julie's name. But it didn't explain the VDG symbol or the grizzly paw necklace.

Later this afternoon, he and other forensic technicians would process the necklace in the hope that they might discover the identity of the owner. They probably wouldn't be lucky enough to find fingerprints—not after it had been buried in the snow at the side of the road all this time.

How the hell had he missed finding the necklace when they first swept the scene? Sure, the leather was the color of dirt and would have blended in when there wasn't snow on the ground. Sure, they'd had other urgent tasks—dusting for prints, measuring skid marks, photographing footprints. Sure, there was a blizzard on the way. But he wouldn't easily forgive himself for overlooking such an obvious clue.

He had to be shown the way by a medium. By Emma. *La loca bonita.* A crazy, beautiful lady in a purple leather jacket.

Dylan came through the front door of the café and joined him in the corner booth. "Sorry I'm late."

"No *problemo.* You okay?"

"Don't worry about me, *vato.*"

Dylan had always been the tough guy, the star athlete, the macho leader of the pack. It bothered Miguel to see his brother rattled.

Annie rushed to their booth as soon as Dylan sat down. She placed a steaming mug of coffee in front of his brother and set down two pieces of apple pie.

"On the house," she said in a throaty voice. She leaned close to Dylan, giving him a glimpse of cleavage. "Is there anything else you want?"

Miguel couldn't resist this setup. "My brother likes whipped cream. All over his pie."

Dylan raised a hand. "Not necessary."

The waitress fluttered her lashes. "You can have all the whipped cream you want. Your name is Dylan, right? And I'm Annie."

And I'm yesterday's fish stew. Amused, Miguel leaned back in the booth and watched as his brother doled out the charm. The guy couldn't help it. He was a *chica* magnet.

When Annie finally moved away, Dylan said, "What's so important that I had to see you right away?"

"The sheriff and I met with a woman today. Her name is Emma Richardson."

Annie rushed back to their booth. "I love Emma," she gushed. "She's a real psychic, you know. She sees things. And she finds missing people."

"Thanks for your opinion," Miguel said in a quiet, firm tone of dismissal. The time for fun and games was over. He needed to talk seriously with his brother. "We'll call you if we need anything else."

"Enjoy your pie." She turned on her heel and flounced back toward the counter.

"A psychic," Dylan grumbled as he dug into his pie. "You interrupted my day to talk about a psychic."

"I was skeptical, too." Miguel kept his voice low so Annie wouldn't come running back over to them. "You know I don't like things that can't be explained by logic or science."

"You were always the smart brother. *El Ganso.*" He smirked. *"El Nerdo Supremo."*

"Because I think with my head, not my *huevos.*" Miguel fixed his twin with a cool gaze. This wasn't a time for joking. "I took the psychic—actually, she's a medium—back to the crime scene where Aspen Meadows disappeared. She had a vision that turned up an important piece of evidence."

Though Dylan continued to eat his pie, Miguel sensed that his brother was interested. "The sheriff still doesn't have any leads on the missing woman?"

"Not yet. I don't have much hope. Somebody who's missing for over a month is either dead or doesn't want to be found." He frowned. "But Emma Richardson is certain that Aspen is alive. They're cousins, and Emma is the guardian for the baby."

"The father hasn't come forward?"

"Not yet." Miguel took out the piece of paper Emma had used to make her notes from the vision. He spread it on the table in front of his brother. "She drew the design of the leather necklace we found at the scene. And also, she drew this."

Dylan picked up paper. His eyes narrowed. "VDG. Vincent Del Gardo."

"There was a symbol like this on that map you showed me—the map that Agent Grainger sent before she died."

Miguel and everybody else in the crime lab had tried every way possible to decipher that map. From satellite GPS to old-fashioned cartography, no one could make sense of those weird twists and turns. It didn't match any known roads. The map could have been the path of a spreading river. Or trails through the forest.

At the counter, Annie was joking and laughing too loudly with a guy who had been sitting there since Miguel came in. He overheard the word *psychic* and glanced toward them. They had to be talking about Emma, and that bothered him. He checked out the guy so he'd remember what he looked like. He wouldn't be easy to forget. Though big and barrel-chested, he was a sharp dresser in a fringed leather jacket with a turquoise yoke. The band around his cowboy hat was snakeskin with the rattles still attached.

Dylan tapped nervously on the tabletop. His voice went low and quiet. "What does this part of the note mean? A tall woman in an FBI jacket."

There was no easy way to say this. "Emma's spirit guide for this vision was Julie."

"She saw Julie?"

"In the same sense that she sees everything. In her head."

"If this is true," Dylan said, "it means that the missing woman is connected to Vincent Del Gardo. Connected to Julie's murder."

"*Sí*, I know."

"This is big. It opens a whole new line of investigation."

"Are you still searching for Del Gardo?"

Dylan nodded. "And for the money he's got stashed away."

Miguel had heard that Del Gardo's illegal fortune was in excess of fifty million dollars. Not an amount that could be tucked away in a tidy little suitcase. "Your map with the VDG symbol might lead to both."

"Let's see if your psychic can point us in the right direction."

BEFORE BABY JACK showed up on her doorstep, the bathroom in Emma's house had been tidy with feminine decorative touches. Now, she had no time for long baths, scented candles and fresh flowers. Her mosaic-tiled countertop held a variety of baby products. She'd known that her life would be different if a man moved in, but she hadn't expected pacifiers and butt wipes.

Confronting her reflection in the mirror, she dabbed a glob of spit-up off the shoulder of her beige turtleneck and ran a comb through her chin-length brown hair. Miguel had called and asked if he and his FBI brother could stop by and ask a few questions.

Miguel. She sighed. *Miguel Acevedo.* She wouldn't mind having him as a houseguest. He was definitely handsome with those green eyes and strong features, but his greater appeal came from his quick mind. She had to be alert when she was around him. He was a challenge.

Also, she needed him to find Aspen. *To follow the trail.* But where was this trail? Discovering the necklace in the snow was a start, but Emma had no idea what came next.

In the mirror, standing beside her, was Grandma Quinn. The resemblance between her and this blue-eyed, elderly lady made her smile.

Grandma said, "Why don't you change that shirt, dear?"

Emma didn't need fashion tips from the other side. "You know I had a vision about Aspen."

"About time."

"I'm supposed to follow a trail or a path. Do you know anything about that?"

"Change the shirt."

Grandma faded and vanished, leaving Emma frustrated. All too often, her spirit visits were cryptic hints and vague impressions instead of direct instructions. Why couldn't Grandma Quinn give her a street address or a phone number?

Grabbing the baby monitor, she hurried to the front door and onto the porch to wait for Miguel and his brother. Jack had finally fallen asleep, and she didn't want the baby wakened by two grown men tromping through the house.

When the car pulled into her driveway, a shiver of anticipation went through her, making her realize how glad she was to be seeing Miguel again. He gave her a lopsided grin that made her heart beat a little faster.

His twin brother resembled him, but she would never confuse these two men. There was something about Miguel that drew her closer. His was a healing presence, like the words inscribed on the back of his silver Chimayo medal.

As she shook hands with Dylan—whose handsome face was somehow enhanced by the scar on his chin—she had the impression that he was kind of scary. His eyes looked haunted. Not in the sense that he had ghosts hanging around him, but he had secrets, many secrets. And he had seen terrible things.

"I hope you two don't mind," she said, "but I'd rather stay outside. The baby's asleep, and I don't want to wake him."

She directed them to a flagstone path that led to the covered patio behind her house. The afternoon sun warmed this western exposure, and there were only a few patches of snow left behind from the blizzard. Within the month, she hoped to start planting her vegetable garden. Most of her other landscaping was shrubs and annual flowers, indigenous to the high plains so they didn't need much watering in drought years.

She sat at the round wrought-iron table with one twin on either side. Miguel held the piece of paper upon which she'd written her impressions from her first vision this morning. "We wanted to talk about the VDG symbol," he said.

With the V *standing for Virgin?* She sucked in a breath to keep from blurting an embarrassing comment. "I really don't know where that came from."

"How does that work?" Miguel asked.

"It's called automatic writing," she said. "Another way the dead communicate through me. I'm holding the pen, but they are directing the strokes. Some people call it channeling."

Watching her intently, he asked, "Does the name Vincent Del Gardo mean anything to you?"

She probed her memory and shrugged. "Nothing comes to mind."

"He's from Las Vegas."

"I've only been there twice." The memory made her smile. "I went to visit Aspen while she was going to college there. She thought, because I'm a medium, that I might be able to beat the odds at gambling. We tried roulette, craps and blackjack. I was lousy at all of them."

Dylan leaned forward. "Your cousin might have mentioned Del Gardo. He had interests in several casinos. Maybe she worked for him."

"I don't recall." In her mind, she repeated the name. *Vincent Del Gardo.* "Are you looking for him? Is he missing?"

"Maybe you can find him," Miguel said. "When you do

that missing persons thing with the sheriff, what's the process?"

"Everything I see or hear in a vision comes from someone on the other side. When I'm asleep, they come to me as if in a dream. When I touch something connected with a missing person, I sometimes intersect with the psychic energy of someone close to them who has passed away. I see them. And hear them."

"Give me specifics," Miguel said. "Last fall, when you told the sheriff that the missing boy was with his father in a motel in Durango, how did you do it?"

"I touched some of the boy's clothing. My vision came from his dead grandmother. She showed me a vision of the room, a wagon wheel and the number seven."

"You're a medium," Dylan said. "The FBI works with mediums. I get it."

Miguel asked, "Were you always like this?"

"When I was ten years old, Grandma Quinn appeared to me. I was old enough to know that my grandmother was dead and to understand what that meant."

"What did she look like?" Miguel asked.

"Just the way she looked in life. But not solid. The best comparison I can make is a hologram. Grandma Quinn wasn't scary, she hadn't come to frighten me. She gave me a warning. It saved my life."

Grandma Quinn had told her there was danger, told her that Emma and her mother had to leave the house. Though ten-year-old Emma wept and pleaded, her mother wouldn't listen.

Later that night, when her mother's abusive boyfriend came home, Emma fled. She ran next door to the neighbor's and hammered on the door. Remembering caused her hands to draw into fists. Sobbing, Emma had begged them to call the police.

They arrived too late. There was a fire in her mother's bedroom. Both she and her boyfriend were killed.

"Emma," Miguel said, "what are you thinking about?"

"A memory." She met his gaze and saw his struggle to accept what she was saying. "A real-life memory. I'm not crazy."

"We get it," Dylan said loudly, demanding her attention. "You knew the missing woman. Aspen Meadows."

"I grew up with her. After my mother died, I went to live with my aunt Rose on the rez." She gestured to her brown hair and blue eyes. "I didn't fit in with the other kids. Aspen used to tease me, and she resented that I was taking Aunt Rose's attention away from her. My main goal in life was to get off the reservation. I studied hard and got a full scholarship to University of Colorado when I was sixteen."

"You sound like my brother," Dylan said.

"El Nerdo Supremo," Miguel said.

"Perfect description." She laughed on the inside. "Anyway, Aspen and I got along better as adults. I kept pushing her to go to college, and she had finally finished her studies. She was coming back to the rez to be a teacher."

A cry from the baby monitor alerted her. "Excuse me? It's almost time for Jack's feeding. I need to get a bottle of formula ready."

She hurried into the house through the back door. Still listening to the baby monitor, she went through the motions of preparing the bottle and measuring the formula. *Vincent Del Gardo.* A casino owner from Las Vegas.

She glanced through the kitchen window. Beyond the patio where the twin brothers sat in conversation, she saw a third person—a man with a shaved head and a white beard. A ghost.

When he looked toward her and waved, she saw his black-framed glasses. He returned to his task, digging with a spade in the area where she would soon plant her garden. The hole grew quickly. He reached inside and pulled out a handful of gold coins.

She blinked, and he was gone.

The noises from the baby monitor grew more insistent, but she rushed outside to the patio table. "Buried treasure. Does Del Gardo have something to do with treasure?"

Dylan stood. "What did you see?"

"An old man with a shaved head and white beard. Thick glasses. He dug up a handful of gold coins."

"That description doesn't fit Del Gardo," Dylan said. "To the best of our knowledge, he's not dead."

"Maybe it wasn't him. The man I saw didn't seem like a crime boss. He was kindly. Like a favorite uncle."

"Do you know his name?" Dylan asked.

"No." If she'd known something as obvious as a name, Emma would have mentioned it. She didn't much care for Dylan's attitude. Though he'd been quick to accept her abilities as a medium, he seemed hostile.

"I want to show you the other VDG symbol," he said. "After I return to headquarters to pick up that evidence, I'll be back with my other colleagues."

"Not tonight," she said.

"What?" His tone was abrupt. Apparently, Dylan wasn't accustomed to having his decisions questioned. "Why not?"

"If this symbol leads to other evidence, I need to be free to follow the trail."

"The trail?" Dylan glanced toward his brother.

Miguel explained, "A trail of evidence that might lead to Emma's cousin."

"Tonight," she said, "I need to stay with the baby. Tomorrow morning, I have someone who comes in to watch him."

"Tomorrow morning, nine o'clock," Dylan said, turning

on his heel and stalking along the flagstone path toward the front of the house. "Let's go, Miguel."

He rose slowly. His gaze focused on the formula bottle in her hand. "If you want, I can stay. I can help with *mijo*."

Though it would be wonderful to have his help, she shook her head. "It's better for me if you go with your brother and calm him down. I don't want him to come back tomorrow with a dozen federal agents. I can't let this turn into a sideshow."

He gently took her free hand. "Dylan plows straight ahead like a powerboat and throws up a big wake. You need a more quiet approach. Like a silent canoe across the waters."

She smiled, appreciating his imagery. A silent canoe.

It had taken five long weeks for her to get any hint about Aspen's disappearance, and she didn't want to jeopardize this tenuous connection with a huge fanfare and many curious eyes watching her. "I want you to come back tomorrow with your brother. Only you."

He gave her hand a squeeze, and she felt a pleasant ripple chase up her arm.

"Tomorrow," he said. "You have my cell-phone number. Call me if you need anything."

She watched as he sauntered along the flagstone path, and she was tempted to call him back. Miguel made her feel safe and protected. She wanted him to stay close to her.

But there wasn't time right now to indulge in such a fantasy. She returned to the house and went directly to her bedroom where Jack's bassinette sat beside her four-poster bed. His little face scrunched up as he let out a loud cry.

"It's okay," she said. "It's okay, *mijo*." Miguel's word for the baby slipped easily through her lips. She liked the way it sounded.

As she lifted him onto her shoulder, she heard the front

doorbell. Was it Miguel coming back? She rushed through the house and opened the door.

Standing on her front stoop was a very large man in a fringed leather jacket with a turquoise yoke.

Chapter Four

Only a flimsy, unlocked screen door stood between Emma and this stranger. In spite of his colorful jacket, he was dark and dangerous. She didn't need a psychic vision to know that she'd be crazy to invite this man into her house.

He must have noticed her hesitation because he stepped back a pace and politely removed his brown cowboy hat. The band was snakeskin with the rattles still attached. His thinning hair, streaked with gray, lay flat against his skull. His attempt at a smile seemed like an aberration, as if his face were unaccustomed to friendly expressions.

"My name is Hank Bridger," he said in a whispery voice. "Are you Emma Richardson?"

"Yes." Still holding Jack on her shoulder, she calculated how long it would take for her to slam the door and race through the house to safety. She had a pistol on the upper shelf in her bedroom closet, but it wasn't loaded.

"Annie at the Morning Ray Café told me that you're a psychic. She gave me your address."

Thanks a heap, Annie. "What else did she tell you?"

"That you can help me." The attempted smile slipped off his long face. Deep lines carved furrows across his forehead and around his mouth. "Ma'am, I'd be willing to pay for your time."

"I'm sorry, Mr. Bridger. Annie gave you the wrong impression. I'm not for hire."

"I'm trying to find my brother. He's been missing since January, and I'm at the end of my rope."

She couldn't help being sympathetic to Bridger's cause. Like her, he was searching for a relative who had disappeared.

Jack wriggled on her shoulder and she lowered him to the crook of her arm. He waved his little arms and let out a yell. "The baby is due for a feeding. This isn't a convenient time."

"I can come back." He slapped his hat back onto his head. "Later tonight?"

"Not tonight," she said firmly. "But maybe tomorrow afternoon. I can't promise that I'll be able to help you."

"How does it work when you get these visions? Annie said you have to touch something that belonged to the missing person."

"Sometimes that helps. If you'll excuse me, I—"

Without warning, he whipped open the screen door, grasped her hand and pressed a round disc into her palm. He stepped back immediately, allowing the door to swing shut.

The suddenness shocked her. Who would have thought such a big man could move so fast? Looking down at her hand, she saw a hundred-dollar poker chip.

"Las Vegas," she said. That explained a lot. Bridger was a Vegas cowboy, not someone who actually rode the range.

"Vegas is my brother's hometown."

Was Hank Bridger somehow connected with Vincent Del Gardo, the casino owner? Though it seemed an unlikely coincidence, she firmly believed that everything happened for a reason. Bridger might lead to the next step on the path to finding her cousin.

She turned the chip over in her hand. The outer circle

of dark gold was edged with green letters spelling out Centurion Casino. She'd been to that Roman-themed establishment when she visited Aspen. She remembered lots of marble and elephant statues.

Bridger leaned closer to the screen door. "You see something. What can you tell me?"

Jack gave a series of yips—sounds that usually led to sustained wailing. And she couldn't blame him. He was hungry. "I have to go."

"Keep the chip," he said. "I'll be back tomorrow afternoon."

As he walked down the sidewalk, she closed the front door and flipped the dead bolt. Though it was possible that destiny had brought Hank Bridger to her doorstep, the fates weren't always kind. In her early morning vision, the man with the leather necklace wanted to kill her. Bridger—in his fringed jacket and snakeskin boots—wasn't that man. But there might be a connection. She needed to be cautious.

While she got Jack changed, she considered taking her gun down from the top shelf and loading it. Probably not a good plan. She hadn't fired the gun in over three years.

Leaning over the changing table, she nuzzled Jack's tummy. "I'd probably shoot my foot off."

He giggled in response.

"Yes, indeedy." She crooned as she picked up his tiny pink feet and kissed his toes. "Yes, I would. I'd probably shoot my footsie right off."

Having a baby in the house changed everything. If Emma had been alone, she wouldn't have been so concerned about Bridger. But there was more than her own safety to worry about. She might need help. It occurred to her that Miguel was only a phone call away.

With Jack freshly diapered and dressed in a green-and-yellow footed sleeper, she settled with him in the solidly built, antique rocking chair with the carved oak back. Before the baby came to live with her, she hardly ever used this piece of furniture. But the rocking chair made a perfect nest for bottle feeding. As soon as she plugged the nipple in his mouth, he slurped vigorously.

Her gaze surveyed her eclectic living room. From the clean lines of the beige patterned sofa to the burgundy velvet Queen Anne chair, she'd picked every piece with care, sparing no expense. She focused on the telephone resting on the spindle-legged table. Would Miguel think she was too needy if she called? Or was she being prudent and sensible? Hank Bridger was a menacing character who had come out of nowhere.

After Jack was fed, she paced with the baby on her shoulder. More than an hour had passed since Bridger came to her door. If he intended to return, he would have done so. Unless he was waiting for darkness.

Better safe than sorry. She picked up the phone and punched in the number on the card Miguel had left behind. He answered after the first ring. "Emma. What's wrong?"

As soon as she heard his voice, she felt like a coward. "I'm probably overreacting. But this guy showed up at my house, wanting me to help him find his missing brother. And he gave me a hundred-dollar chip from the Centurion Casino."

"I'll be right there."

"That's not necessary. I was just wondering if…"

He'd already hung up. As she disconnected, she felt herself smiling. For most of her life, she'd been on her own—proudly independent and able to take care of herself. This was a change. It felt good to have someone to call—a strong, capable man with intoxicating green eyes. A man who could watch over her and *mijo* Jack.

Standing at the front window, she watched through the Irish lace curtains as the sunlight segued into dusk. The house across the street had turned on their lights, probably getting ready to sit down to dinner. Should she offer Miguel something to eat? Like what? She hadn't taken anything out of the freezer this morning to thaw. Her plans for this evening were opening a can of soup or zapping a frozen dinner in the microwave.

His motorcycle thrummed as he swooped up her driveway and parked the sleek, powerful Harley. He wasn't wearing protective headgear. Not illegal, Colorado didn't have helmet laws, but she disapproved of the risk. At the same time, she loved the way his black hair was tousled by the wind. Still astride the Harley, he peeled off his dark glasses and stowed them in the pocket of his denim jacket.

Only once in her life had Emma dared to ride on the back. She'd been terrified. And exhilarated.

She scurried to the front door, flipped the dead bolt and opened it wide. Though the fading sunlight was dim, his green eyes glowed with reassuring warmth.

"I'm glad you called," he said. "I saw what you wrote on that piece of paper where you described your vision."

She'd scribbled a lot of things. "What was that?"

"You made a note. 'Aspen got away, but you will die.'" He stepped inside and looked around, peering into the shadows in the corners. "What made you write that?"

She remembered the faceless man with the knife, the darkness, the blade slashing toward her throat. Some of the things she saw weren't meant to be shared. "You can't take my visions literally. Sometimes, death doesn't necessarily mean physically dying. It could be a death of hope. Or well-being. Or a relationship."

"But I'm a literal kind of guy. You said that you were being chased. Then what?"

"The man with the leather necklace caught me. He had a knife. He said those words."

"The man who came to your door, was it him?"

"I don't think so. He's not the sort of guy who'd wear a beat-up leather necklace. His name is Hank Bridger. He's tall and broad-shouldered. Kind of a snazzy dresser."

"Fringed jacket? A hat with a rattlesnake band?"

She gave a surprised nod. "Now who's the psychic?"

"I saw him in the Morning Ray Café, talking to the waitress." He lifted Jack from her shoulder and nuzzled the top of the baby's head. "Hey, *mijo,* did you miss me?"

Jack gurgled and rewarded him with a great, big smile. He was so sweet, so perfect and innocent. If anything happened to him, she'd never forgive herself. "Bridger claimed to be searching for his brother. He gave me something that belonged to the missing man. A hundred-dollar chip from the Centurion Casino."

"Del Gardo has financial interests in the Centurion."

"I didn't get any particular vibe from the chip."

"No *problemo.* I can."

"Get vibes? How?"

"Fingerprints." He tucked Jack into the crook of his arm. "Show me the way to your computer. Let's do some quick research on Hank Bridger."

She walked through the living room, turning on lights as she went. At the end of the hallway, she opened the door to her office. Very few people had been inside this room. Not the woman who came in twice a month to clean. Not the sitter who took care of Jack in the mornings.

Emma had several reasons to keep her work private. If anyone found out what she was really doing at her computer, her financial well-being would be threatened. This secret couldn't be shared with anyone. Not even Miguel.

As HE WENT THROUGH her house, Miguel switched his brain to analytical mode, as if studying a crime scene. His work included more than collecting trace evidence. The greater clues often came from objects or decoration or color. He could learn much about Emma by studying her home. His first impression: feminine.

Even if he had spent way too much time noticing her slender waist and the way her hips flared into a sexy curve, he would have known a woman lived in this house because of the velvet chair, the lampshade with dangling red crystals and the pastel watercolor paintings on the walls. The paintings were signed, maybe originals. Many of the other items looked expensive. He concluded that Emma was a woman of varied tastes and had the money to indulge them.

Her office was different. Apart from the high-tech equipment, it was as plain as a monk's cell. No plants. No candles. No photos. Papers were stacked and sorted in bins. One wall, floor to ceiling, was solid books. In an alcove that had probably once been a closet, he saw file cabinets and shelving filled with supplies. Two long desks angled to form an L-shape. One side was a workstation with her desktop computer, scattered notes and books. The other held a printer, scanner, fax and copy machine.

Her office was designed for real-life, practical business—nothing psychic or weird. Nothing personal.

"Nice setup," he commented. "What kind of work do you do?"

"This and that."

An evasive answer if he'd ever heard one. "The sheriff said you were a consultant."

"That sounds about right."

Most people liked to talk about their area of expertise, but her lips pressed together as if holding back. Finding out what she did in this office was the key to understanding a different side to Emma.

He checked out the titles on the reference books. *How*

to Build a Bomb. Encyclopedia of Firearms. Deciphering Codes.

"If I had to guess," he said, "I'd say you were doing consulting work for the Department of Defense."

"Why on earth would you think that?"

"Your reading material looks like you're planning to take over the world. Or training to be a spy." The idea of Emma—a woman who wore purple leather—taking on the world of espionage tickled him. "Or maybe you want to be *macho.*"

"I'll leave that to you," she said as she swept her notes off the desktop and dumped them in the top drawer, which she closed tightly. "Why do you need my computer?"

He passed the baby to her and took a seat in front of the flat screen and keyboard. "I'll link with my computer at the lab, using my password. We'll see if your Hank Bridger has a criminal record."

Computers weren't his specialty, but Miguel knew the basics. Hooking up with the lab computer while he was in the field at a crime scene came in handy. He went through the steps, feeding in Bridger's name—Hank or Henry—for a nationwide search.

"Running this data could take a few minutes."

He stood and cleared his throat to cover the growling from his empty belly. The last thing he'd eaten was the apple pie at the café. When Emma called, he'd been in the parking lot of the Morning Ray, close enough to smell the rich, hot, spicy chili.

Food would have to wait. First, he needed to make sure Emma and *mijo* would be safe for the night. "Do you have a security system on your house? Burglar alarms?"

"Most of the time, I don't even lock the doors. Until recently, Kenner City hasn't been a hotbed of criminal activity." Parallel worry lines appeared between her eyebrows. "Can I offer you dinner?"

Mucho gusto. His stomach danced for joy. "I could eat."

"Let's go to the kitchen, and I'll see what I can scare up."

He followed her, catching a glimpse through the open door of her bedroom. The wood on the four-poster bed matched the dresser and side tables. More high-quality stuff. Even Jack's bassinette and changing table were classy. Since he knew she hadn't inherited money, he assumed that whatever kind of work she did in her office paid her very well.

She settled Jack into a baby seat on her kitchen table and flipped the switch on the CD player resting on the countertop. Soft music spilled into the room.

"Classical," he said.

"Not my favorite, but I read somewhere that Mozart is recommended for babies."

Not for any of the babies he knew, but Miguel didn't argue. While she dug through her refrigerator, he surveyed the room from a safety standpoint. The back door seemed solid but didn't have a dead bolt. The three windows looked like they'd been replaced recently and were double-pane. Not that the extra thickness would stop an intruder. If Hank Bridger wanted to get to Emma, those windows wouldn't be an obstacle.

"Do you ever worry about getting robbed?" he asked.

"Not so much. If I'm out of town, I pay someone to house-sit."

The only way for Miguel to guarantee she'd be safe would be to stay here himself. The sheriff didn't have the manpower to provide a bodyguard, and the same was true for the FBI. Law enforcement didn't get involved in protective custody until after an attack. Then, it was too late.

She pulled a container from the freezer. "Lasagna?"

He was starving, and it would take hours to thaw that brick of pasta. "I have a better idea. I'll make a run to the café and pick up a couple of burritos."

"Great idea. Cooking isn't really my thing."

After she shoved the lasagna back into the freezer, she whirled around and beamed an unexpected smile in his direction. The worry in her face disappeared. Her blue eyes shimmered like sunlight on a mountain lake.

The analytical side of his brain shut down. As he stared at her, he forgot the potential danger that brought him here. The soft piano sonata from the CD player painted the air with soft pastels, like her watercolor paintings—colors that suited a gentle, graceful woman with silky brown hair. He almost felt like they were on a date.

"Thank you for coming over here so quickly," she said.

"My pleasure." Earlier he'd been thinking he should stay at her house as a bodyguard. Now he had another reason altogether. He *wanted* to be here, *wanted* to be with her. "I should get going. To the café."

Shyly, she bit her lower lip. "Hurry back."

EMMA WATCHED THROUGH the front window as Miguel climbed onto his Harley and drove away. Calling him had been one of the best decisions she'd ever made.

Humming along to Mozart, she meandered into the kitchen, where she sorted through a few things she could cook for tomorrow. Cooking for Miguel? The thought was both exciting and terrifying. Her culinary talents had never progressed beyond making a salad. Preparing an elaborate dinner for one didn't interest her.

After a little tidying up, she went into her bedroom, placed Jack on the comforter and stretched out beside him. Since her reading time was limited to short spurts between baby care, magazines had taken the place of books. The glossy pages flipped through her fingers and landed on an article titled, "How To Make Him Hot For You."

She scanned the checklist: perfume, lip gloss, smoky

eyes, flirty clothes. Touch him frequently. Find out what you have in common. "Not much," she said to Jack. "We're pretty much opposites."

And she was far too mature to follow the advice of a magazine article. "But maybe a dab of perfume wouldn't hurt."

When she rose from the bed, she saw Grandma Quinn standing in the doorway. Her voice was a thin whisper. "Emma, get out of the house. There's danger."

"What?"

"Take the baby and run."

Chapter Five

Fear chased Emma backward in time—all the way back to when she was a child. Grandma Quinn had warned her of danger, told her to run away and save herself. In a way, she'd been running ever since. She'd spent her life avoiding risk, keeping safe.

"Why?" she asked the ghostly figure. "What's the danger?"

The pale lips of her grandma formed one word. "Run."

The sound raced around the room, bouncing off walls and ceiling, picking up volume and velocity. *Run, run, run, run, run.* It echoed like rolling thunder.

Grandma Quinn vanished.

Emma's course was clear. She gathered Jack into her arms, grabbed a blanket from the bassinette and shoved her feet into shoes. No time for anything else. Get away from here. Get away fast.

Halfway to the front door, she halted. This was her home, a place she'd lived for years and literally put down roots in the garden. Fear couldn't drive her away. She wasn't a helpless ten-year-old girl with no other option than running to the neighbor's house and beating her fists raw against their closed door.

She called the sheriff's private number. "Patrick, this is Emma. I think somebody's trying to break into my house."

"I'm on it."

And Miguel was on his way back to her house. She and Jack would be all right...unless danger hit before help arrived.

Her gun was tucked away in the closet. If she got it down and loaded, she could defend herself. With a baby in her arms? No way, that was impossibly dangerous.

What should she do? The frightened child that lived inside her wanted to run. The more reasonable adult countered with logic. If Bridger lay in wait outside the door, he'd easily overtake her before she made it across the yard to her neighbors. It was smarter to stay here, to wait for help to arrive. But if she waited too long...

As if sensing her internal struggle, Jack let out a wail.

She hugged him close. "Don't worry. I won't let anything happen to you."

In spite of the confusion and fear that clenched every nerve in her body, a plan formed in her mind. Her car was parked in the driveway right outside. If she could get to the car with Jack, she'd make a clean escape.

She raced into the kitchen and got her car keys from her purse. Go out the back door? Or the front?

Under her breath, she whispered, "Hurry, Miguel."

The wall clock slowly ticked off the seconds. He'd be here soon. He'd protect her and the baby.

As she bounced Jack to calm him, her gaze fixed on the back-door knob. It jiggled, started to turn.

She dashed through the house to the front door and flung it open. Crossing the yard in a few frantic strides, she ripped open the car door and dove behind the steering wheel. She slammed the door, locked it. Turning, she settled Jack into his car seat.

She'd made it. With trembling fingers, she plugged the

key into the ignition. She turned the key and heard a click-ing noise. The engine didn't catch. "No, this can't be hap-pening."

Her foot pumped the gas. Again, she tried to start the car. *Click, click, click.*

Her clever plan had left her trapped. In the moonlight, she saw a figure. A broad-shouldered man. Huge. Dangerous.

Stepping out of the shadows, he approached her car. His face was obscured by the flat brim of his hat.

Her hand rested on the door latch. Should she throw open the door and run? No, she couldn't leave Jack here alone.

The man came closer. Why was he after her? What did he want?

The rumble of a motorcycle cut through the night. It was the sweetest growl she'd ever heard. Miguel was here.

As his headlight flashed in her rear window, she watched the man who had been coming toward her turn away. He slid back into the shadows.

Emma leaped from her car and ran toward Miguel. Toward safety.

EYEBALLING THE BAGS OF FOOD he'd brought from the café, Miguel leaned back in his chair at the end of her kitchen table. Emma sat to his right. On the table beside her was the bouncy baby seat where Jack wiggled and added a running commentary of giggles and goos.

His conversation with the lady of the house hadn't been so cheerful. Moments after she threw herself into his arms, the sheriff had arrived with sirens blaring. Her concern about possible danger had turned into a tangible threat. The lock on her back door—a pathetically simple device—had been picked. The battery cable in her car had been de-tached, which was why she couldn't get a spark. Her at-tacker had meant to trap her with no means of escape.

Miguel tamped down his anger. It served no purpose for him to rage against this faceless coward. Better to move on and hope that their luck got better. Unfortunately, the coward had left no evidence.

The sheriff and his deputies spread out and canvassed the area. They found no witnesses. Though Miguel had dusted, he found no fingerprints. There were no footprints on the flagstone path leading around to the back of her house.

"Who was he?" Emma asked for the hundredth time. "You know more than you're telling."

"*Dios mio,* Emma. Let it go."

"I have a right to know who's after me. And why."

He felt guilty, blamed himself for exposing her to danger. The time for casual protection was over. The sheriff had promised frequent drive-bys throughout the night, and Miguel would stay with her as a bodyguard. His hand instinctively went to his gun holster. "I don't want to drag you deeper into the investigation. I've already told you too much."

"Miguel, please. I've spent most of my life running away, and I'm tired of hiding. More information can't hurt me." She straightened her shoulder. "And I might be able to help."

Solving crimes through her visions was a poor substitute for logic and forensics. But she had a point about information. If she knew what she was up against, it gave her an advantage. "I don't know all the answers."

"Tell me what you can." She rose from the table and took down two plates from the cabinet above the dishwasher. "While you're talking, we can eat."

He tore open the bags. Burritos, churros and posole. It was a feast.

She set a bottled water in front of him and picked at her own food. "Let's start with the easy part. Why would anyone come after me?"

He dodged the question. "Any man with eyes would come after a beauty like you."

"Oh, please. I'm an old maid. Thirty years old and not married."

"*Dios mio!* Thirty years old! You're an ancient crone."

In spite of herself, she grinned. "You're older than I am."

"Thirty-three. A decrepit, old bachelor." He bit into his burrito. "And proud to be unmarried."

"Really? No regrets?"

"Not on my part. But Mama says I owe her grandbabies."

On cue, Jack made a noise that was somewhere between the rat-a-tat of a machine gun and the bleating of a goat. His message was clear: pay attention to me. And Emma did. She reached toward him and tickled his tiny foot.

When she looked at baby Jack, her blue eyes filled with love. "Until this little guy got here, I never thought of myself as someone who would have children. I've always been kind of a loner."

"Except for pop-in visits from ghosts."

He was glad to see her hostile glare. When she had first run to his arms, she'd been devastated by terror. Anger was a much healthier response.

"You've gotten off the subject," she said. "Why is someone coming after me?"

"Are you sure it wasn't Bridger?"

Using her fork, she drew a circle around her head. "The man who came out of the shadows had a hat with a flat brim. Not like Bridger."

He shoveled down another forkful of food. His grateful belly had ceased growling. "I don't have solid evidence to prove why someone would attack you."

"I'll settle for assumptions."

"I have two," he said. "No, make that three."

"Just tell me," she snapped.

"*Numero uno.* Your cousin disappeared, and we still don't know why. She might have information that threatens the bad guys. Something she told you." He took a swig of water. "Did she mention any secrets?"

Emma shook her head, sending a shimmer through her straight, brown hair. "Nothing I can recall."

"We move to my second theory." He hadn't put these thoughts into words until this moment, but the logic fell easily into place. "You keep saying that Aspen is still alive."

"That's right."

"Whoever made her disappear the first time might want to make sure that she never comes back. Maybe he thinks you know where she's hiding."

Emma rose from her chair. "That makes sense. Since I have custody of Jack, I'd be the first person Aspen would call."

While she paced and gestured and talked about possible ways Aspen could make contact, he chewed slowly, reconsidering his theory. "The timing is wrong. Aspen has been missing for five weeks. Why wait until today to come after you?"

Her eyebrows lifted. "Coincidence?"

"It's better to stick with logic."

"You're right," she said. "Why today?"

As she considered, the wheels inside her head began to turn. Her fear dissipated. Using her mind grounded her, and he appreciated that trait. Her sharp intelligence appealed to him more than her *loca* visions.

"Are you ready for my third theory?" he asked.

She sat. "Shoot."

"You keep seeing things that are connected to Vincent Del Gardo—a convicted felon and dangerous man. Also, you led me to that leather necklace. The bad guys could be worried about what else you might figure out."

"How would they know about my visions?"

"We made no secret of contacting you." Using a tortilla, he sopped up the last bit of salsa on his plate. "In one day, you had visits from the sheriff, from me and from my brother, an FBI agent. Even a casual observer would notice."

"So this is your fault."

"A little bit. *Poquito.*"

When he came here this morning, he never expected a *loca bruja* to have valid evidence. However, as the day progressed, he should have been more careful in protecting Emma's privacy. Bringing Dylan to her house had been a mistake.

"Who are these bad guys you keep talking about?" she asked. "I want names."

"Put Del Gardo at the top of the list. He's involved in Julie Grainger's murder."

"Who else?"

"There's a hit man from Vegas—Boyd Perkins. He's after Del Gardo's fortune. Without conscience, he'll kill anyone who gets in his way." He pushed away from the table and stood. "And let's not forget Bridger. Even though you don't think he was the man you saw, he could still be a threat. Let's see if your computer gave us any information on him."

She nodded. "I'd forgotten about the computer search."

So had Miguel. A lot had happened since then.

They returned to her monk-cell office. His nationwide search through crime records had produced seven hits. None of the mug shots matched the man who gave her the hundred-dollar chip.

"That's a relief," Emma said, "because he's coming back tomorrow afternoon. It's good to know that he's not a criminal."

"Or he's using an alias."

She grumbled, "Do you always look on the downside?"

"The positive side comes when we nab *el hombre.* You shouldn't have invited him back."

"I didn't know he might be a bad guy."

"Shouldn't be a problem. I'll be here tomorrow." With the stroke of a couple of keys, he closed down her computer's access to his files. "I should get started on that right away. I want to take the hundred-dollar poker chip to the lab and run fingerprints. Then we'll know for certain if Bridger is a bad guy."

She held the door and waited for him to leave the office. "Whatever you need to do."

In the kitchen again, he turned to face her. "You need to come with me to the lab."

"Tonight?" She shook her head. "I don't think so. I don't usually take Jack out at night."

He shouldn't have to explain. She was smart enough to know what might happen. "It's not safe for you to be home alone."

She glanced at the wall clock. "It's almost nine."

"If I run his prints at the lab and find out that he doesn't have a record, we can eliminate him from the list of suspects."

She glanced toward the baby. "Is it safe for Jack to be in a lab? Aren't there a lot of chemicals?"

The crime lab was spotless—more sanitary than the average bathroom. His boss wouldn't have it any other way. But Miguel couldn't resist teasing Emma. "Dangerous chemicals all over the place. Oh, yeah. Every morning I get up and go to work in a biohazard zone. You should wrap yourself in tin foil, head to toe, before you go inside."

She exhaled an angry huff. "Do you ever stop making jokes?"

"Should I weep? Drip tears down my cheeks, wring my hands and wail?"

"Of course not."

Though he got a kick out of her flares of temper, he was

serious about the threat to her safety. "I'm not laughing when I say you're coming with me."

"It's been a long day," she protested.

He caught her arm and gently pulled her closer. "You need to hear what I'm saying."

"There's nothing wrong with my hearing."

"Then listen." He cupped her delicate chin in his hand, compelling her to meet his gaze. "A sleepy little town like Kenner City isn't supposed to be a place where there are murders, disappearances and threats. But the danger has come here. Just beyond these walls. Just outside these windows."

They were standing so close that he could feel the tension radiating from her as she said, "And I can't run from it."

"You're not alone," he assured her. "I'll be with you. Think of me as your bodyguard."

"Interesting. I've never had anyone guard my body."

"I'm glad to. *Me alegro.*" He gazed down at her beautiful face. Did she even realize how lovely she was? If he stayed this close, he wouldn't be able to resist her. "Bring me the chip Bridger gave you. Remember to hold it on the edges so you won't mess up any fingerprints."

She left the kitchen, and he inhaled a deep breath. At the moment, he wasn't thinking about the chip or the danger or the investigation. Emma filled his mind. He wanted to take her hand and pull her against him, to tangle his fingers in her hair, to kiss her lips.

He didn't entertain these thoughts lightly. He'd never been a *chica* magnet like his twin; he didn't have a string of past girlfriends twenty miles long. When Miguel found himself attracted to a woman, his feelings went deep. Too deep.

Emma returned, holding the chip with her fingers on the edges. Before she could give it to him, she stopped short and frowned. "You again," she said.

Her gaze aimed at the back door. When Miguel looked over his shoulder, he saw nothing. "What's up?"

"It's the bald man with the white beard. He's leaning against the door frame, flipping a gold coin in the air and catching it."

Nothing there. Nothing. *Nada.*

The attraction he'd been feeling came to a screeching halt as he remembered the very good reason why he couldn't get involved with Emma. *Oh, yeah. She's crazy. La loca bonita.*

Chapter Six

With a resigned sigh, Miguel said, "Tell me about this ghost."

"I guess it makes sense that he'd show up," Emma said. "I have a hundred-dollar poker chip in my hand, and this guy is obviously interested in cash."

Gruffly, he said, "As long as baldy is here, you can ask him a couple of questions."

"Interrogating the dead presents a challenge. They follow their own path with their own agenda, and they don't always choose to cooperate."

Miguel felt his jaw tighten. Not only did he have to put up with ghosts, but he had to respect their rules. "Try mentioning the Centurion Casino."

Staring into empty space, she asked, "Have you ever been to the Centurion Casino in Las Vegas?"

She paused as if waiting for a response. Then she asked, "Does the name Hank Bridger mean anything to you?"

He couldn't believe he was watching her talk to a man who wasn't there. "Is he saying anything?"

"Yes, but it doesn't make sense."

As if the rest of this made sense? "Tell me."

"He wants Callie to get what's coming to her."

"Callie? Are you sure he said Callie?"

"I'm positive. He said it again."

Once again, Emma had tapped into a part of the on-going FBI investigation. Callie MacBride was Miguel's boss—the head forensic scientist at the crime lab. She'd testified against Del Gardo. "Who is this bald guy? Ask his name."

She shook her head. "I don't think he's been dead for very long. He's already fading."

"Not yet," Miguel said firmly. "Ask him how he knows Callie."

Emma stared as if mesmerized. "A violent death," she whispered. "Cold. Dark."

"Whose death? Who's going to die?"

"His own death."

"Does he have a name?" He needed to pin this ghost down and make him talk. *Dios mio, could this be more frustrating?* "Emma, who the hell is he?"

"There's something about a crescent moon. He's show-ing me a little flag. There's something on it. A sliver of moon in the upper right corner. And a heraldry symbol."

"Of what?"

"It has the body of a lion and wings." She squinted. "He's coming closer so I can see. Too close."

Cold air blasted over Miguel. Icy fingers reached down his throat and clenched his lungs. What was this? What the hell was going on?

Emma must have felt it, too. Her skin blanched. Though trembling, she staggered toward the baby and leaned down to protect him. But Jack seemed unaffected.

Miguel caught her arms and helped her sit in a chair beside the table. The cold vanished.

"The chill of the dead," she said. "It's unlike any other sensation."

"Are you okay?"

Another shudder wracked her shoulders. "I hate when

they talk about how they died. It's intense. It feels like I'm there with them, like I'm dying."

He held both her hands. Her flesh was ice.

He wanted to warm her, to chase away her fears. He wanted to reassure her that everything was all right. But it wasn't.

Even if he surrounded her with an army of body-guards, she wouldn't be safe. He couldn't protect her from the dead.

AFTER SEEING DOZENS of movies and TV shows with forensic themes, Emma expected the Kenner County crime lab would be a high-tech facility where miracles of deduction were performed using a single speck of lint left at a crime scene. Instead, the lab, which was located on the third floor of an office building, seemed like a rather bland space with several partitions.

Miguel relocked the door as soon as they were inside, standing in a reception area. He picked up the baby carrier by the handle. "Here we are, *mijo*. This is where I work."

"He's impressed," Emma said dryly.

"He should be. We solve crimes here."

She peered around a corner. The lab was mostly dark since it was well after regular working hours. "Where do you keep all the really cool stuff? The spectro-analytic magneto machines?"

"This is a real crime lab. Not a movie." He arched an eyebrow. "We don't have billion-dollar tools. Hey, we don't even have theme music."

"I could hum," she offered.

"Spare me the Mozart."

As she trailed him down the hall, she realized that her concern about dangerous chemicals was utterly unfounded. These tile floors were polished to a high gleam.

Beyond the reception area, Miguel showed her to his half-wall cubicle, equipped with an average-looking desktop computer and a metal bookcase packed with volumes on crime scene analysis. Beside his in-box, piled high with work, was a single-framed photograph—exactly the same family snapshot that his deceased sister, Teresa, had shown her. She took a closer look. There were five children, including Teresa and the twins, Miguel and Dylan. A handsome family, all smiling.

He set the baby seat on the desktop and took a plastic baggie from his pocket. "I'll log this poker chip into evidence."

"Wait." She stepped in front of him. "There's no crime connected to that chip. It needs to be returned. Keeping it would be like stealing."

"Fair enough. I'll run the fingerprints, then give it back to you."

"Is it even ethical to investigate a person's prints without telling them?"

"Sure," Miguel said. "Especially if he's got a criminal record."

A slender, blond woman in a white lab coat came toward them. "Hello, Emma. Do you remember me?"

"Ms. MacBride." She'd brought Jack to Emma's house after Aspen's disappearance.

Miguel said, "This is Callie MacBride."

Callie? Her name was unusual; she had to be the same Callie the bald, bearded ghost had mentioned. His voice echoed in her memory. *"I want Callie to get what's coming to her."*

"You're working late," Miguel said.

"There's a lot to do." She peeled latex gloves off her hands, folded them and placed them inside the pocket of her lab coat. Each move was quick and precise. "I've been trying to extract evidence from the leather necklace. I can't believe we missed that clue."

Miguel turned to Emma and said, "Callie is the boss. *El Jefe.* She doesn't like our work to be less than one hundred percent *perfecto.*"

"Forensic science is seldom one hundred percent. I'll settle for ninety-seven. Maybe even ninety-six point four."

"Have you learned anything from the necklace?" Emma asked.

"After being buried in the snow, the fingerprints are too degraded to attempt a match. I checked with Luminol and found no blood trace." Though Callie was talking to Emma, her gaze focused on Jack, who looked especially adorable in his blue snowsuit and knitted cap. "He's grown since I saw him."

"The pediatrician says he's thriving." Emma wanted to get back to the necklace—one of the only clues to Aspen's disappearance. "Is there any way of telling who the necklace belongs to?"

"Not through forensics."

"It'll take research," Miguel said. "Tracking down the maker of the necklace, where it was sold and who bought it."

When Callie moved closer to Jack, Emma sensed the other woman's yearning. "Would you like to hold him?"

Callie needed no further encouragement. She whipped off her lab coat and folded it over the back of Miguel's desk chair. Efficiently, she unfastened Jack's safety belt and lifted him from the chair. He gave her a huge grin, accompanied by cackling noises.

Miguel chuckled. "Ah, *mijo.* He's playing you, Callie."

"He's flirting," Emma said.

"He's beautiful." As Callie snuggled the baby, her features relaxed and her complexion warmed. The cool scientist transformed into an earth goddess. "There's nothing more wonderful than a healthy baby."

Callie's maternal instincts made Emma wonder why she'd never felt that way. Did she lack the mothering hormone? Taking care of Jack hadn't come naturally to her. If she hadn't been able to go online for instructions, she wouldn't have had a clue about how to hold him or change him or feed him.

Nor had she ever experienced a real desire for children. When her friends talked about their biological clocks going off, she'd felt nothing.

Callie rocked on her heels. "You two take care of whatever you need to do. I'll stay with this little one."

Emma placed the satchel with Jack's supplies on the desktop. "He shouldn't be getting hungry for a while, but if he needs anything, it's in here."

"We'll manage." Callie nuzzled the top of Jack's head. "Won't we, sweetie pie?"

Emma hurried to catch up with Miguel, who was already halfway down the hall. He entered a room that reminded her of a high-school science lab with clean countertops, wet sinks and microscopes. The equipment wasn't incredible—not like the array of crime-solving tools she'd seen on television.

Miguel went to one of the stations, opened a drawer and took out a pair of aqua-colored latex gloves. "I want to get the fingerprinting done quickly in case *mijo* decides not to be a sweetie pie, and we have to leave."

She nodded. Though Jack had been behaving like an angel, that behavior could change in two seconds. She perched on a stool beside him and watched as he rolled up the sleeves of his shirt.

"We need to tell Callie," she said. "About the bald man with the beard. We should warn her."

"As soon as I'm done, we'll tell her about the ghost with a vendetta." He snapped on the latex gloves. "Callie can handle it. She's tough. After she testified at Del Gardo's trial in Las Vegas, a hit man came after her. She almost died from smoke inhalation after a fire at the lab."

"Del Gardo, again. He's in the middle of everything, like a spider in his web."

"Things turned out okay for Callie." He removed the chip from the bag. "The FBI bodyguard who was watching her is now her boyfriend. I won't be surprised if they get married."

"And start having babies. Callie looks like she's more than ready for a family." She observed as he lightly dusted the chip. She'd read about the fingerprinting process, but had never seen it done. "What are you doing?"

"Fingerprints leave traces of bodily oil. The powder sticks to them." He held the chip to show her the print. "A unique combination of arches, loops and whorls. We've got at least two distinct prints on this chip."

"One is probably mine," she said. "What comes next?"

"I use tape to transfer the print from the chip to a slide."

Concentrating, he performed this operation. First for one print. Then the other.

Her gaze no longer focused on his hands. She found herself staring at his profile, noticing his firm jaw and full lips. When he concentrated, his eyes narrowed and seemed to glow. His black hair fell carelessly across his forehead.

He stood up straight. "Then I run these fingerprints through AFIS."

"Automated Fingerprint Identification Analysis," she said.

He shot a suspicious glance in her direction. "How do you know about AFIS?"

"Research."

"What kind of research? Tell me about it."

"It's not important." And not something she could share

with him. Usually, she was more careful about keeping her secrets. "Where's this AFIS system?"

"Over here." He led the way to a computer with a large screen. After he accessed the program, he plugged in one of the slides. Half of the screen clearly showed the ridges and whorls of the fingerprint he'd lifted from the chip. The other half was a blur. "Then we wait while the computer compares this print to millions of others."

"You're good at this, Mister Science Guy. How did you get into forensics?"

"I started out in premed. Then I got sidetracked."

As a rule, Emma didn't like to pry into other people's business. Because of her own secrets, she understood the need for privacy. But she was dying to know more about Miguel. Perhaps his interest in law enforcement stemmed from the early death of his sister, Teresa. And what exactly had happened to him? How did he almost die? Why did he wear that medal from Chimayo? "What sidetracked you?"

"If you asked my brother, he'd say I'm too lazy to be a doctor."

"But that's not true."

"How is it that you know me better than my twin?"

She didn't bother running through the obvious deductions. A lazy man wouldn't get through college, follow an intense career, play guitar and fix his motorcycle in his spare time. "Let's just say that a little birdie told me."

"A ghost birdie?"

Teasing, again. "You're such a smart aleck."

"It's my gift."

"Well, it's a very irritating habit." His eyes shimmered. Laughing on the inside? "I don't know whether to punch you in the nose or kiss that smirk right off your mouth."

Kissing? Why did I say something about kissing? "I'm sorry. Um, I didn't mean to—"

"Let me make the decision for you." His arm slipped around her waist. With his latex-gloved hand, he brushed the hair off her forehead. "Kiss me."

She had too much on her plate to even contemplate the possibility of kissing. Or a relationship with Miguel? It wouldn't happen, couldn't happen. No matter how appealing he was. "But I—"

"Kiss me, Emma. It's the only way you'll shut me up."

"Oh, well, if I have to…"

She rose up on her toes, intending to give him a peck on the cheek. Her lips betrayed her. At the last second, she turned her head and kissed him full on the mouth, unleashing a flood of sensations that swept through her body and carried her inhibitions away. A lifetime of caution was gone in an instant.

This wasn't meant to be a real kiss, but her arms wrapped tightly around him. Her breasts crushed against his chest.

His lips parted. His tongue flicked against her lips, and she drew him inside her mouth. Happily breathless, she tasted him.

If this was a mistake, she hoped she would err again. A million times.

Chapter Seven

In the reception area, Emma perched on the edge of a chair beside the boxy sofa where Callie sat with Jack cradled in her arms. Miguel remained standing while he explained to his boss how Emma's visions worked.

She pretended interest in her purple sneakers, not daring to look at Miguel for fear she'd blush. His kiss had surprised her. She wasn't the sort of woman who slipped easily into relationships. Not that she wasn't willing to try, but her lifestyle simply didn't offer many opportunities to meet men. The solitary nature of her work kept her home. The only man she saw on a regular basis was the UPS guy who delivered her online purchases.

And that was okay. She was an introvert; being alone felt natural. And she didn't think of herself as being tragic or lonely. This was simply the way her life had turned out.

At the age when she should have been meeting men and dating, she'd gone to the university in Boulder where there were thousands of available men. But Emma kept to herself. She'd skipped grades and was only sixteen—younger than everybody else. Less experienced and sophisticated, she'd been a skinny, stringy-haired kid who had all the confidence in the world when it came to talking to dead people. But real life? Not so much. Besides, she needed to study furiously to maintain the straight-A average needed for her scholarships.

As a girl growing up on the rez, she'd been an outsider, a teacher's pet, a weirdo who had visions. None of the boys had given her a second glance. Emma had been nothing like her vivacious cousin Aspen, who was popular and always had boyfriends. If only Aspen were here. She'd have some solid advice on what to do about Miguel.

Emma shoved her feelings aside and focused on Aspen. Finding her cousin was all that mattered.

"I understand," Callie said after Miguel's explanation. "Basically, Emma is a medium who contacts people who have passed away."

Emma looked up so quickly that her neck snapped. "I saw a man who spoke of you."

"A man who's dead? Does he have a name?"

"Not that I know."

"What does he look like?" Callie asked.

"Average height and build, maybe with the start of a potbelly. He's completely bald. His beard is white, which makes me think he was older—probably in his early sixties—when he passed. Oh, and he wears black-frame glasses."

Callie shrugged. "Doesn't sound like anybody I know."

"I've seen him twice. He said that he wanted you to get what was coming to you."

"A threat?"

Frowning, Emma recalled the aura surrounding the ghost. "He isn't vengeful. There's something kindly about him. Both times I saw him, he was playing with gold coins. Does that bring up any associations?"

Callie shook her head. "Not a thing."

Miguel said, "Emma sensed that this ghost is recently deceased. Probably murdered."

"That's disturbing," Callie said. She held Jack closer as if to protect him. "How was he killed?"

As was often the case with Emma's visions, the actual circumstances of his death were unclear. The moment of dying seemed to come as a surprise to those who passed on. "Before he died, he was in a cold, dark place. He felt a sudden pain. Maybe he was shot. If I had to guess, I'd say he was attacked from behind."

Jack wiggled in Callie's arms. His nose wrinkled as he started making fussy noises. She stood and rocked him. "Does the baby need a bottle?"

Emma checked her wristwatch. She liked to wait as long as possible before his last feeding so he'd sleep longer. "I should check his diaper first."

"I'll do it," Callie said willingly.

Miguel grinned. "Should I get you a pair of latex gloves?"

"Don't be silly." She unsnapped Jack's outfit. "Miguel, take Emma to the computer with the facial recognition features and put together a composite picture of this ghost."

"Okay."

When he touched her arm to lead her through the lab, her muscles tensed, as if she needed to turn to stone to keep from melting into a puddle of lust and yearning. *What's wrong with me?* This behavior had to stop.

Walking beside him, she straightened her shoulders and tucked hair behind her ear. She needed to be in control. In a measured tone, she said, "I certainly hope I haven't given you the wrong impression."

"I asked for your kiss. And I enjoyed it, *mi loca bonita.*"

"Your what?"

"*Loca y bonita.* It's what I thought when I first saw you," he said. "It means crazy and beautiful."

He thought she was beautiful. Her spirits soared. "But I'm not crazy."

"Whatever you say." He sat in front of a computer screen and inserted a piece of software. "We use this program instead of a sketch artist. I think it works better. We'll start with the shape of baldy's face."

Though she wanted more of his personal attention, the technology distracted her. She'd used this morphing software before. "Start with an oval."

An oblong appeared on a blank screen.

"His eyes," Miguel said. "Close together or far apart?"

"Hard to tell with his glasses. Average spacing. Kind of squinty. And dark."

An image formed in her mind as she directed him through the other features, adjusting as they went. The emerging sketch reminded her of a Santa Claus caricature. "Can you make him older?"

Using the mouse, Miguel selected a box on the left side of the screen. Wrinkles appeared on the forehead and below the eyes. His cheeks hollowed. "How's that?"

"A little scary." In the blink of an eye, Santa Claus had aged by twenty years and looked like a derelict.

"We use this software with missing persons," he said. "If a kid goes missing at age four, we can get a pretty good indication of what he'll look like at fourteen. Or forty."

"Have you done it on yourself?"

He nodded. "I'm a very distinguished sixty-year-old man. Like a wise professor."

She believed him. Miguel had good bone structure; he'd be one of those men who stayed handsome as he aged. The faint lines at the corners of his eyes would deepen with experience. His cheekbones would be more prominent. And his lips...

She turned her attention back to the sketch. "The picture isn't quite right. His face is a bit leaner. And his nose has a bump, like it was broken."

He adjusted the likeness.

"That's it," she said. "I wish I could do better. With the beard, the bald head and glasses, it's almost like he's wearing a disguise."

Miguel printed the likeness. "Let's see if Callie recognizes him."

In the reception area, Callie stood and swung Jack back and forth. He wasn't screaming but not giggling, either. His forehead pinched in a little-old-man scowl. "I really think it's time for his bottle," she said.

Miguel held up the picture. "Do you know him?"

"He's familiar." She leaned closer, concentrating. "Yes, I've seen him. He was outside my house one night. I remember because he was staring. Watching. But I don't know who he is."

Emma took a bottle of formula from the carry-all. "Should I take Jack now?"

"If you don't mind, I'd love to feed him."

Callie took the bottle and settled comfortably on the sofa. As soon as the nipple touched Jack's mouth, he latched on and slurped with greedy abandon. If Emma hadn't known better, she'd think this baby hadn't been fed in days.

The outer door to the office opened, and a tall, rugged man strode inside. His steely-eyed gaze turned gentle as he beheld Callie with the baby.

She introduced him. "Emma, meet Tom Ryan. My very personal FBI bodyguard."

His huge hand enveloped hers. "Pleased to meet you, Emma. I'll be coming to your house tomorrow with Julie's map."

"You work with Dylan," she said.

"Yes, ma'am." He turned to Callie. "You're seven minutes late."

"Unavoidably detained," she said. "Do you recognize this little guy. It's Jack—Aspen's baby."

"Looking good, Jack." He settled on the couch beside her. Gently, he said, "You're going to have to give him back, you know."

"Of course." Callie looked toward Emma. "Is there anything else you can tell me about the ghost? What about the place where he died?"

"Cold and dark," Emma said.

"A cave," Miguel suggested. "Or a basement."

"That sounds right." She related the other details of her vision. "He showed me a little flag with a sliver of moon and a heraldry symbol. A lion with an eagle's head and wings. I think it's called a griffin."

"Griffin," Miguel repeated with a groan. "As in Griffin Vaughn."

"Makes sense," Callie said.

Miguel turned to Emma. "Griffin Vaughn is a wealthy businessman who bought the house that once belonged to Vincent Del Gardo. It's just outside Kenner City."

"Del Gardo had a house here?"

"The house is probably what brought him to this area after he fled Vegas," Miguel said. "Last month, during the blizzard, Griffin had intruders. Probably men who were looking for Del Gardo's treasure."

"Like Boyd Perkins," she said, recalling the name of the hit man.

"As a matter of fact," Callie said, "we found a fingerprint for Perkins at Griffin's house. Maybe your ghost was another of those intruders. You said that he liked to play with gold coins. That suggests a treasure hunter."

"Wait a minute." Tom scowled. "What ghost?"

"I'll explain later," Callie said. "It's complicated."

Emma saw the next step on the path that might lead to

finding Aspen. "We should go to Griffin's house. If that's where the ghost was leading me, I might be able to pick up some kind of clue."

"I concur," Callie said. "I'll arrange it for tomorrow."

"Schedule it for the afternoon," Miguel said. "In the morning, we're going over the map with Dylan and Tom."

Emma's day was filling up. There'd be no time for work, but it didn't matter. One of these clues could lead to her cousin. "I have a regular babysitter who comes in the morning. I'll have to make other arrangements for the rest of the day."

"I'll do it," Callie volunteered. "I'd be delighted to take care of Jack tomorrow."

Emma accepted the offer. One thing she'd learned about babies: you can't have too many babysitters. "We should be getting Jack home to bed. He looks like he's almost done with his bottle."

"Only one thing left to do," Miguel said. "Emma, let's see if AFIS turned up anything on Hank Bridger."

She trotted through the lab behind him, returning to the bland, sterile room where they had shared a kiss. It seemed like the walls should have been colored in passionate pink, but no. Nearing the computer, she recognized the mug shot. "That's him. Hank Bridger."

"That's not the name we have." Miguel tapped a few computer keys. "His original name is Henry Coopersmith, but he's got a string of aliases."

"So he's not an altruistic relative searching for his lost brother?"

"His occupation is listed as professional gambler."

A Vegas cowboy. Her first impression had been correct. "Does he have a record?"

"No outstanding warrants, but there's a record. A long

one. He's been charged with assault, robbery and even murder."

And he'd been standing right on her doorstep—only a few feet away from her and Jack. A belated shiver of fear trickled down her spine.

Miguel continued, "This Hank Bridger also has a very good lawyer in Vegas. With all these arrests, he's never been convicted of a crime, never spent one day in the penitentiary. Each time, he gets off. It's not a good pattern."

"Pattern?"

"Arrest charges combined with a slick lawyer, probably an expensive lawyer, suggests that Bridger considers himself above the law and has a big enough bank account to cover his butt." He swung away from the screen and looked at her. "Not many people can make a living as a professional gambler. Makes me wonder what else Bridger is getting paid for."

"Some kind of criminal activity, no doubt. He's very interested in finding the person connected to that poker chip."

He reached out and gently brushed his fingertips from her shoulder to her wrist. He clasped her hand, laced his fingers with hers. "Until we find out what Bridger is looking for, we'll consider him a threat."

"Sure, why not?" She tried to ignore the tingling in her fingertips. "Bridger. Del Gardo. Perkins. Is there anybody in Kenner County who isn't after me?"

"Maybe we should start an Emma Richardson fan club."

"I don't think these guys want my autograph."

She saw a flicker of amusement in his eyes. He slowly grinned. "You're going to be all right."

"Don't promise something you can't guarantee."

"Trust me, Emma. I'll keep you safe."

He squeezed her hand, probably intending to comfort

and reassure her. Instead, she felt an intense urge to run as fast as she could.

Having Miguel as a bodyguard might be more dangerous than facing criminals and hit men. Miguel had the power to shatter her heart.

Chapter Eight

After they returned to her home, Miguel closed the curtains, locked the doors and took his gun from the holster. He didn't carry a weapon on a regular basis, not like his twin. Dylan was the fighter; Miguel was a lab rat. He'd never actually fired at another human being. There had been confrontations, sure. But showing the gun had always been enough.

Not this time. The threat to Emma came from hardcore criminals. Murderers. It would take more than waving a *pistola* to bring them down.

He placed his gun on the spindle-legged table beside the sofa where he'd be sleeping tonight. Since Emma didn't have a guest bedroom, she'd piled sheets, blankets and a fresh towel on the sofa before she retired to her own bedroom to get *mijo* to sleep. Though the baby should have been tired from being out tonight, Jack was still making fussy noises. This would probably be a good time for Miguel to grab a quick shower. He grabbed the towel and went into the bathroom.

On the way to her house, they'd stopped by his little apartment and he'd picked up a couple of essentials: clean clothes for tomorrow, shaving stuff, a pair of pajama bottoms that had never been worn. Miguel slept naked, but he was pretty sure that Emma wouldn't go for that. After that one hot kiss, she'd retreated like a rabbit into the hole.

Standing in the shower with steaming water sluicing over his body, he remembered how she'd felt in his arms, how she'd pulled him closer. She'd tasted sweet, like warm honey. He shook those thoughts from his head so he wouldn't get hard. Emma the Rabbit would burrow even deeper into her hidey-hole if he went strutting through her house with an erection.

Stepping out of the shower, he toweled dry and dressed in the pajama bottoms and a faded black T-shirt. He returned to the front-room sofa.

The baby noises from her bedroom had gone silent. How many times did *mijo* wake during the night? It was after ten o'clock now. Jack would probably need another feeding around three or four. It would be an early morning wake-up call. Not that Miguel was planning on a deep sleep.

As a bodyguard, he needed to be alert enough to hear everything that went on in the house. The sound of glass breaking. The creak of a floorboard. He left the lights in the kitchen and the hallway on. Sometimes, a light was enough to deter an intruder. He made up his bed and stretched out on the sofa.

He'd never been one who required a lot of sleep; a couple of cat naps were enough to sustain him. He rested until a few minutes after two o'clock, when he heard Jack making restless noises.

Rolling off the sofa, he went to the bedroom door and peeked in. The light from the hallway shone on Emma, who was sound asleep in her four-poster bed. Her full lips were parted. Her breathing was steady.

This woman probably hadn't gotten a full eight hours of uninterrupted sleep since the baby came to live with her.

Miguel figured that—since he was already awake—he could give her that gift.

He went to the bassinette beside the bed and lifted the baby into his arms. "Hush, *mijo*. Let Emma sleep."

This was an exercise he'd performed dozens of times for his sisters and cousins. He changed Jack's diaper, went into the kitchen and prepared the formula. Sitting in the rocking chair while he fed the baby, Miguel realized he hadn't been much use tonight as a bodyguard. But as a nursemaid? He was *primo*.

After Jack finished eating, he looked up at Miguel with his big brown eyes. Wide-awake.

"Now's not the time to be cute," Miguel told him.

Jack giggled and waved his arms.

Putting the baby over his shoulder, Miguel began to pace, bouncing with every step. Instead of calming down and going back to sleep, Jack acted like he was on a carnival ride.

Miguel rocked and paced and hummed a lullaby. If he hadn't been concerned about letting Emma sleep, he would have placed the baby in the bassinette and allowed him to fuss for a few minutes before drifting off. That wasn't an option.

With Jack nestled in the crook of his arm, he strolled into Emma's office. Though it wasn't any of Miguel's business, he was curious about the computer research she did in here. Whenever he mentioned her work, she changed the subject. What was it that she did?

He could have opened the desk drawer and looked at the notes she'd been quick to hide when he was in here before, but that seemed too much like spying. Still, there was nothing wrong with studying objects in plain sight.

Her filing cabinets weren't labeled. Without rifling through the papers on her desktop, he saw nothing obvious that pointed to her secrets. He focused on her bookshelf, which seemed to be divided between reference material and fiction.

One entire row was leather-bound classics. Lots of Jane Austen. The only other author who had several hardbacks in a row was Quinn Richards—a bestselling author who wrote hard-boiled spy thrillers.

Jack wiggled, and Miguel brushed a kiss on the baby's head. "Your auntie has a dark side. She likes to read shoot-'em-up books."

Or not. All of these thrillers were in pristine condition, as if they'd never been cracked open. He read the titles: *Ghost of a Chance. Passing for Dead. Code Breaker.*

He took one of the books off the shelf. "Quinn Richards."

Emma had spoken of her grandma Quinn. Her last name was Richardson. Could she have written these books? Sweet, quiet Emma in her pleasant little house?

On the back cover jacket were several quotes about "pulse-pounding adventure" and a head-and-shoulders photograph of Quinn Richards in a black leather jacket. According to the caption, the author was penning his next thriller in an undisclosed location. Like Kenner City?

Miguel studied the photo. Though masculine, there was something familiar about the blue eyes and the high cheekbones.

Earlier tonight, he and Emma had used software to create the accurate picture of the bald ghost. With the touch of a computer key, he could add twenty years to a person's face. Or change them from blond to brunette. Or from a woman to a man. This cover photo was the result of that same kind of morphing.

Quinn Richards was Emma Richardson.

Miguel looked down at the baby, who had finally fallen asleep in his arms. "For now, we'll keep your auntie's secret. Okay, *mijo?*"

THE NEXT AFTERNOON, Emma followed Miguel into the parking lot outside the crime lab where they'd left Jack with Callie.

On this bright, sunny April day with the snow from last month's blizzard mostly melted, the roads were clear and perfectly safe for riding a motorcycle. She had no reason to be scared, but her pulse was racing at a hundred miles an hour—a speed she hoped to only experience in her imagination. The glare from the chrome on his Harley flashed ominously. A death machine. That was what Grandma Quinn always said about motorcycles.

He unlatched the carrier on the back and took out a black helmet with orange-and-red flames. Not a reassuring design.

She looked longingly at her car. "Wouldn't it be safer if we drove?"

He placed the flame helmet in her hands. "I thought we decided it was best to leave your car here in case Callie needed to use the baby seat for Jack."

"I guess we did."

She hoped Callie wouldn't need the car, but better safe than sorry. And Emma was grateful for Callie's offer to babysit while they went to Griffin Vaughn's house to see if the bald ghost's clue had any significance.

Emma didn't have positive feelings about the path their investigation seemed to be following. Earlier this morning, when she'd met with Dylan and Tom Ryan to see if she could pick up anything from the map with the VDG symbol, she'd felt nothing. This piece of paper supposedly came from Agent Julie Grainger, and Emma had expected Julie to appear. No such luck. The map made no sense— just a tangle of scribbles leading to several dead ends.

Dylan had left her with a copy of the map, and she'd traced the lines several times with her finger. Nothing.

After getting a full night's sleep for the first time since

Jack came to live with her, she should have been sharper and more attuned. Instead she was wildly distracted, unable to think clearly—a state of mind that she blamed entirely on Miguel. All her senses seemed to focus on him. Her vision sharpened when she looked at him. Her ears filled with music when she listened to him speak. His scent was like some kind of wonderful, masculine perfume.

Nonetheless, she didn't want to ride on the back of his Harley. "If somebody is really after me, won't I be more exposed on the motorcycle?"

He shrugged. "On the bike, we can make a fast getaway."

Oh, good. "What does that mean?"

"Off-road." His voice held the teasing lilt that she was beginning to dread. "We can dash across the hillsides to places where cars can't go. Like a Motocross racer."

"Those guys on motorcycles who swoop twenty feet in the air?" Recalling glimpses of that sport on television, she gasped. "They do flips and they crash, Miguel. They crash hard."

"But you like adventure—pulse-pounding adventure."

What was he talking about? He sounded like a blurb on one of Quinn Richards's book jackets. *Pulse-pounding? Fine, bring it on.* She plopped the helmet onto her head. "I'd like to stop at my house first. It might help if I take the chip from the Centurion Casino with me to Griffin's house."

"How so?"

"When I was holding it last night, the bald man appeared and he's the one who pointed us toward Griffin. If I'm holding the chip, he might come again."

"Whatever you need." His own helmet was a Darth Vader black with a visor. He climbed on and waited for her to mount. "Do you need goggles?"

"Will sunglasses do?"

"*Perfecto.*"

After taking her sunglasses from her purse and draping the strap of the purse across her chest, she slipped onto the black leather seat behind him. "Any other instructions?"

"Hold on to me. Don't wave your arms. Don't jump around."

She wrapped her arms around his torso and leaned against him. In spite of her rampant fear, the full body contact felt wonderful. Her heightened sense of touch made her superaware of his lean strength and the wiry muscles beneath his denim jacket.

He cranked the motor; the Harley roared to life, shuddering beneath her. She tightened her grip, holding on for dear life. Though she told herself to lighten up, she couldn't. Her arms clamped around him in a death grip.

The Harley eased forward in a smooth glide. They were on their way with breezes swirling around them.

She stared at the edge of the road, aware that they weren't moving too fast. If she fell off at this speed, she'd probably only break a couple of bones.

When they halted at a stop sign, Miguel turned his head and asked, "Having fun?"

"Not yet."

But the motorcycle wasn't as scary as she'd expected. Miguel handled the bike with skill—not going too fast and carefully obeying all the traffic rules. By the time they got to her house, she'd relaxed enough to breathe normally. It seemed that she had an instinct for keeping her balance, leaning when he did. When she dismounted, her legs wobbled.

"That wasn't so terrible," she said, taking off her helmet and shaking her hair. "And very practical. Good gas mileage."

"Practical." He flipped up the visor. "That's why Hell's Angels ride Harleys."

"I'll grab the chip and we can be on our way again."

She hurried up the sidewalk, taking her keys from her purse. The main benefit to riding behind him was the close body contact. They fit together perfectly.

Unlocking the dead bolt, she hurried through the front room and dining room. She'd placed the chip in a drawer in her kitchen so it wouldn't get lost in the baby paraphernalia that threatened to consume every flat surface in her house. She pulled open the drawer, reached inside and grasped the chip.

A shape flickered in her peripheral vision.

Before she could turn her head, a rough hand closed around her arm. He yanked her around to face him.

She stared up into the expressionless eyes of Hank Bridger.

Chapter Nine

Emma should have been terrified. Bridger's rap sheet included murder charges. Even though he was dressed like a dandy—from the rattlesnake band on his hat to his polished snakeskin boots—he was a dangerous man.

But he had broken into her house, violated her personal territory. She was furious.

"Miss Emma," he said, "we had an appointment this afternoon."

"I don't recall setting a time." Her lips pinched together. "Awfully sorry, Mr. Bridger."

"Tell me where to find what I'm looking for?"

"The treasure," she snapped. "Del Gardo's millions."

"That's right." He easily abandoned the pretense that he was searching for his missing brother. "Del Gardo owed me over a hundred grand, and I can prove it. That money is mine. And you're going to tell me where it is."

Like hell I will. "How did you get into my house?"

"The back door was open."

A lie. She locked the doors before they left. "I'll be happy to return your hundred-dollar chip, but there's nothing more I can tell you."

His grip on her arm tightened. When he leaned close, she could smell his sickeningly sweet aftershave. "I'm a poker player, Miss Emma, and I'm damned good at reading people. I'd advise you to tell me what you know."

He was a huge man. He could break her arm as easily as snapping a twig. But she didn't think Bridger wanted to hurt her. He needed her visions to help him find the money, and he seemed to actually believe that she would do him that favor—track down Del Gardo's millions.

"Do you believe in ghosts, Mr. Bridger?"

His cold black eyes registered no emotion whatsoever. "What do you see?"

Emma cast her gaze to his left. She saw nothing and wasn't a poker player. Still, she bluffed. "There's a ghost beside you. A man who blames you for his death."

When he turned his head and shoulders, the fringe on his jacket bounced. He stared at the empty space where she was looking. "Where?"

"He wants revenge. Can't you hear him wailing? Can't you feel his fiery red eyes staring at you with ultimate hatred?"

He dropped her arm and took a backward step, teetering on the heels of his fancy boots. "I feel nothing."

Another lie. His poker face slipped. Bridger might be a cold-blooded, godless thug, but he was superstitious. That was why he came to her in the first place. That was her advantage.

Emma had no weapon. Her physical strength was no match for Bridger. But her imagination was enough to chase him away. "I'm part Ute, Mr. Bridger. I grew up on the rez."

"So?"

"Unless the dead rest easy, they will rise. Like the dreaded Manitou that kills with one blow and devours souls. The Ghost Dancers of my people call forth the dead and they come, seeking revenge from those who wronged them."

He jabbed a finger at her. "Witch. You tell them to leave me alone."

"No one can stop them."

They both heard the front door open. Miguel called out, "Emma, what's taking so long?"

Bridger went to the back door. "This isn't over. When I come back, you'd better have answers for me."

He dashed through the back door, leaving it swinging open on the hinges.

Her threats of undead vengeance clogged her throat, making it hard to breathe. The anger that helped her face Bridger switched to fear. She slid down the cabinets to the floor. With her knees pulled up, she buried her face and whispered a thank-you to her aunt Rose, who had taught her the lore of her people—so many stories of ghostwalkers and the Manitou. Those myths had saved her.

Although afternoon sunlight poured through her kitchen window, darkness wrapped itself around her. The danger she wrote about and imagined in her Quinn Richards books had become her reality. *This is what it's like to face the threat of death.*

She felt Miguel's hand on her trembling shoulders. "Emma, what's wrong?"

"Bridger. He was here, waiting for me."

"Where did he go?"

"Out the back door." She lifted her head. "Only a minute ago."

Miguel rose, went to the door and stepped outside. She noticed the gun in his hand. A new terror propelled her to her feet. Bridger's superstitions would keep him from harming her, but Miguel had no such protection.

He stormed back into the house, grasped her hand and kept moving, dragging her behind him toward the front door. "I think we can catch him."

"What? On the motorcycle?"

"That's right."

As she stumbled after him, her battered emotions—the terror and the rage—coalesced into one word. "No."

"I can't leave you here alone," he said as they approached the Harley. "Put on your helmet."

"A helmet decorated with the flames of hell? No."

"I want to see what kind of vehicle he's driving. To get his license plate number." He placed the helmet on her head. "Get on."

"There won't be any shooting?"

"Not from me."

Against her better judgment, she climbed onto the back of the Harley. Surely, there were easier ways to get a license plate number, like checking with motor vehicle registration. But Bridger was the king of aliases. His car could be registered under any number of names. There had to be—

Her mind went blank as Miguel swooped down her driveway into the street. The sheer power of the Harley shuddered through every muscle in her body. Holding on took all her strength. She was riding on the back of a rocket.

The familiar sights of her neighborhood whirled past in a wild collage. She saw the tall spruce tree on the corner. Oh, God, they were going to hit the tree.

Miguel turned fast. Disaster averted.

But she was slipping. Her sense of balance was gone. Her clumsy weight would cause them both to fall. To crash and burn.

He circled her block, darted a few streets to the west. Then back.

Then he stopped. "Got it. He's driving a black SUV. I got the plates."

She could only make a small peep.

"Are you okay back there?"

She peeped again.

"Hang on. We're going back to your house."

In just a few moments, they were in her driveway again. Emma caught her breath and climbed off the shiny, chrome beast. From her scalp to her toenails, she was trembling. It took an effort to remove the helmet, walk to her front door and collapse on the sofa in the front room.

While she caught her breath, Miguel strode through her house, making sure no one else was hiding in a closet. He came back and squatted down in front of her. "You did good, Emma."

"I thought I was going to die."

He winced. "I never should have let you come into the house by yourself."

His expression was contrite. She didn't tell him that facing Bridger had been far less terrifying than their wild ride. "I'm all right."

"It's time to find you a real bodyguard, instead of a lab rat. My brother never would have made such a mistake."

"Don't blame yourself."

"Who else? I see no other *estupido* in this room."

"*Estupido?*"

"Idiot. Moron." He took out his cell phone. "I'm calling the sheriff. With a license plate number, he might be able to pick up Bridger and bring him in for questioning."

"Good."

"Then we'll find you another guard."

She didn't want a different bodyguard. Miguel made her feel safe while at the same time not restricting her. When he disconnected the call, she stood on shaky legs and said firmly, "I want you."

"You do?"

"I want you to be my bodyguard. I trust you, Miguel. I can't have someone hovering over me, waving a gun."

He moved closer. "If anything had happened to you—"

"But it didn't." She touched his cheek, reassuring herself

with his nearness. "My mind needs to be free and unclut-
tered if I hope to have more visions. I need to see. It's the
only way I'll find Aspen."

"You're a good woman, Emma."

"And a pain in the neck. A burden."

"A precious burden."

He enfolded her in his arms and pressed his mouth
against hers. His strength absorbed her shivering fear. His
intimate touch roused a passion she'd never experienced
before. She wanted him. In every possible way.

ALTHOUGH EMMA SAID she could manage the rest of the
ride to Griffin Vaughn's house on the Harley, Miguel called
on his twin for help. Dylan showed up with his vehicle,
which Miguel drove with Dylan in the passenger seat,
keeping an eagle eye on the road ahead and the surrounding area. Emma sat in back.

In spite of her reassurances that he was a good bodyguard, he knew he'd made a mistake. Never should he have
allowed her to enter her house alone. The thought of her
alone with Bridger turned his blood to ice. The bastard
could have killed her.

Nor would he be casual about the installation of burglar
alarms at her house. He told her to cancel the appointment
she'd made with a Durango-based company who promised
to be out tomorrow afternoon. Not fast enough! Miguel
arranged with Bart Fleming from the lab to set up a security
system today.

Miguel wouldn't take any more chances with her safety.
She was more to him than a mere witness, much more. He
hadn't felt this way about a woman in years. Maybe ever.

He concentrated on the road ahead, constantly checking
his rearview mirror in case they were followed.

"You're jumpy as a cat," Dylan said.

"Staying alert."

"Relax, *vato*. You've got it under control. Everything is okay."

Easy for him to say. Dylan had been trained in protecting witnesses. This job was new for Miguel.

Dylan glanced over his shoulder toward Emma. "Let me get this straight. Bridger told you that he was after Del Gardo's treasure."

"That's right."

"And he thinks you know where it's hidden."

"But I don't," she said. "I can't imagine where anybody could hide fifty million. That has to be a truckload of cash."

Miguel agreed. "Del Gardo can't be carrying around that fortune with him. He's had plenty of time to convert the money. It could be precious gems. Or certificates of deposit."

His brother was quick to refute. "An amount that large would trigger alarms. The FBI has no record pointing to any such transaction."

"Use your imagination, *vato*." Miguel resented the way Dylan thought the FBI knew everything. In this case, they were as stymied as the Kenner County sheriff's department. "Del Gardo could have loaded his cash on a plane and flown to an offshore bank."

"Oh, sure." Dylan scoffed. "There he was—in a tropical paradise with enough money to last more than a lifetime, then he turned around and came back here. Why? And why did Julie make a map?"

"Maybe he stayed on that tropical island," Emma said. "Are you sure he's in Kenner County?"

"Bridger seems to think so," Dylan said. "So does Boyd Perkins. Just a few weeks ago, Miguel found Perkins's fingerprints at Griffin Vaughn's house. That happened during the blizzard when Griffin and his assistant, Sophie, were snowed in."

In the distance, Miguel spotted Griffin Vaughn's home. Perched on a hillside above an outcropping of rock, it was a modern structure, two stories, with wraparound windows. "Almost there."

Emma craned forward. "Wow! That's quite a house."

With the money she made as Quinn Richards, the best-selling writer of thrillers, she could probably afford a place like this. Instead, she chose to live in her cozy little home and pretend to be nothing more than a researcher. When the time was right, he'd find out why. "Griffin is a millionaire businessman from California."

"Why would he move here?" she asked. "I mean, the house is spectacular. But Kenner County?"

"Haven't you noticed?" Dylan chuckled. "Everybody in California wants a second home in Colorado."

Miguel added, "It's a place where they can escape after the San Andreas fault breaks apart and an earthquake drops L.A. into the Pacific."

Dylan nudged his arm. "All those California guys want to be cowboys like us."

"Some *vaquero* you are. When was the last time you were on a horse?"

"I can ride. Better than you." He looked back toward Emma. "When he was a kid, my brother got thrown from a sway-back mule."

Miguel launched into his own story about how Dylan tried to impress a girl by signing up for bull-riding at a local rodeo. As he told Emma about Dylan's spectacular failure and how he walked with a limp for a week, Miguel's spirits lifted. Picking at his twin felt normal and right.

The door to Griffin's home was answered by Sophie LaRue, his executive assistant who was about to take a more permanent job as Griffin's wife. She was a pretty woman with blond hair and a bright smile.

"Come on in," she said. "Griffin and his son are out, but if there's anything I can do to help, name it."

Miguel wasn't sure what they were looking for, and he didn't want to tell Sophie that they'd been sent here by a ghost. After he introduced Emma, he peeked toward the living room. "You've made some improvements since the last time I was here."

"You know how it is when everything is under construction." Sophie beamed at Emma. "One day, it's chaos. Then next, voila."

She made a sweeping gesture with her hand, nearly knocking a vase off its pedestal.

"Your home is beautiful," Emma said. "Classic."

"She likes classic," Miguel muttered to his brother.

"And you like her," he whispered back. "Remember, *vato*. I'm best man at your wedding."

"And you get your pick of the prettiest bridesmaid."

They watched as the two women oohed and aahed over the view and the new furnishings. Finally, Miguel stepped forward. "I think we need to see the basement."

"Right," Emma said. "A cold, dark place."

"It's still a mess," Sophie said. "But come along."

Emma hesitated. She was staring at a space near the entrance. Nothing there.

Neither Dylan nor Sophie noticed anything odd about her behavior, but Miguel knew what was happening to Emma. She was following one of her ghosts.

Chapter Ten

Descending the staircase into the basement of Griffin's house, Emma shivered. The chill of the dead.

The first time she'd seen Julie Grainger, the murdered woman's presence had been faint. Her voice, a mere whisper. Now her spirit was stronger. Her FBI jacket flapped around her as she darted back and forth, coming too close for Emma's comfort. Anxiously, she beckoned. "This way, this way."

Emma picked her way through the basement. The construction work that had been finished so beautifully in the upstairs was in progress down here. Concrete pylons leaned against half-finished walls. Piles of debris cluttered the cement floor.

Trying to do as Julie instructed, Emma moved deeper into the mess. The cold sank into her bones. The only light came from bare bulbs hung across the ceiling. Shadows loomed all around her.

When Miguel came close behind her, she was glad for his presence and his warmth. "You're following someone," he said. "Is it baldy again?"

She shook her head. "It's Julie."

He winced. "Don't tell Dylan. He still mourns her passing."

Julie's voice intruded. "I'm sorry," she said. "I brought heartache to my friends. I'm so sorry."

Her comment startled Emma. The people she saw in her visions didn't usually acknowledge anyone else. They spoke only to her and often in riddles. In life, Julie must have been an exceptionally straightforward person.

"Tell him," Julie said. "Tell Dylan not to grieve. Let him know I'm all right. Beyond pain, beyond sorrow."

Emma whispered in Miguel's ear. "She wants Dylan to know that she's fine. And she regrets causing him pain."

Dylan tromped up behind them. "Hey, are you telling secrets?"

Miguel held up his hand as if to forestall any teasing from his brother. "I'll tell you later."

In spite of their constant verbal jabs, these twins had an obvious bond of understanding. Their expressions mirrored each other. Dylan immediately comprehended the gravity of the situation. "I can wait."

Sophie stumbled beside them, catching herself before she fell. In her hand, she held a huge flashlight. "Where are we going?"

Emma pointed the way, trailing Julie as she wound around unfinished walls. Taking a quick turn, the ghost disappeared behind a concrete pylon.

Emma hurried to catch up. The others followed.

Julie stood beside a concrete slab that leaned against one of the outer walls of the basement. A stack of old timber from the demolition had been piled in this corner.

Faintly glowing, Julie said, "This is what you're looking for. This is your path."

The path to finding Aspen? Emma could only hope that they were headed in the right direction. Something in this basement could lead to her cousin.

"Dig here," Julie said. "Keep digging."

Like a wisp of smoke, she vanished.

Shivering, Emma pointed. "Here. Dig here."

Sophie came up beside her. "Are you all right?"

This charming woman had been given zero explanation about what they were doing there or about Emma herself. She looked into Sophie's guileless eyes. "I should tell you a few things about me."

While Miguel and Dylan dug through the debris, Emma explained her abilities as a medium. Sophie nodded calmly. She was one of the least judgmental people Emma had ever met.

"I'm not surprised," Sophie said. "I thought there might be ghosts in this house."

"You're quick to accept."

"I'm from California." Mimicking a brainless beach beauty, she fluffed her blond curls. The pose didn't suit her; Sophie was much too intelligent to play dumb. "Half the people I know have regular appointments with psychics. Mostly charlatans. But you're the real deal, aren't you?"

"Afraid so." She was quick to add, "I can't see the future. I don't do counseling and I don't make my living from my visions."

Sophie nodded. "What kind of work do you do?"

"Consulting and research. I work from home on my computer."

The familiar lie slipped easily through her lips. Emma wished she could tell her real profession. Not that she wanted the praises that were sure to be heaped onto Quinn Richards, the bestselling thriller writer. But she liked Sophie and wished she could be honest with her. "And you? You're an executive assistant to Griffin Vaughn?"

"I was. But we fell in love." A simple declaration, spoken with heartfelt tenderness. "We're going to be married."

"Congratulations." If Griffin shared her passion, Emma would venture an obvious predication: these two would be happy together.

"Hey, Emma." Miguel called to her from the pile of clutter that he and his brother were taking apart piece by piece. "Are you sure this is the right place?"

"Positive."

"Aim that flashlight over here."

Sophie moved closer and focused the light on the stack of old wood. As Miguel and Dylan worked, dust kicked up around them. Tiny motes swirled and danced in the bright beam that cut through the semidarkness.

"If you don't mind my asking," Emma said, "why did you think there were ghosts here?"

"The man who built this house was that Las Vegas mobster, Vincent Del Gardo. A convicted felon. I think he brought a lot of bad karma in here with him."

Bad karma made sense to Emma. Her aunt Rose often did a smudging ceremony to purify their house on the rez, burning sage and other herbs in an earthen bowl and using the smoke to chase away negative thoughts or presences.

If she and Sophie became friends, she'd offer to do that ceremony. Right now, Emma had other concerns. Finding Del Gardo seemed to be key. He could lead her to Aspen. If she touched something that had belonged to him, it might call forth another spirit to point her in the right direction. "Did Del Gardo leave anything behind?"

"Bits and pieces," Sophie said. "This basement was his wine cellar. Some of this scrap wood is from the racks."

She doubted that holding the splinters would be useful. "Sometimes when I touch something that belongs to a person, I can pick up a sense of where to find them."

"Terrific." Again, Sophie readily accepted a statement

that many people might consider outrageous. "I'd feel a lot better if I knew Del Gardo was in custody."

"Did he leave any of his belongings?"

Sophie thought for a moment before speaking. "There was the wine itself. A whole case of it. Griffin and I opened a bottle. I'm no connoisseur, but I could tell it wasn't very good."

"A wine bottle probably won't help me. I need something more personal."

"Oh, this wine was personal. He was bottling it himself. There was a symbol on the label—a bunch of vines twisted around his initials. VDG. Vincent Del Gardo."

Emma blinked. Sophie had just given her the explanation for the symbol she'd drawn in a trance—the symbol on Julie's map. "We have to tell Dylan about this."

Before Emma could interrupt the brothers, Miguel made a discovery of his own. He held up a wooden plaque, eight inches square. Burned into the wood was the VDG symbol.

"That's it," Sophie said. "That logo was on the labels of Del Gardo's wine."

Miguel and Dylan exchanged a glance. Though they weren't identical, their expressions matched. Simultaneously, they shook their heads.

"A wine label," Dylan muttered.

"Look at the vines," Miguel said. "It's obvious. You should have figured this out before."

"Me? You're supposed to be the smart one."

"When I have all the facts," Miguel said. "Did you know Del Gardo made wine?"

"Does it matter, *vato?*"

Emma spoke up, repeating Julie's words. "Keep digging."

Miguel turned toward her and held up the plaque. "Isn't this what we were supposed to find?"

"It's a clue, but there's more. A path."

They went back to work, clearing the area until there was only one large slab of concrete leaning against the wall.

Dylan smacked the flat of his hand against it. "We can't move this without a crane."

Miguel reached into the narrow space behind it, feeling against the wall. "There's something back here. It's wood."

They juggled the flashlight between them, trying to see what was behind the slab. After much discussion, they decided the best thing was to try to move it. One twin stood on each side. They braced themselves. As soon as they touched the slab, the concrete moved easily. Both men jumped back.

Emma covered her mouth to keep from laughing out loud.

"Fake rock," Dylan said. "It's lightweight."

Miguel checked the floor. "There are rollers on the bottom. It's on a track."

He shoved the concrete aside, revealing a small wooden door, only five feet tall.

Dylan jiggled the door handle. There was no lock, and it opened smoothly on well-oiled hinges. *"Dios mio,"* he said as he ducked and stepped inside. The darkness swallowed him, then he popped back out. "It's a tunnel."

Miguel was right behind him. "Looks like Del Gardo made himself an escape hatch when he built this house. If the law came looking for him, he'd have a getaway."

"And a way back inside," Sophie said. "When we were snowed in, this must be how the intruders gained access. Del Gardo himself could have been hiding down here."

Miguel took a pair of latex gloves from his pocket and slipped them on. "I don't have enough gloves to go around. The rest of you, don't touch anything."

Sophie moved to the front of their little group. She shone the flashlight into nearly impenetrable darkness.

Emma had been looking for a path. Grandma Quinn told

her to follow the trail. This tunnel had to lead somewhere. Entering seemed like the right thing to do.

But something held her back. She heard Julie's voice. A whisper. One word. "Murder."

MIGUEL HAD REALLY WANTED to explore the secret passageway. As a crime scene, that tunnel presented forensic challenges he'd never face again. Not to mention the potential for uncovering a hell of a lot of evidence. Besides which… it was cool. What guy wouldn't want to crawl around in a mobster's getaway tunnel?

But Emma came first. She'd pulled him back from the entrance, insisting there was something else they needed to do first. A different direction they needed to take.

Miguel had no choice. As her self-appointed bodyguard, he had to stay with her. He'd called in other experts from the crime lab.

Upstairs in Griffin's house, he paced in the living room while Emma stood, glowering through the panoramic windows, impatient to get started. One of her ghosts had given her a new lead, and she wanted to get on it. *Too bad.* Before they went anywhere, Miguel needed to do his job.

Via radio transceiver, he was in communication with the team from the crime lab—Bobby O'Shea and Ava Wright. They'd raced over here as soon as he called and were already making their way through Del Gardo's tunnel. According to what they told him, a narrow bore led from the wood door in the basement and ran for approximately fifty yards before hooking into the twisting tunnels of an underground mine.

Bobby's voice came through Miguel's receiver. "It appears that somebody's been living down here. There's a bedroll, a trash bag, some clothes, discarded water bottles."

"How's the air?" Miguel asked.

"Not bad. There must be shafts to let in fresh air, but I don't see them. When we turn off our high-beam lanterns, it's total darkness. I mean, totally. You can't see an inch in front of your nose."

"No messing around, Bobby. Don't turn off the lights."

"This place is incredible." Bobby was young, inexperienced and enthusiastic. "Like being in the bat cave."

Ava spoke up. "Don't worry, Miguel. Everything is under control. I'm recording our progress on video. And taking lots of pictures."

"Be sure to document the bedroll and keep going. See where the tunnel leads."

"There's a fork ahead," she said. "We're on an incline. We'll go right."

"Keep me posted."

These old mines were dangerous. There could be cave-ins or rock slides. He was glad his crew came equipped with hard hats, gloves and heavy coats.

Emma pivoted on her heel and stalked toward him. "Are you done yet?"

He was sick and tired of jumping every time a ghost said boo. "What's the hurry?"

"It's almost sunset." She gestured toward the windows. "We need to take care of this before dark."

All she'd told him was that this direction was important. He'd resigned himself to the fact that his scientific training and expertise had proven to be less effective than her visions. But he wanted some details. This time, he needed a solid sense of what the hell he was getting himself into. "Take care of what, Emma? What are we looking for?"

She lowered her voice. "I didn't want to mention Julie in front of Dylan, not until you've had a chance to talk to him."

"What did Julie tell you?"

"Murder. That was all she said. Murder." Her full lips pursed. "After that, I had a series of impressions. A road leading away from the house. Three pine trees up on a hill. The VDG symbol. And a crescent moon like the one on the flag baldy showed to me."

Nice list. Murder, road, trees, VDG, moon. Might as well wrap it up with a partridge in a pear tree. "What does it mean?"

"Here's what I think." She spread her hands as if laying out a tidy explanation. "Del Gardo killed somebody and left the body near those trees. As for the moon? I don't know."

These guessing games were driving him crazy. Why couldn't her visitors from the other side be more direct? "But you didn't actually see a body."

"Well, no."

"Julie could have been talking about her own murder."

"I suppose so."

From his receiver, he heard Bobby's voice. "We took a couple of wrong turns. We're back where we started."

Miguel turned on the speaker button. "Try again."

"We need to mark the turns we're taking. Or maybe we could get a really long string to roll out behind us."

"Or leave a trail of bread crumbs like Hansel and Gretel." Miguel couldn't keep the sarcasm from his voice. "Don't mess up the crime scene."

"Got it."

He turned back to Emma. "I should be with them. The tunnels are a real source of evidence. I could be looking at facts, fingerprints and DNA. Julie led us there for a reason."

"Then she pointed me in a different direction." She showed no sign of backing down. "If you don't want to come with me, I can follow this lead by myself."

"I won't leave you unprotected." Not after what happened the last time.

"I'm not in danger from Bridger. He's a superstitious man who thinks I know where Del Gardo's treasure is hidden. He's not going to hurt me until he finds out what I know."

"So he's not going to kill you," he said. "All he might do is abduct you and force you to tell him about the treasure."

"Force me?"

"Break your arm. Shoot off your kneecap. Maybe cut off your fingers."

The worry lines between her fine eyebrows deepened. "I hadn't thought of that."

Of course, she hadn't. Reality wasn't her thing.

Emma wasn't an investigator. She was a woman who wrote novels about crime where the bad guys were always caught and the good guys never got injured. She talked to dead people and turned up clues for other people to investigate.

"Here's another reason I can't leave you alone," he said. "Boyd Perkins? He's probably the first person who tried to break into your house. You remember that, don't you?"

"Of course."

"And Perkins is a cold-blooded killer."

"But he doesn't want me. He's after Aspen."

"Do you think he'd leave you alive? He kills witnesses."

He saw fear in the tightening of her jaw and the darting of her eyes, but she remained determined. "I have to take the risk. This could be the next step toward finding my cousin."

If she was right and there was a body hidden nearby, they'd be smart to locate the corpse before dark. Miguel knew from experience that night predators could do a lot of damage to a crime scene. "We'll follow your lead. But only for half an hour."

"Fair enough." Her features relaxed, and she gave him a dazzling smile. "Thank you, Miguel."

His gaze lingered too long on her lips before he blinked and purposely looked away. He'd be a fool to let her know how easily she could charm him into doing whatever she wanted. All it really took was a smile from her, and he caved.

He followed her to the door. *Vamanos. Let's go. Off on another wild ghost chase.*

Chapter Eleven

Driving his brother's car, Miguel crept along a rutted dirt road that circled away from Griffin's house into rugged mountain terrain. The road narrowed to one lane—not much more than a ledge carved into the rock. He glanced toward Emma. "In your vision, did you see me busting the axle on Dylan's car?"

"I don't predict the future," she reminded him.

"Right." That would make life too easy. At least, this road was on the sunny side of the cliff, which meant all the snow from the blizzard had melted and there was no ice to contend with.

She stared past him through the driver's window toward the arid valley that spread below. "I miss Jack," she said.

"First time you've been away from him?"

She nodded. "Callie would call if there was anything wrong. Right?"

"The only problem might be prying sweetie pie Jack from her arms. We'll pick up the baby after Bart Fleming gets here. He called and told me he's almost done with the burglar alarm system at your house."

"You're coming home with me? I thought you were going to stay here and investigate the mine shaft."

"I stay with you." How many times did he have to tell her? "I'm beginning to think you don't want me around."

"Not true." Her hand rested lightly on his arm, then withdrew quickly. A shy touch. Like a feather in the wind. "You make me feel safe."

And he liked that she felt like that. He'd never been a protector before. "What made you think of Jack?"

"This land. These valleys and mountains. I want Jack to connect to his birthright as a Ute. Aspen would have wanted him to…" She caught herself. "She'll be back. She'll be able to introduce Jack to the land where his ancestors were born."

He wished he could reassure her.

Through the receiver, he heard Ava's voice from the tunnels. "Miguel, I think we're finally headed in the right direction."

"Toward the exit?" he asked.

"You wouldn't believe all the twists and turns. We're going to need a map of this mine system."

"Some of the old silver mines in this area date back to the 1800s," he said. "Those old prospectors made up the rules as they went along, jumping from one vein to another until the ore played out."

He thought there might be a GPS program to map the underground tunnels. "Get back to me when you find the entrance."

"Ten-four," Ava said.

The road ahead branched into a fork. Miguel stopped the car and turned to Emma. "Which way? High or low."

"I'm not sure. The road going up looks a little wider."

He revved the engine and climbed, hoping he'd find a turnaround at the top. Backing down this road would be hell. As he reached a wide level spot, she pointed. "There. Those are the three trees."

He climbed out of the car and trudged behind her as she hiked up the gravelly hillside. The odds against finding a body hidden in the mountains were astronomical. He'd worked with search-and-rescue teams before. Even using heat-sensing scanners and helicopter surveillance, they often failed to locate people who disappeared. This rugged land reclaimed the dead, turning dust to dust.

Emma reached the trees. Standing under the spreading boughs, she rested her hands on the trunk as if to draw a signal from the roughened wood. He didn't question her process; she got results.

As he joined her, she turned in a slow circle. This behavior was new. "What are you doing, Emma?"

"Looking for a crescent moon. Maybe there's a piece of jewelry. Or half of a wheel rim."

In his investigations, Miguel was accustomed to searching for details. He'd developed an ability to focus, shining a mental spotlight on the scene of a crime. The earth beneath their feet was soft, still holding moisture from the recent snows. Only a few yards away, he saw a footprint.

Cautiously, he approached the perfect indentation of a square-toed cowboy boot. Larger than average, it was probably a size thirteen or even fourteen. Boyd Perkins was a tall man, over six feet. As was Bridger. Either one of them might have made this print.

Emma stood beside him. "Looks like somebody besides us has been here."

"It's a good print. We'll make a cast of it. Be careful not to mess it up."

He looked in the direction the toe was pointing. Finding such a precise print was an anomaly in the wilderness, but he made out another heel. And another.

Looking ahead, he saw broken branches on a shrub. Signs of a scuffle. "Stay back, Emma."

Being careful not to disturb anything in the immediate

area, he studied the ground, the pine needles, the vegetation. "Blood."

Across the flat surface of a rock, he saw a smear. Though he wouldn't be sure until he tested, it looked like dried blood. Emma's theory about a murder taking place was gradually being backed up by physical evidence. "There was a struggle here."

"But no body," she said.

He climbed a few steps higher. A fresh nick on the bark of a pine trunk could have been caused by a bullet. He turned a hundred and eighty degrees and stared down the hill.

"What are you seeing?" she asked.

"Ironic." He laughed out loud. "You're asking me what I'm seeing?"

"I am."

"Gathering evidence," he said. "I'm trying to piece together what happened here."

"Well? What happened?"

"I can't be sure. I don't like to make an analysis until I have all the facts."

"Give it a shot." She gave him a wry grin. "I make deductions from almost nothing."

"Which is why we're different," he said. "It seems to me that one man was in pursuit of the other. They struggled. The pursuer pulled a gun and fired. The man being chased continued, trying to get away. But why was he running uphill?"

"Why not?"

"If someone was coming after me with a gun, I'd try to put distance between us. Going downhill is faster." He turned again and looked uphill. "Unless he was running toward something."

The late afternoon sunlight slanted through the trees and deepened the shadows on the rocks. On the flat surface of a heavy boulder, a concave groove etched a shadow in the shape of a crescent. "Do you see it?"

"The crescent moon."

Together, they approached the boulder. The land had been recently disturbed. Branches were torn from shrubs. Stones were overturned, their muddy side facing up. The debris piled against a crevasse on the left side of the crescent boulder.

He shoved aside one of the rocks, revealing part of a leg and a foot in a running shoe.

His fingers itched to tear these rocks apart, but he'd wait for a proper deconstruction of the crime scene. Even if the killer had been wearing gloves, he'd leave traces of evidence.

Emma gasped. "It's a grave."

For someone who routinely hung out with the dead, she seemed shaken. Her arms wrapped around her waist, and she shuddered.

"You're frightened," he said.

"I've never seen a murder victim before. Not in the flesh."

It never got easier. Though Miguel kept his emotions hidden behind an attitude of scientific detachment, he felt empathy for the victims. In his investigations of crime scenes, he always treated the deceased with respect.

Glancing down, he realized that his hand had closed around the silver medallion he always wore around his neck. Silently, he offered a prayer. *May this dead man rest in peace.*

"I know who it is," Emma said. "The bald man with the beard."

"Is he here? Do you see him?"

"No, but I sense him. He suffered before he died. Attacked from behind."

He remembered what she'd told him about baldy's death. "You said he was in a cold, dark place."

"I must have been wrong."

From the hillside above them, Miguel heard a shout. He looked up and saw Ava and Bobby. Looking down from a ledge, still wearing their hard hats, they waved and shouted. "Miguel, what are you doing here?"

He might ask the same question. "Is this where the mine tunnel comes out?"

"This is it. The entrance to the abandoned silver mine."

A cold, dark place. Miguel recast his thinking. If the bald man had been concentrating on those tunnels when he died, it would explain Emma's impression of cold and dark. "He was running *toward* the mine."

"To escape," she said. "The mine was his destination, his safe haven."

"Which explains why he was running uphill."

This simple piece of the puzzle was answered. Now, Miguel faced the big question: who was he running from?

EMMA FELT GUILTY for pulling Miguel away from both scenes of investigation—the tunnels and the grave. But she was glad that he'd come home with her and Jack. Finding the body was an uneasy reminder that these men—Boyd Perkins, Hank Bridger and Vincent Del Gardo—were capable of murder.

The newly installed security system at her house should have made her feel more protected. Not only did it blast an alarm if anyone tried to break a window or open a door, but there were also surveillance cameras at the front and back door. Also, Sheriff Martinez had promised to have a patrol car cruising regularly through her neighborhood.

Lots of people were keeping an eye on her, but she still looked to Miguel as her protector. His presence made her feel safe. In the meantime, as a bonus, she had the pleasure of his company.

They'd already cleaned up after dinner, which was a simple matter of dumping paper plates since they'd ordered in a pizza. In the living room, she spread a quilt on the floor and placed Jack in the center on his back. His tiny legs kicked in time to Mozart from the CD player.

Sitting in the rocking chair, she glanced toward the kitchen, where Miguel was on his cell phone, talking to Callie from the crime lab. Emma saw Grandma Quinn standing in the doorway, waggling her finger in a chiding motion.

Emma heard Grandma's voice inside her head. *Babies shouldn't be on the floor. There are germs.*

In a quiet voice, Emma replied, "Jack needs to be in different places, with different things to stimulate him."

Who told you that? Grandma huffed.

Though she'd read about stimulating baby's senses in one of the baby books she'd purchased online, Emma wasn't about to tell Grandma that she preferred the advice of experts. Instead, she looked up and asked, "What do you think of Miguel?"

Grandma patted her hair as if primping. In her day, she'd been a beauty. *A handsome fellow.*

"I've kissed him. Twice."

Good for you, Emma.

As Miguel strode into the room, Grandma vanished.

He squatted down on the floor beside Jack but looked up at her. "I heard you talking."

Not wanting to relay the message that her deceased grandma thought he was cute, she said, "Chatting to Jack."

"Whatever you say, *loca bonita.*" He turned his attention to the baby. "You're getting a workout, *mijo.*"

"I hope he'll tire himself out before bed," she said. "What did Callie tell you?"

"The dead man had a shaved head and white beard. From his premortem bruising, he appeared to have been in a fight before he was shot in the back, three times. Estimated time of death was forty-eight hours ago."

The bald man had been dead before Emma had her vision about being chased by a man with a knife and her psychic floodgates opened. There must be a connection between Aspen's disappearance and the dead man. "Do they know his name?"

"No identification yet." Miguel picked up one of Jack's toys—a brightly colored plastic rattle—and jiggled it over the baby's grasping fingers. "They'll get started right away on a preliminary autopsy. Once the crime lab has the bullets, we'll know more. Our ballistics expert is *primo*."

Oddly enough, his crime lab shop talk about autopsies and ballistics didn't seem out of place while he played with the baby. "Did they find other evidence near the grave?"

"No fingerprints. The killer must have been wearing gloves." He tickled Jack's tummy. "They've got samples of the dried blood and made a cast of the boot print, which doesn't do us much good until we have a boot to compare it to."

"But the boot print didn't match the dead man?"

"No. Must have been the killer. It's a size-thirteen boot, so he's probably a big guy. Like Bridger or Perkins. Not Del Gardo. He's average height."

"But still dangerous," she said.

"When a man is holding a gun, size doesn't matter."

When Miguel glanced up at her, Emma lost her train of thought. As Grandma Quinn noted, he was a handsome fellow. Even after the long, strenuous day they'd had, his green eyes were sharp and alert. He didn't look tired at all. A teasing smile played on his lips.

She sank to her knees on the floor beside him. As he spoke, she watched his mouth, not really hearing his words as he talked about Del Gardo and his secret tunnel leading from the silver mine into the house he'd built.

The room had gone quiet, except for the noises Jack

made, and she realized that Miguel was looking back at her as if expecting a response. She had no idea what he'd been talking about. She cleared her throat. "Did they find evidence in the tunnels?"

"I just told you that."

"Sorry, my mind was wandering."

"They found clothes, trash, food, water. The preliminary theory is that Del Gardo was living in there, using the tunnels as a hideout."

"Could it be where he hid the treasure?"

"That's another theory," Miguel said. "We'll know more after the evidence is processed. Everybody at the lab is working overtime."

"I feel guilty for pulling you away from your work."

"No *problemo*. I'm exactly where I want to be." His voice was gentle, almost musical. "I like hanging out with a crazy, beautiful *chica*."

She felt a warm flush rising from her throat. "You wouldn't rather be at the crime lab?"

"My brother is the workaholic in the family. As for me? I'm not so intense. Life is too short to spend every minute working."

His gaze warmed her face, and she knew that she was blushing. "I agree."

"You're doing me a favor by getting me away from the crime lab. I haven't had much of a social life since I moved to Kenner City. Everything focuses on the lab." He gave Jack a final pat and stood. "And I have a project that I can do right here. Is it okay if I use your computer?"

Though she liked to keep her office sacrosanct, she couldn't refuse him anything. Scooping the baby off the floor, she also stood. "What's your project?"

"Research. I need to dig up information on the bear claw necklace we found near Aspen's car."

So much had happened that she'd almost forgotten that necklace—their first real clue. "Where do we start?"

"We'll check a couple of search engines to see if we can figure out who made the necklace and who sells similar designs. If we're lucky it'll trace to a shop that keeps receipts."

In her office, Miguel settled into her desk chair facing the computer screen. She noticed him glancing at her bookshelves where the jackets of her several Quinn Richards books stood out in brightly colored relief against her other reference books. Should she tell him her secret?

Long ago, before the first book was in print, she'd signed an agreement with her publisher not to reveal her identity. Their marketing department still thought it would hurt sales if the public knew that these action-adventure espionage books were written by a thirty-year-old virgin who lived quietly in a small town in rural Colorado. After her second book, the true identity of Quinn Richards had turned into a guessing game for critics and fans who supposed the author was a real spy for the CIA or MI6.

It wouldn't hurt to tell Miguel. She wanted to be honest with him. But she'd signed that agreement....

On the computer screen, he pulled up images of leather jewelry from this area. "I'm guessing the necklace was handmade," he said. "It's too crude to be mass produced."

She remembered the bear claw design. "It didn't look like the work of an artisan."

"Crude," he said again.

Her front doorbell rang.

Instantly, Miguel bolted from the chair. His right hand instinctively went to the holster attached to his belt. "Stay back. I'll see who it is."

Still holding Jack, she watched from the dining room while Miguel checked the small screen near the door that transmitted from the hidden camera outside. He turned back toward her. "My brother."

She moved forward as Miguel deactivated the security alarms and opened the door for his twin. As Dylan stalked into her house, she decided that he'd make a very good hero in an espionage novel. He had an intensity, an aura of danger.

In her opinion, his attitude was off-putting. She much preferred a man like Miguel who was intelligent and quietly courageous.

Dylan wasted no time with greetings or friendliness. He strode into her house and announced, "They have an ID on the dead man. It's Vincent Del Gardo."

Chapter Twelve

Del Gardo? Emma couldn't believe it. Her bald ghost with a penchant for gold coins was Del Gardo? She'd come to think of that ghost as a friendly presence. Her opinion of Del Gardo was the opposite. He was an escaped felon, a sleazy casino owner, the primary suspect in the murder of Julie Grainger.

She looked to Dylan. "He can't be Del Gardo. Callie didn't recognize him from the sketch."

"The shaved head, beard and glasses were a disguise," he muttered. "If anybody who knew Del Gardo had gotten close to the bald guy, they would've seen right through it."

"Now we know why he threatened Callie," Miguel said. "She testified against him."

"But the ghost was helping our investigation," Emma said. "He pointed us toward Griffin's house."

"After he was dead, he didn't care if we found his hideout. He must have been trying to get there when he was shot." Miguel turned to his brother. "Knowing his identity narrows the field of suspects. Boyd Perkins was after him."

"So were dozens of other people from Vegas. By the time Del Gardo went on the run, he had a lot of enemies."

"Bridger?"

"I don't care if we find the killer." Dylan flung himself

onto the sofa. "I wanted to apprehend Del Gardo, to make him pay for Julie's death. Now, we'll never know why he killed her."

"Maybe he didn't," Emma piped up.

Both twins turned toward her. Miguel's expression was curious. Dylan exuded angry frustration.

Oblivious to the tension in the room, Jack wiggled in her arms. It was getting close to time for his bedtime feeding.

She continued, "I never knew Del Gardo in life. But when I saw him, I didn't get a negative feeling. He didn't seem like a murderer. Are you sure he killed Julie?"

"Not a hundred percent. The investigation isn't over," Dylan conceded. "We need to locate Boyd Perkins."

Miguel sat beside his twin on the sofa. "There's something I need to tell you."

Dylan rubbed his forehead. "Now what?"

"At Griffin's house, when Emma was telling us where to look, she was being directed by a ghost. It was Julie."

Dylan's eyes squeezed shut as if in physical pain. "She was there? Her spirit was there?"

"She had a message for you," Miguel said. "She doesn't want you to grieve. You should remember the good times."

"That's Julie, all right." His voice cracked. "She was always thinking about other people."

The depth of his emotions caused Emma to wonder if Julie was more than a friend. "I'm sorry, Dylan. I know this is hard. Julie wanted you to know that she's all right. Beyond pain, beyond sorrow."

He leaned forward, elbows resting on his knees. His head drooped. "I don't suppose she mentioned who killed her."

"I'm afraid not."

"If you see her again, tell her that I'll find the bastard who took her life. Tell her that I miss hearing her laugh and the way she talked textbook Spanish." He looked heavenward. *"Via con dios, mi amiga."*

She wished she could comfort him, but his steely demeanor had already fallen back into place. Showing vulnerability wasn't his way. He hauled himself off the sofa, straightened his shoulders and went to the door. "I'll see you both tomorrow."

"Take care, *vato*."

"You, too."

Miguel locked up behind his brother and activated the security system. When he came back into the room, Emma asked, "Were Julie and your brother more than just friends?"

"Not as far as I know, but my brother doesn't talk much about the women he dates. I had a feeling, about a year ago, that there was someone special. But it didn't work out." He came closer to her. "I knew it would hurt him to be reminded of Julie, but we had to tell him."

"Julie wanted him to know."

"Her words are a good reminder. Death isn't the worst thing that can happen to a person." He gazed down into the baby's small face. "Sometimes, it's harder for the people left behind."

"If you're hinting that I should accept the idea that Jack's mother is dead, forget it."

"Aspen has been missing for over a month," he gently reminded her. "The odds are—"

"No." She refused to entertain any doubt. "If Aspen had died, I'd know. There would have been a sign. She'd come here to see her baby. She loved Jack."

"A heartfelt sentiment, but not proof."

"It's enough for me," she said.

"Me, too." A slow grin stretched his mouth. "If anybody had told me last week that I'd accept your visions as fact, I would have said they were out of their mind."

"But now you know better."

"I do." He winked. "If we're going to find your cousin, we better get back to work on that clue. The bear claw necklace."

She followed him into her office, where he sat at her computer and started scanning through Web sites for jewelry makers in Colorado and in Las Vegas. His process didn't seem much different than her own research when writing her books—gliding through various search engines and making inquiries in chat rooms.

Leaving Miguel at the computer, she took care of Jack's last feeding for the day. The baby was tired; he barely finished his bottle of formula before falling sound asleep. After she tucked him into the crib in her bedroom, she went back to the office.

Miguel looked up as she came into the room. "I found something. There's a guy on the rez who sells leather necklaces similar to the one we found. His name is Jerry Burch."

"I know him," she said, remembering a skinny kid with shaggy hair who always had a comic book sticking out of his back pocket. "He called himself The Burch, and he used to draw pictures of superheroes. I think he was a couple of years older than me and Aspen."

"So he knew your cousin," Miguel said. "Did they ever date?"

"I don't think so." In her head, she tried to picture her beautiful, vivacious cousin getting together with weird, skinny Jerry Burch. "He's not her type."

"Maybe he didn't know that. Maybe he had a crush on her."

"Like a stalker?"

"There's one way to find out. We'll take a trip to the rez tomorrow and ask around."

Because of her ghostly connections to Julie and Del Gardo, Emma hadn't thought that Aspen's attacker might be someone she knew. Though none of Aspen's friends had mentioned that she was dating somebody from the rez, they had to consider that possibility. "If Jerry Burch is Jack's father, Aspen would have told me. Besides, the timing is wrong. She got pregnant while she was in Vegas."

"Burch could have gone to Vegas to see her."

"But there's no reason to keep his identity a secret," Emma said firmly.

"Unless he's married," he suggested.

"Even it that's true—and I don't think it is—Aspen would have confided in me that her lover was a married man." In her only conversation with her cousin about Jack's father, Aspen said he was strong and brave. A good man. "She told me that she never expected to see Jack's father again. So he can't be somebody who lives on the rez."

"You think Jack's father is someone who comes from a different world than your cousin?"

She nodded. "An unlikely attraction."

"Those things happen," Miguel said.

When she looked into his face, her breath caught on a sigh. Her thoughts shifted from Aspen to herself and her own unlikely attraction to Miguel.

The house seemed extra-quiet with Jack asleep in his crib. There was only Miguel. Nothing stood between them. Unspoken questions rushed through her mind. What should she say to him? Should she kiss him again? Should she invite him into her bed? *Am I crazy?*

Tearing her gaze away from him, she took a step backward. She'd only known Miguel for a few days. Though she wanted to believe that love could strike as quickly and unexpectedly as lightning on a summer day, that wasn't the way she had lived her life. Emma was a careful woman. Her heart had been bruised too many times.

"G-g-good night," she stammered. "Sleep well."

"You, too."

Moments later, she slipped between the covers. Within seconds, she was sweating. Unaccustomed sensations raced through her. Her skin tingled. God, she was hot. She plucked at her cotton nightie, threw off the comforter. Making love to Miguel, losing her virginity to him, couldn't be a smart move.

Different worlds, they came from different worlds. Though he had learned to accept the validity of her visions, her ability still made him uncomfortable. He was a scientist, a man who relied on facts and logical deductions. Beyond that, she really didn't know anything about him. They hadn't spoken about his family. He hadn't told her the secrets connected to the Chimayo medallion. Not to mention her own big secret—her virginity.

Would he be freaked out? Would he think she was strange? She hadn't planned on being a thirty-year-old virgin; her sexual inexperience didn't signify any sort of ethical stance or need to be pure. It just happened.

If they never made love, she'd never have to tell him. It wasn't as if she had the word *virgin* tattooed on her butt. But she wanted him, wanted Miguel to be the man she remembered forever as her first time.

She rolled to her back and stared up at the ceiling, inhaling and exhaling slowly, willing her muscles to relax. Her eyes blinked closed as the knots of sexual tension gradually loosened. She ought to be able to sleep after the strenuous day she'd had. Quite a day—she'd been accosted by Bridger in her kitchen, gone for a wild ride on a motorcycle, followed a ghost to a mobster's hideout and discovered a dead body. Enough to make anybody tired. Smiling to herself, she thought of Miguel and hoped for pleasant dreams.

Slumber came quickly. No ghosts interrupted her sleep. Instead, she dreamed herself into Miguel's arms while he kissed her forehead, her eyelids and her lips. Downy soft-

ness swirled around them. She felt his embrace. At the
same time, she watched herself and Miguel. They were
beautiful together. He was bare-chested and bronzed. She
wore a long velvet gown, scarlet. Her hair glistened, and
her lips were glossy. She was the star of her own personal
dream movie. Effortlessly, Miguel lifted her off her feet.
Still kissing. He told her she was his *chica,* his *loca bonita.*
Te quiero, I love you. His voice resonated through her,
more musical than Mozart.

Her eyes opened. She was awake. Her dream vanished
like the pop of a fragile soap bubble.

The digital clock beside her bed read 3:37. Almost time
for Jack to be waking up. She yawned, stretched and
climbed out of bed.

The light from the hallway provided enough illumination for her to walk the few steps to the crib. She looked
down. Jack was gone.

Last night, Miguel had fed the baby. But two nights in
a row? Too good to be true. Barefoot, she padded from her
bedroom into the hall and peeked into the front room.

Miguel sat in the rocking chair with Jack on his lap. As he
fed the baby a bottle, his eyelids drooped. His baggy flannel
pajama bottoms puddled on the floor around his bare feet.

Bemused, she watched. This was reality. Instead of a
bronzed chest and flashing emerald eyes, he had stubble
on his chin and a faded gray T-shirt. The odd thing was she
liked this disheveled, unkempt version of Miguel much
better. She decided there was nothing sexier than a man
who was willing to change diapers and get up for the
middle-of-the-night feeding.

Flesh and blood, Miguel made her heart beat faster. He
was the man she wanted. Tonight.

When he looked up and saw her, he nodded. Quietly, he
said, "Go back to bed. Jack's asleep again."

"I want to talk." She crept into the room and sat on the sofa where he'd made his bed. She pulled the burgundy wool blanket over her legs.

Moving Jack to his shoulder, Miguel patted the baby until he heard a healthy burp, then left the room to put Jack back into the crib.

Emma had never been more awake in her life. She crossed one leg on top of the other. Her foot started bouncing. Anticipation hummed through her. She might be on the brink of the best night of her life, certainly the most passionate. *Was she ready for this?* When she reached up, her fingers tangled in her mussed hair. *I need a hairbrush. Some mascara. Oh, my God, I've got to brush my teeth.*

Bolting off the sofa, she dashed into the bathroom. There was enough moonlight shining through the upper part of the window above the café curtains to find her toothpaste. She squeezed a glob. Her fingers were trembling. She turned on the electric toothbrush.

Miguel appeared in the mirror behind her. In the dim light, he was a shadow.

"What are you doing?" he asked.

Making a fool of myself. Having second thoughts. She gestured with the toothbrush. "Since I was awake, I thought—"

He turned her toward him, took the toothbrush from her hand and turned it off. "Dental hygiene can wait. What's up?"

"Apparently, you are." Moonlight slanted across his face, hiding his cheekbones.

"You're shivering, Emma."

"I'm fine." She stepped back, bumping against the tiled counter. "Thank you, Miguel. For helping me out and getting up with the baby. It means a lot to me."

"*De nada.*" He glanced over his shoulders. "When you

said you wanted to talk, I thought you had a visitor. Another ghost."

"Not this time." Ignoring her nervousness, she reached toward him, rested her palm on the center of his chest, near his heart. "We're alone, Miguel. And the baby is asleep."

Just to make sure her invitation was obvious, she tilted her head upward. Her lips parted.

Leaning down, he kissed her slowly and thoroughly. Her shivers of tension transformed into a steady, throbbing pulse. Her hands climbed his chest, and she circled her arms around his neck.

His lean, muscular body pressed against her, trapping her against the countertop. Only a thin layer of clothing separated their naked flesh. She arched against him. The pressure set off a chain reaction of excitement that spread from head to toe.

He glided his hands down her side, grazing her breasts, and cupped her bottom.

Breathless, she gasped. "Miguel."

"Yes, Emma." He kissed her throat.

"There's something I should tell you." Another tremor slid through her. "Something you ought to know about me."

"It's okay. I already know."

How could he know she was a virgin? "What? How?"

With a devastatingly handsome smile, he gazed into her eyes. "Don't worry. Your secret is safe with me."

Her embrace loosened. "What the hell are you talking about?"

"When I was in your office." He stroked the line of her jaw. "I saw that row of books by Quinn Richards, and remembered your grandma Quinn. And your last name is Richardson. Then I looked at the photo on the book jacket— a cleverly morphed picture of you. You're Quinn Richards."

"You were spying on me." She was shocked, appalled,

hurt. Damn him. It felt like he'd thrown a bucket of ice water over her head. "How could you?"

"I'm an investigator. I look at the scene and make deductions. It really didn't seem like—"

"You had no right." She shoved him away from her. There would be no more embraces, no caresses. And, definitely, no lovemaking. "I can't trust you."

"Come on, Emma. You were secretive about your office, and I wanted to know why. I couldn't help figuring it out."

"Congratulations." She wedged out from between him and the counter. "You're much too clever for me."

Before she could leave the bathroom, he grasped her arm. "There's no problem. You were about to tell me, anyway."

"Actually, you're wrong." She slapped his hand away. "I have another secret. A much more important one. And you'll never find out what it is."

He didn't deserve to know. He'd pried into her affairs without her consent. Miguel was an untrustworthy sneak.

She'd never confide in him. It would be a cold day in hell when her sexual experience or lack thereof had anything whatsoever to do with him.

Chapter Thirteen

The next morning as they loaded the baby supplies into the car for the trip to the Ute Mountain Ute reservation, Miguel cursed his bad timing. Last night, he'd chosen exactly the wrong moment to bring up a topic that was sure to make Emma mad—her secret identity as Quinn Richards. *Dios mio,* he was a donkey. No wonder his brother got all the *chicas.* Dylan would have known better.

But Miguel couldn't help who he was. He spoke the truth and didn't play games. However, as a scientist, he could also be patient, *muy* patient. He would wait for Emma to come around.

In the meantime, he was itching to know her other secret. He told himself to let it go, but his brain wouldn't stop chasing after the answer.

Constantly observing her, he constructed theories about her secret, ranging from unlikely espionage plots—she was a smuggler of ancient Incan artifacts—to the mundane. A tattoo? A weird birthmark?

All morning, her attitude toward him had been cool but polite. She didn't pout or give him the silent treatment, for which he was grateful. But he missed those little glances she took when she thought he wasn't looking. Her voice was no longer soft and breathy when she said his name.

Instead, she sounded like Sister Consuelo, his third-grade teacher, who used to smack his knuckles with a ruler.

As they drove east in her car toward the rez, she made a number of calls on her cell phone to friends and members of her extended family until she got a phone number and location for Jerry Burch's studio.

Emma turned to check on Jack, who had fallen asleep in the baby seat. She asked, "Should I call Jerry Burch?"

"It's better if we stop in unannounced." Standard procedure for interrogating a suspect. "If he's somehow involved in Aspen's disappearance, we don't want him to have time to come up with a pack of lies. What did you find out about him?"

"He's been divorced for a couple of years. Has two children with his ex-wife, who lives in Denver. According to Dolly Zeto—a friend of Aspen's—Jerry has a fairly successful line of custom Native American jewelry."

"Did Dolly mention a connection between Aspen and Jerry?"

"None at all. Jerry's a quiet guy who keeps to himself."

With a cynical nod, Miguel digested the brief biography. Jerry Burch sounded innocent enough—maybe too innocent. "It's the quiet ones you have to look out for."

"I thought that was a cliché." Her tone was snippy. "Like when people who live next door to psycho murderers describe them as good neighbors?"

"Most clichés are based on truth." He couldn't help giving her a dig about her secret identity. "You've probably found that to be true in your writing as Quinn Richards."

Her shoulders stiffened. She stared straight ahead through the windshield. "I will not discuss Quinn Richards. I signed an agreement with my publisher to never reveal my identity to anyone."

"Why?"

"Because the Quinn Richards books are marketed as action-packed adventures of espionage. It'd hurt sales if anyone found out that the author is a single woman living in rural Colorado."

"So you're selling the reading public a lie."

"No," she said firmly. "I could have made up an author biography about being a former CIA operative or a world adventurer. Instead, I say nothing."

"There's a phony picture of you on the book jacket."

"But it's still my picture." She glared at him. "How did you recognize me in that photo?"

"I've played around with those morphing programs enough to see through them." He met her glare. "Besides, I'd know your beautiful eyes anywhere."

He wasn't offering an idle compliment. From the first time he'd seen her, Miguel connected with that special glimmer in her eyes—a hot blue spark that lit a flame inside him.

They drove for a while without talking. The rez covered a lot of empty terrain, most of which wasn't good for farming or grazing. The major sources of income for the tribe were the casino and the pottery factory.

As they drove deeper into the rez, Emma's Ute heritage became more apparent. She had stories about powwows and spring rituals. All her directions came from landmarks. Turn east at the seven pine trees. Go south on the hogback ridge.

He pulled up at a stop sign at a crossroads. On the northeast corner was a ramshackle storefront with several hand-painted signs advertising food, beer and—oddly enough—hot espresso. "Which way?"

"East. Toward the red cliffs."

Trying to avoid the bigger potholes in the poorly paved road, he drove slowly. "I'm guessing that Jerry Burch doesn't have many people coming to visit his studio."

"Most of the local artists don't," she said. "Either they have booths at powwows or they sell on commission through established shops in the big cities or tourist destinations."

"I know how it works. *Mi madre* teaches art at Adams State."

"Does she paint?"

"Mostly, she does photography. She's been getting into computer art that's kind of amazing. It looks real and surreal at the same time. I can show you her Web site."

"I'd like that." To his surprise, her voice softened perceptively. "Do you realize that's the first thing you've told me about your family?"

"Is it?"

"You change the subject every time it turns toward you. We've been together twenty-four-seven almost since we met, and I hardly know anything about you."

"You know I play guitar," he reminded her. "And I ride a motorcycle."

"Tell me about your family."

"Five kids. Papa is a lawyer, but not the kind that makes a lot of money. He calls himself King Pro Bono. My sister and other brother are married with kids."

"A sister, brother and twins." She tallied the numbers. "That's only four."

"My sister, Teresa, died when she was fifteen." Not a topic he liked to talk about. He still missed Teresa. "She was murdered."

On the left side of the road, he saw a mailbox with Burch printed in elaborate letters. He took the turn, heading toward two small houses, side by side, both whitewashed stucco. One was two-story with a wide door like a barn.

As they approached, he heard the roar of hard-driving, heavy-metal music. "Jerry Burch isn't as quiet as your friend thought."

After he parked and Emma freed Jack from the baby seat, they approached the smaller door on the side of the tall house. The hyper-amped volume on the music sounded like a heavy-metal concert in progress.

As soon as Miguel knocked, he realized the futility of that motion. No one could hear a tap on the door over the blasting music from inside. Taking his badge from his pocket, he pushed open the door and stepped inside.

He found himself staring down the barrel of a rifle.

Quickly, he held up his badge. "Police."

A man with long black hair flying loose around his shoulders tapped a switch with his moccasin. Silence.

"Police," Miguel repeated. "I'm from the Kenner County Crime Lab."

"You got no jurisdiction on the rez, man."

Emma stepped out from behind him. "Jerry Burch?"

His eyes narrowed as he studied her. "Emma?"

"You remember me." She beamed.

He lowered the rifle. "What the hell are you doing here? Who's the baby?"

As she brushed past Miguel, she said under her breath, "Not calling ahead was a great idea."

"Maybe not," he muttered.

"Let me handle this."

He nodded. Being in the sight of a rifle reminded him that there was more going on than his issues with Emma. This was an investigation, and the danger was real.

While Emma and Jerry hugged and she introduced him to Jack, Miguel took a look around the studio. High windows flooded the one huge room with natural sunlight. A white table in one corner held a clutter of precision engraving and welding tools—apparently the area where Burch did his custom jewelry work. Every bit of wall space was hung with artwork—photographs, portraits and pop art drawings of muscular superheroes from comic books.

Burch came toward him with hand outstretched. "Sorry about the gun, man. I got a lot of silver and turquoise lying around."

Miguel shook his hand. Though Jerry Burch was nearly his height, he was as skinny as Emma had remembered. His rib cage showed through his tight, blue superhero T-shirt. "We need your help with our investigation."

The corners of his mouth pulled down. "Hey, I don't rat out my brothers."

"It's about Aspen," Emma said. "To help find Aspen."

He immediately changed his mind. "Then I'll help. Hell, yeah. What can I do?"

Miguel reached into his jacket pocket and produced a photograph of the bear claw necklace. "What can you tell me about this?"

"Man, I did a bunch of these. Maybe a hundred. Handmade. I burned the image into the leather."

"Uh-huh." Miguel didn't care about the artistic process unless it included a GPS chip to locate the wearer of the necklace. "All bear claws?"

"Different images." He ran his hand through his long hair. "Hawk. Howling coyote. Turtle."

"How many were bear claws?"

"Geez, I don't know. Maybe twenty or thirty. It was a while back. Maybe seven years ago. I'm a better artist now." He turned toward Emma. "Want to see some of my stuff?"

"You bet." She followed him to the worktable.

Miguel didn't want to waste time looking at squash blossom necklaces and concha belts. "I have more questions."

Emma whirled toward him. "Not yet, Miguel. This is how we do things on the rez. We take our time. We socialize."

"She's right." Burch laughed. "Slow and easy. That's why Utes are good lovers."

"Relax," she told him. "Allow the string to unwind."

He adjusted his thinking to her culture, which wasn't so different from his own. As a kid, he'd spent hours listening to the old ones tell stories that circled and looped and came back around to the beginning. Sometimes, there was a point. Other times, not.

Burch's jewelry didn't follow the traditional patterns. Instead, he incorporated Ute designs in braided strands of thin wire and dramatic pendants that showed some of his comic book influence. "You like superheroes," Miguel said.

"Ever since I was a kid and I found Indian superheroes in the comics. I wanted to be like them." He gestured toward a life-size painting. "That's my own creation. Pinto Hawk. He rides like the wind and flies like a bird, wreaking vengeance on evil-doers."

Miguel picked up his thread. "Evil-doers like the man who made Aspen disappear."

"Let me see that picture of the bear claw again." Burch studied his own handiwork. "Most of these were sold through a shop in Durango and here on the rez by a guy who went out of business and moved on."

Tracing the sale through old receipts would be a dead end. Miguel asked, "Who would still be wearing the bear claw seven years later?"

"Somebody who thought the claw brought him luck. Or protected him. You know, like a totem." His dark eyes— nearly black—scanned up and to the right, as if looking for a memory. "There was one guy who lived on the rez. Scuzzy. Kind of mean-looking. I noticed him because I thought it was cool that he was wearing something I made."

"Do you remember his name?"

"Not sure I ever knew it." He darted across the room,

moving silently on his moccasins, and pointed to a photograph. "There. The guy in the flat-brim hat."

The picture showed three men loitering on a wood slat porch. The bear claw was clearly visible, but the face of the man wearing the necklace was in shadow.

"That's him," Emma said.

"You can't see his features," Miguel said.

"Do you see the knife on his belt?" Her blue eyes pierced through him. "That's the man who attacked my cousin."

EMMA HAD SEEN THE faceless man in her vision. He'd been chasing her, trying to kill her with his knife. And she was fairly sure that he was the same man who'd broken into her house and disabled her car. A shadow man.

When they found him, she knew he'd lead them to Aspen.

Tracking down his name was going to take time. "If we showed this picture to somebody at the tribal newspaper, maybe they could identify him."

"Lydia Fife," Burch said. "That lady knows everybody and their ancestors."

"I guess we need to go there." She started the bouncy walk that usually calmed the baby. "It's not really that far. Only about half an hour."

Miguel turned to Burch. "You got a fax machine?"

"Sure thing, man. I'm in business."

In his quiet way, Miguel took control of the situation. He lifted Jack from her arms. "What's your problem, *mijo?* You come with me. Emma, contact the newspaper and get a name for this guy."

"Good plan."

"And you might want to tell her to keep it quiet."

As if that would happen. As soon as they started making inquiries, everybody would know. Gossip on the rez spread fast and wide, like seeds on the wind.

While Miguel fed Jack his bottle and got him quieted down, she and Burch contacted the newspaper office via phone and then by fax. Though it seemed to her that minutes were ticking by like hours, Lydia Fife was able to identify the man with the bear claw necklace.

Before she bid farewell to Burch, she bought a pendant. It had been good to renew their acquaintance, and she sincerely wished him well.

"Sherman Watts." Emma repeated the name as she and Miguel returned to her car. "I recognized the flat-brimmed hat. He was the one who messed with my car."

"Not Boyd Perkins?"

She shook her head. "Watts is the guy. Let's get him."

"Whoa, *chica*. Much as I'd like to make an arrest before he knows we're after him, that's not my job."

"You have a gun," she said. "And a badge."

"Which means nothing on the rez." Carrying the baby, he circled to the passenger side. "You drive. I'll make some phone calls."

"Where are we going?"

"To your house. Where it's safe." He got Jack situated in his baby seat. "We can't chase after the bad guys while *mijo* is with us."

He had a point. Emma was usually cautious to the point of meekness, but her blood was boiling. In her action-adventure novels, she often wrote about men and women engaged in life-and-death struggles. They were brave and proactive. They were steely-eyed predators. Right now, she knew how that felt. Her skin tingled. Adrenaline raced through her veins. She felt the urge to rush forward, no matter what the danger.

Slipping behind the wheel, she scooted the seat forward, fastened her seat belt and adjusted the rearview mirror. "Oh, swell."

"What is it?" Miguel asked.

Her head swiveled as she peered into the backseat. The ghost of Aunt Rose was sitting beside Jack. It made sense that she'd be here on the rez where she'd spent most of her life. Unsmiling, she said, "You be careful, Emma. Sherman Watts is a bad person. Mean in spirit. His heart is stone."

"I know."

Miguel's eyes narrowed. "Another ghost."

"My aunt Rose."

In a low voice, Aunt Rose continued, "Sherman Watts isn't the only danger. Watch out for the Vegas cowboy."

"What else can you tell me?"

"Don't use a pacifier with the baby. It makes his teeth strange."

In a poof, she was gone. Emma muttered under her breath, "Sometimes, I wish my friendly spirit guides would be a little more specific."

"Is she gone?"

"Oh, yeah." She cranked the key in the ignition and headed to her house.

Though the dire warning from Aunt Rose had lessened Emma's desire to strap on a gun and lead the assault team that would track down Sherman Watts, she was still buzzed. They'd had a very productive morning. They'd found the name of the bastard who attacked Aspen. Sherman Watts.

As she drove west, taking the shortest route to Kenner City, she heard Miguel repeat that name several times as he made calls on his cell phone. Who was he talking to? What was the plan? Even though she wasn't technically part of law enforcement, she'd earned the right to know what was going on.

His conversation stopped abruptly. Staring at the phone, he poked the buttons. "No reception."

"There are a lot of places around here that don't get cell-phone reception."

"I guess you'd know all about dead zones. Being a medium."

She was too pleased with herself to be irritated by his teasing. "Very funny. Laughing on the inside."

Miguel turned in his seat so he was facing the back window of the car as he said, "The lab turned up a couple of leads on Del Gardo's murder. Ballistics tests show the bullet to be .45 caliber from a Sig Sauer. No match on file."

She prompted, "Which means?"

"It wasn't from the gun previously used by Boyd Perkins," Miguel said. "But that doesn't take him off the list of suspects. He could have a new gun."

"What else?"

"This is interesting." He played with Jack, eliciting giggles from the baby. "Remember the map with the VDG symbol? The map Julie sent?"

"Of course."

"Those twists and turns seem to match up with the tunnels under Griffin's house. Julie must have gone through those caves. There's something down there she wanted us to find."

"I think we already found it," she said. "Del Gardo himself."

"You're probably right. She mapped the tunnels in case Del Gardo decided to use his hideout. Unfortunately, by the time he was holed up in the tunnels, Julie was already dead."

"Killed by Del Gardo," Emma said. "Supposedly."

"The map is another clue pointing in that direction. Julie was onto him. He had to take her out."

"I still don't believe it." Del Gardo's ghost seemed more like Santa Claus than a bloodthirsty killer. "There's one thing I still don't understand. With all those millions of dollars, why was he hanging around in cold, dark tunnels outside Kenner City?"

"There was something here he wanted. Revenge on Callie, maybe. Or this might be the place where he hid his treasure. Ava and Bobby are going through the tunnels inch by inch looking for signs that something was in there and moved."

"That's possible. The first time I saw Del Gardo's ghost, he was digging up gold coins. Maybe I'm supposed to interpret that to mean that he'd moved the treasure."

Miguel continued to look over his shoulder. "I don't want you to panic, Emma. But I think we're being followed."

Chapter Fourteen

Emma's leg jolted in a reflex action. She pressed down harder on the accelerator, and her car jumped forward like a jackrabbit. *Being followed?* They were in the middle of nowhere—a literal dead zone. "What should I do?"

"He's a good distance back, over half a mile. I can just make out the glint of sunlight on his car."

"If I went faster, I could lose him."

"That's a plan," he said diplomatically. "But there's only one road—this road—leading off the rez. That's why he can stay so far back. He knows where we're going."

"I could take a turnoff." As soon as she spoke, she realized that escape route was iffy. "But it might lead to a dead end. Then we'd be trapped."

His hand lightly stroked her arm. Instead of jerking away and avoiding him, she appreciated the physical contact. No matter how irritated she was with him, Miguel always made her feel safe.

"Here's what we do," he said. "I'll keep an eye on the other car. If he's still following us when we get closer to Kenner City, I'll call Sheriff Martinez for support."

"Who would be following us?"

"Maybe Bridger." He squinted as he peered through the

back window. "Wish I could identify his vehicle. I don't suppose you have binoculars in your car."

"Sorry, I don't generally carry long-range surveillance equipment," she said. "If we were in need of baby wipes, I'd be well supplied."

When she heard him chuckle, her hands almost slipped off the wheel. Was he actually laughing? On the outside? In spite of her stated goal to curtail their relationship, it seemed to be growing of its own accord—like a weed in a garden of roses.

His cell phone rang, and he answered.

Though she checked her rearview mirrors frequently, she only caught faraway glimpses of the car that appeared to be tailing them.

"That was Dylan," Miguel said as he disconnected the call. "There's a jurisdictional problem. The FBI can't arrest Sherman Watts while he's on the reservation. And Sheriff Martinez can't make arrests on the rez, either."

"What about Patrick's fiancée, Bree Hunter? She's a Ute cop," Emma said. "Surely, she can take Watts into custody."

"Dylan talked to Bree. She's not real impressed with our evidence. All we have to link Watts to Aspen's disappearance is the necklace."

"And my vision." Emma knew that testimony from a medium didn't count for much. "Can't the crime lab come up with something more? Like DNA on the necklace? I've read about touch DNA."

He groaned. "So has everybody else. Technically, it's possible to make a DNA identification from a minuscule amount—only a few cells left behind when someone touches an object."

"Right," she said. "They can get DNA from a fingerprint."

"Why bother? A fingerprint ought to be identification enough. It's a painstaking laboratory process to extract those cells for DNA analysis. It could take weeks."

"According to the literature on the subject, touch DNA—"

"Is this research for a Quinn Richards book?"

At the mention of her pseudonym, her jaw clenched. Why had he brought it up? She didn't want to be angry with him. "As I told you before, discussion of my work is off-limits. I won't talk about it."

"I respect your decision," he said. "There's only one thing I have to say, then *silencio*. I'll shut up forever."

There wasn't anything she could do to stop him from making a comment. Since they were being tailed by a bad guy, she couldn't pull over to the side of the road and order Miguel to get out of the car. "Fine."

"I started reading one of your books last night. It was good, really good. I'm proud of you, Emma."

His unexpected statement disarmed her. For the past five years, she'd been writing books that sold very well and were critically acclaimed. Though she took satisfaction from glowing reviews, she'd never been in the spotlight. "Proud?"

"You've got talent. And smarts, too. You're writing about a world you don't know much about."

"I've always been good at research." His praise warmed her. "And my copy editor is good at catching errors."

"You're the one who does the hard part, the writing part. You deserve an Academy Award."

"They don't give Oscars for books, silly." Her hostility toward him began to ebb. "Actually, Quinn Richards has won a couple of prizes. My editor picked them up for me."

"Next time, you should be there to hear the applause."

He sounded sincere; his voice lacked the edge of cynicism that signaled his teasing. But she found his compliments difficult to accept. Throughout her life, she'd never expected others to support her goals, to praise her or be proud.

When she gazed into his green eyes, she knew he was

telling the truth. He honestly admired her accomplishments. "I don't know what to say."

"It's simple, *querida*. Say thank you."

Tenderness washed through her. No way could she hold a grudge against him. "*Gracias,* Miguel."

"*De nada.*" He looked through the back window again. "I think it's a black SUV."

"Bridger," she said. "Is he getting closer?"

"Don't worry," Miguel said. "We're almost at the turn leading toward Kenner City. I can call for backup."

Tension tightened her shoulders. She had no desire to get into a chase, certainly not with Jack in the car. Long, desolate miles stretched ahead of them.

While Miguel made more phone calls, she imagined a hawk's-eye view of the road. Looking down from the skies, her car and the SUV following them would be as small as ants crawling along a mountain pass—separate but on the same trail, a ribbon of road leading to an uncertain future.

At the stop sign, she turned left.

As she proceeded, still following the speed limit, Miguel continued to stare through the rear window. "He went right."

Relieved, Emma exhaled in a whoosh. "He wasn't following us after all."

"Maybe not." Miguel didn't sound convinced. "But it was a black SUV, like Bridger's vehicle."

"We should call Sheriff Martinez. He could—"

"By the time he got anywhere near here, the SUV would be long gone," Miguel said. "For now, we need to concentrate on Sherman Watts."

Logically, she knew he was right. Intuitively, she felt a greater threat from Sherman Watts—a shadow man who threatened her in a vision. But the continued presence of Bridger worried her. He was after a treasure—millions of dollars—and wouldn't quit until he found it.

When they finally got to her house, it was after two o'clock. Jack was awake and wiggling. She lifted him from the car seat. "You've been such a good boy."

He waved his little arms like he was directing an invisible orchestra. And he smiled.

"Good baby," she repeated.

He'd put up with a lot of disruption to his schedule. And so had she. All this crime-solving was exhausting, and she was longing to relax for the rest of the day. Then, maybe, spend a quiet evening with Miguel. After dinner, they might take up where they left off last night.

She'd more than forgiven him for prying into her secret identity as Quinn Richards. As he'd said, he couldn't stop himself from figuring it out.

At the front door, she paused, waiting while Miguel went into the house first and disconnected the security alarm.

Emma turned toward the street.

A black SUV rolled slowly by. Through the open window, she saw Hank Bridger. He grinned at her and gave a wave before driving on.

A FEW HOURS LATER, Emma emerged from the bedroom after putting Jack to sleep. The afternoon had segued into dusk. She sprawled on the sofa and looked toward Miguel who sat in the rocking chair with his cell phone within easy reach.

Though his eyelids drooped at half-mast, he didn't look as tired as he should have been. His first call had been to the sheriff, who had considered putting up roadblocks to catch Bridger. Then, Miguel was in constant communication with the crime lab and with his brother. For the past couple of hours, Miguel had been talking nonstop.

Even so, his steady gaze held a glimmer of energy. A steady flame like a pilot light. She had no doubt that, if encouraged, he could rise from the rocker and sweep her off her feet.

Now might be the perfect time. Her resistance was low, and she was oh-so-ready to be held and cherished. And make love?

She exhaled a sigh, amazed that she could contemplate such an earth-shaking, life-changing event. She cleared her throat. "How did you get to be at the center of all these phone calls?"

"I work at the lab. Normally, I wouldn't have much to do with the FBI, but Dylan is my twin brother—which gives people the mistaken idea that I have some influence over him." He shook his head. "And Sheriff Martinez is my friend."

"Any word from the sheriff? Did he find Bridger?"

"Not yet."

"If they do locate him, can they arrest him?"

"You bet." He cocked his head to one side. "What makes you think otherwise?"

"When we looked him up, he had no outstanding warrants. And he's gotten off on every crime he's been charged with."

"He broke into your house, Emma. That's enough for an arrest. Also, he's a person of interest in the Del Gardo murder."

"But Bridger didn't want Del Gardo dead. All he's interested in is the money." Stretching her legs straight out in front of her, she kicked off her purple sneakers and wiggled her toes. "It doesn't make sense that he'd kill Del Gardo."

"Motives aren't my problem. My job is finding the facts and analyzing them." He steepled his fingers and peered at her over the arch. "So far, we have one good piece of evidence that could point to Bridger."

"What's that?"

"The boot print we found at the crime scene. A size thirteen. The shape is distinctive. It's probably custom-made footwear."

"And Bridger is a snappy dresser. I think his boots were snakeskin."

The cell phone on the table beside him rang. He picked it up and glared at the caller ID. "It's the lab again."

"Go ahead and take it." She pushed herself off the sofa. "I'm going to check my e-mail."

After grabbing a bottle of water from the fridge, she went into the office and turned on the computer. There was an e-mail from her editor asking how she was doing on her latest novel. If Emma could turn it in early, the editor would like to move the pub date up.

In the past, such a request would have thrown her into a tizzy. But now? It was nothing. *Nada.* Emma's life had changed since that moment when she sat at this very desk and had the vision that set her on the path to finding Aspen. Because of that vision, she'd met Miguel. And since she'd met him, many of her priorities had shifted.

The phone on her desk rang, and she picked up.

"Hello, Miss Emma."

"Bridger." She bolted upright in her chair.

"So glad you recognize my voice," he said smoothly.

As if she would ever forget? Talking to him was like sticking her finger into an electric socket. "Why were you following me?"

"You know what I'm looking for. And I've heard tell that there's some kind of treasure map. True?"

She remembered the map Julie had drawn that outlined the twists and turns of the tunnels under Griffin's house. "True."

"I'd sure like to get my hands on that map," he said. "And I think you can help me. I have a proposition for you, Miss Emma."

Common sense told her to hang up; never make a deal with the devil. Still, she asked, "What's in it for me?"

"I have information about the disappearance of your cousin."

She'd be a fool to trust him. But there might be a kernel of truth in what he said. She picked up a pen and held it poised above a clean sheet of paper, ready to write down whatever he said. "Go on."

"Not so fast. We're playing a little game here. You tell me something. Then I tell you."

Her vision went fuzzy around the edges—similar to the way she felt before succumbing to a vision. *Not now. Oh, God. Not now.* She needed to be alert.

"The map," she said. "It starts near three pine trees up on a hill and a marking on a rock that looks like a crescent moon."

"Where do I find these trees?"

"Tit for tat," she said. "You have to tell me something first."

He made a sound that could have been a laugh or a snarl. "You'd make a decent poker player, Miss Emma. With that sweet pink mouth and big blue eyes, you look real innocent. But you're sharp."

On the other side of the office near the bookcase, she saw a shape begin to form. Then another. She needed to talk fast. "Mr. Bridger, you said you had information."

"That's right." His voice dropped even lower. It sounded like he was talking from the bottom of a well.

"Well." The word echoed around her. "Well?"

"Sherman Watts wasn't acting alone."

"Who was he working with?"

"Your turn, Miss Emma."

She figured she'd string him along with a description of the entrance to the tunnel without revealing too much. She'd talk about a cold, dark place and mention a map that had fooled the FBI and the crime lab.

But the atmosphere in her office had transformed. A chill seeped into her bones. The ethereal shapes became more substantial. A dark man and a pretty woman with blond ringlets stood in front of her bookcase.

They were both connected to Bridger.

"Miss Emma," he said. "Don't try my patience."

The sound of his voice gave them life. As the woman came closer, Emma saw the hard lines in her face. Her lipstick was bloodred. "He killed me."

"And me," said the man. He paced back and forth with a limp. "Killed me dead."

"Mr. Bridger…"

The irony of her predicament hit her. When she saw him before, she'd pretended to see the victims of his crimes. Now, they were here. A man and woman. And someone else. A third presence was forming.

Emma looked down at her desk. Though she was unaware of writing anything, two names were clearly spelled out. She read them aloud. "Simone Caparelli. Burton Nestor."

"What the hell are you talking about?"

"You know what I'm saying." She stared at the bookshelf. The third presence took shape. Another man.

"You can't prove a damn thing," he said. "Don't try to threaten me."

She looked into the bearded face of the familiar ghost. His smile was sad.

"You killed Vincent Del Gardo," she said. "He's here. I can see him."

As if from faraway, she heard Bridger say, "You'll be joining Del Gardo. Soon."

The telephone receiver slipped from her hand. She might have hung up. Not sure.

Her vision darkened as her head dropped forward. When

she looked up, the walls of her office had disappeared. Del Gardo held out his hand in a courtly gesture.

She rose to her feet. Accompanied by the ghosts of three murder victims, she stepped into a vision.

Chapter Fifteen

Entering a world beyond reality, Emma strolled across flagstones toward a nighttime fiesta with bright lights strung from the branches of trees. Women in flowing, colorful skirts twirled and clapped in time to lively mariachi music. Even though she knew this was a vision, she found herself searching the faces of the men, looking for Miguel.

"Keep moving," Del Gardo said.

She looked over at his shiny, bald head. "When I first saw you, why didn't you tell me who you were?"

"I had other things on my mind." He scowled. "Like being dead."

She couldn't argue with that logic; death was a difficult transition. Walking abreast, they passed adobe-colored storefronts and crossed a street to enter a town square filled with huge earthenware pots of azaleas, purple pansies and yellow petunias.

In the brightly lit gazebo, the mariachi band played. Four men in sombreros thumped their guitars. Another fingered his accordion. The lead singer, gesturing with his coronet, hit a high tenor note, looking like he might burst right out of his tight black pants with silver buttons down the side.

The blond woman, Simone, took the hand of the limping

man. They danced away together, leaving Emma with Del Gardo, who still scowled, showing no sign of pleasure amid these festive sights and sounds.

"What's wrong?" she asked.

"Others will die."

"Who?"

"And I have no way to stop the murder."

From everything she'd been told about Del Gardo, he was mired in crime—a truly evil person. But that wasn't her impression. His distress about the murders seemed utterly sincere.

"Will my cousin die?" She had so many questions. Bridger had said that Sherman Watts hadn't been working alone. Who was his partner? Where was he? "What else can you tell me?"

Del Gardo took a step away from her.

"Wait," she called after him. Emma knew better than to press for answers to specific questions. Her visions weren't meant to predict the future. She might see future influences, but the spirits never offered specifics.

When Del Gardo turned back toward her, he was wearing a grin and a huge sombrero. Looking down, Emma saw that her outfit had changed. She wore a full skirt of purple with white stars. Though not aware of dancing, her skirt swished back and forth in time to the music.

Del Gardo touched her hand and led her into the throng.

"I'm trying to understand," she said. "What do you want me to see?"

He doffed his Mexican hat and bowed low.

Her feet started moving. She didn't know the steps, but she was dancing, fitting in very nicely with all the other fiesta-goers in the square. As they stomped and twirled, she wished Miguel could see her.

A dark *vaquero* took her hand and spun her in a graceful

circle. He was handsome but no match for Miguel. When she pulled away from him, another man took his place.

"No, no," she protested. "I don't have time to dance."

They laughed…too loudly, slightly maniacal. She didn't want to be dancing when there was so much else to be done. She had to find Aspen.

But the dancing men wouldn't let her stop, wouldn't let her catch her breath. Swirling and dipping and clicking their heels, an endless string of partners yanked her into the center of the dancers. Her shoulders hurt from being pulled in too many directions.

"Excuse me," she shouted. "I have to go."

The thrumming music got louder. The voices of the mariachis howled.

At the edge of the circle, she spotted Del Gardo and his two companions. Their faces were cold. Somber.

She tried to run, but the circle closed more tightly around her. The women rustled their skirts and made yipping noises.

Then she saw Bridger. His fringe on his garish jacket jostled with every step. The snakeskin band on his hat came to life, hissing and rattling. His large hands dripped blood.

She tried to run, but couldn't escape from the circle. A wall of laughing dancers blocked her way.

There was a loud popping noise. Fireworks. All the dancers threw their hats into the air. Dozens of sombreros soared high in the night sky.

Slowly, slowly, they fell.

When they touched the ground, the fiesta was gone.

The night became so utterly silent that she could hear the rapid beating of her own heart. She sat at the desk in her office, staring at the bookcase.

"Emma?" Miguel stepped into the office. "Are you okay?"

She held out her arms, and he drew her from the chair into an embrace.

AFTER A JUMBLED EXPLANATION, Miguel got Emma settled at the kitchen table. He ignored the constant ring tone of his cell phone and concentrated only on her. This vision had taken a lot out of her. She gazed up at him with frightened eyes. "A party doesn't sound terrible, but it was. They wouldn't let me stop dancing. The music was so loud."

"Mariachi music," he said.

"What does it mean?" Tension pinched the corners of her mouth. "Del Gardo showed me the fiesta for a reason, but I can't for the life of me figure it out."

"And the two names you wrote down?"

"That part is clear," she said. "Simone and Burton. They told me that Bridger killed them. And Del Gardo, too."

"And you mentioned these names to Bridger."

"I think so. Things were getting hazy at that point."

This was not good. By telling Bridger that she knew the identities of his victims, Emma put herself at greater risk. If the Vegas cowboy believed she could link him to past crimes, she became a threat. His casual surveillance— following her car from a couple hundred yards away—might get a hell of a lot more personal.

In spite of the security system at her house, Miguel wasn't sure he could protect her from a determined killer. "I think I need more backup tonight."

"Whatever is necessary." She leaned forward, elbows on the table, and rubbed at her forehead. "I wish I could figure out that vision."

"Tell me the details."

She described a town square with azaleas and dancers in bright colors. "My skirt was purple," she said.

"Your favorite color."

"I looked for you in the crowd, but you weren't there."

"Too bad." He gave her an encouraging smile. "I'd like to see you dance."

"In my vision, I was graceful. In real life, I've got two left feet." As if to show him, she staggered to her feet. "I'm thirsty. I should have some water."

"Sit." He touched her shoulder, and she obeyed—too tired to protest. He said, "I was thinking of something stronger than water."

"There's a bottle of wine in the back of the cabinet by the door."

After a quick search, he found a dusty bottle of burgundy. While he dug through drawers, looking for a corkscrew, he asked, "What other details do you remember? How about the music itself? What were they playing?"

"I'm not sure. There was that song that goes like this: Dum-dee-dee-dum-dum. De-dum."

He winced. It was the most tuneless rendering he'd ever heard. Musicality wasn't one of her talents. "Try it again."

"You know what I'm talking about." She went through her humming again, then clapped her hands twice. "Dum-dee-dee-dum-dum. De-dum. Clap, clap. It's the Mexican Hat Dance."

A favorite of grade-school teachers. He opened the wine and poured a glass for her and for himself. "Does that song have any particular meaning for you?"

"I don't know the words." She accepted the wine. "Isn't it something like, dance with your partner, olé?"

"Something like that."

"They all threw their sombreros in the air," she said. "And the mariachis did that song with the dramatic guitar and the high tenor."

"Don't try to sing it." He clinked his wineglass with hers and took a sip. "We'll talk about music later."

Taking out his cell phone, he stepped into the dining

room and speed dialed Sheriff Martinez. After quickly filling him in on the broad outline of Emma's vision, he added two requests. The first was for dinner.

"Fine," Martinez said. "I'll grab something from Mama's café."

"Also, on your way over here, can you stop at my place and pick up my guitar? There's a musical piece of evidence we need to work through."

"Sure." The sheriff paused. "Have you heard from your brother?"

"Only about a thousand times today."

"Recently?"

Miguel thought for a moment. "Maybe an hour ago. Maybe more. Why?"

"I hope he doesn't do something stupid."

Sheriff Martinez didn't need to go into details. Miguel knew how frustrated Dylan was with the slow process of arranging for the arrest of Sherman Watts on the reservation. *Dios mio,* they were all frustrated. But Dylan had the resources of the FBI behind him if he decided to make an abrupt move.

"When Emma talked to Bridger," Miguel said, "he told her that Watts wasn't acting alone."

"Doesn't surprise me. Watts is no mastermind. He's a mean-tempered drunk. Bree tells me that he's rough with women. That could be what happened to Aspen."

Miguel had considered that possibility. Aspen's disappearance might not be part of the ongoing Del Gardo investigation. Emma's cousin was beautiful; she might have been the victim of a simple assault by a local *cabron.* "Why would he go after a woman with a baby in the backseat? Why run her off the road?"

"Good questions," the sheriff said. "And why would Emma link Aspen's disappearance with Del Gardo?"

Miguel grinned at the phone. "I'd almost forgotten that you consider Emma's visions to be valid evidence."

"Admit it, smart guy. So do you."

Miguel looked into the kitchen, where Emma had finished off her first glass of wine and reached for the bottle to pour another. A bit of color had returned to her cheeks.

"I believe in her," he said. "Emma doesn't lie, but some of these visions are *muy loco*."

"See you soon." Martinez disconnected the call.

Miguel returned to the table and sat beside her. The wine seemed to be already having an effect on Emma. The worry lines between her eyes were gone, and she wore a crooked smile.

"I was thinking," she said. "What if the fiesta doesn't have anything to do with the investigation? What if it's meant as a personal message to me?"

"And what would that message be?"

"A cautionary tale." She took another deep sip of wine. "Even when I think I'm having fun, like at a party, it's dangerous. The singing can turn dark. The dancing gets frantic and terrible. Maybe I'm simply not meant to be twirling around in a purple dress."

"What are you meant for?"

"Talking to dead people and writing novels of pulse-pounding adventure." She set her wineglass on the table and shook her head. "I don't mean to sound like I'm feeling sorry for myself. I have a good life. I've been doing this for years, and I'm perfectly content living by myself."

He took her hand. "But you don't live alone. You have little *mijo*."

"Jack is only here until we find Aspen. When she comes back, her baby will go home with her."

"You're not alone," he said. "You have me."

He would never allow Emma—a beautiful flower—to

wither alone and untended. His job was to show her the sun and watch as she bloomed. He stood and gently pulled her to her feet.

"What are you doing?" she asked.

"Teaching you to dance." Though she balked, he held both of her hands firmly. "Simple salsa. Three steps."

"This is silly," she said. "I've always been a klutz, and I don't need to know how to—"

"Everyone needs to dance. It's part of being human. If you want, I can quote anthropological evidence to prove it."

"And it's all about the data. Right?"

"Step forward on your right foot," he said. "At the same time, pick up the left. That's the first step."

Reluctantly, she did as he asked. "Now what?"

"Put your left foot down and put your weight on it. That's the second step."

"Okay," she said.

"Now bring your right foot back so it's even with the left. That's three."

Her feet, in purple socks, moved as he instructed. When she had the simple move down, he matched his steps to hers and counted the beat. "One, two, three. And one, two, three."

He showed her variations on the basic step. Going backward instead of forward. Twice forward. Twice back. "You've got it, Emma. You can dance."

"I can step," she corrected him. "But this doesn't look anything like the salsa dancing I've seen."

"So we add the hip action." He showed her the simple step, moving his hips in time to nonexistent music. Dancing and music came easily to him. "Feel the beat going through your body." He added a shoulder motion and clapped his hands. "One, two, three. And, one, two, three."

She attempted the move, clumsy at first. After a few

tries, her body understood the simple rhythm. Holding hands, they moved together.

"You're dancing," he said, still keeping the beat. "And nothing terrible is happening."

"One, two, three, and…" she counted under her breath.

He twirled her. "Hot move, *chica*. You're not meant to be alone."

"Don't confuse me."

"Relax. Feel the beat."

He pulled her against him. Their bodies moved as one, hips undulating. The tips of her breasts grazed his chest. He tossed his head, and she did the same. Her straight, brown hair flipped across her face.

He cinched her body tightly against his. Purposely, he slowed the count. *"Uno, dos, tres…"*

Her blue eyes flashed. Her lips parted.

Before he could kiss her, the doorbell sounded.

They split apart.

"That must be the sheriff," she said.

Miguel strode through the house, deactivated the alarm and unfastened the dead bolt.

Sheriff Martinez glared through the screen door. "This time, your brother has gone too far."

Chapter Sixteen

Miguel never claimed to be his twin brother's keeper. Dylan was a force unto himself. According to Sheriff Martinez, Dylan and his FBI buddy, Ben Parrish, had entered reservation territory, had gone to the home of Sherman Watts and had busted their way inside. An FBI raid. Totally unauthorized.

"Here's what they found," Martinez said angrily. "Nothing. Watts wasn't there."

The physical presence of their suspect was only part of the story. Miguel seriously doubted that Watts's home was void of evidence. "Did they have a chance to look around?"

"Bree and the tribal cops caught up with them pretty fast. She told them to get the hell off Ute property. The FBI has no jurisdiction on the rez. Your brother's lucky she didn't charge him with breaking and entering."

"Is Bree in charge?"

"Oh, yeah." Martinez had the look of a man who was about to get his butt kicked by his fiancée.

"I want to talk to her," Miguel said.

He needed to convince Bree to let him make a thorough analysis of the scene. Even if there wasn't anything as obvious as a smoking gun, there could be prints, fabrics, notes—some detail that would give them a lead.

Martinez took off his hat and raked his fingers through his hair. "Bree has good cause to be angry. Law enforcement in the Four Corners area is hard enough with four states vying for jurisdiction. Much less the FBI."

"Dylan messed up," Miguel agreed.

The deputy who had accompanied Martinez placed the food from the Morning Ray Café on the kitchen table and handed Miguel his guitar.

"*Gracias,*" Miguel said to the deputy. He turned to the sheriff. "I need to get inside Watts's house. Bridger said Watts had a partner. We need to figure out who that is. If I could explain to Bree—"

"Miguel, you don't know how mad that woman is. She'll chew your face off."

"I could talk to her," Emma offered.

When Miguel looked into her cornflower-blue eyes, it was hard to remember that Emma was part Ute. The way she'd handled Jerry Burch showed that she knew her way around the rez. But gaining access to the scene was Miguel's problem. "This is my job. I've worked with Bree before. We can be reasonable with each other. One law enforcement professional to another."

"It's your funeral," Martinez said.

Still, he got Bree on his cell phone and handed it to Miguel. Her first words weren't encouraging. "I can't believe I'm talking to anyone named Acevedo."

"My brother made a mistake," Miguel readily admitted. "He's not a patient man. Believe me, I know. I grew up with that *vato.*"

"Here's the deal, Miguel. I don't give a damn about protecting the rights of scum like Sherman Watts. And you know I'm willing to cooperate with the crime lab."

"I know," he said.

"But this is out of my hands. The tribal council doesn't

want the FBI thinking they can storm onto our land without consent."

"We'll be fast and respectful," he said. "Let me clean up my brother's mess. Close off the house. My forensic team can be on the road in five minutes."

"I've already secured the house," she said. "It's closed off and I have a man posted outside. But I need a clear directive from the council before you or anybody else gets near this place."

"Watts is connected to our ongoing investigation. And in the murder of Vincent Del Gardo," he said. "We have evidence that could match up to items in his house."

"How did Watts become a suspect?"

He told her about the trip he and Emma took to the rez, explained about the leather necklace and their interview with Jerry Burch. Then, he added the clincher. "More than anything, this is about finding Aspen Meadows, a missing daughter of your tribe."

After a pause, Bree said, "Next time, you set one toe into my jurisdiction, let me know. In the meantime, I'll see what I can do to convince the tribal council to give access to your forensic team. Probably not until tomorrow." She paused again. "From what I hear, you and Emma are getting close."

He shot a gaze toward the woman he'd held in his arms only a moment ago. "That's true."

"If you hurt her, Miguel, I'll track you down like a dog and kick your butt."

"Good to know."

He handed the phone back to Martinez and went toward Emma. Though she considered herself to be a loner, she had a lot of friends. "Bree says hi."

"Is she going to let you investigate?"

"It's up to the tribal council."

Emma groaned. "It could take hours for them to make a decision."

Time they didn't have. The threats to Emma's safety seemed to grow with every minute that passed. Bridger had reason to want her dead. Watts was involved in her cousin's disappearance and might come after Emma if he thought she was close to finding Aspen. Not to mention the unnamed partner of Sherman Watts.

They were like sharks, circling her tidy little house in Kenner City, and he was only one man with a gun. He couldn't stop a coordinated attack from Watts and his partner. Nor could he deal with an explosive device lobbed through a window. Half a dozen other disaster scenarios flashed through his mind.

One thing was clear: to deal with these sharks, they were going to need a bigger boat.

As soon as the sheriff got off the phone, Miguel explained the worsening situation. "I need two of your men. One at the front door. Another at the back."

"Okay, for tonight. But I can't promise bodyguards twenty-four hours a day. I don't have the manpower."

Tomorrow, Miguel might be able to pull in other guards using people from the lab. But bodyguard duty wasn't their training. They were technicians, scientists. What he needed was a man of action, someone who was dying to kick ass, a marksman who was trained in protection.

He needed his brother, Dylan.

AFTER THEY HAD DINNER and finished off the bottle of wine, Emma checked on Jack who, remarkably, hadn't wakened in spite of all the commotion made by Sheriff Martinez. The baby slept so soundly that she rested her hand on his back to make sure he was still breathing. When he wiggled, she quickly pulled her hand away.

It was too early for him to be down for the night, and she worried that Jack would be wide-awake at two in the morning, disrupting her sleep and Miguel's. Still, she couldn't bring herself to wake him. Leaning over the crib, she kissed Jack above his perfectly shaped ear and whispered, "Your mama will be home soon. We're going to find her."

Was that a promise she could keep? Her latest vision had resulted in useful information. She'd given Sheriff Martinez the names of Bridger's two prior victims— Simone Caparelli and Burton Nestor. And she was certain that Bridger had killed Del Gardo. But she couldn't figure out how those crimes linked up with Aspen's disappearance. Unless she was missing a clue from her vision... The mariachi music? The sombreros?

Sherman Watts was the more likely lead. She sensed the aura of danger around him, sensed that he was the man who had been chasing Aspen near the river. Also, there was the fact that Watts's bear claw necklace was found near Aspen's car.

The light strumming from Miguel's guitar led her into the front room. He sat on the edge of the rocking chair tuning his six-stringed instrument. The golden wood of the body gleamed softly in the light from a table lamp with a beaded shade.

Without disturbing him, she lowered herself onto the sofa and stretched out her legs. In her mind, she took a snapshot of this moment, hoping always to remember Miguel as he concentrated on his guitar. His hair fell loose across his forehead. He'd taken off his outer denim shirt. His black T-shirt revealed strong forearms and wrists that tapered to his long, sensitive fingers. Like her, he'd taken off his shoes and was barefoot.

When he looked up at her, she noticed the silver medallion that hung at his throat. Without looking down, he plucked the strings in a classical melody.

Emma wasn't a musical person, but she knew what she liked. And she definitely enjoyed the subtle blending of sound that came from his guitar. The vibration of the strings resonated inside her.

When he paused, she said one word. "Beautiful."

"Better than the Mozart you play for *mijo?*"

"Much better."

"Actually, that was Mozart. An adaptation of a piano adagio."

Could he possible be more perfect? "How did you start playing the guitar?"

"I was about twelve. My uncle got a new guitar and gave me his old one." He continued to finger the strings. "At first, I thought I should be in a band. Figured it was a good way to get girls. Every *chica* loves a rock star. But my uncle told me that this was an expensive guitar and I shouldn't play around with it."

He tapped a rapid tattoo on the body of the instrument as he continued. "Don't play around? That's what I said to him. What else are you supposed to do with a guitar?"

"And then?" she asked.

"He showed me. My uncle is a good musician. He taught me a lot. Then I took some other classes."

"The lessons paid off." She exhaled a contented sigh. Though there were deputies posted at the front of the house and the back, she felt like they were in a special, secluded space. A private world.

Miguel grinned. "My guitar still didn't help me get a date."

While he held the guitar, she could feel him opening up to her. "Ever since we met, I've been wanting to ask you about something."

"Go ahead."

"That medallion you always wear, it's from Santuario de Chimayo in New Mexico," she said. "I've never been there, but I've heard of it."

"It's a place of miracles," he said, accompanying his words on the guitar. "Long ago, a friar from Chimayo discovered a mysterious crucifix buried in the earth. He took it with him to Santa Cruz, but the crucifix disappeared. He found it back in the original hole where it was buried. This happened twice. A small adobe church was built on the site where the crucifix was found. Later, it was discovered that those who came to worship were cured of their ills."

"By praying to the crucifix?"

"By the dirt," he said. "The sacred soil from El Posito—the pit where the crucifix was found—has healing powers."

She raised a skeptical eyebrow. "I'm surprised that a guy like you, a scientist, believes in miracles."

"Hey, I was an altar boy." He stopped playing and held the medallion between thumb and forefinger. "Some things can't be explained by facts. Like your gift."

"Talking to the dead? I'm not so sure it's a gift."

"Your visions can't be rationally dissected. I can't put them under a microscope or through a computer program, but I believe you see them."

When she first saw him standing on her doorstep, watching her through suspicious eyes, Emma never would have predicted that he would accept her so completely.

Throughout her life, she'd been made to feel like she was weird or different. "You don't think I'm a witch? A *bruja?* Or mentally disturbed?"

"For sure, you're crazy," he teased. "*Loca bonita.* But crazy in a good way."

"Do I have Chimayo to thank for your open-mindedness?"

"Chimayo changed me," he admitted. "When I was growing up, I was nearly as wild as Dylan. *Dos perros,* we were like two dogs out howling at the moon. I got in a fight, got shot."

"My God, how old were you?"

"Sixteen." He shrugged. "Just a flesh wound in my shoulder, but we were a long way from the doctor. I lost a lot of blood. For a few minutes, I was dead. Then I went into a coma."

"You saw the light," she said.

"Pure white. Like angel's wings." His eyes took on a dreamy expression. "I was at peace. I wanted to stay in that beautiful place, but my mama wasn't ready for me to die. She went to Chimayo and brought back the soil from El Posito, which she rubbed into my hand."

"And you woke up?"

"A day later." He strummed his guitar for emphasis. "The doctor said I would have come out of the coma, with or without the soil. But it was important to me. And to Mama. She'd already lost one child."

"Your sister," she said. "Teresa."

His gaze rested gently on her face. "You've seen her."

"Dressed in white," Emma said, remembering her vision of the lovely young woman. "She wants you to know that she's all right."

"I miss her. Will always miss her. She was killed a few months after her *quinceanera*. An accidental shooting. After her death, Dylan and I went even crazier than before. It's probably why I got myself shot."

She knew that grief took many forms. Sometimes, people came to her, looking for their loved ones who had passed away. Often, they were angry. They wanted to curse the dead person for leaving them alone. "You were angry."

"Angry at death. I was only sixteen but living on the edge, taunting death. If fate could take my sister—a good girl who never did harm to anyone—I dared death to take me, too."

"And got yourself shot," she said.

"*Muy stupido*. I think Teresa's murder is what made Dylan decide to go into the FBI."

"And you?" she asked. "What did you decide?"

"I was different after my coma. More serious. I got into medical science and thought I might become a doctor. That's when I went to Chimayo myself and got this medallion. On the back, it says, Protect and Heal."

"But you went into forensics instead."

He played a chord on his guitar. "And that's the story of Miguel Acevedo. A rational man who believes in miracles."

The perfect man for her. At this moment, she felt so close to him. She knew that she was meant to be with him. Her virginity and lack of experience in lovemaking weren't an issue. She knew Miguel would understand. He'd be gentle.

"Now," he said, "we get back to work. I have this guitar for a reason. In your vision you heard mariachi music. If we can figure out what they were playing, the lyrics might be a clue."

But she wasn't interested in deciphering clues. She wanted to make love. "I already told you. The Mexican Hat Dance."

"Here's another." His fingers plucked out a familiar song.

"La Cucaracha," she said. "Yes, they played that. But I can't think of any clue that might relate to a cockroach."

"Unless it refers to Sherman Watts," he said.

He changed the rhythm. His left hand darted along the frets while he picked out individual notes on the strings. In a warm tenor, he sang in Spanish, the ballad of "Malagueña."

She leaned back against the sofa and closed her eyes. His voice mesmerized her. Though she didn't understand the lyrics, a plaintive tone of desperation and yearning touched her heart. Unexpected tears burned behind her eyelids.

He finished with a dramatic guitar flourish. "Well, Emma? Was this song in your vision?"

She pushed herself off the sofa and stood. "Tell me the words."

"A lover sings the praises of his Malagueña. He longs for her. Without her love, he will surely die of grief."

She stood before him. "We can't let that happen. Lovers are meant to be together."

He set his guitar aside and pulled her tight against him.

Chapter Seventeen

Still hearing the echo of his music inside her head, Emma submitted to her desires. She kissed Miguel with a passion so intense that it seemed to lift her off her feet. He cinched his arm around her waist as if to anchor her. He deepened the kiss with his tongue. Sensation raced through her veins.

She wanted to savor every touch, to fully experience this moment. But it was all happening so fast. They fell into an embrace on the sofa. He rose above her, his eyes shimmering like emerald stars, and she was overwhelmed. Unable to think, she didn't know what to do or what move to make next.

Doubt crept in. Was her inexperience showing? Would she make a fool of herself?

As if sensing her hesitation, Miguel spoke. "I've wanted this since the first time I saw you."

"Me, too."

He stroked her cheek, and she did the same to him. When his hand glided down her throat to her breast, an amazing thing happened. Her body reacted to his caresses as if she knew exactly what she was doing. She responded on pure instinct.

When he took off her shirt and her bra, she felt no shame. Not even when his gaze lingered on her breasts. He touched her as gently and skillfully as he stroked the strings of his guitar.

Again, she responded. Though she'd never done this dance before, she trusted him to take the lead. The rest of their clothing slipped away, almost like a miracle.

She placed her hand on his bronzed chest. His lean muscles quivered.

"Truly," he whispered as he kissed her again. "You are a crazy and beautiful lady."

"I must be crazy."

"And beautiful," he said. "Don't forget beautiful."

She didn't protest this extravagant compliment because she knew his sincerity was real. Miguel wouldn't lie. He thought she was beautiful, and she felt like the most fantastic creature on the planet.

Their bodies glided together. The rhythm of passion grew inside her—a throbbing, inexorable beat that would not be denied. He stroked between her legs, creating a new tempo, a trembling counterpoint.

When he paused to sheath himself in a condom he took from his wallet, she could hardly stand the brief moment away from him. She'd been waiting for this moment for a very long time. All her life.

He poised above her, gazing down. Slowly, slowly, he entered her. Her breath caught. She was on the verge of fainting but, at the same time, intensely involved with each thrust. This was more than she'd imagined. Better.

His body tensed. At that very second, she was rocked by surging emotions, like being caught in a churning ocean wave and tumbled to the shore.

They climaxed together—a thrill and a relief. She must have done something right.

Breathing hard, they lay tangled together on the narrow sofa. Fireworks burst behind her closed eyelids. She reveled in the sensations, taking a full measure of enjoyment. And then, she sighed. "That was worth waiting for."

"Worthwhile," he said.

"If I'd known…" Her voice trailed off. "I'm a virgin, Miguel."

"What?"

She opened her eyes. "I mean, I *was* a virgin. Used to be. Until just a few minutes ago. You're my first lover." Amused, she rolled the word in her mouth. "Looov-ah."

His gaze darted, but he didn't move away from her. "I didn't know."

Of course, he didn't know. Virginity was her secret. Perhaps she shouldn't have mentioned anything, but he'd been open with her. It didn't seem right to hold back. "You couldn't tell, could you? Did I make mistakes?"

"No mistakes, *querida*." He kissed her forehead. "You were perfect."

She cleared her throat. "I'd like to do it again."

"That can be arranged."

However, before they had progressed beyond one kiss, she heard Jack fussing in the bedroom. As she'd feared, the baby wasn't going to sleep well tonight.

She eased away from the wonderfully cozy spot on the sofa beside him and went to care for the baby, gathering her clothing along the way. After slipping into a nightshirt, Emma performed the familiar baby care routine—changing his diaper, wiping and powdering. These were actions she'd done hundreds of times. And yet, as she lifted the baby to her shoulder, she was aware of the difference. Her life had changed. More than the slight tingling between her legs, she felt an afterglow of the passion she'd shared with Miguel. Not a virgin anymore.

She wished she could call Aspen and tell her.

LYING ON THE SOFA, Miguel took a moment to digest Emma's secret. A virgin? How could a woman as beautiful as Emma be a thirty-year-old virgin? She'd talked about being an outcast on the rez, about going off to college when she was only sixteen, about working alone in her office. But a virgin?

As the first man who had slept with her, he felt a certain responsibility. This couldn't be a one-night stand. He couldn't hop onto his motorcycle and ride off into the sunset.

Not that he had considered either of those alternatives. From the start, he knew that he wanted something more with Emma. A relationship with her would be a constant amazement.

He pulled himself off the sofa. This was all working out for the best.

While she fed *mijo,* he stayed with her, playing his guitar and thinking of the next time they would make love. He'd be more careful with her. He'd tenderly introduce her to the pleasures of her own body.

After his feeding, Jack was wide-awake. His schedule had been disrupted, and he wasn't about to let them rest when he wanted to play. It took over an hour to get him back to sleep.

Miguel collapsed on the bed beside her. He could tell that she was exhausted. Gently, he kissed her smooth forehead. "Tonight, we'll sleep. Tomorrow, we'll make love again."

Her blue eyes, lined with black lashes, gleamed in the faint light of the bedside lamp. She whispered his name. "Tomorrow is a very long time to wait."

"Hours." Having her so close, lying beside her on the bed, he was already aroused. But he wouldn't push her.

She coiled her arms around him and pulled him closer. "I can't wait until tomorrow, Miguel. I want you."

She'd gone from virgin to wild cat. He couldn't have been happier.

After they made love, he closed his eyes and sank into dreams of Emma that lasted until early morning when Jack was awake again.

MIGUEL EXPECTED THIS to be a very long day. With luck, he would be given permission from Bree to process the scene at the home of Sherman Watts. New evidence could be uncovered.

With Jack tucked into the crook of his arm, he made his first phone call to his brother. "Dylan, I need you at Emma's house."

"Why? What's your problem, *vato?*"

His tone was surly, and Miguel answered in kind. "After what you did last night, you should take a step back from this investigation. I need a bodyguard for Emma and little *mijo.*"

"I'm not a babysitter."

"Maybe you should be. That's something you can do right."

Miguel imagined his twin seething. Dylan wasn't accustomed to failure. Tersely, he said, "I'll be there."

He watched Emma as she bustled around her kitchen, putting together trays of coffee and cereal for the two deputies who had spent the night guarding her house. She wore a cotton shirt the color of lilacs in spring, and she reminded him of a graceful flower, bobbing in the mountain breezes. Such poetry! She inspired him. *Te quiero,* Emma. He thought the words but didn't say them.

Once, he noticed her laughing to herself. Was she talking to her ghosts? Telling them that she was no longer a virgin?

Unexpectedly, she bounced over to him and kissed his cheek. "Don't look so worried, Miguel. Everything is going to be all right. We'll find Aspen. Soon. I can feel it."

"You've been talking to your ghosts again."

She shrugged. "I just have a feeling."

A bizarre and disturbing thought occurred to him. "Last night, when we were making love—"

"Twice," she reminded him with a sexy grin.

"*Sí*, both times when we were making love, were we…alone?"

She cocked her head to one side and gave him a quizzical look. "Of course, we were."

"I mean *completely* alone." He gestured to the air around them. "No ghosts."

She gave a throaty laugh. "Did you think my grandma and Aunt Rose might be around?"

The thought of two little old lady spectators made him cringe. "They have a habit of popping in unannounced."

"Not to worry. They come to me in response to something I'm thinking about." She glided her arms up his chest and around his neck. "Last night, my every thought focused on you."

He gave her a quick peck on the cheek. "You're sure?"

"Positive."

His cell phone rang, and he disentangled himself to answer. It was Callie at the crime lab. After she gave him an update on their progress, she had another proposition. "I'd like to have you bring Emma over here."

He figured that Callie wanted to see baby Jack again, but that wasn't going to happen. After last night's fussing, it was obvious that they needed to keep *mijo* on a more regular schedule. "The baby needs his rest."

"This isn't about Jack," she said. "Emma is a valuable resource that we haven't been using. I want her to take a look at the evidence. Maybe she'll get a sense of where to go from here."

"We'll be over later," he said. "Any word from Bree

on whether or not we can go onto the rez to process Watts's house?"

"Nothing yet."

After ending his call, he paced through the house, carrying Jack and thinking. He expected that the evidence they'd find at Watts's house would point to a partnership with Boyd Perkins. In prior investigation, the crime lab had already found fingerprints and a bullet from a gun owned by Perkins. Their operating assumption was that Perkins— a known hit man for another Vegas crime ring—had been sent to this area to kill Del Gardo. It seemed rational to assume that Perkins had hooked up with Watts—a man who knew the territory.

After he put Jack down for a nap, Miguel tried to discuss this possibility with Emma. But she wasn't interested in talk. In spite of the deputies in the kitchen, she shoved the bedroom door closed. The intensity of her kiss shocked and amazed him.

It seemed that her intention was to make up for thirty years of virginity in one day. Which was okay by him. The next time he left the house, he'd pick up a crate of condoms.

IT WAS AFTER LUNCH when Miguel opened the door for his brother. As soon as their eyes met, Miguel knew Dylan was *muy furioso.* That attitude always meant trouble.

Carrying his cardboard cup of coffee, Dylan strode through the house. Wearing his FBI jacket with the letters stenciled on the back, he wasn't exactly undercover. "I've been ordered to stand down. For the rest of the day, I'm supposed to back off."

"What did you expect?"

"I expected to catch Watts." He pivoted on his heel and glared. "It's what you should have done."

Miguel knew better than to get into a spitting match with

his twin, but he couldn't let that statement stand. "You think I should have gone after Watts?"

"As soon as you had the suspect's name, you should have taken action."

Not when Emma and Jack were in the car with him. Should he have dragged an infant into a dangerous situation? "I did take action. Big mistake. I called you."

Dylan set down his coffee on the dining-room table where Jack sat in his baby seat, waving his arms and kicking his legs like a swimmer who didn't know he was out of the water.

Turning away from the baby, Dylan faced him. He tore off his jacket and squared his shoulders, ready for a fight. "If I had been where you were—on the rez—I would have made my move. Watts would be in custody."

"Listen to me, *estupido*. If I had—"

"Don't call me stupid."

"What else would you call your unauthorized raid?"

"At least, I did something," Dylan said.

"Something stupid."

Are we in grade school? His twin had always known how to provoke him. Miguel's fingers curled into fists. It'd be dumb to get into a fight in Emma's dining room, but punching Dylan would feel so damned good.

"Here's how I see it," Dylan lectured. "The only way to nab Watts—a *gallito* who knows every hiding place in these hills and valleys—is to strike fast. Grab him before he figures out we're onto him."

"Grab him? Even when you have no authority on the rez to make an arrest."

"Jurisdiction be damned," Dylan said. "You know this guy was involved in Aspen's disappearance, right?"

"That's right," Emma said as she entered from the kitchen. Fearlessly, she positioned herself between them. "Watts is the man I saw in my vision. We found his necklace near the place where Aspen lost control of her car. He's definitely involved."

"He's the best lead we have. *Dios mio,* he's the only lead."

"Is that so?" Emma shot him a hostile glare that told Miguel she'd been eavesdropping. "My, Dylan. It almost sounds like you're actually beginning to care about what happened to my cousin."

"Yes, I care." His voice was strained. "I care about Aspen. And Julie. And even Del Gardo. I want this case closed."

"We all do," Miguel said. "But you've been warned off. You need to take a step back."

"Are you telling me what to do?"

"Leave this to me, Dylan."

"You? You've never even made an arrest." Dylan stuck out his chin, a tempting target. "Oh, maybe you've read a suspect his Miranda rights after he's been taken into custody. But you don't know what it's like in the field."

"Kicking down doors. Racing in hot pursuit. Waving your gun." Miguel's anger simmered, close to boiling over. "That's not my job."

"Because you hide in the lab. You stay safe."

"I stay smart. I think before I act."

There were times—plenty of times—when he'd prefer the release of action. If anyone threatened Emma or baby Jack, he'd be hard-pressed to hold himself in check.

He glanced over at her, where she stood watching their argument like a spectator at a tennis match. Then, he turned back to his brother. "Kicking ass? That's the easy part."

"You think my job is easy?"

"Not when it's done right," Miguel fired back. "It's tough to put together enough evidence for a conviction. You know that, Dylan. You know that when you angered the tribal elders, you made everybody's job harder. Because of you, we can't get into Watts's house and do the forensics."

"I was just trying to—"

"You didn't even apprehend the suspect."

Dylan winced. The fight went out of him as he dropped into a chair beside the table. His gaze cast downward. He was in pain—genuine pain. And Miguel felt his agony.

A few seconds ago, he'd wanted to punch his brother in the nose. Instead, he rested a comforting hand on Dylan's shoulder. "It'll work out. We'll get this guy."

Looking up, Dylan's face was troubled. "I lied just now when I said I don't make mistakes. Some of the stuff I've done is beyond fixing. I'll never make it right."

Miguel assumed he was referring to a serial killer case he'd been on before coming to Kenner City. Though his brother hadn't told him details, he knew that case had been intense. "Whatever you need, I'm here."

He stood and gave him a hug. No matter how much they fought, they were part of each other. Twins.

Over his brother's shoulder, he saw Emma smiling warmly. She'd fit well into the Acevedo family, where passions ran high but they never stopped caring for each other.

Dylan stepped back. "Okay, Miguel. What do you want me to do?"

He pointed to Jack. "This little *mijo* has been through hell. He's lost his mama. He's been dragged all over the countryside looking for bad guys. Today, he needs rest and the best protection the FBI can provide."

"You weren't joking? You really want me to spend the day as a babysitter?"

"That's right."

Dylan lifted Jack from his baby seat. When Jack burst into a spontaneous grin, Dylan had to respond. "I care about this case," he murmured. "More than you know."

Chapter Eighteen

At the crime lab, Emma stood beside Miguel and watched while Ava and Bobby displayed the bagged and tagged evidence they'd gathered from inside Del Gardo's tunnels. Supposedly, Callie wanted Emma here as a resource—a psychic translator of these physical clues. She hoped she could help, but the debris from the tunnels looked like garbage to her.

Ava held up plastic evidence bags containing candy wrappers, an empty aspirin bottle, used tissues and a personal music player. "Because of fingerprints, we assume all these items belonged to Del Gardo. Emma, is there anything here you'd like to look at more closely?"

Bobby O'Shea watched her with a curiosity that was both insulting and flattering. He asked, "Exactly what do you need to get your vision started? Should we hand you things in a certain order?"

"She's not a psychic computer," Miguel informed his colleagues. "Emma gets her insights from people who have passed away. Sometimes they cooperate. Sometimes, not. These ghosts are as unpredictable as the weather."

She smiled at him—Miguel, her lover. Her first lover. Being with him made it difficult to concentrate on anything else, but she had to try. For Aspen's sake. "I wish I could guarantee accuracy, but it doesn't work that way. It might be best if I just watch while you show Miguel the evidence."

"Okay," Miguel said as he looked over the array. "From this stuff, we can deduce that Del Gardo liked chocolate with peanuts and probably had a head cold. What did you get from the music player?"

"Frank Sinatra, Tony Bennett and jazz," Ava said.

"Tell me about the prints."

"Almost all were from Del Gardo. Likewise with DNA extracted from hairs we found on the bedroll."

"But his head was shaved," Emma said.

Ava stroked her own chin. "From his white beard."

Callie joined them. "The Santa Claus beard. It's hard to believe that such a simple disguise was so effective. When I saw his body in autopsy, I barely recognized him." She gave Emma a quick nod. "Thank you for coming."

"I hope I can help."

"I have a bit of good news," Callie said. "I just got off the phone with Sheriff Martinez. He said that the Colorado state patrol sighted Bridger's black SUV outside Telluride."

"Yes!" Emma gave a fist pump, a gesture she'd never before used in her life. "He's on the run."

"Was he arrested?" Miguel asked.

"Afraid not."

Callie's expression was troubled, and Emma sensed an undercurrent of strong emotion. Patting Callie's shoulder, she said, "You must be relieved. Del Gardo is no longer a threat to your safety."

"I've been worrying about him for months, looking over my shoulder, never knowing when he might attack. And yet, there's something poignant about the death of an adversary." She picked an invisible piece of lint off her white lab coat. "It's hard to believe he's finally gone."

Miguel nudged Bobby's shoulder. "What else did you find in the tunnels?"

"Not the millions of dollars in treasure. Ain't that a shame." A goofy grin made his face look lopsided. "I already figured out how I'd spend my share."

"You don't get a share," Callie said. "We're not treasure hunters."

"Beagles," Bobby said. "I read about this guy online who made a fortune raising and training purebred German shepherds. I could do the same thing. Buy a couple of acres and set up a beagle ranch."

"Bobby," Miguel interrupted. "The evidence."

"Right. There are other prints, mostly smudged and probably old. From clerks in stores. Stuff like that." He shuffled through evidence bags until he found one containing a plastic comb. "This is the prize. A nice, clear thumbprint from our Vegas hit man—Boyd Perkins."

"Unfortunately," Ava said, "one print isn't enough to draw conclusions. We can't say for sure that Perkins was in the tunnels. Del Gardo might have picked up the comb."

"That print shows Perkins was close," Bobby said. "That's significant."

"But did Perkins kill the old fox?" Miguel posed the question. "What else does the evidence say?"

On this topic, Emma needed no further validation from the physical evidence. Because of her vision, she was certain that Bridger was the man who murdered Del Gardo. She'd seen Bridger with blood on his hands. As the memory flashed in her mind, she heard echoes of the fiesta music.

The raucous sounds of the mariachis faded into the sweet resonance of Miguel's guitar playing, the memory of his voice singing softly. She thought of his skillful hands, plucking the strings of his guitar and caressing her body. A rush of passion coursed through her veins, raising her temperature. She fanned her face.

"Are you all right?" Callie asked.

"I'm great," she said. And she meant it. Emma was no longer a timid old maid. Not a loner anymore.

"Over here," Ava said as she led the way across the lab to the evidence wall where several items were displayed. "I've made a preliminary sketch of the inside of the tunnels. As you can see, it's very similar to the VDG map made by Julie Grainger."

Emma compared the two drawings. It was obvious that Julie had been in those tunnels. Had Del Gardo found her snooping around in his lair? Had he killed her?

Though Julie's murder was important to Emma, her focus remained on her cousin. She needed to know how Aspen fit into the picture that was emerging from the evidence. Moving along the wall, she studied the other information that had been posted. A map of Kenner County and the reservation took up a large portion of the wall. Various locations had been labeled. Griffin's house. The spot where Aspen's car was found. Sherman Watts's house. He seemed to be equal distance from Towaoc, the casino on the reservation and a little town just outside the rez called Mexican Hat.

Her gaze moved down the board to a series of mug shots, labeled with tags—a Rogue's Gallery of suspects. She saw Bridger with his several aliases listed. And two photos of Del Gardo: a death shot of an old man with a beard and a picture of what he looked like without his disguise. Comparing the two, she decided that Vincent Del Gardo was definitely more sinister with hair.

Emma barely glanced at Boyd Perkins. Though central to the investigation, he didn't make much of an impression on her. Sherman Watts was different. His flat, black eyes seemed to follow her as she moved. He looked older than she thought, probably in his late forties. Hard living had carved deep lines in his face. Danger emanated from him.

Farther down the wall were photos of Simone Capparelli and Burton Nestor, easily recognizable as her two ghosts—the victims of Bridger. She pointed to them. "Did you find any information about these two?"

"We checked with Las Vegas homicide," Callie said. "Both of these murders are open investigations. Bridger was interrogated, but he had airtight alibis for both incidents."

Now would have been a good time for Simone and Burton to appear. Emma gazed intently at the photos. All she had was a memory of her vision where these two victims danced at the fiesta.

"There's something I want to see," Miguel said. "The cast of the boot print we found near Del Gardo's body."

"Got it." Bobby's grin couldn't get any wider. Clearly, he was proud of his work. As he loped toward a computer, Emma was reminded of one of the beagles Bobby hoped to raise.

He tapped on the keyboard. "Here are the digital photos we took at the scene. Check out the surrounding area. It's all bushes, shrubs and rocks. We were lucky to get this boot print."

Bobby scrolled through a photo array. Pictures taken from every angle. Several included measuring instruments placed beside the print to indicate the size in inches and centimeters.

"It's a size thirteen," Bobby said. "Big foot."

Miguel leaned closer to the screen. "The heel box doesn't look like any cowboy boot I've ever seen."

"That's right," Bobby said. "These boots weren't made for riding. They're meant to be stylish. Custom-crafted."

He rose from his seat at the computer. With a flourish,

he unveiled the cast he'd made of the footprint. Emma reached over to touch the surface. "It's perfect. How did you get so much detail?"

"It's a diestone material. Mix the powder up, pour it in, let it set. And then spray with sealant."

"This would be great for arts and crafts projects," she said. "I could make little prints of Jack's hands and feet."

Callie beamed. "How is my favorite baby?"

"Taking a day off to rest. Dylan is watching him."

"He ought to be good at babysitting," Callie muttered. "He acts like he's about two years old."

Emma suppressed a chuckle. "I have the feeling that Dylan was one of those kids who never learned to play well with others."

"Hey," Miguel interrupted. "Can we focus on the case?"

"I saved the best for last," Bobby said. "Remember how I said the boots were custom? They're also new, barely worn. I checked with the Las Vegas PD, and they referred me to Ostrich Al's Custom Shoes. When I described the boot print to Al, he didn't even need to check his records. Two weeks ago, he sold a pair of snakeskin boots, size thirteen, to Hank Bridger."

That was enough proof for Emma. "So we know he was there. At the tunnels. We know he killed Del Gardo."

"Not necessarily," Miguel said. "We've placed him at the crime scene, but we still need to put the gun in his hand."

"I wonder if he knew," she mused, "how close he was."

"To what?" Callie asked.

"Bridger is obsessed with Julie's map, thinks it will show him where the money is hidden. If he knew that map was of the tunnels, he'd be there right now. With a shovel and a pickax."

She turned to see Miguel watching her. "Bridger wouldn't go back there now. We have the area marked off as a crime scene."

"But we're done with forensics," Bobby said. "And we don't have a guard posted."

"Bridger and the tunnels," Emma said. "They go together like…"

Tongue-tied, she tried to come up with an apt comparison. She was, after all, a writer of pulse-pounding adventure, and she ought to have a ready phrase. But when she looked into Miguel's green eyes, the only simile she could come up with was her and Miguel. They belonged together. Their names should be carved in the trunk of a tree with a big, sappy heart drawn around them.

She felt a blush creeping up her throat, and she shrugged. "That's my hunch."

"Bridger and the tunnels," Miguel said. "I'll remember that."

He turned to the others, and they discussed other evidence that was yet to be processed. Though Miguel had been absent for most of the work at the crime lab, he was clearly in charge of analyzing the crime scene evidence. Was there anything sexier than a competent man? Anyone sexier than Miguel?

Listening to their discussion with only half an ear, she turned back to the wall. She touched the VDG map, hoping she'd make a connection with Julie. The spirit of the deceased FBI agent had led her into the investigation. It made sense that Julie would show the next step.

Everyone else was working hard, putting forth an intense effort. Emma had nothing but the echo of that annoying mariachi tune. She must have been humming it because Callie came closer. "What's that song?"

"Something I've got stuck in my head," Emma said. "I heard the tune in a vision, and it keeps playing over and over."

"Could be significant," Callie said.

"I don't think so. It's a kid's song. La-la-di-dah-dahdi-dah." She clapped twice. "It's called 'The Mexican Hat Dance.'"

Callie raised an eyebrow. She pointed to the map. "Like this town. Mexican Hat."

Emma's focus zoomed in on the tiny dot on the map. The San Juan River etched a path near the town of Mexican Hat.

The music inside her head went silent as she remembered the end of her vision with dozens of sombreros tossed in the air. Mexican Hat. This was the clue she'd been waiting for. Her vision had been important after all. The mariachi song pointed the next step on the path to finding Aspen. "I need to go there."

The receptionist Emma had met at the front desk strode into the room. "I got the call from Bree," she announced. "The tribal elders will allow a CSI team to process Watts's house. You should leave right away."

Immediately, they went into action. Finding Sherman Watts was the number one priority.

THOUGH MIGUEL WAS ITCHING to get his hands on the evidence he was sure they'd find at Watts's house, Emma came first. He drove her car back toward her house. "Are you sure you don't want me to stay with you?"

"It won't be easy, but I can force myself to wait until you come home." As an afterthought, she said, "I'll save you a space on my bed."

Condoms, he remembered. He needed more condoms. "You'll be safe with Dylan."

"When you come back to me tonight, we might want to take some risks."

She leaned toward him, as far as her seat belt would allow, and stroked his jaw. When her thumb traced the line of his lips, he caught hold of her hand and kissed her palm. "You have risky business in mind?"

"Dangerous liaisons." Her voice was husky. "I've never felt like this before. I want to throw caution to the wind, to storm forth and conquer the world."

"Making love doesn't mean you've turned into a super-hero, Emma."

"Really?" She pulled her hand back. "I'm not invincible?"

"Not likely."

"And I can't fly? Except in the metaphorical sense."

"Metaphors?"

"My heart takes flight. Fly me to the moon. Be the wind beneath my wings." She heaved a sigh. "All those romantic song lyrics. I never understood them until now."

"Speaking of songs…"

"Mexican Hat," she said. "As soon as Callie pointed it out on the map, I saw the connection to my vision. All those sombreros must mean something. We need to go to Mexican Hat."

"Tomorrow," he promised.

"I'm not sure I can wait." She fidgeted in her seat. "But it's important for you to go to Watts's house on the rez. He's the best link we have to Aspen, and I want the best person handling the evidence. That means you."

"You just saw the crime lab in action. They're all good."

"But you're the best. Everyone else defers to you when it comes to crime scene evidence. Even Callie."

Without being too cocky, he knew she was right. In addition to gathering evidence, he had learned—through study and experience—how to take an overview of the scene. The application of inductive and deductive logic showed him where to look and what was significant.

He turned onto her street. "In case you need your car, I'll take my bike to the rez. It's parked in your driveway."

"By the time you get there, it'll be dark. Is it safe to ride your motorcycle at night?"

"I'll be fine."

As soon as he parked her car at the curb in front of her house, she unsnapped her seat belt and kissed him. Her mouth pressed hard. He pulled her onto his lap, wedged against the steering wheel. Her hair brushed his cheek, and he smelled the scent of her shampoo—fragrant as a night-blooming flower.

When they separated, his heart was beating faster. "I almost forgot what it was like to make out in a car."

"What's it like?"

"Uncomfortable."

Holding her, he gazed through the windshield. Daylight was fading. He needed to get moving, get to the scene. But he longed to stay here with her, to make love until dawn. "I'll miss you, *querida.*"

"What will happen," she asked, "after we find Aspen and all the thugs are in jail?"

"Fiesta?"

"When you no longer need to stay with me as a body-guard, what will you do?"

He wasn't about to plan the rest of their life in the two minutes that it took for him to walk from her car to his Harley. "Emma, this is a talk that needs more time than we have."

"Just wondering," she said.

She looked away from him. Was she hurt? *Dios mio,* that was the last thing he wanted. "I need to go."

She followed him to the Harley for another long, linger-ing kiss. Then she stepped back. "Be careful, Miguel."

He cranked the motor and flipped down the visor on his helmet. As he powered into the street, he looked back at Emma standing in front of her house. The wave of her hand tugged at his heart. He never wanted to leave her.

Logic told him that he would never find another woman like her. *Te amo, Emma.*

Chapter Nineteen

Emma turned on her headlights as she drove east through the settling dusk. She lowered the driver's-side window halfway, and the evening breeze whisked across her face. Hoping to drown out the insistent mariachi music that still played inside her head, she reached for the buttons on the radio. Instead of the Mozart she usually played for the baby, she tuned to the oldies station.

The song on the radio made her grin. An old Frank Sinatra hit. Vincent Del Gardo would have loved this music. She sang along with the classic "My Way."

Her way. That was where she was headed. Her way.

Following her own path, even though she was pretty sure Miguel wouldn't approve. When he'd dropped her off, he'd expected her to march inside the house, lock the doors and stay there. He'd promised to take her to Mexican Hat tomorrow.

But she couldn't wait. In the crime lab, when she'd figured out the meaning of her fiesta vision, she knew that she had to follow that lead as soon as possible. Between her visions and Miguel's evidence, they were close to finding Aspen. Only inches away. With one final clue, the mystery of her cousin's disappearance would be solved.

Glancing to her right, Emma saw Grandma Quinn sitting in the passenger seat. "Go home, Emma."

"Why should I?"

"Because I said so." Grandma's voice was thin but firm. "You shouldn't be out here by yourself."

Since childhood, Grandma Quinn had watched over her like a guardian angel. Emma took her warnings seriously, but it wasn't as if she was plunging forward with no regard for her own safety. "I'm only going to look around at Mexican Hat. I have no intention of getting out of the car."

"Not even if you're led toward Aspen?"

Of course, that was what Emma hoped for. The best possible scenario would be for Julie Grainger to show up and point the way. "I won't rush in. I'll call for help."

"Tomorrow is soon enough."

"Then why was I given this vision?" She was so close to finding Aspen. "Can you tell me if she's there? Is Aspen in Mexican Hat?"

"This isn't like you, Emma. You're usually such a sensible girl."

She pulled onto the shoulder of the road and let the car behind her pass. In her encounters with her grandma, she tried to be respectful. Literally, she owed Grandma Quinn her life. "Please tell me. Will I find my cousin in Mexican Hat?"

"You know better than to ask. I'm not a fortune teller, dear." Her outline softened. "I want you to have all the happiness you deserve."

Emma remained adamant. "Aspen is there, isn't she? You can't deny it."

"Go home," Grandma Quinn repeated. "Be safe."

Then she vanished.

An old pickup truck rumbled by. This wasn't a busy road, but there was a fairly steady stream of traffic. Nobody would attack her with all these witnesses; she ought to be safe.

The cell phone in her purse rang. Caller ID showed it was Miguel. Explaining herself to him would be far more difficult than dealing with Grandma Quinn. Reluctantly, she answered.

"Dylan called," he said. "It seems that you never made it into the house. He stood at the front window and watched you get in your car and drive away."

She tried to change the subject. "How was his afternoon of babysitting?"

"Where the hell are you, Emma?"

"Going to Mexican Hat."

"Not anymore. Turn the car around and go home."

"I'm not being reckless," she said. "Bridger was sighted near Telluride. He's probably on his way back to Vegas. In any case, he's far away from me."

"What about Sherman Watts? And Boyd Perkins?"

"They're both on the run for their lives. Nobody has seen Perkins in days. By now, Watts knows he's the target of a manhunt. Why would either of them bother with me?"

There was a pause as Miguel considered her words. "I don't know."

"You see? No need for worry. I'm only going to drive through Mexican Hat near the San Juan River. In my first vision, I saw a river."

"You also saw someone who wanted to kill you."

A shudder went through her. She hadn't forgotten the faceless man with a knife. "He was chasing me. If I don't get out of the car, that can't happen. I'll be safe."

She couldn't say the words that poised on the tip of her tongue, couldn't bring herself to tell him that she probably didn't need a bodyguard anymore.

Parked at the edge of the road, she watched as headlights approached and drove on.

Earlier, when she'd asked him what would happen when

his presence wasn't necessary to keep her safe, she'd made a mistake. She had no right to push him or make inappropriate demands. Just because they'd made love, it didn't mean they were going to be together forever. Plenty of women—sophisticated women—were able to have sex with a man, then say *adios*. At least, that was what Emma had heard. She'd read about casual sex in novels. Seen it in movies.

But there was nothing casual about her feelings for Miguel. She wanted him with a passion that was bigger and more powerful than an avalanche. But she couldn't force him to feel the same way about her.

"Where are you?" he repeated. "On what route?"

"Why do you want to know?"

"I'll join you, *querida*. I think you need a motorcycle escort through Mexican Hat."

Her heart took a happy leap. She'd love to have him with her, but she didn't want to tear him away from his investigation. "I'm all right, Miguel. Stay where you are."

"I'll find you."

Before she could object, he disconnected the call.

AFTER A QUICK EXPLANATION to Callie, Miguel remapped his route. Locating Emma wouldn't be difficult; there weren't that many roads that went through Mexican Hat near the river.

Though her rationale about being safe made a certain amount of sense, she wasn't acting on logic. Emma was following her feelings. *That's what she did.* Her actions were directed by ghosts and emotions. *That's why she needed him.*

He brought reality and common sense to her life. He wouldn't take any chances with her safety, not even if the odds were a hundred to one. She meant too much to him.

Stubborn woman. He wheeled around on his Harley. Fortunately, Mexican Hat wasn't far from the rez. He might even get there before she did.

APPROACHING THE RIVER, Emma slowed her car. The traffic was almost nonexistent. A desolate night had descended, sprinkling stars across the black velvet skies. In the distance, she saw the lights from the town of Mexican Hat, but there were no houses nearby. On one side of the road were open fields leading toward forests and jagged cliffs. On the other was the river—about forty yards away and down an incline.

She pulled off and parked in a wide area overlooking the river. Gravel crunched under her tires. She'd promised not to leave the car, but there was no rule against lowering the window. She turned off her engine and listened to the rush of cold, white water. A chill slid down her spine.

Among the cottonwoods near the edge of the river, she saw the figure of a woman. Aspen? Was she here? Anticipation mixed with dread as Emma watched the ethereal figure approach. A spirit. If this woman was Aspen, it meant her cousin was dead.

In a logical sense, Aspen's death was likely. Why else would she be gone for so long? Why else abandon her baby? For the first time since this investigation started, Emma allowed herself to consider the horrible possibility of her cousin's death. She didn't want it to be true, didn't want to step out of her car and find Aspen's body.

Hands gripping the steering wheel, she watched as the woman came closer. Her FBI jacket caught on the breeze. Julie Grainger. Emma whispered her name.

A vision flashed before her eyes. Julie in a life-and-death struggle, fighting off two men.

Emma blinked and the vision was gone. Julie came closer. The wind tossed her hair. Moonlight shone on her pale face.

Purposefully, Emma closed her eyes. She needed to know what had happened, needed to see. Julie's lifeless body was being dragged across dirt and rocks.

Then she saw Aspen. Like Emma, Aspen watched as the men disposed of Julie's body.

The vision dissipated. When Emma looked up, she saw Julie striding closer. Even in death, she was strong and full of purpose. She spoke one word. "Witness."

Aspen had been a witness.

Julie disappeared into the night, leaving Emma shaking with anger and regret. Finally, she knew how Aspen was connected to Del Gardo and these other crimes. She knew why Aspen had been attacked. Her cousin had done nothing wrong. Aspen had merely been in the wrong place at the wrong time. She'd seen something she shouldn't have seen. And she'd paid the price for her bad luck.

But was she dead? Emma wished that Miguel was here; he could translate her vision into logic. When he was with her, she felt grounded and safe. She needed him. Alone, she had too many questions and too few answers.

Aspen's abandoned car with Jack in the backseat had been found far away from this place. Why had she come here?

Mexican Hat was close to the rez. Had Aspen been trying to get back home?

"Julie," Emma whispered, "come back."

She needed more information. Her hand rested on the door latch. Julie had come from those trees by the river. Should she go there?

This area was not well-traveled. It had been several minutes since any cars passed the overlook where she was parked. She glanced toward the road and saw the outline of a pickup truck pulled off on the shoulder about twenty yards behind her. Its lights were off.

She didn't remember passing a parked truck before she pulled off which meant that he must have been following her. But she hadn't seen his headlights. She remembered the careful way Bridger had kept his distance when he followed them from the reservation. This couldn't be him. He drove an SUV, not a truck. And he'd been sighted in Telluride, far away from Kenner City…unless he'd turned around and come back…unless the state patrol had made a mistake in identifying his vehicle.

This was enough investigation for tonight. She cranked the key in the ignition.

Before she could back up and pull away, the truck was behind her. Its lights were still off. She tried to drive forward, making a sharp turn. The nose of the vehicle tapped her bumper. She jolted.

The only escape route was straight ahead. Her foot jammed down on the accelerator and the engine whined. She drove off the gravel overlook onto the moist earth. Her car wasn't made for off-road driving. Her undercarriage crashed over rocks and ditches.

She tried to turn, but her steering wheel wouldn't respond. Forward momentum carried her toward the trees at the river's edge. She jammed on the brake but couldn't stop. Her car wasn't going fast. Just fast enough to keep rolling. Her front bumper smacked the trunk of a cottonwood.

The impact was painful. The air bag exploded in her face.

Frantic, Emma fought the bag. Her car was dead. Her window was still open. If she sat here, he'd grab her.

Struggling, she stumbled out of her car. Pain shot up her leg from her ankle. She must have injured herself when she hit the tree. No time to think about that now. She lurched forward.

To her right, the river roared. The bare branches of trees rattled in the wind. Gritting her teeth, she forced herself to run. To run for her life.

Adrenaline surged through her body, giving her much-needed strength. If she got back to the road, there might be another car. She might find someone to help her.

"Help me," she cried out. "Someone help me."

She turned and saw the dark figure of a man coming after her—moving fast while she was clumsy. Her ankle must be sprained. Her whole leg felt numb. Still, she dodged around a clump of sagebrush.

Her pursuer came closer. She could hear him.

She had no way to fight him off. No gun. No weapon.

His hand gripped her arm. He spun her around.

Off balance, she fell to the earth. Her bare hands scraped against the rocks.

He loomed over her. Like her vision. But she clearly saw his face, and she recognized Sherman Watts from the photographs.

"Where is she?" he demanded.

He must be talking about Aspen. Emma took a breath, hoping to calm her racing pulse. The only way she'd survive was to outsmart him, convince him that he was better off keeping her alive.

She sat up, brushed the dirt off her arms and tried to sound like she was in control. "Why were you following me?"

Beneath the flat brim of his hat, his dark eyes glittered in the moonlight like hot coals. "Following you?"

"That's right."

She tried to sound confident, but she feared this encounter would not turn out well. Dealing with Bridger, she'd been able to engage his intelligence, to mess with his head. Watts wasn't a thinking man. She could smell the cheap whiskey on his breath.

"Where is she?" he demanded.

"You must have been following me."

"You got it wrong, bitch. You came to me."

To Mexican Hat. Her vision had led her into a trap. "Why are you here?"

"I don't have to answer any damn questions from you."

He yanked her to her feet. Her ankle throbbed, and she let out a yip.

"You're hurt." His lip curled in an ugly sneer.

"My ankle." She supported her weight on her other leg. "I think it's sprained."

He shook her. "You came here to meet your cousin. Tell me where the hell she's hiding."

"I don't know."

He drew back his foot and kicked her injured ankle.

She hated herself for whimpering, but the pain was so intense that she felt light-headed.

"Where is she?" he demanded. "I should have killed her when I dumped her here. I never thought she'd survive in the river. But nobody found her body."

"You showed mercy," Emma said. "That was wise. You don't want to kill a daughter of your tribe."

"Mercy." He scoffed. "I won't make that mistake again."

He drew a hunting knife from a sheath fastened to his belt. The moonlight gleamed on the blade. "Where is she?"

Playing for time, Emma bluffed. "I have to take you there. I can't tell you exactly where it is. I have to show you."

He stroked the flat of the blade against her cheek. "If you lie, you die."

"It's the truth," she said desperately. "I swear."

A gunshot exploded through the night.

Sherman Watts shoved her away, and she fell to the

ground. She curled into a ball to ward off any blow. Her arms covered her head.

Another shot.

Watts took off running like the coward he was.

Emma stayed where she was, breathing in heavy gasps. She'd been close to death, almost a victim. Waves of pain washed over her. Pain and relief.

Miguel must be coming to her rescue. He had to be the person who'd fired the shots.

She heard him tromping through the sage, coming closer. Thank God, he hadn't listened when she told him to stay at the other scene. Thank God, he'd come for her.

She opened her eyes and looked up into the face of Hank Bridger. This nightmare wasn't over.

Chapter Twenty

On his Harley, Miguel rode slowly along the road that bordered the San Juan outside Mexican Hat. He hoped that Emma had already made this drive and was safely on her way back to the house, but he needed to be sure before he returned to his forensic team on the rez.

Pulling off on a graveled overlook—the only good stopping place along this stretch—he took out his cell phone and speed dialed her number. All he heard was a lonely buzz before it switched over to her voice mail.

Annoyed, he snapped the phone closed. She was probably right in assuming there was no reason for worry. Chasing after her was an overreaction on his part.

But what if he was right?

In the light from the waning moon, he noticed tire tracks gouged in the gravel. He dismounted from his bike to take a closer look. These were recent tracks, not eroded by wind or weather.

Miguel stepped back to get a better perspective. He'd done this sort of crime scene investigation dozens of time, reconstructing an accident. Based on skid marks and tire tracks, he could see that there were two vehicles. One had a wider base, probably a truck, and it had come too close to the first vehicle. There was a possible collision at slow speed, less than ten miles per hour. The smaller car, the one in front, had driven over the edge of the overlook and across the rutted landscape.

His gaze followed the path that car had taken. He squinted through the night. About twenty-five yards away was Emma's car. She'd run headlong into a tree.

He knew this wasn't an accident. The truck had forced her off the road. Someone had been chasing her.

Grabbing his flashlight, Miguel ran down the incline toward the river. His heart beat so fast that he thought it would jump out of his chest. He reached the car in seconds.

The front bumper had crumpled on impact. Her air bag had deployed. The driver's-side door hung open. She was gone.

"Emma," he called out. "Emma, where are you?"

He listened hard, hoping to hear her voice over the rush of the river and the wind.

Inside his head, his thoughts careened. A few days ago, he hadn't even known her name. Now, she was everything to him. She was his future. The only woman he ever wanted to be with. He never should have left her alone, not for one minute.

The Chimayo medal he wore around his neck burned against his skin. He held the silver disk between his thumb and forefinger, absorbing the words on the back: Protect and Heal. That was his mission. He must find Emma. Protect her.

He could do this. The evidence was here. All he needed to do was process the clues correctly.

The beam of his flashlight followed the tire tracks that led from the overlook to this tree. Shrubs lay flattened. There were deep ruts where her tires had churned on the rugged soil. She'd been trying to drive fast, but the terrain was too much for her little car. She'd lost control and hit the tree.

His attention turned to the car interior. Her purse sat on

the passenger seat. In the back was Jack's baby seat. Nothing inside the car resembled a clue.

He focused on the ground beside the car, trying to see which way she'd gone. He saw a partial print from her purple sneaker. Then another. She'd been on her toes, running. Running for her life.

Miguel seldom feared for his own safety. When faced with danger, his mind became calm and even more rational than usual. He thought ahead, trusted himself to do what needed to be done.

But when he thought of Emma—frightened and alone— his gut clenched. His ability to reason was replaced by fierce emotion. Fear surged inside him. Panic at the edge of a scream. He feared for her.

"No." He stood upright and inhaled a steady breath.

Overhead, the stars scattered across the night sky. After Teresa died, he imagined her in heaven, being a distant star that would guide him. He couldn't lose Emma, too. Fate couldn't be so cruel. *Think,* vato. *Think and you will find her.*

Concentrating on the trail she'd left as she ran, he came to an area where the ground was more disturbed. Someone had fallen here. He squatted down and carefully inspected the ground with his flashlight. There had been a struggle. *Emma,* mi amor, *you fought hard.*

Then he saw the boot print—size thirteen, square-toed, custom made. Hank Bridger's boot.

He remembered what Emma had said at the lab. *Bridger and the tunnels.* They went together.

He took out his cell phone, called for backup.

Miguel knew where Emma had gone.

BARELY CONSCIOUS, Emma slumped in the passenger seat beside Hank Bridger. He'd been considerate enough to fasten her seat belt, but her hands were cuffed in front of her. Her wrists chafed. When she moved, her ankle throbbed.

"You awake?" Bridger growled.

It might be safer to pretend that she was unconscious, but she was too exhausted to come up with a clever plan. Unrelenting fear had sapped her strength and intelligence. "Where are we going?"

"Where you told me," he said. "The place where Del Gardo died."

"The mine tunnels."

Was he still searching for the treasure? Surely, he knew that the crime lab had been all over Del Gardo's hideout.

"You told me," Bridger repeated, "that you were the only one who knew where to look. Del Gardo's ghost showed you the way."

Emma truly didn't remember telling him anything, much less spinning a fantastic yarn about how she could find the treasure when no one else could. Nor could she recall how she'd gotten from the field by the river to his car.

When she'd looked up and seen Bridger instead of Miguel, her hopes shattered. She'd been overwhelmed by a dread certainty that she would never get out of this alive. She'd never see Miguel again, never know what they might have shared together.

Knowing she had nothing to lose, she asked, "How do you know where Del Gardo died?"

He turned to her and smiled—wolflike, predatory. "I think you know that answer."

"You killed him. And those other people, too."

"You're too smart for your own good, Miss Emma." He maneuvered onto the turn below Griffin's house. "When you said their names, my first plan was to cut my losses and head back to Vegas. I talked to my lawyer. He said evidence from a medium would never be allowed in court."

"He's right. No one would believe me."

"Your testimony carries even less weight than circumstantial evidence." He drove slowly on the narrow road. She noticed that he wore black driving gloves, leaving no fingerprints. "But I changed my mind."

"Why?"

"I like a sure bet. If I eliminate you, the proof is gone. As a bonus, you can show me where to find Del Gardo's millions."

"Why should I? What's in it for me?"

He stopped at almost the exact same place she and Miguel had parked when they were following her hunch. "We might be able to work out a deal. I'd give you ten percent to pay for your silence."

"Only ten? That's not much of an incentive."

He unsnapped her seat belt and grabbed the front of her jacket, pulling her close to his face. "Ten percent. And I don't cut out your tongue."

She swallowed hard. "I have a better deal. A really sure thing."

"I'm listening."

"You said that Del Gardo owed you a hundred thousand. I'll pay you that much if you take me home."

His gaze turned blank. Talking about finance, he put on a poker face. "If this is a bluff—"

"It's not," she said desperately.

"How would a mouse like you come up with that kind of dough?"

"I make a lot of money and my needs are simple. My profits are all in the bank. All I have to do is talk to my financial advisor."

"You? You have a financial advisor?"

"It's true." When she'd lied to Bridger about the Manitou, he'd readily believed her. Now, she was telling the truth, and he was suspicious. "You can call my accountant. He'll tell you."

He leaned back in his seat. "Even if you're not shining me on, why would I make that deal? You've seen things that would put me in jail."

"Nobody will believe me. You said it yourself. My visions don't count for a damn thing in a court of law."

He shoved open his car door and got out.

Terror crashed through her. A suppressed sob escaped her lips. She was going to die.

The passenger's-side door whipped open. Roughly, he pulled her out. When her foot hit the gravel road, she winced in pain.

"Please." She gasped. "I'll pay you."

"Why would I settle for your money when I can have Del Gardo's millions?"

"Getting my money is easy. Just a phone call." She gestured with her cuffed hands. "A transfer of funds. From my account to yours."

"And that might be a reason to keep you alive until morning when the banks are open." He shoved her shoulder. "For now, I want Del Gardo's treasure. Show me where it is."

She hobbled forward.

"Let's go. Move it."

She stumbled. "I have a sprained ankle. I can't go any faster. Maybe if you take off the handcuffs."

He whirled her around. Using a key, he unfastened the cuffs that bound her wrists together.

With her hands free, there might be something she could do to protect herself. If she could get her hands on something she could use as a weapon. A rock. A tree branch.

She studied the huge man in the fringed jacket, taking his measure. There was no way to overcome him.

And he held a gun. His voice was low and calm. "Make no mistake, Miss Emma. If you try anything cute, I will hurt you."

To illustrate, he delivered a glancing blow to her right temple. The burst of pain made her gasp. When she touched the spot, she felt wet blood.

A sudden certainty hit her. "This is what happened when you killed Del Gardo."

"That's right." He nudged her arm with the barrel of his gun. "Start moving."

She limped uphill toward the three trees. "You brought him here. He promised to lead you to the treasure."

"He took some convincing."

She remembered the coroner's report. Del Gardo had been beaten before he was shot. "Then what happened?"

"He started running. I had to chase after him. His old-man disguise tricked me. I forgot how strong he was."

Emma dragged herself forward, putting as little weight on her sprained ankle as she could. "But he was taking you toward the money. Why did you kill him?"

"He had a rifle stashed over by that rock. When I saw the gun, I thought he brought me here as a ruse. So he could get to his weapon."

"You were so close," she said, thinking of the tunnels.

"The bastard was never going to hand over the money. I had to kill him. Or be killed."

But the treasure might actually be here. She couldn't imagine how Bobby and Ava could have overlooked millions of dollars hidden in the caves. But it was possible. Del Gardo could have changed his cash into diamonds or gold coins. When she first saw him, he was digging up coins.

If she could find his stash, she might figure out a way to survive.

She heard a rustling in the trees and glanced in that

direction. For an instant, she thought she saw the shape of a man. Now would be a good time for a vision. "Del Gardo," she whispered.

She needed his ghost, needed him to show her the way.

They had reached the place where she'd found his body. Bridger tore aside the yellow crime scene tape with a gloved hand. "Keep going," he growled.

She heard the hum of a motorcycle. *Miguel.* Her fear trebled. She'd rather die than have anything happened to Miguel. But if she died, Jack would have no one. *Oh, Miguel.*

"Your boyfriend," Bridger said. "I hate to shoot a cop, but I will. Keep moving."

Struggling, she pulled herself up the steep incline toward the entrance to the mine shaft.

The sound of the motorcycle went dead. How was she going to get free? She peered into the rustling trees. Somebody had to help her.

"How much farther?" Bridger demanded.

"Not much." She paused, catching her breath. "This is a hard climb."

"Keep going."

She knew what he wanted. If they made it to the ledge, he'd have an advantage. He could look down on anyone approaching. Taking aim at Miguel would be easier.

And she couldn't let that happen.

Glancing over her shoulder, she saw Bridger below her. His eyes cast downward, picking out careful steps on the loose dirt of ancient mine tailings. She couldn't let him get his footing. He had to be stopped. This was her best chance.

She gathered her strength. Using her body as a missile, she launched herself into his huge, barrel chest. Off balance, they both tumbled down the hill to the spot where he'd killed Del Gardo.

Emma tried to move, but she couldn't.

Bridger grabbed for her.

"Don't move," a voice shouted through the trees. She knew that voice. Sheriff Martinez.

"You're surrounded," came another shout from another direction.

"Let her go." It was Miguel. He'd come for her. He'd arranged this trap.

As she watched, Bridger leaped to his feet. He raised his gun. The barrel pointed directly at her. Horrified, she watched. Time slowed. Seconds passed like hours as she waited for death.

When the first gunshot rang out, he stumbled. Other shots followed in rapid succession.

Bridger fell to the ground, twitched once and went still.

Miguel came to her, gathered her into his arms. She rested her head against his chest, too weak to embrace him.

"You're all right, Emma. You're going to be all right."

"How did this happen? How did you—"

"Logic, *querida*. I found your car. I saw Bridger's boot print, and I remembered what you said about the tunnels."

"But how—"

"I called for backup. I'm the smart twin, remember?"

She lifted her chin. His smile was the most wonderful sight she'd ever seen. "You're brilliant."

"Martinez and his men had enough time to set up an ambush before you got here."

She counted three other men besides Martinez. The sheriff felt for a pulse in Bridger's neck. Then, he shook his head. The big man was dead.

"Died with his boots on," Martinez said.

She nestled against Miguel. "I never should have taken off by myself."

"I'll never leave you alone again. I want to be with you for all time. Even when you don't need a bodyguard. I love you, Emma."

"In Spanish?"

"Te quiero. Te amo."

"And I love you, Miguel. With all my heart."

Epilogue

Some days later, Miguel's love for Emma had grown deeper. He'd put down roots, moving his belongings into her house. More important, he'd taken up permanent residence in her bed, where she continued to amaze him with the intensity of her passion. Ever since she abandoned her virginity, she couldn't get enough of lovemaking. *Sí*, he was a lucky man.

He leaned over on the sofa and gave her a little kiss on the forehead, just below the bandage that covered the spot where Bridger struck her.

"Lovebirds," his brother muttered.

Dylan sat in the rocking chair, feeding a bottle to the baby. It seemed that he couldn't get enough of Jack. Since the day he'd spent babysitting, he had bonded with the motherless child.

"Maybe," Emma said, "if you'd stop being so macho, you might find a woman who could put up with you."

"I have plenty of *chicas*," Dylan said.

But love was different. Deep and powerful and strong. Miguel was glad he'd been patient enough to wait for Emma to come into his life.

When she shifted her weight, he asked, "How's the ankle?"

"Almost better. I'm feeling good enough to hobble around in the kitchen and make dinner tonight."

"No need, *querida*." He'd tasted her cooking. He was the better chef. "I like making food for you."

Dylan groaned. "I can't stand all this lovey-dovey goop. Can we talk about something important? Like Sherman Watts?"

"Have they found him?"

"Not yet, but the search is—"

When Emma stood, Miguel was at her elbow. "Do you need something?"

"I'm perfectly capable of walking to the kitchen," she assured him. "You two can talk. I have nothing to say about Watts."

As soon as she left the room, Dylan lowered his voice. "Unless we find Watts, I'm afraid we'll never locate Aspen. We've searched all over Mexican Hat. There's no sign of her."

"Watts doesn't know where she is. He's looking for her, too."

"How could she vanish?" Dylan looked down at the baby in his arms. "Where the hell is your mama?"

"Maybe somewhere on the rez. Have you made your peace with Bree?"

"No *problemo*," Dylan said. "I apologized. She accepted."

"So you're back in everybody's good graces."

Dylan's late-night raid on Watts's house hadn't really done any harm. The forensic investigation at his place hadn't turned up anything of significance.

When Emma came back into the living room carrying a bottle of water, she halted. Standing very still, her blue eyes focused on a spot near the front door.

Miguel recognized what was happening. She was seeing

one of her ghosts. He rose from the sofa and went toward her. "What is it, Emma? What do you see?"

A beautiful smile broke across her face. Excitedly, she said, "We'll find her. I know where Aspen is...."

* * * * *

Mills & Boon® Intrigue
brings you a sneak preview of…

Jessica Andersen's Internal Affairs

Sara is shocked when her ex-lover, an internal affairs
investigator, returns from the dead. Injured and
unable to remember who he is, all he knows is
theirs is an urgent mission he must complete.

Don't miss this thrilling new story in the
BEAR CLAW CREEK *mini-series, available next*
month from Mills & Boon® Intrigue.

Internal Affairs
by
Jessica Andersen

The pain speared from his shoulder blade to his spine and down—raw, bloody agony that consumed him and made him want to sink back into unconsciousness. But at the same time, urgency beat through him, not letting him return to oblivion.

The mission, the mission, must complete the mission.

But what was the mission? Where was he? What the hell had happened to him?

Cracking his eyes a fraction, careful not to give away his conscious state if he was being watched, he surveyed his immediate surroundings. Tall pine trees reached up to touch the late summer sky on all sides of him, their bases furred with an underlayer of smaller scrub brush. There was no sign of a cabin or a road, no evidence of anyone else nearby, no tracks in the forest litter but his own, leading to where he'd collapsed.

He was wearing heavy hiking boots, dark jeans and a black T-shirt, all of which were spattered with blood. Something told him not all of it was his, though when he moved his arms, the agony in his right shoulder ripped a groan from his lips. He felt the warm, wet bloom of fresh blood, smelled it on the moist air.

Shot in the back, he knew somehow. *Bastards. Cowards.* Except that he didn't know who the bastardly cowards were, or why they'd gone after him. More, he didn't know who the hell *he* was. Or what he'd done.

The realization brought a sick chill rattling through him, a spurt of panic. His brain answered with *I've got to get up, get moving. I can't let them catch me, or I'm dead.*

The words had no sooner whispered in his mind than he heard the sounds of pursuit: the sharp bark of a dog and the terse shouts of men calling to one another.

They weren't close, but they weren't far enough away for comfort, either.

He struggled to his feet cursing with pain, staggering with shock and blood loss. He didn't know who was looking for him, but there was far too much blood for a bar fight, and the pattern was high velocity. Had he killed someone? Been standing nearby when someone was killed? Had he escaped from a bad situation, or had he *been* the bad situation?

He didn't know, damn it. Worse, he didn't know which answer he was hoping for.

The mission. The words seemed to whisper from nowhere and everywhere at once. They came from the trees and the wind high above, and the bark of a second dog, sharper this time, and excited, suggesting that the beast had hit on a scent trail.

One thing was for certain: he needed to get someplace safe. But where? And how?

Knowing he wasn't going to find the answer standing

there, bleeding, he got moving, putting one foot in front of the other, holding his right arm clutched against his chest with his left. The world went gray-brown around the edges and his feet felt very far away, but the scenery moved past him, slow at first, then faster when he hit a downhill slope.

He saw a downed tree with an exposed root ball, thought he recognized it, though he didn't know from when. His feet carried him away from it at an angle, as though his subconscious knew where the hell he was going when his conscious mind didn't have a clue. Urgency propelled him—not just from the continued sounds of pursuit, which was drawing nearer by the minute, but also from the sense that he was supposed to be doing something crucial, critical.

His breath rasped in his lungs and the gray-brown closed in around the edges of his vision. He tripped and staggered, tripped again and went down. But he didn't stay down. He dragged himself up again, levering his body with his good arm and biting his teeth against the pained groans that wanted to rip from his throat.

Instead, staying silent, he forced himself to move faster, until he was running downhill through trees that all looked the same. He saw nothing except forest and more forest. Then, in the distance, there was something else: a rectangular blur that soon resolved itself into the outline of a late-model truck parked in the middle of nowhere.

Excitement slapped through him, driving back some of the gray-brown. He didn't recognize the truck, but he'd run right to it, hadn't he? It stood to reason that was because he'd known it was there. More, when he'd climbed into the driver's seat, he automatically fumbled beneath the dashboard and came up with the keys.

It took him two tries to get the key in the ignition; he was wobbly and weak, and he couldn't lean back into the seat without his shoulder giving him holy hell. But he had wheels. A hope of escape.

He couldn't hear the dogs over the engine's roar, but he knew the searchers were behind him, knew the net was closing fast. More, he knew he didn't have much more time left before he lapsed unconscious again. He'd lost blood, and God only knew what was going on inside him. Every inhalation was like breathing flames; every exhalation a study in misery. He needed a place to crash and he needed it fast.

After that, he thought, glancing in the rearview mirror and seeing piercing green eyes in a stern face, short black hair, and nothing familiar about any of it, *I'm going to need some answers.*

Knowing he was already on borrowed time, he hit the gas and sent the truck thundering downhill. There wasn't any road or track, but he got lucky—or else he knew the way—and didn't hit any big ditches or dead-falls. Within ten minutes, he came to a fire-access road. Instinct—or something more?—had him turning uphill rather than down. A few minutes later, he bypassed a larger road, then took a barely visible dirt trail that paralleled the main access road.

The not-quite-a-road was bumpy, jolting him back against the seat and wringing curses from him every time he hit his injured shoulder. But the pain kept him conscious, kept him moving. And when he hit a paved road, it reminded him he needed to get someplace he could hide, where he'd be safe when he collapsed.

Animalistic instinct had him turning east. He passed street signs he recognized on some level, but it wasn't until he passed a big billboard that said *Welcome to Bear Claw Creek* that he knew he was in Colorado, and then only because the sign said so.

His hands were starting to shake, warning him that his body was hitting the end of its reserves. But he still had enough sense to ditch the truck at the back of a commuter lot, where it might not be noticed for a while, and hide the keys in the wheel well. Then he searched the vehicle for anything that might clue him in on what the hell was going on—or, failing that, who the hell he was.

All he came up with was a lightweight waterproof jacket wedged beneath the passenger's seat, but that was something, anyway. Though the fading day was still warm with late summer sun, he pulled on the navy blue jacket so if anyone saw him, they wouldn't get a look at his back. A guy wearing dirty jeans and a jacket might be forgotten. A guy bleeding from a bullet wound in his shoulder, not so much.

Cursing under his breath, using the swearwords to let him know he was still up and moving, even as the gray-brown of encroaching unconsciousness narrowed his vision to a tunnel, he stagger-stepped through the commuter car lot and across the main road. Cutting over a couple of streets on legs that were rapidly turning to rubber, he homed in on a corner lot, where a neat stone-faced house sat well back from the road, all but lost behind wild flowering hedges and a rambler-covered picket fence.

It wasn't the relative concealment offered by the big lot and the landscaping that had him turning up the driveway, though. It was the sense of safety. This wasn't his house, he knew somehow, but whose ever it was, instinct said they would shelter him, help him.

Without conscious thought, he reached into the brass, wall-mounted mailbox beside the door, found a small latch and toggled the false bottom, which opened to reveal a spare key.

He was too far gone to wonder how he'd known to do that, too out of it to remember whose house this was. It was all he could do to let himself in and relock the door once he was through. Dropping the key into his pocket, he dragged himself through a pin-neat kitchen that was painted cream and moss with sunny yellow accents and soft, feminine curtains. He found a notepad beside the phone and scrawled a quick message.

His hands were shaking; his whole body was shaking, and where it wasn't shaking it had shut down completely. He couldn't feel his feet, couldn't feel much of anything except the pain and the dizziness that warned he was seconds away from passing out.

Finally, unable to hold it off any longer, he let the gray-brown win, let it wash over his vision and suck him down into the blackness. He was barely aware of staggering into the next room and falling, hardly felt the pain of landing face-first on a carpeted floor. He knew only that, for the moment at least, he was safe.

2 FREE BOOKS
AND A SURPRISE GIFT

We would like to take this opportunity to thank you for reading this Mills & Boon® book by offering you the chance to take TWO more specially selected books from the Intrigue series absolutely FREE! We're also making this offer to introduce you to the benefits of the Mills & Boon® Book Club™—

- **FREE home delivery**
- **FREE gifts and competitions**
- **FREE monthly Newsletter**
- **Exclusive Mills & Boon Book Club offers**
- **Books available before they're in the shops**

Accepting these FREE books and gift places you under no obligation to buy, you may cancel at any time, even after receiving your free books. Simply complete your details below and return the entire page to the address below. You don't even need a stamp!

YES Please send me 2 free Intrigue books and a surprise gift. I understand that unless you hear from me, I will receive 5 superb new stories every month, including two 2-in-1 books priced at £4.99 each and a single book priced at £3.19, postage and packing free. I am under no obligation to purchase any books and may cancel my subscription at any time. The free books and gift will be mine to keep in any case.

Ms/Mrs/Miss/Mr _____ Initials _____

Surname _____

Address _____

_____

_____ Postcode _____

E-mail _____

Send this whole page to: Mills & Boon Book Club, Free Book Offer, FREEPOST NAT 10298, Richmond, TW9 1BR